ALSO BY THERESA RIZZO

He Belongs to Me

THERESA RIZZO

Published by Theresa Rizzo
www.theresarizzo.com

ISBN 978-0-9890450-2-5

Cover design by Kim Killion, Killion Group
Book design by Donna Cook

Printed in the United States of America

For Dad,
who always encouraged me.

Acknowledgments

Any work of fiction is a collaborative effort and this one is no exception. I heartily and sincerely want to thank the many people who contributed their time and knowledge in helping me create this story. Any errors in this work of fiction are completely mine.

To Jayne Reardon, Robyn Meinhardt, and Dayna Matthew, for their legal advice and critiques. Mike Reardon, whose debate first sparked my interest in the ethical ramifications behind postmortem sperm retrieval and subsequent pregnancy. Dr. Jacques Beaudoin for information regarding diagnosis of brain death. Jennifer at Gift of Life Michigan for current organ donor information.

To Courtney Gambrell for her sensitivity and great insight into characterization. To Philip Sutherland for his paramedic knowledge and advice. Danny Myers, Marj OReiley, and Laura Burleigh for quick reads and helpful critiques. Paul and Marilyn Rizzo for their contributions concerning Grosse Pointe and medical issues.

As always, I need to thank my great writing pals, Noelle Gracy, Judy Duerte, Kerri-Leigh Grady, Donnell Bell, Leslie Sartor, Kally Jo Surbeck, Audra Harders, and Kaki Warner, who help me be true to the characters and story, and inspire me. You guys are awesome.

To Ellis Vidler, my talented freelance editor. To Alex Logan and Beth de Guguzman, editors at Grand Central Publishing, for wonderful feedback that compelled me to strengthen the story. To Donna Cook, book formatter extraordinaire, for making my print copy so lovely. To Kim Killion for designing another beautiful cover.

To Mike Rizzo, for his medical counsel and master critiquing skills. Thanks Mike, for challenging me to write the best story I can and for always encouraging me to stretch and grow in my craft.

To my wonderful beta readers, Jill Cullinane, Jessica Brooks and Allison Brooks whose critiques are brutally honest and helpful.

Lastly I'd like to thank my husband, John, and children, Jillian, Brian, Jessica, and Allison for years of patience and encouragement.

Prologue

Steve Grant's heart pounded as if it might hammer its way right out of his chest. He took a measured breath, stretched an arm across the back of Annie's chair and settled into his stadium seat. *What's the problem, man? You've faced down Billy Ray Butler and Crush Davis, stared them down across home plate, in front of a sold-out crowd without breaking a sweat; you can do this. It's the right thing to do.*

The band's drums, trumpets and trombones belted out the Michigan fight song. "Let's! Go! Blue!" The Ann Arbor crowd cheered as one.

"Why'd you give up your fifty-yard-line seats for these nosebleeds?" Annie raised her eyebrows.

"Lemme go," the three-year-old behind her shrieked as he strained and bucked in his mother's arms.

Annie winced, covered her ear and gave Steve a knowing look. When they went out without her children, he knew she wanted a break from *all* kids. These seats cost a small fortune; who in the hell brings their kid along? Steve scanned the packed seats around them—not a damn kid in sight. What were the chances they'd be sitting right in front of the only holy terror?

"One of our paralegals, Pete McGaffy, has his dad in town this weekend to celebrate his first year cancer free. Pete helped me a couple of times so when I found out his dad's a huge Michigan fan, I gave them my tickets and got these instead." He glared at the kid beating an annoying tattoo on the back of Annie's chair, tempted to grab the little ankle to still him. "We have a great view of the whole field from here. Besides, I thought you'd enjoy sitting with Notre Dame fans instead of the enemy for a change."

Annie had gone to Notre Dame and was a die-hard Irish fan, where as a Michigan alum, Steve's season tickets bordered the Michigan sideline. She held out her hand for the binoculars and jerked forward as the kid pounded her chair with both of his feet. Stiff backed, Annie scooted forward in her chair.

"Switch seats with me." Steve stood and pulled Annie out of her seat. She should be safe in front of the dad.

Annie stood and threw the little brat that warning look mothers seem to perfect, before slowly lowering herself into the other seat. Not exactly the mood he wanted to set. He hoped it wasn't an omen. *Chill, man. She's gonna love it.*

He looked at the giant scoreboard—five minutes to halftime. Steve settled back in the seat, rubbed tight neck muscles, and rolled his shoulders.

He'd chosen these seats carefully. The first row in club level seating had lots of leg room, a bird's eye view of the whole field, and the cameramen should have no trouble zooming in on them. It was perfe—the boy put a sticky hand on Steve's head and lunged over his shoulder, nearly falling into his lap. Steve caught him and shoved him back at his parents.

"Henry. I'm sooo sorry. Really. Sorry. I..." His mortified mother tried to lift him onto her lap, but the little boy arched his back and bellowed.

"That's enough!" the father said. He handed his wife his beer and reached for the boy at the same time the kid jumped up, knocking her arm.

The halftime buzzer sounded loudly as Steve lunged forward, but he couldn't right the cup before a wave of beer cascaded over the lip, splashing all over Annie's shoulder, arm, and chest.

Annie gasped, jumped up and whirled on the threesome. Fury burned in her eyes as she shook her arm, spraying beer. "Are you freaking kidding me? What's *wrong* with you people? Haven't you ever heard of a babysitter?"

Steve stepped back and stared in horror. The pink of Annie's shirt grew increasingly dark as it soaked up the beer.

"I'm *so* sorry." The woman rummaged in her bag, yanked out some baby wipes and held them out to Annie. "I... please. We'll pay for dry-cleaning."

Annie snatched the wipes, made a few futile dabs at her arm before throwing them on her seat and pushing past Steve.

"Laaadies and geeen-tlemen," The announcer drew out.

Steve grabbed her arm. "Where're you going?"

"Preee-sent-ing the two-hundred thirty-five member Michigan marching Band. Baaa-nd... take the field."

Annie frowned as if he was crazy. "To the bathroom."

"Now? You can't go now."

Eyes widening, she plucked the wet shirt from her chest. "I'm *covered* in beer."

Shit. Shit. Shit. "Uh... there'll be a long line. Just wait a little bit." He turned her toward the field. "Watch the show." He glanced at the forty-seven by eighty-five-foot screen to see the camera zooming in on them. He pointed toward the field. "Look, they're spelling out something."

"I don't care." She tried to pull free.

Steve tightened his grip on her shoulders. "Listen. It's that Bruno Mars song you love."

"What is wrong with you?" She glared. "I'm soaked and smell like a frat party."

Steve pivoted her toward the field and locked his arms around her. "*Look.*"

The band had spelled out "M-A-R-R-Y M-E" and dissolved to reform one last word. "A-N-N-I-E."

The announcer boomed, "Weeeell, Annie?"

Annie looked toward the huge board where the camera had zoomed in on them and they stood larger than life. Her glare melted as awareness set in. She brushed her hair back and a tentative smile flickered across her face.

Steve released her. He wiped damp palms on his thighs, then dropped to one knee and took her hand. "Will you marry me, Annie?"

Hand covering her mouth, Annie dragged her gaze from the huge screen long enough to nod at him. Her glance darted back and forth from the screen to him. She thrust out her left hand. He took the ring box from his pocket, then slid the ring onto her finger.

Annie yanked her hand back and after a quick inspection of the 3-carat marquise, held it up for everybody to see as if she were a winner lofting her trophy. Steve pulled her into his arms for a hug while the crowd cheered and clapped.

Smile, Steve. Even if he couldn't give her his heart, he'd embarrassed himself in front of millions of people and given her her dream proposal. The love would come.

Chapter 1

Even the best-made plans were subject to the whims of fate, and Jenny Harrison believed in embracing Lady Destiny's cues. She grabbed her list and the gallon-size baggie of cookies, whistled for Ritz and rushed through the hedge separating the driveway from their neighbor's. With the golden retriever prancing at her heels, she breezed through Steve's back door, calling out, "Hey, Grant?"

"Kitchen." Steve, with his maroon silk tie tucked into his white dress shirt, leaned over his sink and bit a pickle. He saluted her with the dill. "Lunch?"

"No, thanks, we'll catch something on the road. Save room; I made your favorite, pecan chocolate chip." She held up the cookies.

Steve took the bag. "Mmmm. They're still warm. You didn't have to do that."

"Yes, I did. We really appreciate your taking care of Ritz and the house. With the trial ramping up, I know you're crazy busy."

"No problem." He polished off the pickle and pulled the cookie bag open.

The sweet scent of fresh-baked cookie and warm chocolate commingled with the acetous pickle smell. Jenny winced. Gross. Shaking her head, she laid down the list. "Here's the number of the Saugatuck Inn—in case of an emergency—though we'll both have our cells." She frowned and craned her neck to read the upside down list. "And... you have a key to the house. We won't set the alarm. There should be plenty of dog food in the garage, and I stopped the newspapers." She looked up. "Questions?"

"Jen, you'll only be gone three and a half days." Then at her steady look, he sighed. "Got it."

Jenny reached for her back pocket and fingered the bulky line there, thinking. She couldn't wait to share her good news. Ordinarily she'd want it to be Gabe, but under the circumstances, maybe a test run on Steve might be good.

"What?" He raised his eyebrows and polished off the cookie. "Out with it. You look like the cat who swallowed the canary and got her cream too."

Jenny smiled, whipped the plastic stick from her back pocket and waved it around. "I'm pregnant."

"You're...?" His eyes widened and his jaw dropped. "That's great. Right? Is it great?"

She nodded and smiled. "It's amazing."

"Pregnant? Wow. What'd Gabe say?"

"He doesn't know. I just found out myself. I'm going to tell him this weekend." She grinned a wide silly, grin, then bit her lower lip. "I'm going to have a baby."

"Congratulations, kid. You're gonna be a great mom."

"Thanks." Jenny smiled, still a little shocked. She fingered the stick, staring at the blue line, then slipped it back in her pocket. That wasn't so bad. In just a few minutes Steve had lost that stunned look. It'd be fine. Everything would be fine.

Jenny crouched down and rubbed the big dog's head between her hands. "Be a good girl, Ritz." Out of the corner of her eye she glimpsed her husband's red Volkswagen zipping up their driveway. She stood and headed for the door. "Gotta run. Thanks."

"Have fun."

"See ya." Jenny rushed out the door and trotted across the drives to her Jeep. She faced Gabe with a cheerful smile. "Hi."

Gabe walked over and planted a quick kiss on her lips. "Ready to go?"

"Car's all packed, but—" She reached out and took his hand. Threading her fingers between his, Jenny held on to keep his attention. "I have a tiny favor to ask."

He raised his eyebrows. "Tiny, eh?"

She nodded. "Hardly anything at all."

"Shoot."

"Would you mind very much stopping by the clinic on the way out?"

"Be-cause..."

"Because... I sort of promised Tommy you'd take a look at his little brother. You know, the eleven-year-old boy I interviewed for the foster care article. His half brother and sister live with their grandma, and his little brother's been sick for the past week. Grandma works as a cleaning lady and doesn't have insurance, so she won't take the boy to the doctor."

"So you told Tommy I'd examine him." Gabe looked down at her, his expression hard to read.

"I did." She winced. "Do you mind very much? It shouldn't take long and it's on the way. I was hoping that if I got a chance to talk to the grandma, I could help her see that the clinic isn't such a bad place."

"What time are we supposed to meet them?"

She pulled her hand free to look at her watch. "Eleven forty-five—shoot, we're gonna be late."

"We'd better get a move on."

Relief lightening her heart, Jenny ran around the Jeep and jumped into the passenger's side. They drove down Lakeshore Drive. The huge century-old elms shading Grosse Pointe neighborhoods gave way to the stark, concrete city streets of Detroit.

Settling back in her seat, Jenny took in the tired neighborhoods, pausing on the occasional abandoned home where the peeling paint of white-framed windows highlighted dark, gaping holes. A few windows had unbroken, grimy glass, but most held jagged broken panes looking like sharp wicked teeth in a monstrous dirty brick face.

Green bushes and weeds grew three feet tall around the decaying buildings, as if trying to hide the dangerous eyesores.

Jenny turned to Gabe wondering if the worn dereliction saddened him as it did her, or, since he drove this route once a week, had he become immune to the neglect. His attention seemed focused on avoiding the potholes rather than inspecting the neighborhood.

Ten minutes later, they pulled up outside the one-story red brick clinic. Tommy stood beside an elderly lady with white hair and a ramrod-straight back. She wore a dark woolen coat and no-nonsense shoes. A little girl about four years old clutched the woman's hand while a boy about seven slumped against her as if exhausted.

"Hi, guys." Jenny smiled broadly and held out her hand to the woman. "You must be Tommy's grandmother. I'm Jenny and this is my husband, Gabe."

The woman stared at her several long seconds, then looked at her hand before slowly raising her own and shaking Jenny's. "Abigail Johnson. Tommy said you might could help Sammy here."

"Why, sure we can." She smiled reassuringly at the little boy. Poor little guy's eyelids drooped over eyes dulled with pain. "Hi, Sammy, I'm Jenny."

"Miss Jenny," his grandma corrected and gave the boy a raised eyebrow and a telling stare for emphasis.

Sammy's head rolled up and the edges of his lips rose in a weak smile. "Miss Jenny."

Jenny turned and bent until she was face-to-face with the little girl. "I like your pigtails. What's your name?"

"Clarisse," she whispered, in a darling little lisp.

"Isn't that a pretty name?"

Gabe rested a hand on Jenny's back. "Why don't we move inside? Jenny will get the paperwork from Sharon while I find us an empty exam room."

Gabe urged the group toward the Plexiglas, bulletproof door. The thin, bespectacled guard sitting behind a scarred desk gave them a broad smile and buzzed them in.

"Hey, Doc."

"How's it goin', Max?"

"Fine. Jus' fine. You workin' today?"

"Nope, just got a friend here I need to take care of and then we'll be out of your hair."

Jenny ushered them toward the receptionist, stopping when she felt a tug on her arm. Abigail Johnson looked her in the eye. "I don't have money for this. Wish I did, but with the two little ones and... well—I just don't."

"Grammy J, I told you, Miss Jenny said it's free," Tommy broke in.

She scowled at him. "Hush now. I'm talkin' to Miss Jenny."

Jenny leaned close. "Please, it's just Jenny. Don't worry, Mrs. Johnson, he's right; it is free. We just need you to fill out some forms, but there's no charge."

The woman nodded and put a bony hand on Jenny's arm. "You can call me Grammy J."

Jenny smiled. She'd never had a grandma she remembered, and this stern old lady warmed her heart. Jenny seated her charges and got the new patient forms from the receptionist. Grammy J sat with the little girl on her lap, clutching her like a shield. Her nostrils flared wide and her knee bounced so hard Jenny worried little Clarisse's eyeballs rattling around in the poor mite's head would give her permanent eye damage—that is, if she wasn't catapulted off her grandma's knees.

Sitting next to them, Jenny handed the clipboard of papers to Grammy J.

She stopped her nervous galloping and accepted the board. After several seconds of peering at the paper over Clarisse's shoulder, Grammy J passed the clipboard to Tommy. "I can't concentrate."

Tommy obediently took the forms and slowly, with meticulous printing, began to fill them out. Occasionally he whispered a question to Grammy J, who murmured an answer. Then he handed her the pen and pointed to the spot on the consent form needing her signature.

Gabe came back to get Sammy. "Mrs. Johnson, would you like to come too?"

"No, I'll keep an eye on this one. Tommy'll go along." She nudged Tommy, then grabbed Sammy's thin arm. "You do what the doctor says, hear?"

"Yes, ma'am," he muttered. Sammy slipped his hand into his brother's and followed Gabe down the hall.

"I can watch Clarisse if you want to go with Sammy," Jenny offered.

"Tommy'll do."

"You've done a wonderful job with the children. They're very polite and sweet."

Staring at the hall her grandsons disappeared down, Grammy J sighed. "I try. It about tore me up to have to send Tommy away, but he better off outta that neighborhood." She looked at Jenny. "You know, you try to do the right thing. You take 'em to church and try to raise 'em right, but with the gangs and the drugs, they just won't let 'em be. Them kids were after Tommy for weeks to join up, but I sent him away. He better off."

"I'm sorry. It sounds like you're doing the right thing. I know Tommy misses his brother and sister, but the Jeromes are nice people and make sure he visits, right?"

"Not enough. I shouldn't have to get permission from nobody when I needs to take my own flesh and blood outta school to he'p his brother," Grandma J whispered. She looked sideways at Jenny. "You got kids?"

"Me? Uh—" Jenny resisted the urge to put a hand to her stomach; instead she shook her head. "Stepchildren. But they're in college."

"None of your own?"

Not really. Not yet. "No. Children are a lot of responsibility."

Grammy J's head bobbed. "Amen to that."

"Well, I think you're doing an awesome job." She smiled and ducked her head to look at the four-year old. "Isn't she?"

Clarisse nodded shyly.

"Would you like a juice box Miss Clarisse?" At the enthusiastic nod, Jenny looked at Grammy J. "Can I get you both a juice, or perhaps you'd like coffee?"

"No. Thank you."

Jenny went off to the kitchen to get drinks. On her way back, she ran into Gabe and the boys.

"Will he live?" Jenny teased.

"Should." Gabe looked at Grammy J. "He's got a pretty good ear infection going, but after a few days of antibiotics, he'll be fine. I'll get the medicine, then we can be on our way."

Jenny handed out the juices. Grammy J sat stiffly in the plastic chair. Her knee began fanatically springing again as she constantly scanned the near-empty waiting room as if expecting an attack. Poor thing couldn't have looked more uncomfortable.

Jenny turned Tommy aside so they faced the wall. "You know there are free programs to help her learn to read."

"What?"

"She can learn to read; she's not too old." Jenny looked into his eyes. "You can't always be there to help her."

Tommy stood up tall and lifted his chin. "Who says she can't read?"

"I says."

"She's too proud," he whispered.

"Maybe I can talk to her after I get back from vacation."

"Maybe." He gave her a considering look before breaking into a broad smile. "She likes you."

"I like her too."

Gabe returned, gave Grammy J the medicine and explained the dosage. He looked at Jenny. "How about we give these nice people a ride home?"

Grammy J frowned. "We don't want to trouble you."

He held the door open for them. "No trouble. I insist."

"Thank you." She looked up with solemn eyes and nodded. "For everything."

"You're welcome."

Jenny's heart swelled with pride. She caught Gabe's eye, and mouthed, "I love you."

He winked and opened the car door for her.

They piled into Jenny's Jeep, dropped the Johnsons home and Tommy at school. After Tommy disappeared behind the dark wooden doors, Jenny turned in her seat. "You're a good man, Gabriel Harrison."

Gabe stretched out in the passenger's seat. "I try."

She smiled at his glib answer. "I know how precious your free time is. Thanks for doing that for me."

He gave her a warm look. "My pleasure."

Some husbands would be seriously derailed at starting their vacation several hours late because their wives committed them to a good deed, but not Gabe. Her husband was a sweetie, a real angel. She just hoped what she had to tell him wouldn't wreck things.

"What would I do without you?"

He threaded his fingers through hers. "Don't worry, you're never gonna get the chance to find out."

∾ ∾ ∾

Driving down I-94 in her new sapphire blue Jeep, they sped past Detroit Metro airport before Jenny remembered the present. "Oh. With all the commotion, I forgot about your anniversary present. Look in the glove compartment."

Gabe pulled out the flat, square gift. Though the distinctive shape pretty much precluded the reason for wrapping the CD, Jenny had chosen brightly colored paper and tied a stylish gold wire-rimmed bow around it. "Guess who."

"Isn't the appropriate gift for a second anniversary paper or tin foil or pottery?"

"Close. Guess who."

"Kelly Clarkson?"

"Would I get you *my* favorite singer as a present?"

"You got me headphones for Christmas so *you* could sleep while I watched TV in bed."

"That's different," she dismissed airily. "That was a gift to both of us. You get to watch the whole TV show in bed, and I don't have to harass you to turn it off when I want to go to sleep."

"And that's different... How?"

"It's cheaper than marriage counseling," she said in mock warning.

Gabe laughed and tore open the wrapping, revealing a classic Chuck Mangione recording. "Jazz. Great. Thanks, honey." He reached out a hand to massage her shoulder. Jenny leaned into his touch, enjoying the way his fingers lingered at the nape of her neck and toyed with her hair.

"You're welcome. Why don't you pop it in?"

They drove west across Michigan to the relaxing sounds of the horn while the tension lines eased from around Gabe's eyes. The hectic pace of his general surgery practice combined with his volunteering at the inner city clinic took its toll.

The breeze from the open window whipped Gabe's short hair. He propped one sneaker-clad foot on the dash and slumped deeper in his seat. "Are you in mourning yet? Now that Steve and Annie are engaged."

She wrinkled her nose. "Funny. She's not who *I* would've picked for him, but I'll be nice to her."

Gabe chuckled. "You hate her."

She shot him a quick, accusing look before returning her attention to the road. "You don't like her either."

"He could do better."

"So why Annie? And proposing at a football game?" She rolled her eyes. "How private and romantic."

"It had national coverage. She loved it."

"She would," Jenny muttered. "Think she's pregnant?"

One eyebrow arched over mirrored aviator glasses. "*Not* nice."

Yeah... this "nice" thing would take some practice.

Gabe rummaged through the cooler for a Coke Zero and opened it with a loud pfft. Holding it out to Jenny for a sip, his hand jerked, sending soda splashing across the center console.

"Shoot." He grabbed a Kleenex to swipe at the drops sliding down the side of his seat.

Jenny swallowed a quick gulp and handed the can back. "Thanks."

Out of the corner of her eye, she saw Gabe's hand tremble violently as he raised the can to his lips. This wasn't the first time she'd noticed his hand shaking, but it seemed to come and go.

He glanced sideways and flashed her a rueful grin. "Better lay off the caffeine."

She gasped. "Leadless?" They'd always disdained decaf coffee.

He stared at the black can in his hand and sighed. "Soda, too."

Jenny laughed at his sorrowful look. Gabe loved his morning coffee and was a bear until he'd downed at least half a cup. The hand jitters made him more nervous than she would have thought. Did he know something he wasn't telling her? She peeked at him out of the corner of her eye again. It was probably nothing a little less caffeine wouldn't cure. They'd give it up together. Caffeine wasn't good for the baby anyway.

Before Benton Harbor, they turned north onto a less-populated road. They drove up the coast past near-empty beaches now lying dormant in the off-season. The musty smell of lake water gave way to the distant scent of burning leaves. Harbors sat quiet, where a few remaining boats waited patiently to be dry-docked and stored for the winter.

"Hey, Gabe?"

"Hmm."

Jenny kept her eyes on the road. Her fingers flexed around the steering wheel. "What would you think of our having a baby?"

Chapter 2

Gabe's sunglasses hid far too much of his expression, Jenny only had the momentary tightening of his lips to gauge his reaction. He paused long nerve-wracking seconds before answering. "I thought you didn't want children."

"I know I said that, but... what if I do?"

"We already made this decision—it's what we both wanted."

"Maybe I changed my mind."

"You were pretty emphatic about not wanting children, Jen."

"I know," she said in a conciliatory tone. "But I was a little overwhelmed with my job, the wedding, and the house renovation. I really thought I didn't want kids. I figured I'd be busy with my career and being a wife and stepmother, but maybe I was wrong," she finished softly.

"I got you Ritz."

"A dog's not quite the same as a child."

Gabe sat quietly for what seemed like minutes. "You want a baby?"

His obvious reluctance kept her from blurting the truth. Jenny kept her eyes on the road, afraid to look at him. Afraid of the anger and betrayal she might find in his face. Her grip tightened around the steering wheel until the tendons in her hand rose up and fanned out in four taut lines.

"I... yeah. You're a great dad to Alex and Ted, but I missed out on sharing those times with you. And being divorced, even you missed a lot." She paused and snuck a sideways look at him. "What do you think?"

Gabe sat in the seat with his eyes closed so long she feared he'd gone to sleep. Only a rhythmic clenching of his jaw betrayed his feelings. Darn, this hadn't been the right time to bring it up.

"Gabe?" she ventured softly.

"I'll think about it."

∾ ∾ ∾

As if he could think of anything else—and he'd tried. Over the next two days, Gabe tried hard to let the fall country beauty distract him from Jenny's proposal. She didn't press the issue, which in itself made him nervous. Her continued silence indicated how serious she was about wanting this baby.

When Jenny wasn't interviewing the proprietors of the Saugatuck Inn for her article or typing up notes, they took long walks on the beach or in the woods. Hand in hand, they shuffled through the blaze of autumn colors littering the ground, absorbing the earthy scent of dirt mixed with the unmistakable smoky smell of burning leaves.

Fond memories of a radiant Jenny raking the leaves in their yard back home were intruded upon when the images suddenly contained a bundled, runny-nosed toddler waddling across the lawn. Trying to dismiss the picture, Gabe spent hours staring at his suspense novel until the words blurred before him and he read the same page at least five times, but even Harlan Coben couldn't compete with Jenny's bombshell.

Damn. She wanted a baby.

A part of him was tempted to experience parenthood again with her. The thought of a tiny newborn nursing at her breast stirred something deep and primitive within him. But a larger part, the selfish part, wanted another child like he wanted a Drano enema.

He'd gone through the long, sleepless nights caring for his sick children. He'd celebrated their freedom from diapers, each lost tooth, and mastery of riding two-wheel bikes without training wheels. He'd sympathized at the funerals of six goldfish, three hamsters, and one cat. He'd spent years juggling his schedule to attend soccer, little league games, and tennis matches, feeling guilty when his job made him miss a crucial birthday or school event. Though rewarding, parenthood was difficult, time-consuming, and sometimes heartbreaking. And long—definitely long.

Gabe washed a hand over his face. Marriage was about compromise and sacrifice. But in this situation, having a baby was a hell of a sacrifice for him. He did not want to start all over again at forty-three. Then again, he supposed never experiencing pregnancy and parenthood from conception was a hell of a sacrifice for her.

The morning of their last day of vacation, Gabe waited out front by their bikes, admiring his wife as Jenny skipped down the wide porch steps. She'd pulled her brown hair back in a ponytail and covered her worn jeans with his blue and gold striped rugby shirt that fell mid-thigh on her. Smiling widely, she looked at him with those guileless, translucent blue eyes. Lord she was beautiful. A shiny silver helmet dangled from her finger.

"Glad to see you've come prepared," he said, nodding at the helmet.

"It's for you. Your other anniversary present. It's about time you retire that old, hot relic." She stretched out her hand to take his black helmet.

"That's sweet of you, but I like this one."

"Look at all these ventilation channels to keep you cool." She flipped it over to show him the inside. "And quick-drying padding made with some fancy material to inhibit nasty smelling bacteria. Try it on." She held the helmet out to him. "I had to go to four stores to find this helmet in a color you wouldn't hate."

He took it from her and plopped it on his head. Stiff, but it fit. Hand halfway to his chinstrap, he looked at her. "What about you? What're you going to wear?"

"Me?" Not riding often, she obviously hadn't thought about herself. "I'll wear your old one."

"Take this one." He thrust the new helmet at her. A sly look crossed his face before he contrived to look innocent. "A really considerate wife would break it in for me."

Jenny snatched the new helmet. "When we get home, you are *going* to wear this one." She glared at him while tugging the chinstraps until it fit snugly, grumbling, "I'm gonna burn that ugly old thing."

"Thanks, sweetheart. Although your head's a bit big, you'll break it in just fine for me."

Jenny gave him the evil eye and pushed her bike toward the deserted road.

Peddling down the black top, they soon reached a designated trail that wound between large oak trees, through a meadow, and around a little pond. The few remaining dandelions relinquished their fuzz to loft above decaying fields of wildflowers and thistle patches, floating lazily about in the cool morning air. Straggling songbirds foraged for one last meal before heading south for the winter.

Gabe breathed in deeply, loving the earthy scent of the lingering summer warmth melding with the inevitable fall decay. Stealing a glance at Jenny, he read the contentment in her expression. Regret weighed heavily on his soul. What he had to do would shatter nature's soothing influence as surely as a rock shatters a windshield. He fervently hoped it wouldn't destroy anything more important— like her heart. Or their marriage.

Spotting a huge log that looked like the perfect resting place, Gabe pulled over and dismounted. Jenny pulled up behind him, straddling her bike. "Tired already, Harrison? This vacation was supposed to rejuvenate you."

"I'm rejuvenated." He snagged her shirt and pulled her close. With a gentle hand at her jaw, Gabe tilted her head up so he could memorize every curve, every nuance of her heart-shaped face before settling on her intelligent eyes. Good Lord, she was beautiful. She was energy, and laughter, and love; everything he had ever wanted. Jenny filled his heart with warmth and light.

"I love you."

A smile curved her lips and lit her eyes. "I love you, too."

Gabe fumbled with the hem of her shirt until he could slip his hand beneath, where he caressed the warm silkiness of her waist. He loved her soft skin—could spend hours stroking it, like rubbing a good-luck charm. His hand splayed, spanning her small back, pulling her close.

Lowering his head, Gabe feathered light kisses over her lips. Jenny's arms snaked around his neck, pressing him closer until he couldn't tell her heartbeat from his. With a little sigh, she toyed with the hair at the base of his neck, sending shafts of delight down his spine and heat pooling in his groin.

Gabe kissed his wife long and deeply. Remorse intensifying his passion, he molded Jenny's hips to his, hardly feeling the cold metal of her bike gouging his thighs. Eyes shut, he devoured her lips, as if his love alone could bend her will to his. A tremor moved through him as he thought about how much of his soul this woman owned. She was his heart. His life. He didn't want to share her—he didn't want to lose her.

Jenny moaned in appreciation. Her bike crashed to the ground.

Chest heaving, Gabe eased away from her. "That's no way to treat an expensive bike."

She looked at him from beneath passion-drooping eyelids and licked her lips. "Then you shouldn't seduce me with a kiss like that."

"That good, eh?" He stood a little taller.

She stepped over the bike, feigning nonchalance. "Not bad—for an old married man."

Gabe took Jenny's hand, so small and delicate, so trustingly curled around his own fingers, and guided her to the large log. Straddling the trunk, he pulled her down to face him. "Jenny. About the baby—"

"You don't want to," she broke in.

He looked up. The disappointment deep in her eyes weighed on his chest, crushing his heart and conscience. "I love you and I understand your wanting a baby. I have no doubt you'd make a wonderful mother." He paused and looked out over the lake. "It's me. I'm a selfish bastard. I can't help thinking of all the negatives. I'd be in my sixties by the time this child graduated college."

"Sixty's not all that old."

"Not from our perspective, but would our son or daughter think it was? And we'd probably have to have two kids, because it wouldn't be fair to only have one so much younger than Ted and Alex. And then Ted and Alex would be old enough to be our children's aunt and uncle."

"They adjusted to your divorce and to our marrying. They'd get used to having younger siblings."

Probably. His kids were remarkably resilient and independent. That wasn't a very solid argument. He stared at her hard, trying to make her determine if this was really a true desire and need, or just a fleeting sentimental idea.

"Is this is what you *really* want? Are you sure this isn't like wanting us to become foster parents?" Low blow. It was unfair to throw that incident up in her face, yet he had to know.

"This is different. I know it's not fair to change my mind. But I ache to feel your baby growing inside me." She cupped her hands over her lower abdomen. "I want to create a new life with you—a legacy of our love."

He didn't know what to say. "You could've just stopped taking birth control pills."

Jenny frowned and leaned back. "I don't want it that way."

He'd never believe her now. How could she tell Gabe she was already pregnant? It would devastate him. He'd feel betrayed—or tricked. Gabe would never believe it'd been an accident. Even though Jenny took the pill religiously, she was two weeks late. Her boobs were fuller and painful. She felt pregnant.

"I could never be happy if you didn't want the baby too."

He took her hands in his. "How about this... we stop using any birth control for six months and see what happens? We'll let fate decide it. No drugs, no operations, no assisted measures," he warned. "And if you get pregnant, we have a baby. If you don't, you don't. We're on our own. What do you think?"

Sounded reasonable given the fact that she was already pregnant, but on principal alone, Jenny wasn't impressed. She wanted him to want this baby. She wanted enthusiasm, not a compromise. "That's not exactly fair. What if I have some medical problem?"

Gabe sighed loudly. "It's a compromise, Jen."

"Six whole months?" She pulled her hands away. He didn't want a baby. Didn't want their baby.

He threw his arms wide. "Well, what do you want? A year? Two? How long do you want, Jenny? Enough time to have three kids? *That's* really fair." He planted a hand on his waist and cocked his head. "That's sure leaving it to destiny."

"Six months is stingy."

He looked away and swallowed hard. "A year?"

He spoke as if the two words were dragged from him. Jenny stood and turned her back on him in one fluid movement. "Forget it."

He vaulted to his feet. "What? I'm trying to compromise here."

She whirled to confront him as angry tears flooded her eyes. "I don't *want* to compromise," she shouted. "If you don't want it, just forget it."

This was a disaster. Gabe didn't want their baby and he'd never believe she hadn't gotten pregnant on purpose. She had to get away.

Gabe took a startled step backward, away from the force of her anger and disappointment. His mouth dropped open as she jumped on her bike and wobbled toward the path.

"Jen, wait. Come back. We can work this out."

They could work it out? That was just man-speak for "I can talk you out of it." Infuriated at his attitude, she headed for the trail.

On the path, Jenny quickly gathered momentum. She swiped at the tears blinding her and swerved sideways, narrowly missing a low-hanging branch in her determination to put some distance between them. She heard Gabe mount his bike and race after her, but that only served to panic her.

As they broke out of the stand of trees and darted into the street, he pulled alongside. "Jen, stop. Let's talk."

Peddling furiously, she surged ahead. He moved alongside her. "Jenny, I'm sorry. Pull over. We can have the baby."

God, when he found out she was pregnant he'd hate her. She had to get away.

Without sparing him as much as a glance, Jenny burst ahead, swinging toward the center of the street to circumvent a long stick blocking the edge of the road. Gabe dropped behind her and rounded the stick.

"Hey. Watch out!" Gabe yelled.

In a mighty surge, he sprang forward and shoved Jenny sideways. Eyes wide, unable to believe that he'd deliberately pushed her, she tumbled off her bike.

Chapter 3

"Ugh." The breath shot out of Jenny as she hit the ground hard. She skidded across the stinging coarse gravel and rolled down the embankment. Musty leaves crackled loudly in her ears and sticks scratched her face, but she still heard the unmistakable squeal of tires. Bang! She crashed into a large bush. Stunned, Jenny lay motionless for a moment, catching her breath and waiting for the sky, clouds, and trees to stop whirling around so she could focus.

"Oh, my God!" a voice said.

Jenny sat up, tentatively testing her muscles while looking around. Her hand went to her smarting cheek, then pulled away; blood smeared her finger tips. She looked up to where her bicycle teetered on the edge of the hill, the wheels spinning madly.

"Gabe?" He'd shoved her off her bike. Why would he do that? Where was he?

"Gabe?" she called louder this time, amplifying the pounding in her head. Jenny pushed to her feet. She steadied herself on a nearby tree trunk and stumbled toward the sound of the frantic voice up the hill. Higher on the slope to her right, Gabe's old, black helmet rested at the base of a narrow tree trunk; it lay open, empty, the ends frayed where the chinstrap had snapped in two.

"Ga-be!" Jenny scrambled up the steep slope, ignoring the stinging scratches on her palms. Topping the embankment, the pungent smell of burned rubber assaulted her nose. A large rumbling SUV idled nearby. The gleaming black hood was dented and the windshield shattered into a spider web of millions of glass pieces.

Gabe's mangled bike lay beneath it. A young man shouted into a cell phone as he rushed over to her.

"Are you okay? I didn't see you. The water bottle fell and I reached down to get it and... the shadows..." His mouth opened and closed wordlessly.

Head snapping from side to side, Jenny brushed by him. A lone shoe sat in front of the vehicle and then she spotted a hairy male leg and foot on the far side of the truck. She sprinted around the car and fell to her knees beside Gabe.

He lay curled on his side as if asleep. Legs and arm scrapped, face ashen, his eyes were closed—not pinched shut as if in pain but lightly, as if resting. He wasn't the bloody mess she'd feared when she'd seen that lone foot and leg, just a little blood seeped from his ear. His head was bare. Maybe he was just knocked out. A concussion. You weren't supposed to move an accident victim, were you?

Jenny's hand hovered over him, afraid to touch yet desperately needing proof that he still lived. She stroked his stubbly cheek and was reassured by its warmth. He was breathing and warm; that had to be good.

"Gabe?" she whispered.

"I didn't see him," the man sobbed. "The shadows—I'm so sorry."

"Gabe? Honey? Wake up." Jenny lightly caressed his face. "Gabe."

"Help should be here any minute," the man rasped. "I tried to stop. I tried. But..."

Chills chased through Jenny as she pressed against Gabe's inert form. Shivering, she inspected his body, looking for broken bones and signs of injury. She picked up one limp hand. "He's cold. He needs to be covered."

The man ripped off his coat and handed it to her. "Here, use this.

She spread the khaki jacket across Gabe and then hovered gently over him, mindful of possible internal injury, but needing to warm him with her own body heat.

"It's okay, honey," she crooned. "You're gonna be okay. The ambulance is on the way. See? Hear the siren? It'll be here in a minute and you'll be fine." Her voice clogged with tears as she wiped away the blood trickling from his ear down his cheek.

"I love you. You're going to be okay." She sniffled. "You'll be fine."

Her eyes never left Gabe's face as she willed him to wake. When the ambulance pulled alongside, Jenny allowed the paramedic to back her away from Gabe. She shook her head when asked if she was hurt. With her arms wrapped tightly over her stomach, Jenny hovered nearby, scrutinizing every move the paramedics made.

One man ran skilled hands over Gabe from his face to his toes, while the other carefully strapped an oxygen mask around his head and then fitted a thick collar around his neck. Together they rolled him onto his side and then back again onto a board. They worked in tandem to a script they'd practiced and perfected.

Each paramedic knew his role, and there was no fumbling or getting in the way of the other. One of them started an IV while the other put the oxygen tank between Gabe's legs and checked his blood pressure, scribbling numbers on his glove like an ugly tattoo. When they loaded him onto the truck, Jenny tried to climb in behind them.

"Ma'am, you need to ride up front." The paramedic helped her off the bumper step and slammed the doors shut.

"Hey, what about the police?" the driver yelled.

"Wait for them and then send them to Saugatuck General." The paramedic helped Jenny into the front seat before jogging around the truck.

Jenny twisted around until the seatbelt gouged her waist. She watched the paramedic in the back tend to Gabe. Her hand touched the cold glass partition, needing to be closer to him. Gabe lay so still on the stretcher.

The paramedic spoke into a black disk CB radio. "We've got a truck versus bicycle; male, Caucasian, mid-forties."

"Forty-three. He's just forty-three," Jenny mumbled.

"Unconscious. BP eighty over fifty. Respirations, thirty-five. Pulse one-thirty and thready. Pupils, seven millimeters, fixed and dilated. We've got him on oh-two at fifteen liters and normal saline drip running wide open. ETA, ten minutes. Any further orders?"

A voice crackled back, loud and clear, "Nothing further. Expect in ten."

The paramedic hung up the radio and pumped up the cuff around Gabe's arm. Deflating the cuff, he fiddled with the IV, opening the line wide, forcing fluids into Gabe's veins. He checked his pulse, then his blood pressure again. Frowning, the paramedic deflated the cuff and grabbed the radio. "Med Control from unit twenty-four. Pressure's dropped to sixty over forty, Requesting orders for Dopamine."

"Affirm. Start dopamine. Ten micrograms per kilogram per minute and get a second line in if you can."

The man flipped open what looked like an orange toolbox. With quick efficient movements, he withdrew a syringe and vial of clear liquid. Poking a needle in it, he drew some up into the syringe, injected it into a small bag, and then attached it to the IV.

Jenny's eyes never left her husband and the man working to save his life, as if she could will it to turn out right. The brakes squealed in protest as the ambulance stopped next to the Emergency room's sliding glass doors. The paramedic hopped out and ran around the back to help unload Gabe. Jenny jogged behind the paramedics, doctor, and nurse, as they rapid-fire reported Gabe's condition in what seemed like abbreviated code language.

The nurse directed the group into the second treatment room on the right, then stepped in front of Jenny as she tried to follow. The exam door slowly drifted shut, cutting off Jenny's view. Her last picture of her husband was of yellow-gowned people swarming Gabe like a hungry pride of lions at a fresh kill.

ल॰ ल॰ ल॰

Hours later, Jenny stood in the hall outside Gabe's room. Flattening her back against the wall, she drew in and pushed out measured breaths in an attempt to clear her numb brain. The doctor's earlier words still echoed through her head, meaningless. She probably should have grasped what Dr. Collins said; the doctor hadn't used any confusing medical terms, but Jenny needed it spelled out.

She swallowed the sour feeling and tried to paste an optimistic smile on her trembling lips before following a nurse inside. The young blonde woman with her hair pulled back in a tight ponytail fiddled with a machine, then smiled kindly at Jenny.

"Mrs. Harrison? Come on in. Don't let all these leads and tubes intimidate you."

Jenny moved closer, stepping around various IV poles. Gabe lay still in the bed. A clear tube was taped to his mouth and several smaller lines disappeared into his arms. A bag hooked onto the side of his bed collected pink-tinged urine. Dark bruises circled his eyes. Mesmerized, she moved closer.

Jenny turned to the nurse, speaking softly. "Can I touch him?"

"Absolutely." The nurse ran a hand lightly down Gabe's arm. "And talk to him too. You never know what he might hear."

"They said he has no brain function."

The smile faded. "I know. But I believe his spirit's still here."

Jenny watched Gabe carefully, wistful. "He looks so peaceful— like he's sleeping."

"He's not in any pain." The nurse paused at the door. "If you need anything, just ring his button."

"Thank you." Jenny moved closer to the bed, dropped the plastic hospital bag and helmet to the floor before stroking Gabe's cheek. His warmth reassured her.

"Hi, honey." She lovingly scanned Gabe's face, searching for some response to her voice. Finding none, she leaned forward and pressed a tender kiss to his warm cheek. She eased back and her hands gripped the cold metal bed rail as she studied his face. Nothing. No twitch. No eyelids fluttering. No slight lifting of his lips. Nothing. Breath rushed from Jenny's chest, crushing her aching heart in disappointment.

Well, what had she thought? That he'd magically awaken at the sound of her voice or her kiss. He wasn't sleeping beauty and this wasn't a fairytale. Jenny was trapped in a nightmare. Blinking rapidly, she blew out another hot breath and moved her hand up and down his arm.

"That's okay. You've got some mending to do. The doctor said your head took quite a hit. It's probably good you're not awake because you'd have a whopper of a headache."

Talk to him. You never know what he might hear. The nurse's advice echoed in Jenny's tired head. People who came out of comas often recalled what had gone on around them. Maybe Gabe would. Maybe that was the key to her miracle.

Jenny's hand cupped her stomach. Gabe couldn't die. They had too much to do, too much to share. If he remembered how much they loved each other, if he knew how much she needed him, he'd never leave her. Spirit or coma, Gabe would fight to come back to her. Jenny sniffled and swallowed the lump clogging her throat. He would come back. She'd bring him back.

She dragged the chair closer and perched on the edge of the seat. "Gabe, remember the day we met? I'd snuck into the hospital to stay with Michael, and you caught me while making rounds." A smile lightened her voice. "That was the luckiest day of my life. I was so nervous. You were this gorgeous guy; older, sophisticated, and my little brother's doctor for Pete's sake. I was just an insecure kid a couple of years out of college, struggling to support myself at the *Chronicle*, and in trouble with my mom. I was hardly in your league. But you—" Jenny smiled at the memory; warmth and happiness flooded her. "You smiled at me as if I was perfect and asked me out."

She stared at the white cotton blanket. Her vision blurred until she could clearly see the past. "You took me to the Hunt Club for our first date, remember? And when you showed so much interest in my article on the Donnatelli Clinic, I felt a real connection with you before dinner was even over.

"And then we kissed." Jenny sighed and smiled warmly at her husband. She squeezed his unresponsive hand and stood to press a tender kiss to his cheek. Blinking back tears that blurred Gabe's beloved face, Jenny blew out a deep breath and forced a smile to her lips, whispering, "You had me at that first kiss."

Nurses and lab people came in periodically to take blood and urine samples and to check on Gabe. They all kindly offered Jenny words of sympathy and encouragement, but she just wanted to be alone with her husband. She smiled wistfully, lowered Gabe's bed rail and sat next to him. Hip pressed tightly against his side, she raised his slack hand to her lips and kissed his knuckles. She nuzzled his hand, wishing he would cup her cheek as he often did before kissing her.

"Gabe? Can you hear me?" Jenny stared intently at his face, but Gabe didn't so much as twitch. Heart heavy, she sighed and gently placed his hand on the bed. If she hadn't run from that stupid fight, he wouldn't be lying in that hospital bed. Her lips trembled. "I'm *so* sorry. This is all my fault."

She reached for the rough tissues on Gabe's bedside stand and blew her nose. Her gaze dropping to the helmet and bag on the floor, she slid off the bed, opened the plastic hospital bag and looked inside. Lying on top of Gabe's jeans was the vintage Tissot doctor's watch George gave Gabe for his graduation from medical school.

George claimed the watch had been given to grandfather Harrison in nineteen thirty-eight when he graduated med school—a real family heirloom. She stared at the watch until it blurred. She couldn't remember a time when Gabe didn't wear it. She scooped it up and stuffed it in her pants pocket. Gabe would be upset if anything happened to his beloved watch.

Jenny returned her attention to the bag and his wallet, peaking out of the neck of his navy knit shirt. His wallet was brown leather, creased and worn, like all Gabe's favorite things.

Taking the billfold out, Jenny sank into the nearby chair. She moved her thumb back and forth over the cool rawhide. One side was curved, bowed from years of being stuffed in Gabe's back pocket. Maybe she'd get him a new one for Christmas.

She slumped in the seat until her head rested against the chair back. Rolling her head sideways, she looked at Gabe. His eyes remained closed, his body still but for the rhythmic breathes the ventilator forced into his chest.

She toyed with the billfold and looked at Gabe's face. His eyelids didn't even flutter. With a sigh, Jenny dropped the wallet to her lap and leaned forward to stroke Gabe's warm, hairy arm. She laid her cheek on the back of his hand and laced her fingers through his slack ones. The wallet plunked to the floor. When Jenny's back began to ache from the awkward position, she gave his hand one final pat, straightened and stretched her sore muscles. Picking up the wallet, she put it on his bed.

The night crept on and the nurse brought Jenny a dinner tray. She tried to eat, knowing she'd need the strength, but could only force down the salty meatloaf and soggy green beans. At ten o'clock, Ken Stanley, the chief of St. Francis's neurosurgery department, entered Gabe's room. Tall and balding, wearing wide, wire-rimmed glasses, Ken exuded confidence, even casually dressed in navy corduroys and a cream cable-knit sweater.

He put a warm hand to her back. "Jenny."

"Ken. Thanks for coming." If anybody could help Gabe, it'd be Ken. Not only was he a friend but Gabe had always respected his skill as a doctor, so Jenny had asked Dr. Collins to call Ken for a second opinion. Surely he'd find something the others here had overlooked.

"How're you holding up?"

"Okay." Alone in his room, Jenny could pretend that Gabe was just like any other sick patient—just resting deeply—perhaps drugged by pain medication. But with the appearance of this doctor she recognized from social functions, reality suddenly came crashing back. Fear and impotence filled Jenny, like a dam broken loose. She grasped Gabe's hand in a crushing grip. "They say he's got no brain function, but they're mistaken, right? There must be some medication, some surgery, *something* you can do to help him. *Please*, tell me there's something you can do."

"I'll try." He squeezed her shoulder. "I talked to the admitting doctor and looked over his chart. Let's see if there's been any improvement."

Jenny watched carefully as Ken pried Gabe's eyes open and flashed a light in them. He tapped his knees and elbows with a small rubber mallet. When he pinched the muscle on the back of Gabe's neck and then pricked his thigh with a safety pin, Jenny flinched—unfortunately Gabe didn't.

Finally the doctor's experienced hands traveled Gabe's arms and legs, testing his muscle tone, before frowning intently over his chart again. He carefully read each page, flipping back to an earlier page to reconfirm something. Sighing, Ken pulled a chair over next to Jenny's. He sat down heavily and turned sad eyes to her.

She scowled and looked away. *No. No. No. Don't look at me like that. He's not gone. He's not!*

"I'm sorry, Jenny."

"No." She frowned fiercely and slowly shook her head. "Don't you say it. Fix him. Just make him better." *Bring him back to me.*

"I can't. You know I would if I could but—"

"Yes. Yes, you can. Fix him."

"I'm sorry. I can't fix Gabe. Nobody can."

She glared at him. "I don't believe you."

"Jenny, Gabe is completely unaware of any internal or external stimuli. He has no pupillary response. No gag or cough response. No spontaneous reflexes. The exam and test results indicate that all functions of his brain have been irrevocably lost."

All functions irrevocably lost. She slumped in her seat and clutched her aching stomach. "Nooo," she drew out.

"If there was anything at all—I'd do it." He pursed his lips. "But there's no point."

"So, he's..." Jenny cleared her throat. Trying again, she whispered. "He's really gone?"

"I'm afraid so." Ken's head bobbed in a slight nod. "The damage to his brain was just too massive."

And it's my fault. If I hadn't run... If I'd told him about the baby instead of manufacturing some fake scenario... If the truck hadn't come along... she looked at Gabe, then dropped her head. *I did this. It's my fault.*

"I'm very sorry. They've done two EEGs, brainstem evoked potentials, and four-vessel cerebral angiography. It's been twelve hours since he came in and there's been no improvement at all— despite all the steroids and medication they've pumped into him. The ventilator is breathing for him."

She lifted her gaze. "Twelve hours? Twelve hours isn't long. It's—it's not even twenty-four hours—not even a day. You're ready to write him off after just twelve hours?"

"I know it seems a short time to you, but given all the tests and medicine and the total lack of response, I'm afraid it's not good." Ken waited as if giving her time to assimilate the bad news before speaking gently. "They'll maintain his respiration and heart with the machine but only long enough for you to adjust and make plans."

"Plans?"

"We could keep his body alive for months like that, until an infection killed him, but we won't. Letting Gabe continue like this only perpetuates unrealistic expectations. I'm sorry." Ken gently squeezed her forearm. "You need to gather the family to say your good-byes and let him go with dignity."

"*Me?*" *She* had to gather the family and tell them Gabe was gone? *She* had to let him die? Was he crazy?

"Yeah." He nodded. "It's your decision when. Technically he's already gone, but nobody's going to turn off the respirator before you're ready. In all fairness to you both, it needs to be soon."

Jenny's gaze darted to Gabe's chest. She watched it rise and fall in a perfect steady rhythm. He wanted her to stop that? He'd disguised it as "letting him go with dignity," but as far as Jenny was concerned, as long as Gabe breathed, assisted or not, he was alive. And this supposed friend, supposed expert doctor, wanted *her* to kill Gabe.

"I can't do that," Jenny said. "What if I was wrong? What if he came out of it?" She wanted to turn from the pity in his eyes, but made herself focus on Ken's words.

"I don't want to sound cruel, but you need to know the reality of the situation. *If* a miracle like that happened," Ken's forehead wrinkled over wide eyes, clearly doubting the possibility, "I *guarantee* you he'd be a vegetable." He paused, letting the statement sink in. "Gabe was a doctor—the best. He'd have seen poor souls like that and I don't know a man who would want to exist that way."

Jenny wanted to shout, "Who cares? *I* want him alive. *I need him.*" Images of Gabe flashed through her mind. Sweaty Gabe gliding up the driveway after a long ride with Steve. Grinning in satisfaction, he'd salute Steve as they headed for their showers. Gabe's face lifted to the sun, at the helm of their boat. Gabe serving, then rushing the net to best his son at tennis. Jenny saw him confidently striding down the hospital hallway, hurrying to surgery or to check on a patient. Tears filled her eyes with the weight of the truth. Gabe was a dynamic man. If he could breathe without the machine and was even remotely aware of his helpless condition, it'd kill him.

"He'd hate it." She blinked back tears. "It'd break my heart too, but I can't. I can't do it."

"You don't have to make a decision right away, but you do need to gather the family." Ken looked hesitant, like he had something to offer but was unsure.

"What?"

He expelled a breath. "Have you thought about organ donation?"

Jenny stared at Ken and blinked.

"Most of his organs are in good shape. Gabe could live on through other people."

"Are you kidding me?" She vaulted to her feet and rounded on him. "Cut Gabe up and give bits and pieces of him to other people? Are you nuts?"

"I know it sounds callous, but he could save a lot of lives."

"No!" Jenny glared at him.

"I understand. But as Gabe's friend, I had to bring it up. As a doctor I want to give you as much information as possible. You need to fully understand the gravity of the situation—"

"He's dead. I get it." Jenny wrapped her arms tightly around her quivering stomach.

"Jenny, you need to consider what Gabe would want." He picked up Gabe's wallet from the foot the bed and held it out to her. "I suspect he wanted to be an organ donor."

Jenny stared in horror at the billfold, then looked at Ken. The sympathy in his eyes gave her courage. She reached out and took it. Her hand sank as if the wallet weighed twenty pounds. With a deep breath and trembling fingers, Jenny flipped the billfold open.

She ignored the driver's license tucked inside the slot under the credit cards and slowly turned the plastic rectangles protecting his family pictures. The first was a photo of her, then one of her and Gabe, then Alex and Ted's high school graduation pictures. The regular assortment of insurance cards stacked the back. Jenny pulled out Gabe's Blue Cross Blue Shield card and blindly handed it to Ken, mumbling, "They'll need this."

Though sorely tempted to slam the wallet shut, Jenny worked the driver's license back and forth until she'd freed it from its plastic slot. God, her husband was a handsome man. She loved the way his light brown hair lay close-cropped to his head in tidy layers, and the deep crinkle lines at the corner of his pewter gray eyes made him look totally adorable. Though not pretty-boy handsome, he had that Harrison Ford every-day rugged look.

A smile creased Jenny's face when she looked at his documented weight, one hundred seventy pounds. Hmmm. He'd put on a few pounds since then. Moving her thumb, Jenny looked for the little red heart signifying an organ donor. She flipped the card over. Eyes popping wide, she looked at Ken. "It's not there."

Ken frowned. "Really?"

Jenny felt lightheaded, almost giddy. Knowing Gabe, she'd fully expected to find the heart, but it wasn't there. Though Jenny believed in organ donation, even made sure she was registered as an organ donor when she'd changed the name on her driver's license, it wasn't appropriate now. Gabe's circumstances were different.

Her hand trembled as Jenny handed him the card. She stifled a nervous smile. Nothing would change. They had a respite.

"This must be a mistake." He frowned, then handed the card back to her. "Even so, you can still donate for him. It's your decision."

Jenny's relief evaporated and tears stung her eyes.

"You know it's what he would have wanted. Just think about it." Ken wrapped an arm around her shoulder, holding Jenny close as she sobbed until her chest hurt. She actually felt her heart tearing, painfully ripping apart, exposing jagged raw edges. Ken allowed her to ease away and handed her the tissue box.

"Gabe was a talented doctor—a really great person. If there was any hope, any chance at all, I promise you, I would do whatever it took to help him. But there just isn't. I'm sorry." His voice broke. "I'm going to miss him like hell." He paused for a moment. "Is there someone you can call? Your mom?"

She shook her head.

"Have you notified his children? His parents?"

"His parents are..." she stumbled over the word *dead*, as if she said the word then Gabe would be dead too. "Gone. And the kids are—" My God, Alex and Ted. Jenny hadn't given them a thought. How could she tell them their father was dead? "I'll call their mother."

"I'll write up my consult and then talk again with Dr. Collins. If there's anything else," he handed her a business card, "my home phone's on the back. Please call if there's anything I can do."

Jenny nodded and turned away, unable to look at him. He was healthy. He got to go home to his family. Her husband would not.

Numb, she moved closer to Gabe's bed. A quick scan showed everything to be the same. She slid a hand up his warm arm. Gabe couldn't be dead—dead people were blue and cold. Jenny's pain in her pelvis intensified and then eased. Her eyes opened in horror, recognizing the familiar spasms. No. No. It couldn't be cramps. She pushed back in the chair and rested her feet on the bed. She just needed to rest. She'd be fine. They'd be fine.

Chapter 4

After another twenty minutes of painful cramping, Jenny hurried out of the room to the nurses' desk. "Can you help me? My husband is Gabe Harrison." She pointed to his room. "I'm pregnant and I'm cramping and bleeding. Is there a doctor I can see?"

The nurse sent her down to the ER where a doctor examined her, ran an hCG test, then came back to tell her she'd lost the baby.

Her beloved baby was gone. Lying alone on a gurney in the ER, Jenny rolled onto her side and cried and cried. She cried for the little one she'd lost and cried for herself. She begged God to wake her from this nightmare. Then she bargained with God, the baby's life for Gabe's. Surely he wasn't cruel enough to take them both?

Jenny dried her eyes, cleaned up, dressed, and rushed back upstairs, convinced Gabe would be better. She rushed into Gabe's room, sure she'd find him awake—or at least curled on his side as he preferred to sleep.

Gabe lay on his back, bruised eyes closed, the ventilator tube still protruding from his mouth. His chest rose and fell to the rhythm of the machine. No improvement—for either of them. Jenny kept backsliding, losing more and more.

She dropped in the chair next to his bed. Not fair. This was *not fair*—none of it. First God stole her husband and now her baby? What was going on? Jenny stared at Gabe, longing to feel his strong arms wrap around her, reassuring her everything would be okay. But nothing would ever be okay again.

Gabe couldn't hold her. And now she wouldn't even have his baby to hold onto. And they wanted her to stop the machine. They wanted her to give away his organs. It was her decision. Jenny kissed Gabe's knuckles, then rested her cheek on their clasped hands.

"Gabe, help me. What should I do?" She gulped and tried to force her trembling lips into a smile. "You said we'd be together forever. You said—" The breath flew from her lungs. "You said—"

Jenny broke down and wailed, deep, gut-wrenching sobs.

∾ ∾ ∾

The next morning, people came and went from Gabe's room, but none offered Jenny a miracle. Jenny called Alex and Ted's mother, Judith, about the accident and Gabe's condition. To her relief, Judith offered to tell the children and Gabe's uncle, George. Jenny hadn't the energy or emotional fortitude to deal with his uncle.

Gabe had gone to live with his uncle George and aunt Adele when he was only eight years old. His parents had worked for the Peace Corps and both died of amoebic dysentery in a little village in Columbia. George had had no children of his own; perhaps that's why he was so obsessively close to Gabe.

Though George was always polite to Jenny, she got the feeling he didn't really like her. He displayed no outright hostility, but Jenny sensed an underlying chill and tolerance from Gabe's uncle that hadn't lessened over the years of their marriage. She refused to let her feelings get hurt, figuring that her patience and kindness would wear George down. Besides, Gabe's love more than made up for his uncle's indifference.

Jenny lifted Gabe's hand. She stretched his long fingers out and moved her thumb over his palm. Surgeon's hands. Warm hands. Could he really be dead?

Gabe's face remained unlined and peaceful. If his brain had stopped, had his spirit already departed while the machine kept his body warm? Was Gabe somewhere in this room, hovering above, trying to come to grips with death himself, like people from near death experiences claimed? Was he confused? Scared? Jenny hoped not. Senses straining, she tried to feel something ghostly. Any subtle indication that Gabe's existence had really changed so dramatically beyond the calm sleep that seemed to have claimed him.

God, please don't take him from me. If this is my punishment for Michael or for wanting a baby, it's not fair. Don't punish Gabe because of me. It should have been me.

"Mrs. Harrison?"

Jenny looked up into the chocolate-colored eyes of a tall, thin, dark-haired woman clutching a clipboard to her chest. But for the short, dark hair feathered away from her face and the pointy, pinched nose supporting wire-rimmed glasses, she very much resembled Popeye's Olive Oyl.

"I'm Amy Bromley from Save a Life. The hospital thought I might be of some help to you."

"Why? Can you save my husband?" Jenny raised her chin, challenging.

Amy looked at Gabe, then back at her. "Not the way you're hoping."

She turned away. *Didn't think so.*

Amy moved to the other side of Gabe's bed, back into Jenny's field of vision. "I'm very sorry for your loss. I'm here to present you with an opportunity to have your husband live on through other people as an organ donor. Have you and your husband ever discussed this possibility?"

Feeling ashamed at taking her frustrations out on the woman, Jenny shook her head. "The subject never came up." She paused. "Gabe's a doctor. A colleague of his was here last night and broached the idea of organ donation. I practically took the man's head off."

"I understand."

Really? How could she understand? Jenny tried to shake off her annoyance at the woman's agreeability. "When he suggested I consider donating Gabe's organs, all I could think was, he'd have to be dead to do that. And I wasn't convinced he was gone. I mean intellectually I know. I've seen the test results, I've talked to the experts, but it doesn't feel so in here." She tapped a hand over her heart.

"That does make it more difficult," Amy agreed. "But the hospital has quite specific criteria in determining brain death. A lot of families take great comfort from knowing that their loved one's death wasn't for nothing.

"You can choose which organs and tissues he would have wanted recovered or you can donate his whole body, in which case as many as fifty people could be helped. Your husband could live on in as many as fifty people. That's quite a legacy."

Not the legacy that would bring Jenny any comfort. She looked at her beloved husband. How could Gabe really be gone? She dragged in a deep ragged breath, struggling to get oxygen past her raw, constricted throat. With one trembling hand, she rubbed the tears from her eyes.

"I don't know. If Gabe wanted to be an organ donor, why didn't he check the box? He knew how important it was." She looked at Amy, puzzled. "You'd think a doctor would know better." Why on earth would he leave such and important decision unmade—up to her?

"I'm not surprised. Only about forty-five percent of Americans have joined their state's organ donor registry, even though, according to Gallup polls, more than ninety percent of people support organ donation and think it's a good thing." She pursed her lips and shrugged. "People just don't get around to it, or they aren't asked when they renew their license, or they want to discuss it with their family first but have trouble starting the conversation—or any number of reasons. But you can do it for him. You can give your husband a wonderful legacy and make something positive come from his loss."

I can, but should I? She'd lost so much during the past twenty-four hours. Gabe. Their baby. They'd left her to go on alone. Jenny's top teeth clamped down on her bottom lip.

She looked at the lady. "Okay, I'll do it. I'll sign. But I want something first." Jenny paused. "I want Gabe's sperm saved so I can still have his baby. That's the legacy *I* want. Can you do that?"

Amy frowned. "I don't know. I'd have to check with our director. As far as I know, it's never been done."

"But it's possible?"

"I don't see why not. But I'm not sure they have the facilities here to store the sperm."

"I don't live here anyway. We're from Grosse Pointe."

"Let me talk to my boss and do some research." With her index finger tapping her flat lips, Amy raised unfocused eyes to some distant point while she thought out loud. "If the hospital has an ethics committee, we'll probably have to get permission from them. Then I'll have to find a doctor willing to perform the surgery... and then get hold of a sperm bank."

"Will that take long? I assume they'll want to take his organs soon."

"Which organs would you want to donate?"

Decision made, a shot of adrenaline raced through her. Oh no, what had she done? *What Gabe would have wanted,* her little voice whispered. Gabe might have chosen this, but *she* wasn't ready. *He's gone; it has to be now.* But—*He'll always be with you, imprinted on your mind and heart. You know it's true.*

A peaceful feeling settled over her, slowing her tripping heart. This was right. A tender smile curved her lips as she looked at Gabe. "He'd want to help as many people as possible."

"Wonderful." Amy beamed. "I'll contact the transplant teams immediately and let them know you've consented to donate. They'll give him some medicine to thin his blood and maximize the health of his organs, so don't be alarmed when you see him getting extra medication." She stood and headed for the door. "I'll get the consent forms and make those phone calls."

"Wait," Jenny called out. "Before I sign any forms. For my own peace of mind, could we turn off the ventilator just to be sure he can't breathe on his own? I know they said the machine's breathing for him, but I need to see it for myself. Please."

The lady frowned, clearly uncomfortable with the idea. "I'll talk to his doctor. We may be able to arrange something."

"Thank you."

Two hours later, Dr. Collins returned to Gabe's room. "Jenny? I hear you've consented to donate your husband's organs."

She nodded. "But I need to be sure. I know you said he's gone, but what if it's a mistake? What if he's just in a coma? Can you turn the ventilator off so I can see for myself?"

Hands deep in her lab-coat pockets, Dr. Collins listened. "There's just one problem. If we turn it off—his heart can only survive a very short time without oxygen before it'll stop—there's a very real possibility that we couldn't start it again and then his organs would be unsuitable for recovery." She paused before simplifying it for Jenny. "You wouldn't be able to see the flat line on the EKG—we couldn't let it go that far."

"But there's a little time?"

"Only about a minute."

Hope swelled from desolation. A minute could be a long time. It could be enough. "Could we try? Please? I have to give him that chance."

Dr. Collins hesitated, clearly reluctant to take the risk, but she relented. "Sure." She turned to a nurse who entered the room. "Cindy, get the crash cart."

When the nurse wheeled the big red metal cart resembling a huge mechanic's toolbox into the room, Dr. Collins turned to Jenny. "Ready?"

Jenny stood next to Gabe's bed. In two and a half short years this man had become her life. He meant the world to her. Without him, Jenny was nothing. She would not give up on him now. Gabe was all that was good in her, and she couldn't accept his death without proof. Maybe they were wrong. Maybe he was locked deep inside a coma recovering from the trauma of the accident. He might still be able to come back to her. He might not really be dead. God couldn't be that cruel.

She looked at the doctor and nodded for her to turn off the respirator.

Gabe's chest jerked a little, rose, and then fell on his own. Jenny's heart soared. See? They'd all been wrong. They hadn't had enough faith, she thought as she watched his chest jump again.

"He's breathing! Did you see that? He's breathing on his own." Grinning like a fool, she looked at the doctor, but no triumphant smile lit her face, only a deep frown of concentration as she split her attention between her patient and the EKG machine.

Jenny turned back to watch Gabe's chest rise and fall sporadically. "He's breathing. He's doing it." She grinned and picked up his slack hand, squeezing it. "Gabe, it's me. Wake up, honey. You're gonna be all right. Everything's gonna be all right."

Jenny's smile faded, wilting like a rose out of water, as she scanned Gabe's slightly graying face. He lay perfectly still. No breathing, no twitching. Nothing. The EKG monitor blipped erratically, nowhere near the steady reassuring blipping inspired by the ventilator. Eyes wide, Jenny stared at Gabe's chest willing it to move.

"Oh, no." She shook his hand. "No. Come on. Don't do this to me. Breathe."

His face took on a definite blue tinge.

"Gabe, breathe," she whispered. Panic raced through her. "Breathe. Please, breathe."

His chest remained still.

She reached out a trembling hand to his face, half afraid it would be cold. It wasn't, but no soft breath exhaled on her hand either. Her tear-filled gaze darted between the frowning doctor and Gabe's inert form.

"Help him! Turn it on. Turn it on! Don't let him die," she begged, fear constricting her throat. "I'm not ready. I'm not ready. I'm not ready," she chanted through trembling lips. She pressed her folded arms against the crushing pain souring her stomach. "I can't do this. Please, don't let him die."

Dr. Collins flipped the switch and Gabe's chest rose and fell again as the respirator inflated then deflated his lungs for him. After listening to his heart and checking the machines one last time, the doctor nodded for the nurse to wheel the crash cart out of the room. She rounded the bed and put an arm around Jenny's shoulders. "I'm sorry."

Jenny nodded as the tears cascaded down her face. She clutched Gabe's hand while watching his color gradually return. The doctor slipped a box of tissues within her field of vision, but Jenny couldn't bring herself to let go of his hand or tear her gaze from his precious face.

He was really gone. She bowed her head and sobbed. What was she going to do?

With one trembling hand, Jenny rubbed the tears from her eyes. She took small shallow breaths to calm her galloping heart. Refusing to turn away from Gabe, Jenny forced herself to give them the answer they all wanted—the answer Gabe would have wanted. "All right. I'll sign."

"I'll let them know. If it's any consolation, I think you're very brave. I'm sure your husband would be proud." Dr. Collins left the room.

Why not just pat me on the head too? Jenny wanted to be polite and say thank you, but the words stuck in her throat. She couldn't be gracious. She wasn't thankful about any of this. She just wanted her husband back.

Gabe, what am I supposed to do without you?

∾ ∾ ∾

Jenny dozed fitfully in the chair at Gabe's bedside. The kitchen staff brought her breakfast and lunch, and Jenny did her best to choke down some of it. The phone in her pants pocket pulsed. She checked the number but didn't answer it. Steve. Pulling herself out of the chair, she glanced at Gabe before going downstairs to the lobby to call their friend back.

"Jenny? Are you all right? I heard about the accident on the news. Is Gabe okay?" The worry in Steve's voice suddenly made it all real again.

"No. Gabe's... Um..." She pushed a lock of hair behind an ear. Turning away from eavesdropping people, Jenny rested her head against the wall and lowered her voice. "Gabe's not all right."

"Sit tight. I'll be right th—"

"No, don't. There's nothing you can do. Gabe's gone." Tears flooded her eyes and stung her nose. She swallowed hard. "The damage to his brain was too much."

"I'm on my way."

"No, please—really." She didn't want Steve—didn't want anybody. Just Gabe. "Judith and the kids will be here soon." *I can't take anymore.* She wanted them all to go away and leave her alone with Gabe. "Stay home," she pleaded.

"Jenny, I can—"

"No!" *Damn it. Just leave us alone.* "Please, just take care of Ritz."

"Okay," he said quietly. "If that's what you want. If you change your mind, I can be there in three hours."

"I have to go." Jenny slid the phone closed and sagged against the wall, exhausted. Several minutes later, she returned to Gabe's room, hoping she'd find him sitting up in bed, alert and hungry, but one look at his peaceful face and her heart dropped anew. Nothing had changed.

Nurses fiddled with his IV and adjusted lines here and there, but Jenny ignored them, tuning them out, until her stepchildren arrived with their mother.

"Jenny?" Alex and Ted hesitated in the doorway, as if worried they'd be intruding. "Mom's talking with Dad's doctor. She said it was all right to come in," Alex whispered. The wide-eyed girl stood slightly behind her frowning big brother, clutching his arm.

Jenny smiled, wanting to look strong and confident for Gabe's children. Though in college, right now Ted and Alex resembled much younger kids. Many wonderful things had come from her marriage and these two kids were one of her best blessings.

"Hey, hi." Jenny waved them in and stood. "Come on in."

Being a stepmom hadn't always been easy—especially when Jenny was closer to her stepchildren's ages than her husband's, but Gabe had always been supportive of her relationship with his kids.

They each gave her a long tight hug before lining up behind her, making sure Jenny was between them and their father. They cast worried looks past her at the bed. Putting an arm about each kid, Jenny urged them closer. "It's okay. There's no need to be frightened."

Ted stared at his dad. "He looks like he's sleeping."

"I know."

Alex frowned at Gabe and then quickly looked away. "Mom said he's dead," she whispered, as if it would hurt Gabe's feelings to hear.

Jenny swallowed against the tears swelling the back of her throat and nodded. She cleared her throat. "I talk to him. I think his spirit's still hanging around." A smile trembled on her lips. "You know your dad. He'd want to say goodbye and let you feel how much he loves you."

"Did he say goodbye to you? Did you get to talk to him?" Alex asked.

Jenny pursed her lips and shook her head. No; no goodbyes. They'd been having a fight. A stupid argument. Her last words to Gabe had been mean and hurtful. God, she hated herself.

She moved around Ted. "I'll go find your mom."

Jenny raised Gabe's hand and kissed the back of it, then pressed her mouth to his cheek in a brief, tender kiss, showing the kids that being left alone with their father wasn't scary.

She found Judith at the nurses' station reviewing Gabe's chart. Tall and well proportioned, Judith had a commanding presence. As an older woman and a doctor, she always managed to make Jenny feel stupid and immature. From a distance, she watched Judith pore over the reports, desperately hoping that maybe she could find a miracle everyone else overlooked.

Gabe always claimed Judith was an extraordinary doctor. Judith and Gabe had been great friends for years and he'd fathered her children. She'd save Gabe if it were within her power. Judith slowly closed the blue plastic chart and placed it to the side of the nurses' desk. Her eyebrows pulled together until two vertical parallel lines creased her forehead. She slumped in the chair and stared at her Dansko clogs.

"Did you find anything?" Jenny had to ask, then exhaled in disappointment at the raw grief in the other woman's eyes.

"No." She took a deep breath. "There's no consent to donate organs in his chart. You're going to donate, aren't you? He'd want that."

"How do you know?"

"We discussed it when we were residents." Judith rose and came over to her. "He never wanted to be on a respirator and he wanted to be an organ donor."

Jenny didn't know what to say. Jealousy ripped through her. Here was Gabe's ex-wife, cool as can be, bugging her about giving away his organs. She'd had her time with him. She'd gotten her children and then discarded him for another man. Judith would always have a living reminder of Gabe, but Jenny had nothing. Nothing but memories that would fade in time.

She opened her mouth to explain about the sperm recovery, then closed it. If Judith thought it was a bad idea, could she block the procedure? Just then the organ donor lady rounded the corner. Jenny was forced to introduce them. Knowing that Judith respected strength, Jenny straightened her shoulders and pretended a confidence she didn't feel.

"I've agreed to donate Gabe's organs, but first they need to recover his sperm for me." Should she tell them about the miscarriage? She frowned—no, it was too new—too personal, but she felt compelled to explain the odd request. "This way I can still have our baby."

Judith raised her eyebrows but didn't comment.

Jenny turned to Amy. "So where do we stand?"

"I have good news and not so good news." Amy glanced at Judith, as if wondering if she should share this in front of the other woman or speak to Jenny privately. "Dr. Steinmetz is a urologist on staff here, and he's consented to recover your husband's sperm. This hospital doesn't have an ethics committee, so we don't have to wait for approval. However, I'm having a hard time finding a sperm bank willing to store it for you."

"Why?"

"Well, this is a very unusual situation. So far, four out of the five sperm banks in Michigan have refused to store your husband's sperm. The Kalamazoo lab is dragging its feet. I've called dozens of companies, and the only one willing to take it right now is located in California."

"Really?" Jenny deflated. California was so far away. How could California be the *only* one?

"I'm afraid so."

"Since you have a urologist willing to do the surgery, I'd advise you not to let him know you've run into this much resistance to storing the sperm." Judith said. "He might change his mind."

"Why?"

"Well, this is pretty controversial." Judith crossed her arms over her chest and gave Jenny a censorious look. "What you're asking him to do isn't exactly illegal, but it *does* stretch ethical limits."

"How? Gabe's my husband and I want to have his baby."

"Sperm banks are under intense scrutiny. A lot of people are unaccepting of the work they do. Not quite as bad as abortion clinics, but I imagine they have to be careful."

"If he backed out, could you do it?"

"What, sperm retrieval? Me?" Judith raised her eyebrows. "Not a chance."

"Couldn't or wouldn't?" she challenged. "Gabe said you're a remarkable doctor. You could do it if you wanted to."

"I'm a heart surgeon, Jenny. I have no idea what that kind of procedure entails. I wouldn't know what to do with the sperm once I had it. Not to mention the ethics of a doctor operating on her ex-husband to remove his sperm for future conception.

"It'd have to be a urologist or maybe even a fertility specialist. I don't know. If I were you, I'd get it done as soon as possible. Harvest the sperm, send it to California and then worry about transferring it closer to home."

Jenny turned to Amy. "Okay, let's do that. Now what?"

"Are his children here?"

"They're with him now."

"Well, as soon as you sign the papers and all say good-bye, we'll turn him over to the transplant team. They'll collect his sperm and recover his organs, and it could be all over with by tonight."

Amy was wrong; tonight wouldn't be the end of this nightmare, it'd be the beginning.

"I'll see you later this afternoon." She dismissed the woman, stifling the urge to run back to Gabe's bedside and hide. Strangely, even inert and unconscious, Gabe gave her a sense of comfort and feeling of security.

"Have you gotten hold of George yet?" Judith asked. "He wasn't home when I called, so I left a message on his machine."

"I left a message too." Did he really have to know?

"You can't do it without giving George a chance to say goodbye," Judith admonished, as if reading her mind.

Jenny sighed. "I'll try again."

"How about your parents?"

"They don't need to come. I'd rather tell them in person."

"Have you made any arrangements?"

She slumped, suddenly weary of being pummeled by Judith's questions. "Not yet."

"I could help—if you want."

Her eyes narrowed on Gabe's ex-wife. "Why would you do that?"

"I want to help." Judith wouldn't hold her gaze and a red rash flushed her chest and her lower neck.

The ice lady embarrassed? She couldn't be. "Why? Afraid I'll screw it up?"

Judith's eyebrows rose. "No, I'm not afraid you'll screw it up. The funeral director pretty much guides you through it any way. I just thought it'd be something I could do for him. It would make Gabe happy, knowing I was helping you."

"He's dead," she bluntly reminded in an effort to shock her nemesis and, in a perverse way, to prove her toughness. "You think he'll know the difference?"

Tears glistened in Judith's eyes, although her voice was firm. "He'll know. His spirit lives on. Through Alex and Ted, and that little baby you'll carry. He'll always be with us."

And that little baby you'll carry. She looked at Judith, curious. "So you think I'm doing the right thing?"

"If that's what you want."

"Even the baby?"

"What baby?" As they talked, Alex left Gabe's room and eased into her mother's arms. Alex's face lit with hope and a tentative smile softened her lips as she looked at Jenny. "You're pregnant?"

"Not yet, sweetie." Judith stroked her daughter's hair. "They're going to save Dad's sperm so Jenny can be inseminated."

"About time," Alex said.

Judith patted her arm. "Check on your brother for me, will you?"

Jenny's eyes widened. Alex wanted a baby brother or sister? "About time?"

Judith shrugged. "You're young, Jenny. We've been expecting an announcement that you were pregnant."

"But Gabe wasn't—isn't," Jenny corrected, unwilling to declare him past while his body still lay warm mere yards away. "Gabe isn't that young to be starting all over again."

"He *wasn't* that old," Judith corrected, silently chiding Jenny to accept the inevitable. "Besides, he loved you. He loved kids. I expected that he'd want to have children with you."

Her assumptions were a balm to Jenny's soul. Of course Gabe would want her to have his baby.

Chapter 5

George came home from fly-fishing totally beat. He threw his canvas duffel down and walked into the kitchen. Ignoring the blinking red light on his answering machine, he turned on the TV and snagged a cold root beer from the refrigerator. He sat at the counter, hoping to catch the score of the Tigers' game on the noon news. If they beat the White Sox last night, they'd go on to the playoffs. He reached in a cupboard and opened a new bag of Fritos.

"And in the local news, a prominent Grosse Pointe surgeon and humanitarian, doctor Gabriel Harrison, is in critical condition at Saugatuck General Hospital."

George's head whipped up. Hand pausing half way to his mouth, he stared at the screen.

"While vacationing in Saugatuck, he and his wife were riding bicycles when Dr. Harrison was hit by a car."

"What the hell?" George said.

Mrs. Harrison was treated for minor abrasions and released. The driver has been charged with reckless endangerment. And," he paused for dramatic effect, "if Dr. Harrison dies, the driver could be charged with manslaughter—which carries a possible three- to five-year prison sentence in the state of Michigan. So our prayers go out to the Harrison family. Now onto..." The rest of the newscaster's speech fuzzed over.

Fury burned in George's chest. Why hadn't they called? He grabbed his coat and hurried to his Saab. Numbness spread through his body as he imagined a car plowing into Gabe's bike. He raced onto I-94 and accelerated to eighty miles an hour.

Gabe was critical? He couldn't be dead or the driver would've been charged with manslaughter. He could be in a coma. Did Judith and the kids know? He picked up his cell phone, searched his recorded numbers, and then threw it back in the seat. He didn't have her number with him. Alex and Ted's numbers were programmed in, but if they didn't know about their dad, he didn't want to alarm them before he had any facts.

George pulled out and raced around a slower Toyota, giving the driver a dirty look as he flew by. "Damn tortoise."

The burning in his gut prodded George to flatten the accelerator with complete disregard for the posted speed limit. Spoiling for a fight, he almost welcomed a vigilant police officer, then he eased off the pedal, realizing he didn't want to waste time with a traffic cop. He couldn't afford the time; Gabe may be dying.

It was late afternoon by the time George located the hospital and stormed the receptionist's desk demanding information. He took a deep breath and stiffened his resolve when the volunteer confirmed that Gabe was in the ICU. Gabe would be all right. He'd be fine. The elderly volunteer cautioned George that he might not be able to visit his nephew because of their strict visitation policy, but her voice trailed off as she spoke to his retreating back.

George punched the round pewter disk and waited impatiently for the ICU doors to swing open. Entering Gabe's quiet room, his glance slid past Alex, Ted, Judith, and Jenny to where Gabe lay peacefully sleeping. The tightness gripping George's chest ever since he'd heard the news broadcast eased. Although a white tube protruded from his mouth connecting Gabe to some machine, numerous electrodes covered his chest, and an IV line ran in one arm, he didn't look as banged up as George had feared.

Big black bruises ringed Gabe's eyes, like a raccoon's, and a few scrapes scabbed over on his arm, but his color was nice and pink. George let out the breath he'd been holding. All things considered, Gabe looked okay. And Judith was here. His shoulders relaxed. With her here, he was certain his nephew would receive the best care.

George moved into the room and hugged his great niece and nephew before turning to their mother. "Why didn't you call? I had to find out about Gabe on the news."

"The news?" Judith looked at Jenny.

He turned from Jenny to Judith. "Yeah. I got back from fishing, turned on the news, and they said some idiot creamed Gabe."

"How'd the press find out?" Judith asked Jenny.

"I don't know." Then her frown eased. "It must have been Ken Stanley. He was here." Jenny turned to him. "I had them call St. Francis's chief of neuro for a consult. We called you," she looked at Judith for confirmation, "and left messages. Several."

"Didn't you check your answering machine?" Judith asked.

"No. I left as soon as I heard." Ignoring Jenny, he looked at Judith. "So how's he doing? What's the damage? Is he in a coma or what?"

Judith's gaze slid from Jenny to her children. "Ted, why don't you and Alex get a snack?"

Ted shifted uncomfortably. "Do you want us to bring you anything?"

"There's no food allowed in ICU." She looked to Jenny, "But you could eat in the hall."

Jenny looked away, speaking softly. "No, thank you."

Since when had Judith cared about feeding Jenny? George thought she had little use for the girl, barely tolerating her. Stress did strange things to people. The kids left, Alex sniffling and avoiding everybody's gaze, and Ted guiding her with a hand on her shoulder. Poor guys. Did they really need to be here? What was the matter with Judith? Couldn't she have waited until Gabe looked a little better before bringing the kids to see him?

He looked at Judith. "Now that you've gotten rid of the kids, how's my boy?"

She looked at Jenny and some silent communication passed between them before Judith stood. "He's gone, George. He suffered a severe intracranial injury. I talked with the specialist, but all the tests indicate that Gabe has no brain activity. The machine is maintaining his respiration."

He frowned. "Wha'da ya mean, gone? Like dead? Look at him— he's not that bad." He gestured to Gabe. "He's just in a coma or something. He'll come out of it."

Judith sadly shook her head. "That's not going to happen. We've been waiting for you. We've kept him going so you could say good- bye."

George sank into a nearby chair and stared at Gabe. "You're kidding, right? This is some kind of a sick joke." His gaze bounced between the two women, trying to find some scrap of hope in their expressions, but he only found abject misery. This was no joke. No mistake. He turned on Judith. "What's the matter with you people? Fix him."

"There's nothing we can do, George."

"Nothing?" The fight went out of him at the miserable shake of her head.

Jenny stood with her arms wrapped around her stomach.

"We need to say good-bye," Judith said.

Tears filled his eyes as he stared at Gabe. Swallowing hard, he swiped an unsteady hand across his mouth. "When?"

"Now that you're here, there's no reason to prolong it."

"Now?" He'd just gotten here and they wanted him to say good- bye and walk away?

"We can give you a little time alone with him, but we need to do this before long. It's for the best."

"Whose best?" George railed. "It's only been a day, for Chrissake."

"All our sakes. His sake. He needs us to let him go."

George stared at Gabe's still form, allowing the truth to sink in. His lips began to tremble; his hand covered his mouth, stilling them. He stared at the man in the bed, the man he'd raised and loved like a son. He'd gotten Gabe through his parent's deaths, he'd taken him fishing, and taught him to drive on his old Ford Taurus. They had season tickets to the Tiger's games. Gone? Fuck.

He closed his eyes against the truth. "What now?"

"We'll call the mortuary and let them know we're ready. When the kids get back, we'll say our good-byes... and leave."

He blinked furiously to stem the tears. With his thumb and index finger he pinched his nose. He forced his eyes open and looked at Judith. "Nobody's going to be with him in the end? That's not right."

Jenny reached for Gabe's hand. "I'll be here."

An immediate protest formed on George's lips, but he saw the grief etched on her young face and remembered how Gabe always jumped to her defense. He'd been crazy about the girl. Totally blind in love. Much as he wanted to deny it, Gabe would want it to be her. He blew out a deep breath, nodding.

It'd been hard burying his wife, parents, and sister, but this was infinitely more difficult. Too soon. Adele's death had been a heartbreaking tragedy. George's mother had been older when she died, and his father—his death had been hard, but they'd lived productive lives. For the most part. And his sister, Jan? Well, she'd simply been dumb and careless.

She'd followed that do-gooder husband all over the world to any unsettled third-world country when she should have been home taking care of herself. Plain stupid was what she was, but her son never went looking for trouble: Gabe was a good boy—a good man, George corrected. The best. He didn't deserve this.

When Judith left the room, Jenny gave him one last stern look before slowly following.

What the hell does she think I'm gonna do to you? He scowled back at her and pursed his lips hard against a caustic comment. *Jesus, Gabe, I'll never understand why you married that one. Never mind her—I don't know how much time they're going to give me with you.*

What in the hell happened? How can you be gone? I wasn't expecting this yet. I should have had more time with you. He paused and closed his eyes against the pain tightening his chest. He opened his eyes and looked at his nephew's face, hoping to see a reaction, desperately hoping they'd all been wrong. *I never really came out and said it, but you know how much I love you and how proud of you I am, right? I mean, sure, we had our little quarrels—mostly over that girl—* He shook his head. *Sorry.*

It's just… I tried to give you a happy life. I worked so damn hard to protect you—but I couldn't have seen this coming. Dead at forty-three? Shit. What a waste. I am so damn tired of the waste. After your mother died, I should have been prepared for another life taken too soon, but it wasn't supposed to end like this. Maybe it's for the best, but damn it hurts. He dropped his head and hot tears scalded his hand. *I'm just not ready for you to leave me too. Not yet.*

But you'll be okay. He blew out a deep, hot breath. *Jan. Adele. Those girls'll take good care of you. It's me I'm cryin' for, you know that, right? You were my son. My best friend. I've never known a better man, and that's the truth.* He sobbed. *I love you, Goddammit, and I miss you so damn much already.*

George heard footsteps and clothing rustling at the door. He took his handkerchief from his back pocket and turned his back on Judith, Jenny, and the approaching kids. He wiped his eyes and blew his nose, a loud honking sound.

A blue scrubs-clad doctor and nurse and some Amy chick, probably a bereavement counselor, paraded in after them. With apologetic eyes, the doctor instructed them to say their good-byes. One by one, they hugged Gabe and whispered some last words of love in choked voices, leaving the room blinded by tears. First Alex and Ted, then Judith, and then himself.

My God, he'd just got here an hour ago and already they were making him go. They didn't give a man much time, did they? Maybe it's just as well. Jenny took the longest, but they didn't have too long to wait before a nurse escorted her from the room.

He watched in astonishment as Judith and Alex both wrapped comforting arms around a sobbing Jenny and led her down the hall.

Grief did strange things to people, he thought as he and Ted followed. The Amy lady trailed behind, like the caboose on a train. She was probably just as useless. When they reached the elevator, he turned back and out of the corner of his eye, he saw them wheel Gabe away in the opposite direction around the corner.

Although he was now on a gurney, George was sure it was Gabe. What in the hell was going on? Why was he still hooked up to the breathing machine? George turned around and sprinted down the hall. Pain from arthritis in his hip caused him to limp, but he caught up to them. "Hey, what're you doing? Where are you taking him?"

They paused but didn't stop until he passed them and blocked the hall.

"Where are you taking my boy?"

The doctor looked beyond him to where Amy had come up behind them.

George narrowed his eyes. "What's going on?"

"It's okay, George. This is how it's done." Judith said. The others gathered behind her.

"How *what's* done? When you die, your body stops breathing and they cover you with the sheet. Or they put you in some giant black baggie or something." He pointed at Gabe lying on the gurney, chest still rising and falling with the machine. "That is *not* how it's done. He's still breathing."

"Gabe wanted to donate his organs," Judith said.

"The hell he did," he exploded.

"It's what Gabe wanted. Jenny signed the papers." Judith looked at the waiting team. "Go ahead."

"You can't do that." Donate his organs? He looked at his helpless nephew, picturing them slicing him open and hollowing him out before giving him back to them to put into the ground. He didn't deserve that. He was a good man. He deserved to be buried whole, with honor. Rage and betrayal ripped through George.

The team resumed pushing Gabe's gurney.

"You do and I'll sue you and this whole damn hospital," he snarled. He pointed an accusing finger at Jenny. "I don't give a damn what she signed, nobody's carvin' up my boy."

Amy eased around the others, little miss meek preparing to confront the lion. "Mr. Turner, I understand your concern, but—"

"You understand *nothing*, lady." He turned back to the doctor. "You're not taking him anywhere. You turn that machine off right here and let him die with dignity."

"We can't do that," the doctor said.

Jenny, her face red and blotchy from crying, looked at the waiting team. Squaring her shoulders, she said, "Please. Take him."

The team wore varying degrees of relief and acceptance on their faces as they escaped. They'd actually listened to the little twit. Astonished, he turned on her. "Stop them."

"It's what he wanted, George," she choked out.

"How the hell could you know what he wanted? You only knew him a few years, I knew him his whole life, and I'm tellin' you it's not right." He chased after the team. "Wait," he yelled as they pushed Gabe onto the elevator.

They hesitated long enough to look past him to Jenny, who nodded miserably as the stainless steel doors glided shut.

Gabe was gone. He had to get him back. He couldn't let them do this. It was inhumane.

"Goddammit, come back here. I'll sue!" he yelled, smacking his palm against the cold pewter doors.

Judith put a hand on his arm. "George, calm down. The decision's been made. And I think it's the right one."

"Then you're an idiot." He shook loose, giving her a stony glare of betrayal. They were going to carve Gabe up over his dead body. He'd lost enough. Gabe *would* be buried with the same parts he came into the world with. Mind racing, he struggled to gather his scattered thoughts. It's clear they wouldn't listen to him, but they'd have to listen to a judge. "Let go me. I've gotta call my attorney."

"Don't be ridiculous, you can't stop it. Gabe believed in organ donation, and as his closest living relative, Jenny's wishes take precedence."

He glared at the bereavement counselor. "Is that true?"

She nodded. "Yes, but most people—"

"Stop them." He hovered over Jenny, crowding her, intimidating. "You can stop it. They're going to carve him up and hollow him out like a Thanksgiving turkey. How can you let them do that? And you claimed to love him," he scoffed.

"I *do* love him," Jenny whispered, anger glistened in her tear-drenched eyes.

"Then stop them." Tears burned his eyes. He wasn't too proud to beg. He looked at Jenny, letting her see his gut-wrenching sorrow and desperation. "Stop them. Please."

"I can't." She held his gaze. "It's what he wanted."

He bent his head and pinched the bridge of his nose. Tears eased around his fingers in a steady, uncontrollable flow. There had to be a way. He raised his head to the ceiling, blinked hard and took a deep steadying breath.

"She's right," Judith said.

"And the baby. Daddy wanted Jenny to have his baby," Alex said, as if offering hope.

George froze, then slowly turned around to stare at his great niece.

Alex's eyes widened with the sudden realization that she'd told a secret.

"What baby?"

Everybody started talking simultaneously, but George waved them aside, zeroing in on his great niece.

"What baby, Alex?" he asked softly.

Stuttering, she eased closer to her mother. "I... the one Jenny's gonna have."

His gaze settled on Jenny's flat waist. "You're pregnant?"

Her mouth opened and closed wordlessly. Tears filled her eyes as she shook her head.

"Gabe and Jenny were trying to get pregnant when this happened," Judith said. "They're going to save Gabe's sperm for her so she can try again to conceive."

Save Gabe's sperm? How would they even get it? More surgery? There? Eyes wide, his neck extended in disbelief. "That's sick."

"It is not," Judith said.

"He's dead."

"All the more reason to want his baby. She wants a living part of him. There's nothing wrong with that."

"It's illegal. Why... it's rape—that's what it is. It's rape. You can't do that." He jabbed a finger at them, before gripping his waist with tense fingers that he longed to curl around their collective necks and shake some sense into them. Sick. Crazy. Illegal. It had to be illegal.

"He's her husband. It's hardly rape, George," Judith maintained.

"There's no law specifically forbidding sperm recovery in situations like this," Amy stated.

George glared at the five, hardly able to comprehend their madness. His gaze honed in on the counselor as she spouted her ridiculous statement. Apparently he couldn't stop them from taking Gabe's organs, but he could handle this little grief mouse. Furious, he turned on her, jabbing the air in front of her. "*You. Stay out of it.*"

He glared a long minute at Judith, then Jenny. "First I find out Gabe's been injured on the afternoon news; when I get here I find that he's brain dead and only the machine's keeping him alive." He ticked the offenses off on fat, short fingers. "Then I find that you're about to desecrate his body, and *now* you think you're going to steal his sperm and have his baby—after he's dead?"

He shook his head. Calm defiance settled over him. "No way, lady. No. Fucking. Way."

Chapter 6

Jenny didn't know how she'd make it through the following few days when she had trouble just leaving the hospital. After George stormed away to call his attorney, Jenny, Judith, and the kids gathered their few things and headed down the hall. Jenny lingered as long as she could, surprised to find herself reluctant to leave.

She'd spent every minute of the past two and a half days within these cream-colored walls, and suddenly the prospect of stepping out into the world frightened her. Given the circumstances, she should have hated the place, but walking toward those gliding doors made her increasingly nervous.

Something lodged deep in the heart of the hospital pulled at her as if by some strange magnetic force. She'd lost so much here—her baby and her husband—and she wanted them back. Both of them.

She'd barely had a chance to get used to the idea of their baby before that dream had been ripped from her—but Gabe was reality. It wasn't right leaving without him. She'd come with him; she should leave with him.

While at the hospital, Jenny felt this vague connection to Gabe even though he was gone. Now she was abandoning him. She didn't say anything because the others would think her nuts, but she felt this urge to ask if she could wait for Gabe and drive to the funeral parlor with his body. Knowing how crazy the thought was, Jenny kept quiet and followed them into the chilly evening air.

Clutching the white plastic bag containing Gabe's belongings, Jenny paused in the open car door and watched a red and white life-flight chopper approach through the dim evening light. It hovered over a cordoned off area of the blacktop above a large red circle surrounded by neon orange cones, before gently setting down.

Were they bringing in a critical patient or were they here for Gabe's organs? No medical personnel rushed out to greet them. A man and women left the helicopter before the blades had a chance to slow. Both wore ugly, wrinkled, green scrubs and white running shoes. The man carried a red and white cooler. Jenny turned away. There was her answer.

Judith drove them to the bed and breakfast. While Jenny quickly packed her and Gabe's stuff, Ted secured the bikes on her jeep. She checked out in a numb haze, signing where indicated and responding to the owner's condolences with a nod and murmured thank you. She pushed through the door, anxious to get away from the inn.

"Jenny," Ted called after her.

She continued walking toward the car as if it were her lifeline.

"Jenny." Ted darted in front of her. Jenny pulled up short of running into him and stared at the hand he held up. She scrutinized at her maroon leather wallet as if she'd never seen it before. "You forgot this."

Ted awkwardly pushed it at her. "Why don't I drive you home?"

Jenny looked at Gabe's son a long minute. Why did he have her wallet? She took her wallet and stuffed it in her purse before moving around him. Ted put an arm around her shoulders and guided her to the passenger's side.

He held out his hand. "I'll drive."

She handed Ted the keys, and they set off with Alex and Judith leading the sad, short procession.

The ride home passed in a surreal blur. Ted drove through the darkening country roads and the light highway traffic with smooth confidence, reminding her of his father. If she looked at his hands only, she could almost pretend it was Gabe behind the wheel. Long slender fingers with short, clipped nails. Strong hands. Caring hands. She abruptly turned away, not wanting to encourage the fantasy.

Lip trembling and eyes stinging with welling tears, she watched the blurry landscape flash by. Gabe was gone. To pretend otherwise would be foolish and painful. Luckily, they didn't need to pass the road where the accident had happened. Poor Ted tried to make conversation, but she even had trouble responding with monosyllabic answers.

Once home, Judith and the kids tried to persuade her to stay with them, at least until the funeral was over. Their concern touched Jenny. She wasn't looking forward to staying alone in the house, but she gracefully declined their kind offer. There was no use putting it off.

With a brave smile, Jenny stood outside in the crisp night air and waved them away. She watched the headlights disappear and wrapped her arms tightly around her waist in a feeble attempt to ward off both the cold and the house full of memories that awaited her.

A high-pitched whine and yelp drew Jenny's attention to a large shadow standing in the path between their and Steve's houses. Ritz leaped forward, her golden coat glowing copper in the bright moonlight. Jenny wondered how long the man and canine had been standing there. She crouched down to ruffle the dog's soft coat and inhale her dusty doggie scent.

Holding Ritz close, she buried her face in the dog's neck, happy to have something solid and familiar to hang onto. Thrilled at her mistress's return, Ritz squirmed out of her embrace and enthusiastically licked her face until she tipped Jenny backwards, plopping her onto her bottom in the middle of the drive. With a choked laugh, she pushed the dog away and took the hand Steve extended to her. He pulled Jenny off the ground, then released her.

Steve took in her appearance. With one unsteady finger, he gently brushed her tangled hair away from her face. His mouth opened and then he bowed his head and washed a hand across his face. He didn't know what to say. He couldn't imagine the depth of her loss. Jenny had loved Gabe so much. And Gabe had adored her.

Jenny had basked and blossomed in Gabe's love and approval. And now he was gone. She must be feeling so alone and empty.

Abruptly he turned from her and walked behind the house to the lawn overlooking the lake. The covered speedboat hung high over the glistening water, ready for winter. Waiting, yet prepared. There hadn't been any preparation for the tragedy now confronting them. No warning at all. Hands on his hips, Steve's shoulders rose and fell with his struggle for composure.

He felt Jenny behind him but couldn't look at her—he needed a minute. *Get it together, Grant.* He swallowed hard and cleared his throat. "When's the funeral?"

"Friday. Judith helped with the arrangements. She's been really great."

"Are the kids okay?"

This was good. She could talk about mundane facts. It helped push the pain aside. "They will be. Ted drove me home—which was a good thing. I've been in such a fog I'd probably have ended up in Canada."

"I would have helped." He sounded gruff, almost hurt.

"I know—but there was really nothing for you to do."

Steve stared at the lake. "He didn't suffer any, did he?" He alternately frowned and blinked, before sinking to the ground as if his legs could no longer support him.

Jenny looked at the top of Steve's bent head through wide eyes. This strong man who'd endured so much—the precipitous end of his professional baseball career followed by the indignity of constantly having to prove he wasn't a dumb jock. He'd fought it all with very little complaint, but now he sat crumpled in grief, brought down by the thought of his friend suffering a painful death.

"No." She knelt next to him. "Gabe didn't suffer at all. He never knew what hit him."

Steve buried his face in tented arms, shutting out the world, alone in his pain. Jenny's shaking hand hovered over his back before gently patting him. At her tentative touch he turned from her.

Jenny wrapped her arms loosely around him in an awkward hug. She rested her head on his shoulder and closed her eyes. She was tired. Bone deep tired. And he hurt so much, it radiated off him in waves, pulsing through him in an all too familiar rhythm.

Steve slipped his arms around her, seizing her waist in a grip of steel, making it impossible for Jenny to draw in a deep breath. They clung to each other for a long, calming minute, silently waiting for the grief to lessen.

These past miserable days she'd been so afraid, so alone. God, it felt good to be enclosed in strong male arms again. To feel comforted and secure. In his arms, she could pretend the nightmare of the past few days never occurred.

But it had. Heated and soaked by tears, Jenny peeled away. The cold autumn air chilled her as she inched back, suddenly self-conscious.

"Sorry." Steve rolled to his feet and put a good yard between them.

Sorry for hugging her or sorry for crying in front of her? The bright moon highlighted the flush darkening his face. Steve thrust his hands in his pocket and scowled at the ground. Jenny slowly got to her feet. Great, now everything was weird between them. She couldn't do *anything* right. She bit her bottom lip hard, then released it.

"Nothing to be sorry for." And everything. "This sucks. It just... sucks." She threaded shaky fingers through her hair in an impatient gesture. "It's just—" She frowned and closed her eyes against the tears. "It's just *so hard*." She bowed her head, then whispered. "And I lost the baby."

"What?"

She blinked up at him. "After the accident, I miscarried. I don't know if it was the fall or the stress... they said it was most likely a chromosomal abnormality," she shrugged. "Doesn't matter why, it's gone too."

I'm such a failure. Everything I love leaves me.

"Ahhh, com'ere." Steve reached out and hauled her into his arms in a light grasp. With a hand at the back of her head, he pressed her tightly against his chest. His button dug into her cheek. "It's all right. Cry. Let it out."

Jenny wiped remnant tears from her eyes and ran a hand under her nose. Turning her head sideways, she stared at the darkened house she and Gabe had spent hours planning to remodel, sharing their lives, and talking about their dreams. They'd picked out every tile, every faucet, every paint color—everything—together. They'd debated and compromised over each piece of furniture. There was so much of them in that house. So many memories embedded in every wall, in the very air.

Jenny had thought their home would embrace and comfort her, making her feel safe, like wrapping herself in an ultrasoft blanket and reading a book in front of a fire on a blizzardy day, but now that she was here, it wasn't that way at all. Those same memories felt like ghosts waiting to prey on her pain. Suddenly anguish and aching loneliness branched out from their home, reaching out with invisible stinging tentacles.

"I can't go in there," she whispered. "I thought I could." She pulled away. Her eyes widened in panic as the words spewed out of her in a desperate, chaotic hurry. "It's our—and I know I should—but I just can't." Her voice cracked.

"Hey, it's okay. You don't have to."

"No. I have to." She nodded. "Because he'll—he'll be—" She drew in a ragged breath. "I have to—" she spit out in between sobs. "Oh, God. He's—not—there," she wailed, clutching her stomach.

Steve caught Jenny as she crumpled. Scooping her up in his arms, he cradled her close like he'd done to Sophie a hundred times, and carried her into his house. Unlike his girlfriend's daughter who always circled his neck with her chubby little arms, Jenny curled in on herself, lost in misery.

Moving into his family room, Steve pushed Ritz aside and settled on the leather couch. Jenny sat on his lap, coiled against his chest.

Her sobs eventually quieted, but her breathing still sounded ragged, as if dragging the very life from her throat one rough, raw gasp at a time. He stroked her arm and brushed the damp hair from her face, wishing he could take on her agony.

"It's okay. It's okay, Jen. You'll get through this." He gulped. A lone tear seeped out the corner of his eye. "We'll get through this."

"I—I—," she sobbed.

"I know. I know. It's okay," he murmured.

Her chest lifted in a big sigh. "I'm *so* tired."

Looking at her bruised, closed eyes, he continued stroking her hair. "No doubt."

"Don't wanna be alone." She rubbed her cheek against his chest as if snuggling into a pillow.

"You're not alone. I'm here." He patted her back. "Go to sleep, Jenny."

Jenny sighed. Her body relaxed heavily against his chest and side as she drifted off to an exhausted slumber. Steve stared at her small hand, now lying over his heart. Her diamond engagement ring twinkled in the moonlight, mocking him. It seemed like she'd always held his heart in the palm of her hand. Pretty much from the very beginning.

As Jenny slept, he memorized every line of her face, determined to imprint this forbidden moment forever. He was engaged; they'd never be this close again. They shouldn't be this close now—and wouldn't be if grief and exhaustion hadn't consumed her.

He should shift her off his lap and onto the couch. Put a little distance between them. He could tuck the afghan around her and she'd never miss him. He wouldn't leave, just move to the chair—or the floor. The chair. That's what he'd do.

After twenty minutes, Steve reached out and snagged the blanket his mother had knitted for his high school graduation from the back of the couch. Carefully settling it around her, he shifted under Jenny and gently pressed a feather-light kiss to the top of her head.

Just a few more minutes.

∿ ∿ ∿

Early the next morning Jenny stretched, trying to ease the painful crick in her neck. She burrowed close to the hard chest, seeking the comforting warmth and steady heartbeat next to her ear. Ritz whined and licked her hand. Why hadn't Gabe let her outside?

Jenny pried one arid eyelid back and looked around the room, frowning at the unfamiliar framed pictures on the mantel and the leather Lazy boy recliner with a picture book lying across the arm. Large white Reeboks, still knotted as if they'd been carelessly kicked off, rested under the glass coffee table. Steve's family room.

Gabe's accident. Leaving the hospital. Their empty house. Jenny inched away from a sleeping Steve, putting a few centimeters between their bodies. She carefully lifted her leg from across his. Last night came flooding back. The tears, the pain of loss... oh Lord— he'd carried her back here and held her until she'd fallen asleep—like a baby or...

Her eyes slowly widened, then she winced at the memories. A low moan of embarrassment started in her throat; she slapped a hand over her mouth. Shoot! She didn't want to wake him. Slowly she rolled her head sideways, fearing she'd find him awake, watching her.

Steve slept inches away, sprawled on his back with one arm pinned behind her shoulder and the other thrown across his lean waist. With full lips slightly parted, he puffed out tiny breaths as he slept. Faint morning stubble bristled his jaw and upper lip, and a restless night mussed his light brown hair.

In the weak morning light none of the crushing sorrow or fear of being alone that tormented Jenny last night surfaced, making her feel foolish and threatened.

They'd cried together. He'd held her. Carried her. She closed her eyes and wished the memory away. How awkward. She was married for God's sake and Steve was her friend. Steve was Gabe's friend. It was weird. Wrong. It was wrong. She was wrong. Again.

Chapter 7

Ritz licked her face and nudged her arm. Jenny patted her head and pushed her back. *I know you need to go out.* She slowly eased out of the crook of Steve's arm and slid off the couch onto the floor. Not wanting him to miss her warmth, she quickly tucked the blanket around him before slipping from the room.

Like a teenager breaking curfew, she and Ritz snuck out the back door. She scanned the neighborhood for snoopy neighbors and the newspaper boy before running across the drive through the path to her own home.

In her bedroom, Jenny paused by Gabe's side of the bed and the framed picture of them in Maui. One finger lightly traveled the cold glass above Gabe's face. A roving photographer at the luau had snapped the photo of them. Gabe had surprised her with it on the last night of their honeymoon.

Their faces were softly illuminated by the firelight as they shared a tender look. They'd been so happy. Just being together had lit a comforting glow in her soul. Jenny sighed. Now she was cold, empty, and alone. And she deserved it. She'd snuffed out their glow, first with rash, harsh words and then last night's... weakness.

She reached into her pocket and pulled out Gabe's watch, warmed by the heat of her thigh. Holding it tightly she stroked the back. "I'm sorry." She rubbed it harder as if she could erase her misdeed. "Sorry. Sorry. Sorry."

No matter how innocent, she'd still fallen asleep with a man who wasn't her husband. Even if it was just Steve, they'd been too close. Jenny wanted to scream at her stupidity; instead she carefully placed the watch on her nightstand and stripped her clothes off on the way to the bathroom.

Under the hot shower spray she scrubbed her body pink. Nothing happened. Sure, they'd spent the night together, but not romantically. She hadn't been unfaithful. She wasn't a horrible person.

Jenny wished she hadn't awakened to find herself snuggled against Steve, but like words spoken, as much as she wanted to, she couldn't take it back. He'd taken her home and they'd fallen asleep together. And, God forgive her, it was the first night since the accident that she'd actually slept.

Collapsing against the cold tile wall, hot water pelted Jenny's head and sluiced down her face, flushing away her tears. How could she? How could she have betrayed her husband like that? Not even buried yet, he lay in some satiny coffin waiting for her to visit. She banged her forehead against the wall, welcoming the pain.

The phone rang. Afraid it would be Steve, she let the answering machine get it. The phone kept ringing. The answering machine must be full. Jenny twisted off the water and wrapped a towel around her as she left the shower and bathroom. Taking a deep breath, she snatched the phone from the cradle. "Hello"

"Jenny? It's Judith. What took you so long to answer?"

"I was in the shower."

"Oh. The funeral home called when they didn't get an answer at your place. They'll be ready for the wake tonight from five to nine. Do you want us to pick you up?"

"No, I'll drive myself. How're the kids?"

"Okay. I don't think they slept much, but that's to be expected."

Guilt hammered her conscience; she'd slept great. "I guess so. Well, I'll see you then. I've got to tell my family and... um... do stuff."

Jenny hung up the phone and sank to the bed. Her husband had spent the night in some cold, foul-smelling mortuary while she had lain safely cocooned in his best friend's arms. *What a whore.*

And how could she face Steve? Steve was the confidant/big brother she'd never had and would be lost without. She couldn't stand it if she destroyed that relationship. Jenny had always gotten along well with men, but Steve was different. The first time they'd traded confidences it'd been so easy—felt so right. She'd been sitting on the dock wallowing in self-pity one evening when Steve had joined her.

"You looked lonely. Gabe still working?"

"He's stuck at the clinic. I'm meeting him at the Hunt Club for dinner at seven thirty."

"So what're you doing out here?" Steve shrugged out of his suit coat and draped it over the dock post.

He unbuttoned his white dress shirt cuffs and with quick, efficient twists of the wrist, had both sleeves rolled halfway up tanned forearms. He lowered himself to the wood, disregarding potential damage to his expensive slacks. Resting a forearm on one bended knee, he squinted into the fading sun. The breeze rustled his hair, giving him an attractive mussed look. All he needed was to loosen his tie and he'd make a great cover shot for some men's magazine, Jenny thought.

"Contemplating life. It's been a rotten week."

"It's only Tuesday."

She paused, then raised her dark sunglasses and gave him a long, sideways look. "Really rotten."

"Because?"

Pulling her knees up to her chest, Jenny drew her windbreaker around her bare legs to shelter them against the cooling breeze. "I make so many mistakes."

"What'd you do this time?" Steve reached up to the crown of her head and gently lowered her sunglasses, easing a small measure of her discomfort.

She groaned and washed a hand over her face. "Instead of sending Alex to her mother to talk about sex and birth control, I told her that abortion was killing a tiny baby and that if she was smart—with all the

STDs and AIDs out there, she should always make the guy wear a condom."

"Sound advice."

"Judith didn't think so when she found condoms in Alex's bag. Alex told her I said she should use them."

"O-h, shit."

"Ye-ah. Judith wanted to know if I taught Alex the different positions too."

"That's a little harsh." Steve paused before raising an eyebrow. "Did you?"

She swatted his arm.

"Was Gabe mad too?"

"No." She grinned. "And I did qualify it with a 'I don't think you're ready—don't think any teenager could be ready for the emotional impact of sex... yada, yada, yada,' but still. It was pret-ty ugly."

"I wish I had some words of wisdom, but I don't." He paused. "Things may be hard sometimes—complicated, but you and Gabe have a great relationship." Steve shook his head, smiling wistfully. "Those other things, parenting, people doubting you—that's their problem, don't let them project their issues onto you and ruin what you have with Gabe. Just be true to yourself and Gabe, and everything will work out."

Be true to yourself and Gabe. If only Steve knew what a fraud she really was. If he knew her secret would he hate her too? Jenny brushed the hair from her eyes and stared at Steve. This prophetic, philosophic counsel was a new side to him. "That's pretty sage advice, counselor. How'd you get to be so wise?"

He pursed his lips. "The hard way. By paying too much attention to what others thought."

"When you stopped playing ball?"

He nodded. "Then too."

"It must have been tough, going from being famous to a regular person overnight."

"It was an adjustment." Steve stared at a rusty buoy bobbing gently in the pewter water, then plucked at his perfectly creased pant leg.

"Somehow, I'd always expected that the decision to quit would be mine. I mean, it was baseball, not football or hockey. I worked out regularly with a trainer specifically to avoid this type of injury."

"But all's well that ends well. You excelled at law school and now work for one of the most prestigious firms in the Detroit area."

He grunted. "They just took me in to use my name. They parade me out in front of important clients like cheap entertainment. I never get assigned the interesting cases." He glanced sideways at her before going back to his inspection of the wood splinter he'd ripped off the dock. "Do you know what I'm doing now?"

She shook her head.

"Cite-checking an article one of the partners wrote about civil procedure. There can't possibly be more boring work." He paused. "But I can be patient. Soon the right case will come along and they'll see I'm not just a dumb jock playing attorney."

Steve called from downstairs, jolting her out of the past. "Jenny?"

Panic dashed through her. "Be right down."

Throwing on the first thing she saw, a pair of jeans and Gabe's polo shirt, she whipped the towel from her head and grabbed her brush. Yanking the brush through her wet hair as she descended, Jenny found Steve in the kitchen.

Unshaven and tousle-haired, Steve rested his jean-clad hips against the kitchen counter. A couple of buttons peeked halfway through the buttonholes of his wrinkled navy-checked shirt, as if hastily done up. His eyes locked on hers, wary, as he ignored Ritz's pawing his topsiders. Other than the uncertainty stamped on his face, he looked refreshed and disgustingly unrepentant.

"We need to talk," he said.

Jenny called to Ritz, let her outside, and then returned to the kitchen. Not having the faintest idea what she should say or wanted to say to him, she put the round table between them, crossed her arms over her chest, and looked at him expectantly.

"Last night—" he frowned, then extended his hand to her before allowing it to fall, slapping his thigh—"was a little weird. I'm sorry. I fell asleep. I meant to move to the chair, but I fell asleep."

"No—it's all right." She nodded, wanting this awkwardness to be over. "It's not as if anything happened."

"Gabe's my best friend," he said softly. "I don't want you to think I'd take advan—"

"No. I know." She shoved an impatient hand through her hair. "I—uh—look. Let's not make a big deal out of it. Let's just forget it."

His blue gaze sharpened on her. "Forget it?"

"Yeah. It's fine. We're good."

"O-kay." He nodded in slow motion. "I really value our friendship and I'd hate like hell to think things would be weird between us because of last night."

"Don't worry about it." She waved a hand, feigning nonchalance. "Last night-psh. Nothing happened. We're fine. We're good."

Steve watched her carefully, as if expecting her to break down. Well, she wouldn't. The old Jenny might have, but that was before her husband died. She made a mistake, but she'd go on and it'd be okay. It had to be.

"Riiight," he said slowly, as if trying to piece everything together. "So... do you need help with anything?"

"No. I was just on my way out," she lied, ignoring her wet hair and bare feet. "I'm off to break the news to my folks." She went into the laundry room and retrieved a clean pair of socks from the dryer.

"Want me to come with you?"

"No, thanks."

"Want me to get your mail from my house or take the garbage out?"

"It's Tuesday?" She took in his casual attire. "How come you're not at work?"

He stared at her so long, that she looked away and shifted her weight from one leg to the other. Was that a dumb question?

"I thought you might need help," he finally said.

"That's sweet, but I'm fine. Really. I've had a bit longer than the rest of you to accept his... being gone." She inwardly cringed. She still couldn't say Gabe's name and the word "death" in the same sentence. "I'll be okay."

The house seemed to close in on Jenny, causing a vacuum, making it hard for her to breathe. Whether it was grief or guilt, she couldn't tell—all she knew was she had to get out. Jenny thrust her feet into her socks, laced her shoes, picked up her purse and whistled for Ritz.

"Ritz, come on."

"She's already out."

"Oh, right. I've really got to go." Jenny shoved her arms in the coat sleeves and passed him, careful not to let their bodies touch.

She'd almost reached the shelter of her car when Steve called her name. Jenny was tempted to ignore him, but she pivoted on her heel. "What?"

He closed the door and approached. Her car keys jingled loudly as he passed them to her on his way out. "You'll need these."

Jenny watched Steve roll her garbage cans out of the garage to the driveway where the garbage men could empty them. Shoulders hunched as if weighted down, he plodded through the passage between their homes without looking back.

ŵ ŵ ŵ

Jenny refused to give in to the grief consuming her. She had a myriad of things to do to honor her love before he could rest in peace. Family and friends were counting on her to organize this last farewell and she would not disappoint them. Mourning was a luxury she'd indulge in later.

After creating a detailed to-do list, Jenny made all the funeral arrangements. She'd swallowed her pride enough to consult with Judith to see if Gabe had any favorite hymns or bible readings—she'd wanted everything to be perfect for him this one last time—but the rest of it she did alone.

She agonized over the difficult decisions, but forced herself to make them. She picked out his coffin, found a distinguished picture for his mass cards, ordered two limos for the family's use during the funeral procession, and decided to have the brunch afterward at the Hunt Club. She didn't want hordes of people invading their home.

She spent at least fifteen minutes lingering in Gabe's closet, swamped with beloved smells and memories, before she was able to pick out his favorite suit, dress shirt and tie to be laid out in. Since being a doctor was such a huge part of who he was and since he'd been wearing it the first time they'd met, she considered going to the office to get his lab coat, but she allowed tradition to prevail and chose a gray wool suit coat that complimented the gray at his temples. Gabe had been a wonderful man—so much more than just a doctor.

Hot, wet tears ran in long rivulets down her cheeks as Jenny typed Gabe's obituary. Clutching his gold watch, she stroked it like a talisman—as if rubbing the metal would bring back memories of Gabe's arms wrapped around her. She went through a whole box of Kleenex and her gritty eyes burned before she finished. Writing was her God-given talent. She spent hours choosing the exact right words, pouring her heart and soul into the piece, determined to pay this last tribute to her love.

But most importantly, Jenny initiated the fund for the clinic in Gabe's name. She certainly didn't want a profusion of flowers at the funeral home and house to deal with, so in his obituary, she'd asked people to send donations to the Gabe Harrison fund for the Donnatelli clinic where he'd volunteered. Jenny was certain Gianna, the woman whose family had founded and ran the clinic, would find an appropriate use for the money as a memorial to Gabe. He would've loved that.

∾ ∾ ∾

Weeks later, Jenny pulled into a tight ball under the down comforter, trying to warm the coldness deep within her. She pulled Gabe's pillow closer, deeply inhaling his scent. Why hadn't the car hit them both? She sobbed. Going on without Gabe *and* their baby was doubly intolerable. She just couldn't do it. She didn't even want to try. Life before Gabe had been challenging, but nothing compared to this.

Her existence felt like a big, empty cavity that echoed her loneliness. Exhausted by life at twenty-eight. If this was growing up, it stunk. She reached for a Kleenex, blew her nose, and threw it on the floor to join a dozen more. If the rest of her life was to be filled with heartache, what was the point?

She sighed deeply. Ritz nudged her arm with a cold wet nose. She heaved her sore body out of bed. Looking in the mirror, the gaunt woman with stringy, straggly hair staring back was a stranger. For once she looked her age—older even. Gabe would've allowed her time to grieve, but her weeks spent wallowing in self-pity would have exhausted even his patience. What should she be doing?

Jenny stripped off her smelly nightshirt on the way to the shower and then detoured into the closet. She ran a loving hand over Gabe's suits, shirts, and pants. When she came to his maroon robe, she pulled it from the hanger and crushed it to her. Rubbing her cheek against the terry material, she inhaled his scent, still strong. She swung the robe around her shoulders and firmly knotted the belt while walking to the bathroom.

Bleep, bleep, bleep. Jenny looked at the caller ID on her phone—Michael. Her hand hovered over the cell, then dropped to her side. She couldn't talk to him now. There was little Jenny wouldn't do for her baby brother, but she just didn't have it in her to be cheerful today.

She looked at the clock—lunchtime. What if Michael had a problem? Maybe he was sick and the nurse couldn't get hold of Mom. He started high school this year and so far he'd transitioned nicely, but fourteen-year-olds were quixotic and hormonal. She picked up the phone and played back his message.

"Hey, Jen. You didn't forget my game today, right? It's home. Mom said to ask if you're eating with us." He lowered his voice, "I wouldn't—she made beef stroganoff *again*. Let's go out. You ask. She won't say no to you."

Jenny smiled and shook her head as she erased the message. That kid always had an angle and wasn't above using her to get his way. Too bad he was so damn cute. She sighed. Maybe it'd be good for her to get out and go to his game.

She picked up her phone, texting, 3:30. Be there.

After showering and dressing in ratty sweats, she let a whining Ritz out of the house. The poor dog had been totally baffled by the continual flow of people and Jenny's weepiness. She sometimes whined and looked at the door, then ran from room to room, searching for Gabe. Or maybe she sensed his spirit watching them, Jenny fantasized. Whatever Ritz's canine intuition, she rarely left Jenny's side for more than a few minutes, as if fearing Jenny would fall apart without her.

Well, no more. Jenny was going to pull herself together. She'd start by collecting the mail, then going to Michael's soccer game. It was a beautiful crisp day, but she didn't stop to appreciate the smells and sunshine as she normally would have.

Jenny hurried to the mailbox and was surprised and disheartened by the volume of mail stuffed inside. A few were bills, but most were private cards. For once Jenny longed for more bills and junk mail instead of the well-meaning condolences she knew awaited her behind the flowing handwritten envelopes and gold Hallmark seals.

She tossed the mail onto the desk in the study, took out Gabe's letter opener, and began slashing open envelope after envelope until all the mail lay exposed like her raw nerves. Carefully, she placed the bills to one side and then turned her attention to the much larger stack of correspondence requiring a response.

When the doorbell rang, she wanted to ignore it; on the other hand, it gave her an excuse to escape the sentimental notes sure to make her cry. A glance through the peek hole showed a messenger. She opened the door, allowing Ritz's head to protrude.

"Jennifer Harrison?"

"Yes?"

"This is for you." He handed her an envelope, then walked away.

Jenny frowned at the envelope, showing the return address of Schimmel and Rinehardt, Attorneys at Law, as she pushed the door closed. Ripping open the envelope, she stood stunned. He'd done it. George was actually suing her.

How dare he? Anger rippled through her, building in furious waves. Having Gabe's baby was *none* of his business. She wasn't going to let him get away with this. Gabe was gone, but she could have his baby and she would. George Turner could go to hell.

Jenny picked up the phone but didn't know whom to call. Judith would be at work, and although they'd achieved a weird sort of friendship, they weren't all that close. Though Jenny had to give her credit, Judith kept calling weekly and offering to help in any way she could.

Jenny's parents didn't know about her plans to have a baby. Knowing her mother, she'd probably protest something so nontraditional. Nope, they wouldn't be supportive. Which left... who? Steve? She hadn't seen much of him lately. He'd attended the wake and funeral, but Annie had pulled him away as soon as they'd left the graveyard, and she hadn't had a chance to talk to Steve since.

In all honesty, after what happened that night, she wasn't sure they'd be able to recover their old friendship. Things had changed between them. No matter how hard she pretended otherwise, she knew it was true. But still, he might be willing to help. She looked at the clock. He'd be at work now.

Before she attacked this latest crisis, Jenny decided to pull herself together. She'd take care of her backlogged correspondence, then deal with George Turner and get on with her life. She'd be free to concentrate on her and Gabe's baby.

Jenny stared at the answering machine she'd been avoiding these past weeks. Nineteen messages had been recorded before the tape filled. She found a yellow legal pad and a pen, and punched the play button. The first two messages were old ones from Michael one reminding her about his soccer game, the other giving her movie times. Then Gabe's deep voice came on the machine.

"Jen? Are you there? I guess not. I'm going to be a little late tonight, but if you want to pack a dinner, we can eat on the boat and still catch the sunset. It'll be cold, so bring a blanket. They're paging me. Gotta go. Love you."

All Jenny's newfound courage evaporated in an instant. She dropped the pen and covered her face with trembling hands. God, it was so *good* to hear his voice. Although it'd only been a few weeks since the funeral, it seemed an eternity since she'd heard Gabe's voice or cuddled against his warm body.

Hugging a soft pillow to her aching heart, Jenny replayed his message and sat back, savoring the sound of his beloved voice. She pushed the replay button again. And again. And again. She swallowed hard against the tears, frantically wondering how she could save just Gabe's message.

My God, how pathetic am I? Trying to save his message so I can play it over and over again, tormenting myself. Damn you, Gabe. Why'd you leave me? Suddenly furious, she threw the pillow to the floor and stormed into the garage.

She punched the garage door opener to get light and then stalked over to what was left of Gabe's bike. She kicked the tires and handlebar. She jumped on the wheels, trying to balance and hop up and down to break the spokes. When that didn't accomplish enough damage, Jenny grabbed a hammer and beat the mirror and speedometer, over and over again, welcoming the pain vibrating up her arm.

Ignoring flying glass and sharp metal bits, she pounded away until the bike lay in pulverized, shattered pieces. Chest heaving, Jenny turned her fury on the new helmet Gabe had insisted she wear. Tears blinded her as she fell on the silver helmet, hammering away, pocking it like the surface of an old battered golf ball.

"Damn you." Pound. "Why," pound, "didn't," pound, "you," pound, "protect him?" she sobbed through clenched teeth.

Intent on destroying the helmet, Jenny barely noticed the hammer being removed from her grasp. She clutched her heaving stomach and rocked back and forth. Debris littering the cold cement floor dug into her knees. Her breath came in tortured gasps, ripping past her swollen, raw throat.

"Damn you. Damn you. Bring him back. Give him back to me," she wailed.

Strong arms pulled her close, rocking with her, until the anger burned away. Worn out, she leaned into the comforting hold and then stiffened.

"I'd bring him back if I could."

Chapter 8

Jenny looked up into Steve's glistening blue eyes. Steve, not Gabe held her. She'd never again know the comfort and security found in her husband's arms. She frowned and twisted out of his embrace.

He immediately released her, stood and backed away, as if remembering where their emotions had led them last time they'd cried over Gabe. Avoiding Steve's gaze, Jenny wiped her nose on her sleeve and surveyed the broken glass sprinkled beneath the mangled bike and dented helmet.

"Want me to get rid of it for you?"

She nodded. The bike was a constant reminder of the accident.

"Not the helmet." She flashed him a sheepish smile. "I might need something to hit. I nearly broke my wrist on that damn bike." She flexed her wrist, then wiped remnant tears from her eyes.

Steve helped her to her feet. He led her inside, pulled out a chair for her at the kitchen table and handed her a box of tissues. Just like the old days before guilt made them polite, he snagged a Coke Zero from the refrigerator and poured half in a glass with ice for her and kept the can for himself. Leaning against the counter, he faced her.

He frowned and pulled his phone from his pocket. He swiped it open, tapped out a quick text, then placed it on the counter. "So, other than beating the hell out of Gabe's bike, what've you been up to?"

Her lips twitched in appreciation of his attempt to lighten her mood. She shrugged. "The usual; paying bills, cleaning house, the dog, acknowledging condolences, you know. Stuff," she said, pretending that the house wasn't a mess, that the sink wasn't filled with dirty dishes a week old, and that clumps of fur sticking out of Ritz's normally smooth coat didn't give her away.

His phone vibrated as Annie's face showed on the screen. Steve glanced at his fiancé's picture, then took another sip of his drink. "How're the notes coming? There were a lot of people at the funeral."

Jenny nodded at the phone. "Do you need to get that?"

"No. She knows where I am." He raised his eyebrows. "Got a lot of notes left to write?"

She thought about bluffing, but decided it took too much energy and brainpower. "It's awful." She glanced at the basket of condolence cards, florist and gift basket cards. "There are over hundred. Do you think I have to write a personal note to all of them? It's bad enough addressing them."

"Why don't you go to a printer? They should have a stock thank you and then you could just sign them. What about Judith and the kids? Haven't they offered to help?"

"The kids shouldn't have to do this." She looked away, embarrassed. "Judith offered, but I don't want to take advantage."

"What about your folks?"

She shook her head. She didn't want them writing her thank you notes.

He sat at the table across from her. "I'll address them."

"I couldn't ask—"

"You're not, I'm offering. Gabe was my friend, I want to help."

"Thanks."

"Anything else I can do?"

Jenny looked at Steve, considering. It was kind of personal, but she needed help and he offered. "Be right back."

She hurried to the study then returned to the kitchen. Envelope in hand, she stood next to him, not quite sure how to start. She sucked in a deep breath, then pushed it out. "At the hospital when I lost both Gabe and the baby, I was completely devastated. Then it occurred to me. I couldn't bring Gabe back, but I *could* have another baby. So when they recovered Gabe's organs, I had them freeze his sperm so I could be artificially inseminated. I know it's unconventional, but this way I can have our baby."

Jenny watched Steve, closely assessing his reaction, deciding he would be a formidable foe at poker. "Anyway, George pitched a fit when he found out about the organ donation, but he couldn't stop it. When he found out about the sperm recovery, he went ballistic. He actually accused me of raping Gabe." She rolled her eyes. "Then I got this today." She handed him the restraining order. "That jerk's taking me to court to keep me from using Gabe's sperm. Can you believe his nerve?"

Steve slid the sheaf of papers from the envelope and scanned the documents. Could he believe George's nerve? He couldn't believe *any* of it. Steve stared at the document in his hand. What the hell was this, a restraining order for sperm? He looked at Jenny. "Tell me again."

"I donated Gabe's organs and they saved his sperm so I could be artificially inseminated."

Eyebrows raised, he looked at her. "You can do that?"

"Yup." She nodded.

"How? I mean, he never regained consciousness. He was brain dead, right?"

"Yeah."

"Then how'd they get his sperm?"

It was Jenny's turn to look perplexed. "I don't know. Surgery, I guess. That's how they got the rest of his organs. The important thing is they did it."

Steve mentally winced and resisted the urge to cup his balls. Yow. How painful would that be? But then Gabe was dead, so he wouldn't have felt anything—but still. Owww. He looked at Jenny, curious. "Why?"

"Why what?"

"Why would you want to have Gabe's baby after he's gone?"

Her eyes widened as if his question was incredibly stupid. "Because I love him. Because I want a living reminder of him. He was an amazing man, who has wonderful traits to pass onto our children."

Children? Was she nuts? She'd do this more than once? Well, with Gabe's sperm frozen, he guessed she could conceive a whole brood of kids without the guy. Just how much semen were they able to get?

He'd like to hear her explain that one to her future five-year old. *Yes, Mommy's going to have another baby. How? Oh, don't worry, honey, it's easy. You don't need a daddy to have a baby. Heck that's the old-fashioned way, all you really need is a petri dish and a tube of frozen semen.* Too weird.

He brought his wandering thoughts back to the situation at hand and tried to sound reasonable. "Raising a baby alone would be hard. Not to mention that if the baby looked like Gabe, it'd be a painful reminder of him. You'd have to go through the pregnancy and birth without a husband. I'd think it'd make it harder to cope with his death."

Jenny smiled gently and got a faraway look in her eyes. "Just the opposite." She looked at him, pleading. "I need this baby, Steve. I need this piece of Gabe. Besides, who's George to say I can't? It's none of his business. It's not as if under ordinary circumstances we'd consult him before starting our family."

"This is a little different, Jenny." The circumstances were light-years from ordinary. He rescanned the document in his hand but had trouble concentrating. "So tell me again how this all came about. From the beginning."

Jenny heaved a sigh. "It's simple. The organ donor lady was telling me about all the people that could be helped with his organs, and I thought, what about me? If they could recover his sperm and freeze it, then I could be inseminated. I could have another baby."

"And this didn't seem a little crazy to you?"

"No—okay, maybe." A deep frown creased her brow and she crossed her arms over her chest. "But the more I thought about it, the more sense it made. I'd just miscarried my baby and lost my husband—it seemed like a blessing. But now I got this." Jenny leaned across the table and pointed to the paper. "I have to show up in court November sixteenth. Will you represent me?"

He paused, trying to think of a way to soften his response. "Jenny, I can't."

"Why not?"

"Well... To be honest, I'm not sure I agree with you." He held up a hand to forestall her objection. "I'm not sure how I feel about it. There's a lot to think about. Secondly, this is a very sticky legal issue that I'm totally unfamiliar with—I'd be out of my depth. I think you'd be better off with someone else."

Jenny studied him one long minute, as if trying to puzzle something out. Then her eyes went big as she came to some conclusion. "Oh, my God. You blame me. You're mad at me because we spent that night together."

"What?"

"You won't help me because you feel guilty about the night we spent together." She cocked her head. "You didn't tell Annie, did you?" She glanced at his phone on the counter. "Is that why she's calling you all the time?"

"No." Only an idiot would tell his fiancée he'd spent the night with another woman—even if it was innocent. There was simply no reason to hurt her like that. Annie texted and called him frequently because she liked to stay in touch.

"No what?" She crossed her arms over her chest and pinned him with cool blue eyes. "Not guilty or didn't tell?"

He pushed away from the table to stand. His chair cracked loudly against the wood floor, making Jenny startle. "Didn't tell." He righted the chair. "Of course I feel a little guilty—more weird than guilty, really, but I thought we were beyond that."

"I did too. That's why I want your help. You're the only one I can trust with this."

"Look, Jen. I wouldn't be your friend if I wasn't honest with you." He picked up the document. "This is a complicated subject. I know it seems like a nuisance suit to you, but George might actually have legal grounds to block you. It's a very touchy issue. I know you don't think it should be, but legally it is."

"Why?" She looked young and genuinely confused.

"Because. Forget the fact that Gabe's your husband. You took his sperm without his consent—when, in fact, he was incapable of objecting should he have wanted to—for the express purpose of reproduction."

"But he *was* my husband."

"That doesn't matter."

"Yes, it does."

"No, it doesn't." He shook his head. "It does *not* give you the right to invade his body, taking sperm from him to make a baby that would have half his genetic makeup. A lot of people would see that as disrespecting the deceased."

"But I *do* have the right to give away his organs? They even would have let me pick and choose which organs I wanted to give. 'You can have his heart, nope, sorry, not his lungs'" she played out. "I can give away his organs and help as many as fifty people, they said, but I can't save his sperm to conceive *one* child for me? Where's the logic in that?"

She could pick and choose which organs to give away? He didn't know anything about organ donation beyond the little red heart marking his driver's license.

"I don't know this area of the law well enough to debate it, but some would consider it the difference in altruistically *giving* a gift to save other's lives and *taking* something from Gabe for yourself. What you're trying to do breaches many legal, medical, and ethical areas. This is going to create a lot of controversy."

"But why?" she wailed. "It's a *personal* decision."

"The decision might be personal, but implementing it isn't. You need advanced medical technology to help you do what you want to do—what you already did. You didn't just take Gabe's sperm and get pregnant on your own. That's where you open yourself up to criticism and interference. Are you sure you want to pursue this?"

Jenny's lips pinched tight, her expression angry. "Yes. Nobody's going to tell me I can't have my husband's baby."

He dropped the document on the table. "Frankly, I'm surprised you found a doctor willing to take the sperm. He must have understood how controversial this would be."

"He was very kind. He just wanted to help me."

Steve looked at the papers again. "Why was the sperm sent to California instead of a sperm bank here?"

She glanced away, avoiding his look.

"Jenny?"

She raised her chin and looked at him. "The facilities here were reluctant to take it."

"Be-cause..." he drew out.

"Because. Of the lack of consent," she admitted.

He sat. "Look, Jen, ask me to draw up your will or write a nasty letter to the insurance company. Hell, ask me to do your taxes, but don't ask me to do this."

Her shoulders drooped; all the fight seemed to drain away. "You think I should forget about it?"

He *did* think she should let it go, but in all honesty he couldn't be sure he was being completely objective. "I think I'm not the right attorney to advise you."

"Just think about it. Please."

Steve hardened his heart against her pleading. He knew it was difficult for Jenny to ask for help, but he couldn't. This trial would be messy and highly publicized. He wasn't experienced enough. Besides, he didn't like what she was trying to do—it just felt wrong.

"I can't. I want to help you, but I'm sorry, you're going to have to find someone else."

She stared at him one long minute through wide, wounded eyes, making him feel like a heel. A few more seconds and he would have broken down, agreeing to whatever she wanted as long as she didn't look at him with that betrayed disappointment.

"Okay," she said in a flat voice.

Relief coursed through him. "I'm sorry."

"I understand." Slumping in her seat, she looked sad and lost. She didn't understand at all.

He stood and slid his phone into his pocket. "Let me know when you get the notes from the printer."

She nodded and forced a smile to trembling lips.

God, please don't let her cry.

"Well," he headed for the door and Ritz, who watched the door hopefully, wagging her tail. "Want me to let her out?"

She nodded.

"Bye." Steve let Ritz out into the backyard, then walked back to his kitchen.

Jenny wanted to have Gabe's baby after he's dead? In his mind's eye, Steve morphed her belly until it swelled huge, heavy with child. Crazy. He grabbed a beer from the fridge and the bottle opener off the counter. With a quick flick of his wrist, he popped the cap and pitched the opener back in the drawer.

"So what da ya say, Gabe?" He looked up into the air. "Do ya want to become a daddy from where you are?"

He listened carefully, not sure what he was expecting, but hoping for some divine guidance. Nothing? Fine. He threw his head back and took a sip of beer. The hoppy, bitter taste of the pale ale suited his mood.

He walked into the family room and threw himself into his lounge chair. "I don't know, somehow it just doesn't seem right." He slowly wagged his head from side to side. "Sometimes we humans frighten me with the things we discover. I mean, look at cloning. Man, there's a dangerous field.

"Some things are better left alone. You know what I mean, Gabe? I mean, just because we *can* clone animals, doesn't mean we *should*. It's like all those thousands of times doctors step in to prevent death but maybe shouldn't have.

"You were lucky, buddy. She let you go. I gotta give her credit," he inclined his head. "Took a lot of guts to turn off that machine. She could have kept your body going for months, costing society a ton of money and grinding her down with false hope, but she didn't." He took a long pull of his beer.

"By now you know I feel." He smiled wryly. "I sure didn't plan it. You might have a talk with the Man upstairs and tell Him I didn't appreciate that joke. Fallin' for my best friend's wife? That's just plain cruel. Nothing would have come of it—I swear. Neither of you would've ever known. You two were so damn happy—so good together. I envied you that. Hopefully I can get it with Annie."

He stared at the label on the beer bottle till it blurred. "I gotta tell you, Jen wanting your baby now really threw me. I didn't even know you could do things like that. This is nuts. You're gone. Jen's alone and hell-bent on having your baby. And she wants me to help. Fuck."

He'd see what Allen Blakeman knew about cases like this. Allen was the firm's best family attorney. Maybe he'd take Jenny's case. Probably not. The firm had a reputation for being conservative. They'd probably run from this case faster than loan sharks from the IRS. But he'd try.

His cell buzzed, announcing a text. Annie was confirming Saturday's date. He quickly tapped out a response. A barbecue with her kids he could handle. Play a little ball, feed them hotdogs, pickles and fries, and they were happy campers. Simple. Uncomplicated. Perfect.

Chapter 9

Steve rose up out of the pile of leaves, snarling and growling ferociously.

"Where are they?" he bellowed in a deep, dramatic loud voice. "Where are those little children?" He looked at his fiancée, who sat on the steps and raised a questioning eyebrow as she leafed through a bridal magazine.

A high-pitched giggle erupted from a bush to his right. Annie grinned and pointed to the side of his house.

"Ah, ha." Steve ran to the bushes and scooped up the giggling three-year-old. He tossed her over his shoulder like a sack of potatoes and captured both of her ankles in one hand to steady her.

"Where's the boy?" he roared, tickling Sophie until she shrieked with delight.

"Twee." She gave up her brother.

Steve stalked over to the crabapple and snagged Josh as he tried to scramble higher to safety. With the preschooler draped over his shoulder and her brother slung under one arm, Steve lumbered back to the huge pile of leaves.

He tossed the kids in the pile and tickled them before raining leaves all over them. Out of the corner of his eye, he saw a flash of blue. He stilled and looked next door.

"Be right back." He gave them a mock fierce scowl. "Don't run away again."

∾ ∾ ∾

Annie lifted her gaze from the lawn where Steve wrestled Josh and Sophie in the leaves, to the blue Jeep pulling in the Harrison's drive. From her seat on the front steps, she smiled and swung her arm wide in a big wave. Jenny got out of the car and flapped her hand in Annie's direction—almost as if swatting an annoying bug, before heading for the trunk.

Steve broke away from the kids and trotted across the lawns. He greeted Jenny with a heart-melting grin, before lifting two large paper grocery bags from the truck and slamming the lid closed. With the springy step of an athlete, he followed Jenny into her house.

Hmm. Jenny didn't put up any protest, casually accepting his help as if almost expecting it. *Figured.*

"Joshie, be careful you don't land on your sister," Annie called out when the five-year-old began launching himself into the pile of leaves. She looked next door at the open garage. How long does it take to drop off two bags of groceries?

"Sophie, come here, honey. You've got leaves in your hair," Annie said, but the preschooler ignored her.

She licked her finger and flipped the magazine page while watching the Harrison's house out of the corner of her eye. Annie snatched up her phone and sent Steve a quick message. Finally he strolled back across the lawn.

"She's not completely helpless, Steve. She only had two bags."

"Jenny's going through a rough time."

"Her husband died, it's not as if *she* has a terminal illness."

"That's right," he nodded. "Her husband died. Have a heart, Annie."

Steve stood there with a lock of hair draped across his forehead and his hands anchored at his lean waist. A University of Michigan T-shirt molded nicely to his defined chest muscles. Even sweaty and messy her guy was hot.

"You don't have to rush to her side every minute."

"I don't. And maybe if you made a little effort, I wouldn't have to. Did you see how sad she was? Why don't you take her some ice cream and try to cheer her up?"

"Ice cream?"

"Yeah. Peppermint's her favorite. There's a new carton in the freezer."

"Ice cream's so fattening."

"Jenny could use fattening up; she hardly eats since Gabe died, and you—" Steve grabbed Annie's arm and pulled her to her feet. Swinging an arm around her waist, he brought her tight against him. "You, have a stunning body. You hardly need to worry about weight."

Soothed by the compliment, she smiled. "Okay. For you."

"That's my girl. Meanwhile, I'm going to find me an Englishman," he growled and turned away from her. Steve made a big show of sniffing the air. First to the right, then to the left. "Fee, Fi, Fo, Fum. I smell the blood of an Englishman," he roared and rushed to the giggling children hiding beneath the leaves.

Annie smiled wistfully. Steve was so good with Josh and Sophie. He'd make a wonderful stepfather—far better than their real dad. Ryan had always been off playing sailor. Every darn summer she'd had to plan their lives around that stupid Mackinac race. Every winter he'd tried to get her to spend more and more time at his parents' second home in Florida, just so he could sail. Like he was ever going to be in the America's Cup. He needed to grow up and face reality.

But he hadn't. And when he did spend time with their children, he took them to inappropriate movies, stuffed them with ice cream and cotton candy at the zoo, allowing them to eat until their tummies hurt. And who got stuck with sick kids? Her. Her ex was a juvenile pain in the butt. Sometimes she suspected he ignored her rules and advice to punish her. Steve was much more mature—and trainable.

Annie was having loads of fun planning their spring wedding. Steve had wanted to elope, but no way was she going to miss out on a wedding with all the trimmings. Though not a baseball player anymore, Steve still had fans who would love to see pictures of their special day. After all, it was his first wedding and he could afford it.

She picked up her thick magazine and entered the dark foyer. Padding through the house, she glanced at the sparse living room with its ugly leather couch and modern glass coffee table. Leather and glass? She wrinkled her nose. Framed photos of Steve's family lined the marble fireplace mantle. He even displayed his nieces' and nephews' school pictures.

Now all she had to do was convince Steve that a fresh start required a fresh house. Perhaps a classic Tudor on the country club golf course. She wanted to start their new life together without any baggage—and Jenny Harrison was pretty obvious baggage.

In the kitchen, Annie dropped the magazine on the counter, wandered over to a stack of stationary sitting next to a pile of ripped envelopes. Recognizing Steve's handwriting, she picked one up.

"Doctor and Mrs. Henry?" She frowned. It wasn't enough to invite Jenny everywhere with them, but now he was carrying her groceries and writing her thank you notes? What else was her fiancé doing for his friend? She needed to have a talk with Steve—right after she made nice with Jenny. Maybe she was overreacting.

In the freezer, Annie found two quarts of Dryer's Slow-Churned Peppermint ice cream. She pulled one out and moved aside a container of Denali Extreme Maximum Fudge Moose Tracks, looking for strawberry or vanilla, or anything she remotely liked, but that was it. Chocolate or peppermint. Maybe she wasn't overreacting.

Annie found a scrap of paper and started a grocery list. Strawberry ice cream. Not that she even liked ice cream, but it was the principle. She grabbed her Coach purse and fished around for her lipstick. With two quick swipes, she refreshed her makeup and smacked her lips together. She ran a brush through her straight blonde hair then fluffed it before stuffing the brush and lipstick into her bag and tossing the purse back onto the table. She snatched the ice cream from the counter and headed for the path between the side-by-side driveways.

At the Harrison's back door she knocked twice. Maybe Jenny was napping or in her bedroom crying. She shifted the cold dessert and backed away from the door, suddenly nervous. This was so awkward. She must care for Steve a lot to try to cheer up Jenny Harrison.

Ordinarily she and Jenny hardly said more than a few sentences to each other in a whole evening, and now she was trying to comfort her fiancé's friend. What was she supposed to do? What could she say? Annie heard rustling in the kitchen and then footsteps. Jenny opened the door.

She pasted on a big smile on her face. "Hi, Jenny. I just thought I'd come over for a little visit and see how you're doing."

Wow, Steve was right. The poor thing didn't look well at all. There were huge dark craters under her eyes that no amount of makeup could hide. And her skin looked pale—almost pasty. Was she sick? Annie took a step back, hoping she wasn't contagious.

She had the kids this weekend and Ryan was totally incapable of getting Sophie to Pee-wee tennis and then Joshie to Coleman's birthday party—she hadn't even wrapped his gift yet and Ryan was hopeless at wrapping. Nope—she couldn't afford to get sick.

"I'm fine," Jenny said.

"I can come back later if this is a bad time. I know you're probably busy with work, and Gabe stuff. I..." She shrugged. "It's just that we didn't get to talk much at the funeral."

"I'd ask you in, but the house is really a mess." Jenny picked nervously at her navy sweatshirt.

"Oh, that's okay." Annie waved a hand. "I don't mind." She raised the melting container and smiled brightly. "I brought you ice cream. Peppermint."

"Peppermint?" Jenny's looked at the container before pushing the door open. "That's my favorite."

"Mine too," Annie said with a bright smile as she rushed into the kitchen. It wasn't very messy—a few dishes out—certainly no worse than her own kitchen after Bunko night. Jenny left the inside door open. Folding her arms across tiny breasts, she tucked a chunk of hair behind her ear. Poor thing, didn't anybody ever tell her that doing that would make her ears stick out like Dumbo's?

"Thanks for the ice cream." She took it and put it in the freezer. "Would you like something to drink?" Jenny peered inside the nearly empty refrigerator. "I have Coke Zero and... I'm sorry, I only have Coke Zero and water."

Annie internally shuddered. Soda was *so* bad for you. It accelerated aging, wrecked your complexion, the caramel coloring was made of carcinogens, and even diet soda contributed to belly fat. *No. Thank. You.* "Water will be fine."

Jenny reached into the cabinet for a clean glass. "So... I saw Steve out playing with your kids. His case must be going well."

"What case?"

"The hazing one."

Annie frowned and took a seat at the counter.

"Fraternity," Jenny said, trying to prod her memory. "The kid who was beaten in the fraternity hazing. They started the trial this week."

"Nope." She shook her head. "Doesn't sound familiar. Steve doesn't really talk about work much. We're busy with the kids and planning our wedding."

"Ah-h." Jenny nodded, but Annie had a feeling she didn't really understand.

"So... well, I'm not sure how to go about this—nobody's ever died on me," she waved a nervous hand at her chest. "But, is there some way I can help? Maybe... take you out to lunch? Oh, I know. I know." She bounced on her stool, impressed with her brilliant idea. "How about a girl's day at the spa? We could get facials, mani-pedis, and then finish up with a massage and an affinoderm seaweed wrap—they're all the rage now." She smiled encouragingly. "It'd be fun."

Jenny put down her glass and stared at her. "Annie, why're you here?"

"What do you mean?"

"Why are you sitting in my kitchen trying to pal up to me?"

"I'm just trying to be nice."

"And you feel sorry for me."

"No—well, of course I do. Your husband died."

"Well don't. I'm fine."

Annie felt insulted at the rejection. Like she wasn't good enough to be Jenny's friend. "Why don't you like me?"

Jenny blinked stupidly. "Excuse me?"

"You've never liked me and I want to know why. What'd I ever do to you?"

"I don't dis—"

"Yes, you do. Do you think I'm stupid? It's Steve, isn't it? You're jealous that I'm marrying him."

Amusement brought a spark to Jenny's dull eyes. "Hardly. Steve's just a friend—a big brother really."

"No-o-o, women like me—unless they're jealous of my man. So you should like me. It must have something to do with him." Her eyes narrowed, watching Jenny for a telltale blush or any sign of guilt or embarrassment, but Jenny just stood there swallowed by sweats two sizes too big, staring at her with those dull blue eyes.

"Okay, you want to know the truth? The truth is, I do care about Steve. He's a good friend and I don't want to see him hurt."

"You think I'll hurt him?"

"Look, I really don't want to get into this. Thanks for the ice cream—" Jenny moved toward the door.

"No. I really want to know." Annie hurried after her. "You think I would hurt Steve?"

Jenny sighed and folded her arms across her chest. "Look, I just think you're not right for him, that's all."

Well, that stung. "I'm not *right* for him? What? Like I'm not good enough for him? Then who is? You?"

"Don't be ridiculous."

Annie raised her chin and leaned forward. "Well, I've got a news flash for you, little Ms. Widow Reporter, no one will ever be good enough for Steve in your eyes 'cause you're in love with him yourself. But you'd better get over it." She held up her left hand and waved her diamond at Jenny. "I'm the one wearing his ring and I'm going to marry him. So you can forget your pitiful little poor-me-widow tricks."

Jenny's eyes sprang open and her jaw dropped wide in a satisfyingly shocked look. "My *what?*"

"Oh, yeah, I'm onto you, sister." Annie waved an index finger. "I've watched you manipulate your husband and Steve." She raised her voice and opened her eyes wide in imitation of Jenny, "Oh, honey, I left my coat in the car. Would you be a dear and get it for me?" She fluttered her eyelids. "Oh, Steve, I'm too short to reach the wine glasses. Would you mind?"

"I can't help that I'm short."

Short, beautiful, and vulnerable. Annie simmered. "Get a step stool. You've had two men at your beck and call—"

"*Two* men?" Jenny raised an eyebrow. "I *am* good."

Annie narrowed her eyes, pissed that Jenny dared mock her. "You just sit around batting those big blue eyes to manipulate men to do whatever you want. I bet you're even a crier—of course you're a crier, it's the best way to get to men. You're a spoiled brat is what you are.

"Now that your husband's not around to dance attendance on you, you turn to Steve—knowing full well that he's such a sweet guy that you can pull that sympathy card into the *next century* and he'll keep falling for it.

"Well, I'm sick of it. Steve's engaged to *me*, not you. Find another man to wait on you, princess. Just friends, my ass." She paused before adding, "And if it's true that you're really just friends, you're even more despicable than I thought. Friends don't use friends. If you had any decency, you'd leave him alone."

Annie brushed past her and through the door. Pausing in the driveway, she looked back over her shoulder. "Enjoy your ice cream, princess."

Annie walked across the yard, adding a little extra swing to her hips when Steve turned and spotted her. *I'll be damned if that little widow's gonna take my man.*

He tossed Sophie onto his shoulders and came over. "Well? Did she like the ice cream?"

Annie shrugged. "She kept it and said she'd eat it later." She leaned in and brushed her breast against his arm. "You're right, babe, she did need cheering up. I offered to take her to lunch. She wasn't keen on that, but she *did* like the idea of a day of pampering at the Coloseum International."

Steve raised his eyebrows. "Really?"

She nodded. "Especially when I told her it was your treat and that you insisted—that's okay, right?" She opened her eyes wide. "I figured you'd be happy to chip in—after all I'm taking a day off work to keep her company, and it was your idea to cheer her up."

"Well, sure. I'm happy to pay. I just didn't think Jenny was into that type of thing."

"Well, I guess you don't know her as well as you thought you did." Annie held out her hand, palm up. "I need a credit card to make the reservations."

Steve swung Sophie to the ground, pulled out his wallet, and handed his VISA to Annie.

"Oh, and Jenny felt a little weird about you paying," she wrinkled her nose. "So it's probably best if you don't make a big deal about it—don't want to spook her." She smiled and flipped Steve's credit card back and forth in her hand. "Thanks, sweetie."

And thanks to you too, Jenny. Too bad you're going to cancel on me. How could you be so mean when you know how badly Steve wants us to get along?

She held out her hand to Sophie. "Come on, honey, let's go inside and get a popsicle." She looked over her shoulder. "Joshie, coming?"

"The grill's on. We're eating in twenty minutes, Annie," Steve said.

"Psht." She waved a dismissing hand. She was in a great mood and felt like celebrating with her kids. She smiled brightly at her son. "One little popsicle won't hurt. They'll still eat dinner."

Ignoring the way her son peeked at Steve out of the corner of his eye, she spun on her heel and headed for the house.

∾ ∾ ∾

Jenny stood in the open doorway, staring at the woman marching back to Steve's house. *Well, that was fun.* She'd felt Annie's jealous hatred hitting her in waves. Beware blondes bearing gifts. Annie *was* right about one thing. Jenny had never really liked her. And now she liked her even less.

Her and Steve? Romantically involved? Ridiculous. Sure they'd shared that one night, but they'd been under incredible stress and it'd been the only time. Heck, Steve bossed her around and treated her like a kid sister.

Actually, Jenny felt sorry for Annie. She had some real insecurity issues. Then again Jenny already knew that; Annie was constantly texting and calling Steve. Sad, really. Jenny shut the door and backed into the kitchen. She sat in a chair at the table.

But Annie might have a point about her taking advantage of Steve. She'd been leaning on him too much. He shouldn't be addressing her condolence notes. And she wasn't helpless. She could carry her own groceries, put out her garbage cans, and rake her own leaves. This winter she could even shovel her own walk. The driveway was a bit much—she'd have to get the number of a snow removal service, but she could take care of herself.

Steve just did all those things for her automatically—it's not like she asked him to.

But you allow it.

True. Truth be told, she liked being taken care of. Now that Gabe was gone, Jenny appreciated someone thinking of her. It was comforting. But still, she'd probably be a little upset at her husband showing that much consideration for another woman too.

After all, Steve *did* invite her to go out with them—as if she'd ever willingly spend an evening being a third wheel to Steve and his fiancée—but it must piss Annie off that he always asked. It'd bug her if Gabe had always tried to include a female friend on their nights out.

Much as she disliked the woman, Annie had a point. Maybe Jenny should apologize. She didn't want Steve's friendship with her to come between them—not if Annie was really what he wanted.

Jenny wrinkled her nose. Nah, no apology needed. She'd just stop relying on Steve and be nicer to Annie. She'd wean herself from Steve's help, starting today. She'd taken care of herself before she married and she could do it again. Hopefully, pretty soon she'd be taking care of herself and a baby.

Tomorrow she'd attack that huge to-do list. She tucked a lock of hair behind her ear and looked around the kitchen. Today she'd put away the groceries and actually cook herself a healthy dinner. She'd grill a steak and steam some asparagus to go with it. Not exactly gourmet fare, but it'd do.

∾ ∾ ∾

Sunday afternoon, Jenny reached above her head and clasped her hands. Leaning to the right and then to the left, she stretched sore shoulder muscles. One pile on her desk was almost clear. Still three piles of condolence cards six inches high remained on her to-do half of the desk, but at least she'd paid the bills.

Jenny glanced at the calendar. Wednesday the fourteenth she had her first appearance in court. She picked up the list of attorneys with more than a half-dozen names crossed off. How could it be this hard to find a lawyer willing to take her case? Maybe Steve was right and this was a bigger deal than she'd thought.

She frowned, then shook her head. Naw, it couldn't be that complicated when she could simply walk into any old sperm bank, fill out some papers, pay a fee and buy some stranger's sperm to help her get pregnant. But why do that when she had her husband's sperm? It couldn't be this hard; surely the judge would agree with her.

Only a few more days to find a lawyer; she'd better make more calls this afternoon. Tomorrow she returned to work and wouldn't have much time to interview attorneys.

Tck. Tck, tck. The tapping of freezing rain on the glass drew her attention. Jenny stood and walked over to the window to stare out into the cold, dreary day. It was the perfect day to clean. She located her favorite country station on Pandora and loaded the dishwasher, washed and dried the few dishes that needed it, and scrubbed the counters until the granite gleamed. That was better.

She got the vacuum from the closet and had just plugged it in when the phone rang. "Hello."

"Miss Jenny?"

"Hi, Tommy, what's up?"

"The clinic's not just for kids, is it?"

"No. Why?"

He turned aside, voice muffled. "I told you, Grammy." Then he spoke to Jenny. "Grammy J's sick an' she won't go to the clinic 'cause she thinks it's just for kids. It's free for adults too, right?"

"It's free for anybody who needs it. What's wrong with her?"

"She's got a real bad cough and she's so tired she can hardly get outta bed."

Jenny looked outside at the stormy weather. A sick person shouldn't be riding the bus in weather like this. "Give me ten minutes, and I'll come and get her."

"Thanks." Jenny heard the relief in his voice. At eleven, Tommy shouldn't have to be worrying about stuff like this. He should be obsessed with video games and baseball, not taking care of his family.

Jenny turned off the music, snatched her purse and had reached the garage door before she looked down at her plaid PJs. "Crap."

Darting upstairs, she threw on some jeans and, mindful that she'd probably run into Gianna, she put on a nicer sweater and took the time to apply a little lipstick before hopping in the car.

Twenty minutes later she pulled up outside the modest bungalow. Grammy J left the house, then stopped halfway down the walk and brought a handkerchief to her mouth. Her slight shoulders hunched, rising and falling with each cough. She pocketed the handkerchief and resumed her trek to the car. The three children trailed behind her.

"Tommy shouldn't have called you." She stood in the open car doorway.

"I'm glad he did. Now hop in and we'll get you all fixed up."

Grammy J huffed and puffed as she seated herself in the Jeep. That little exertion shouldn't have had her breathing so hard. She must really be sick.

"Thank you for fetching us." She fastened her seat belt and then clutched her purse on her lap.

"Happy to help." Jenny looked over her shoulder to where the children climbed in the backseat. The kids would be bored at the clinic and this time of year waiting rooms were a breeding ground for bacteria and every the other germ that crossed through the clinic doors. "Tommy can stay home with the kids—they don't all need to come."

"No, can't trust 'em home alone. Never know what mischief they get into."

Jenny doubted they'd get into any trouble. Tommy was pretty responsible, but she wasn't going to argue the point. Jenny winced as Grammy J coughed, a deep hacking sound, like she could rip out a lung. She drooped in her seat and closed her eyes, exhausted.

At the clinic, Jenny supported one of Grammy J's arms and Tommy held the younger kids' hands. The little group moved up to the doorway and Jenny waved at the guard. Inside, the waiting room was packed. They passed people of all ages, lounging in the hard plastic seats, waiting their turn.

Tommy took the last free seat and pulled Clarisse onto his lap while Sammy sat silently at his feet. Jenny escorted Grammy J to the receptionist to sign in. Just as before, Grammy took the clipboard and passed it off to Tommy, trading it for his seat. Tommy quickly filled out the necessary paperwork, pointed out where Grammy J needed to sign, and handed it in.

A flushed older gentleman in the corner sat blowing his nose and coughing so badly that Jenny put her body between the sick man and the Johnsons. With her weakened immune system, Grammy J didn't need whatever it was that guy had. Several babies whimpered and fussed, another poor mite wheezed so loudly she could hear him easily from twenty feet away, and a woman in the corner argued with someone on her cell phone.

Clarisse squirmed and grunted when Sammy poked her. Then he pulled her braid and looked the other way. Jenny turned to the receptionist. "How long's the wait?"

She winced. "Probably about an hour. Bad weather seems to bring everybody in."

Jenny strained to hear her over the din of a crying baby and now arguing kids. "Is Gianna here?"

"Yup. Go on back."

Jenny went to Gianna's office—a little more than a closet actually. She wasn't there, but came hurrying down the hall. Gianna Donnatelli Scarfili's white lab coat flapped, snapping her legs, as she tossed instructions to the other nurse. Though a petite, tiny woman, she epitomized harnessed energy, making Jenny tired just at the thought of keeping up with her.

Gianna broke out in a wide smile when she spotted Jenny, which melted into concern. Reaching out, she squeezed Jenny's arm. "Hey, how're you doing?"

"I'm okay."

Her gaze sharpened on Jenny's face. "Really?"

Jenny nodded.

"Then what're you doing here?"

"A friend's sick and needed a ride."

"Really? Who? I'll see if Joe can slip them in—"

"No—but thanks. There's a huge line out there and she wouldn't feel right about that." No way would Grammy J stand for any preferential treatment. She'd wait her turn, even if she were dying. "I was looking for some books or magazines or something for the kids."

"Books don't last long here. If there aren't any out there, then..." She bit her lip and looked beyond Jenny into her office. "I think..." she rummaged though papers on her desk. "Yep, here." She handed Jenny a crumpled *Ranger Rick*. "Chris finished this and I brought it in days ago and forgot to put it out."

Jenny took the magazine. "Thanks. Hey, you don't happen to have any pamphlets on literacy programs, do you?"

Gianna walked with her toward the waiting room, then plucked a pamphlet off a wall filled with brochures. "ProLiteracy Detroit. Great people."

Gianna turned as the doctor called her. "I've gotta run, but we'll get you back as soon as possible."

"Thanks." Jenny folded the leaflet and tucked it in her back pocket.

In the waiting room, she sat Indian-style on the floor. Crooking a finger at Clarisse, she held up the magazine. With a shy smile, the four-year-old hesitated a second before darting over and climbing into Jenny's lap. Jenny relished feel of the solid little bundle that fit so perfectly in her arms and the fresh smell of her shampoo. This is what her own little one would feel like one day. She couldn't wait.

The *Ranger Rick* cover had a close-up frontal picture of an enormous, sloe-eyed hippo in a pond with a baby in front of her. The little hippo's whole head and neck were smaller than the end of the mother's nose. "And the caption read, 'Meet Mom and me and our whole hippo family.'" Jenny bent to look at Clarisse. "Do you want to meet his whole hippo family?"

She grinned. "Ye-th."

"Me too," said a voice to her right.

"Me t-o-o," chimed a little boy in front of Jenny.

Jenny looked up and while she and Clarisse had been studying the picture on the cover, four other children had crept near, and Sammy was craning his neck from five feet away. A half a dozen pair of eyes stared curiously at her. Jenny scanned her small audience and smiled.

"Okay. Everybody settle down. Make room." Jenny scooted over to accommodate a boy wedging closer. "And we'll all learn about the hippo family."

When they finished with the hippos, they moved on to learning about the care of little orphan bats, the world of sea turtles, and an article about "neat feet," but the hippo family story was the favorite. Perhaps because Jenny made fun little-boy voices when she read the baby hippo lines and used a deep "papa" voice for the daddy.

As Jenny read and showed the pictures, their little group grew and the room quieted until she could hear the receptionist talking on the phone and the shush shush shush of a blood pressure cuff being pumped up. Jenny added more animation and embellishment, to the delight of her audience.

Feeling eyes on her, Jenny looked up to see Gianna huddled with another nurse, whispering and nodding in her direction. They stared, making her feel self-conscious. Weren't doctors' wives supposed to sit on the floor entertaining children?

She raised an eyebrow and looked over the children's heads. "What?"

Gianna strolled forward. "Wow. It's as quiet as a library in here."

"We're enjoying *Ranger Rick*."

"I can see. You didn't even notice when Mrs. Johnson was called back."

Jenny scanned the room and saw Grammy J standing at the receptionist desk. She stood Clarisse up and slid out from under her. She handed Tommy the magazine and looked at all the expectant little faces. "Tommy'll finish the story for you."

"We'll have to start calling you Pied Piper," Gianna teased.

Jenny brushed away the compliment. "All done?"

"Yup." Gianna handed Grammy J a small plastic bag of medicine. "She's got an antibiotic for the infection, cough medicine so she can sleep, and an inhaler. She should be feeling much better in a couple days."

Jenny beamed. "Great." She looked at Grammy J. "Ready to go?"

"If you can pull the young ones away from that magazine of yours." She nodded to Sammy and Clarisse, still on the floor.

"Come on, guys," Jenny called out as she helped Grammy J on with her coat.

The little group moved out into the blustery day. Once settled in the Jeep, Jenny pulled out into the street. "Now that wasn't so bad, was it?"

"It was fine. Though I was hopin' to see your fine young man again, but Dr. Joe was real nice too. He took good care of me."

Jenny froze. The breath caught in her throat as they cruised past the Johnson's street.

"Jenny?" She heard the concern in the old woman's voice.

She pulled to the side of the road and looked straight ahead. "Sorry. I... um... Gabe was killed in a biking accident last month."

"Oh, honey. I'm so sorry," Grammy J reached out for Jenny's hand.

The younger children leaned forward. "What? What happened, Grammy?"

"Hush, now; never you mind." She patted Jenny's hand. "I been without my Herb now goin' on twenty years. It's hard, but you get by."

Jenny nodded. "Let's get you home now."

At home, Jenny got Grammy J and the kids settled inside the house. She made sure Grammy J understood which medicines she was to take when, and how to use her inhaler. Hesitating by the front door, she reached into her back pocket and pulled out the pamphlet.

"I got this from Gianna." She held up the flyer. "ProLiteracy Detroit is a free program that helps folks learn to read—mostly adults, and they meet in the basement of the church around the corner every week."

Jenny ignored the old woman's set features and the stubborn thrust of her chin, saying gently, "I know it's none of my business, but you're a smart lady. You can learn to read. And Tommy won't always be there to help you."

Grammy J took the flyer. She stared at the map and phone number on the front. "I'll think about it." She coughed, a raspy bark that sounded like something was caught in her throat. The little woman's shoulders hunched and her chest caved in deeply with each breath.

Jenny urged her to sit in a nearby chair until the coughing fit passed.

Grammy J grabbed Jenny's hand in a crushing, bony grip, as she fixed her with a stern stare. "I wish there was something I could do for all you done for us."

"You know I'm happy to help."

Grammy J lifted her chin. "Me too."

This sweet old lady was proud and didn't want charity; Jenny could understand that. She glanced at the pamphlet in Grammy's lap. "Maybe there is something..."

Chapter 10

Steve came home from work to find Annie's black Audi blocking his garage. His shoulders drooped. After the day he'd had at work, he'd been looking forward to vegging out in front of the TV with a beer or two. He parked under the basketball hoop and followed the sound of childish chatter around the side of the house to his back patio.

Josh and Sophie sat barefoot in a huge turtle sandbox, digging and flinging sand while Annie stretched out on a padded lounger, chatting on the phone.

"St-e-v-e," Sophie squealed, scrambling out of the box and running over.

He squatted down and frowned. "Hey, muffin head. Aren't you cold?"

She wagged her head back and forth.

Annie ended her phone call and jumped up. "Surprise." She gave him a quick kiss. "This darling little sandbox was half off—I just couldn't resist. I thought it'd be a great way to entertain the kids while we grilled and had drinks."

No doubt it was a great sale; there probably wasn't much demand for sandboxes in the fall. "Isn't it a little cold to be playing in a sandbox?"

"Don't be silly. We can always move it to the lawn or driveway if you want, but I can see the kids through the kitchen window."

Sophie manned the yellow watering can and sprinkled water on a bucket of sand while Josh smacked the top. "More, Soph."

"No, it's fine. What're you doing here?" he asked.

Annie pointed to a cloth Trader Joe's sack. "I thought we'd surprise you with fajitas."

"Steak?"

She smiled. "No, silly, chicken. We're cutting back on red meat, remember?"

Since when? He loved steak. But he also loved Annie's fajitas. Chicken would do.

"I would've had it ready by now, but I forgot the code to your garage and we were locked out."

Steve didn't remember ever telling her the code, but as his fiancée, she probably should have a key to his house—after all in about five months she and the kids would be moving in.

"The kids are starving. They should have eaten half an hour ago." She headed toward the house.

Steve accepted the grocery bag she handed him, unlocked the back door and stood aside for Annie to precede him.

He glanced back at the kids. "You guys don't leave the patio without me or Mom, right?"

"Uh huh." Josh slapped the shovel on the top of the bucket of sand.

Steve changed out of his suit and into a T-shirt and jeans. He rummaged through his desk. "I must have another spare key..." He'd gotten two when he'd made a copy for the Harrisons. Reaching deep into the drawer, he fingered an envelope with a key in it. Pocketing the key he headed to the kitchen.

Steve mixed Annie a gin and tonic and got himself a beer while she microwaved macaroni and cheese for the kids and prepared a salad and fajitas for them. The second dinner was over, the kids wanted to go back in the sandbox. Steve opened the heavy sliding door for them. "Watch your sister and remember not to leave the patio, okay?"

Josh nodded and ran over to the dump truck as Sophie headed for the watering can.

Steve stacked the dinner dishes and, with a finger in each glass, carried them to the sink. "Have you decided between the Country Club or the Yacht Club yet?" He squirted dish soap on the sponge.

"We picked the Yacht club weeks ago, remember? And Debra almost has the save-the-date video ready to send out, and I sent you the link to our website earlier this week. Did you like it?" She sat on a stool and leaned on the counter.

"Yeah, it was great." He vaguely remembered clicking through some silly, frilly website filled with sappy pictures Annie had hired a photographer to take of them after they'd gotten an engagement photo to satisfy her. Save-the-date video? Come on, it was just a wedding, not a state dinner. He scrubbed the stainless steel salad bowl, around and around.

Look at her, she's happy. Don't bring her down. Be supportive.

He tossed the spotless bowl in the drying rack. "So. What now? I have some time tonight; want to go over the guest list?"

"Done."

"Right." Of course it was. O-kay. "Do you need help picking out the invitations or," gulp, "flowers?" He knew *nothing* about flowers, but he wanted to be supportive and involved. "Or maybe we could pick a honeymoon spot?" *That* he could do. "How about a tour of Italy? Rome, Florence, Venice, Tuscany? Or—" he dried his hands and circled her in his arms, "a romantic ten days in Paris?" He turned Annie so she faced him. "I've never been to Italy or France, have you?"

Annie pulled out of his arms. "After college Suz and I bummed around Europe for a month." She wrinkled her nose. "You're not missing anything. They don't even speak much English—I mean they *can*, they just *won't*—unless you make them. They want to make tourists try to speak their language—not very friendly."

Okay, so Europe was out.

"A Bora Bora honeymoon would be romantic. All that sugary white sand and clear, warm water." She drifted off, her expression softening in a faraway dreamy look. "Everybody raves about the St.

Regis." She brightened and her body fairly hummed with excitement. "We could stay in one of those gorgeous over-the-water villas like Nicole Kidman." She snuggled against him. "Wouldn't that be wonderful?"

A beach vacation? That was kind of sedate, but... "If that's what you want."

Annie looked outside and frowned. She got up and slid the door open. "Where's Sophie?"

Josh sat alone in the sandbox, using a truck to demolish a huge sand hill. "She wanted more water for her moat." Josh looked at the hose lying curled next to the house, then whipped his head back at his mother. "Where is she?"

"Sophie?" Annie left the house looking right and left. "So—phie?"

Steve hurried after her. "Sophie." She wanted more water? He looked toward the lake in time to see the three-year old waving her yellow watering can a foot from the beginning of the dock.

"Sophie, no!" Steve bellowed. His heart flipped into overdrive as he leapt over a lawn chair and sprinted down the hill. "Don't move!"

With one foot on the edge of the dock, Sophie swung around and froze. Her eyes widened in surprise, seconds before her face crumpled into a hurt, frightened look. Steve scooped her up before he'd even stopped moving, and jogged in a semicircle away from the water. Chest heaving, he pressed her close as anger swamped him. "Jesus fucking Christ!"

"Dad—dy" Sophie sobbed. "Dad—dy."

He carried the howling child a hundred feet from the lake and set her down on the grass. "Are you okay?" Hands on his knees and chest still heaving, he bent over to look at her face. "Why're you crying?"

"Mom—my!" she wailed. "I. Want. My. Mommy," she sobbed, stopped between words to gasp and shudder as she stumbled toward the house.

Annie swung Sophie onto her hip and cuddled her close. "You're okay, baby. You're not hurt."

"Steve yell at me." Sophie hiccupped, rested her head against her mother's neck, and scowled at him, accusing.

Damn right he yelled. She could have drowned.

"He said a bad word." She had the nerve to tattle.

Annie frowned at him over her daughter's head.

"Uh-oh—You're in trouble," Josh said.

Steve slammed his hands on his hips and scowled at Annie. He cocked his head sideways and raised his eyebrows in silent question. Really? Seriously? The kid disobeyed the rules and Annie's going to censure *him*?

He took a deep breath to summon patience. Steve ducked his head to look Sophie in the eyes. "Sophie, you know the rules. It's not safe for you or Josh to go near the water without an adult. We talked about it." Almost every damn visit.

Sophie turned her head away and started crying again.

Annie rubbed her back and cuddled her closer. "Shh. Shh. You're okay. Steve doesn't know what a great swimmer you are." She kissed her forehead. "You just scared him."

Steve froze. He jabbed his index finger toward the lake. "That water's like forty-five degrees." She could have died from hypothermia if she hadn't drowned. He knew they should present a united front, but this was a safety issue he would not give on.

He clamped his jaw shut to keep from scaring Sophie more and stalked away. Goddamit. Now he was going to have to put up a fucking fence. He looked over his shoulder and scowled at Annie, letting her know that this was *not* over. He marched to the patio.

"You're mad," Josh said, galloping at his side.

Steve slowed so Josh could keep pace. "Yup."

"Sophie was bad. She broke the rules."

Steve looked down at Josh's guileless upturned face. "You're the big brother. You were supposed to be watching her," he reminded.

"Sorry." Josh hung his head. "Do you still love us?"

Steve sat on a chair and pulled him onto his lap. "Of course. We're buds. But you've got to follow the rules because they keep you and your sister safe, right?"

Josh nodded.

Steve hugged him close as Annie approached with Sophie. Annie set her daughter down. The preschooler studied the flagstaff and poked her bare toe at an anthill. Annie nudged her.

Sophie wrapped her arm around her mother's leg and peeked at him. "Sorry for scaring you."

"And?" Annie prompted.

"I won't do it again."

Steve leaned forward. "You've gotta follow the rules, Soph. I have to be able to trust you, right?"

She popped her thumb in her mouth and rubbed her head up and down against her mom's leg.

"You're forgiven." Steve held up his palm. "High five. Thanks for apologizing." He kissed her cheek.

"Mama made me," she whispered.

"I know," he whispered back, then blew in her ear to make her giggle.

"Hello? Sorry to interrupt..."

Annie whipped around and frowned as her ex-husband approached.

"Daddy!" Sophie screeched, bolted from Steve's embrace and threw herself at her father. Ryan scooped her up and settled the preschooler on one arm, then stretched out a hand to Steve, "Steve. Annie." He looked at her and then back at Steve. "Sorry to barge in like this, but I saw what happened," he inclined his head toward the lake, "down by the water, and I'm afraid it's my fault."

Annie stared at her ex-husband, having trouble comprehending that he was actually there in Steve's backyard, when his words sank in. Of course it was his fault. Ryan always screwed everything up.

"Ryan." Steve shook his hand and stood back, waiting.

"Thanks for reaching Sophie before—he frowned and swallowed hard. "When I waved, it never occurred to me that she'd run down to the water—she about gave me a heart attack. Thank God you saw her."

"You waved to her?" Of all the stupid things. What kid wouldn't run to see her daddy? Of course it never occurred to him. Nothing ever occurred to Ryan. "What were you doing out there?" She didn't even know he knew where Steve lived. She narrowed her eyes. "Were you spying on us?"

Steve put a hand on her shoulder. "Annie..."

"I was giving my new boat a test run—"

"And you *just happened* to run by Steve's house?" She crossed her arms over her chest. How dare he spy on them? She knew her engagement so shortly after the divorce would upset Ryan, but she'd just thought it'd shake him up, not turn him into a stalker.

He nodded. "When I saw the kids playing outside, I waved. I wasn't even sure Sophie saw me until she ran down the hill." He hugged her close and looked at Steve. "Thanks."

Annoyance rose in her as Ryan spoke directly to Steve, ignoring her as if she had no part in watching her kids—like he was the responsible adult. Ha! Like Ryan had a responsible bone in his body—who was he to judge? She was a responsible parent. She hadn't taken her eyes off Sophie for more than a minute. If Ryan hadn't lured her down to the water, none of this would have happened. As it was, Sophie had been perfectly safe. Thanks to Ryan, she'd been raised around the water and learned to swim before she could walk.

She crossed her arms. "It's not as if she can't swim."

Ryan frowned at her over their daughter's head. "Nobody could survive long in that cold water, Anne."

Annie scowled at him. He knew she hated being called Anne.

Sophie tucked her head into Ryan's neck and he kissed her forehead.

"Is that your new boat, Daddy?" Josh asked, his eyes lit with an excitement that fueled resentment in Annie. All Dad had to do is show up with a new toy and he was golden.

"Can we go for a ride?" Josh looked from Ryan to her and back again.

Great. Now she had to be the bad guy. Again. She gave Ryan a hard look.

"Sorry, Pal." He handed Sophie to her. "Another time. It's getting late and you guys probably should be in bed."

He stood there looking tan and fit in his usual Gore-Tex khakis, topsiders and a windbreaker. The wind ruffled his short auburn hair. Annie watched him, surprised her ex was behaving responsibly.

"Aww, pleeease?" Josh looked at her, pleading. "Mom?"

"Don't bug your mom," Ryan said. "Maybe next week after school. I'm off early Tuesday, if it's okay with Mom." He looked at her for permission. She had the kids during the weeks and every other weekend.

Annie nodded.

Ryan smiled and nodded. "Then it's a date. Well, I've got to get back." He looked to the water where a huge sailboat waited, gently bobbing in the waves.

Steve turned with Ryan and headed down the hill toward the dock.

"I'll talk to a fencing company next week," Steve told Ryan.

"Not a bad idea. I've seen some unobtrusive iron fences."

Annie put Sophie down. "You guys get your backpacks ready and then stay here. I'll be right back."

She followed the men down the hill, half listening to their discussion about fences, still having trouble believing Ryan had just dropped by. Both men were broad-shouldered and fit, though Ryan was several inches shorter than Steve. But Ry had a smile that could charm a beggar out of his last dollar. And he could just turn it off, because Annie didn't like her fiancé and ex being so comfortable with each other. Suddenly the idea of a house on the golf course seemed a necessity—at least there Ryan couldn't just pop in. Though Steve didn't seem too annoyed at her ex's impromptu visit.

She paused as Ryan shook hands with Steve and got into his little dinghy. Ry sped back to the huge sailboat. As he approached the back of the boat and climbed aboard, she frowned at the large slanted script across the stern. Annie Girl?

She hated sailing. Why'd Ryan named his boat after her? She *wasn't* impressed—okay, she was a little impressed. What girl wouldn't like a boat named after her? And he'd told Josh no himself and hadn't made her be the bad guy. Maybe their divorce was finally making him grow up. Good for him. His next wife would thank her.

Steve took her hand and together they climbed the hill to the waiting children. Earlier anger apparently burned away, he thanked her for dinner and helped buckle the kids into their car seats.

Annie rolled down the window. "Oh, I almost forgot. Emma cancelled on me for Thursday night. Is there any way you can watch the kids from seven to ten? I've got Bunko at Shirley's."

"What about Ryan?"

"I didn't ask him."

"Ask him. He'd probably enjoy the extra time with them." Steve took out his cell phone and checked his calendar. "If Ryan can't do it, then I will. But check with him first."

She pouted. "Fine." Then she brightened. "Thanks, honey. Love you."

"You too." Steve leaned in and kissed her goodnight, then backed up as she zipped down the driveway.

He headed back toward the house, then turned at the low drone of the Harrison's garage door opening. Jenny backed out and executed a three-point turn. She saw him, and a big smile broke across her face, warming him. Tension eased with each step as he strolled over to the idling Jeep.

"Hey. Where're you off to?"

"Barnes and Noble."

"Need something to read or research?"

She cocked her head sideways. "I'm teaching a friend to read and I thought I'd see if there were any basic books that might appeal to an adult."

"Really? How'd this come about?"

Jenny waved a hand. "It's a long story, but it's good. I needed a project—something to get me focused on other people instead of obsessing about my own problems."

"Good for you. Does that mean you found an attorney?"

She pursed her lips. "No, still looking. I've got a few feelers out."

"I asked Allen Blakeman, but—"

"He didn't want anything to do with it," she broke in.

"I was going to say," he raised his eyebrows in reproach, "that he was too busy." He gentled the truth. *Why'd you do that, Grant? Not helping her any, hiding the truth.*

"And he wasn't interested."

True. No money to be made in losing. "You'll find somebody," he offered halfheartedly.

She nodded. "Gotta run before the store closes. See ya."

Steve watched her drive away.

She wasn't going to find a lawyer to take her case, but there was no need to remind her of that. Jenny seemed less sad than she'd been since Gabe died, and he didn't want to wreck that. Besides, he was confident he didn't need to be the bad guy. Time would prove him right.

Chapter 11

Monday morning Jenny pulled on dressy jeans and a bulky cable knit sweater that hid the fact that she'd lost ten pounds. For the first time in weeks, she went to the trouble of using cosmetics. She carefully applied foundation to hide the dark patches under her eyes and blush to give her pale face some color. No amount of makeup could make her skin and hair glow again, but at least she didn't look ill.

Jenny slipped into work earlier than usual, hoping if she was already there when her co-workers arrived, she'd miss that embarrassing moment when she drew attention, like a kid coming into class late. She scrolled through the daily news on her computer, hoping for inspiration for her next piece. A new yoga studio was opening on The Hill, maybe something about how yoga seemed to be growing in popularity?

She could use some zen in her life—what she *really* needed was an attorney. She'd made light of it when Steve asked, but she'd just about reached a dead end. *Focus, Jenny. Worry about that later.* She glanced at the time. *Staff meeting in ten minutes and you got nothing.*

"Hi, Jenny. How're you doing? I'm sorry about your husband." Betty McIntyre paused beside her desk.

"Thanks, Betty. I'm fine." Jenny looked at the middle-aged advice columnist. Betty had a daughter graduating from high school this year. Ordinarily Jenny would have enjoyed chatting about her, but she wasn't in the mood for chitchat and had work to do.

"If there's anything I can do—"

"Thank you," Jenny cut her off and smiled to take the sting out of her abrupt reply, then turned back to her computer. She flipped through several more pages and then moved to MSN headlines. Breakup relationships? The holidays were coming... how to survive the holiday with your mother-in-law? Or your husband's ex-wife.

Judith kept calling, bugging her about Thanksgiving. She'd tried not answering the phone, but then she just left messages. And messages.

People left their desks and walked toward the meeting room. Jenny grabbed a notepad and her favorite pen, hurried in and took a seat along with five others and their boss. Karen kept the meeting blessedly short as she handed out assignments and listened to their brainstorming ideas. Jenny was rounding the conference table when Karen stopped her.

"Condolences, Jenny." Karen smiled. "It's good to have you back."

"Thank you."

"I like the piece about people with food allergies surviving the holidays. Very timely."

"Good." Jenny had thrown that out at the last minute.

Karen softened her voice. "If you need a little extra time or anything, just let me know."

"Thanks, I appreciate that. I *will* need to miss Wednesday's staff meeting. I have a meeting with an attorney that couldn't be scheduled any other time." Jenny didn't explain the nature of her appointment, hoping that Karen would assume it pertained to settling Gabe's estate.

Karen's face dissolved into a sympathetic look. "Certainly. Whatever you need. Just let me know if you're going to be late with that piece—we have a little wiggle room."

"No need. I'll get it in. Thanks." She'd never missed a deadline and she wouldn't start now—she wouldn't allow George the satisfaction of messing up her life further.

She really didn't want George's lawsuit making her private life public knowledge with a protracted lawsuit. She didn't need people gossiping about her any more than they already were. Surely she could convince the judge that this suit was stupid and unnecessary, and then Jenny could move on with getting pregnant.

Heck, if she could get this taken care of quickly and was lucky enough to get pregnant right away, people might even assume that she'd gotten pregnant right before Gabe died. *You were pregnant—at least for a little while.* She pushed the sad thought aside. She'd be pregnant again and this time she'd protect their baby better.

∾ ∾ ∾

Wednesday afternoon Jenny warily examined the judge's chambers, trying to ignore the men facing her across the gleaming wood conference table. She'd never seen the inside of a courtroom, let alone a judge's chambers.

Stately walnut bookcases neatly filled with volumes of legal books stood floor to ceiling. Flanking American and Michigan flags guarded a big wooden desk, with several hard-backed chairs clustered nearby. Framed credentials and scholarly achievements decorated the cream wall behind the desk. It looked pretty much like what Jenny had seen on television, with the exception of the scattered profusion of live plants, the sprinkling of family photos, and the row of fiction books lining the bottom shelf of the credenza.

Susan Wiggs, Kristin Hannah, Julie Garwood and Stephen King and Dean Koontz? Romance and horror, how interesting. She thought about the painful, scary weeks surrounding Gabe's death. Loving left one vulnerable. Perhaps romance and horror weren't that far apart.

Jenny had arrived twenty minutes early, hoping to have some time to mentally prepare, but George and his attorney were waiting in chambers. Dressed in dark suits with hair slicked back, the two huddled men looked up at her entrance. George stared at her while his attorney quickly dismissed her with barely a glance and reclaimed his client's attention. A woman sat in front of a small gray appliance that looked like an old-fashioned adding machine, reading something on her iPad.

Jenny took a step backward, longing to escape. A fine sheen of sweat glossed her body, chilling her, despite the heavy sheepskin coat she wore. Feeling alone and threatened, she avoided looking at the men and perched on the edge of the seat next to the court reporter.

Her heart dropped as she took in the scene. This official room suited the serious men, and her aloneness hit her like a slap in the face. This was *not* going to be quickly resolved. She was in way over her head. Her abdomen cramped painfully; Jenny hoped she wasn't getting an ulcer.

A woman with coal-black curls breezed into the room and the court reporter immediately put away the e-reader and turned on her machine. Judge Christina Moore wore a white silk shirt and camel-colored suit with matching high heels. She glanced at the waiting group as she rounded the table and picked up a file. Resting a hip against the desk, she put on her tortoiseshell reading glasses, opened the folder and scanned it. She consulted the small gold watch on her arm before looking at Jenny.

"We'll wait a little longer for your attorney, but if he doesn't show we'll have to reschedule."

Jenny glanced uneasily at George and his attorney. She licked her dry lips. "I don't have an attorney yet, Your Honor."

"Why not?"

"My husband died just five weeks ago." She gave George a reproachful look. "It's been difficult interviewing attorneys under the circumstances."

The judge pinned her with a firm look. "I understand how difficult this time is for you; however, you really must give this your full attention." She paused. "I'll give you an additional forty-five days to find counsel."

"Judge, we all sympathize with Mrs. Harrison's loss, but there are major issues at stake here and my client strongly believes that Dr. Harrison cannot rest in peace until the fate of *all* of him has been laid to rest." He glared at Jenny. "Therefore, I'd ask that the court not be overly indulgent in granting a continuance. Frankly, I don't think her difficulties in obtaining the services of an attorney are limited by any time constraints."

The judge glanced sharply at the lawyer. "That's enough, counselor. I've made my ruling." Sitting, she picked up a ballpoint pen and studied the stand-up monthly calendar. She reached out and flipped forward to the next month, then tapped the pen against her lips.

"Let's see... forty-five days from now puts us just about at Christmas, then there's New Years... We'll set the pretrial hearing for Monday January fourth." She looked from George's attorney to Jenny. "I assume that's all right with everybody?"

Thank God for holidays. Jenny nodded, feeling the pressure ease from her chest. "Thank you."

She fumbled with her monthly planner and painstakingly shaped each letter and word to record the appointment. Head down, she rearranged the contents of her purse until she heard the door close behind them.

"They're gone," the judge said.

Jenny looked up, embarrassed that Judge Moore knew she'd been procrastinating to avoid them. With a mumbled thank you, Jenny quickly gained her feet and headed for the door.

"Mrs. Harrison?"

Jenny slowly pivoted, feeling like a child about to be reprimanded by the teacher for dawdling.

"I'm sorry for your loss."

Jenny forced a stiff smile. "Thank you."

She hurried out the door and paused in the hallway. The meeting had been so formal—so official. George's attorney seemed cold and heartless. He was *not* going to be civil about this. She shuddered, shaking off the uncomfortable feeling of being targeted by a bully. By refusing to give in to George, she'd put a big bull's-eye on her forehead. Geeze, was it really worth it? All she wanted was a baby; why did it have to be this hard?

Jenny put a hand to her pounding head and headed for the parking garage. Several people clustering around the elevator prompted Jenny to veer right toward the stairs. Her steps faltered as George moved out of a doorway to her left. He smoothed the brim of his plaid cap. "Can I have a word with you?"

She kept moving toward the staircase. "I think you and your attorney have said enough."

He fell into step beside her. "It'll just take a minute."

Jenny pushed through the metal door into the stairwell, then faced him. "One minute."

He cleared his throat, frowned and then looked away as if having trouble starting. "Ya look like hell."

She spun toward the stairs, releasing the heavy fire door. She knew she looked like a mangled kitten and didn't need the reminder.

"Oh, hey. I'm sorry." Her foot rested on the first step when she felt a light grip on her arm. Jenny froze and looked up at George before staring pointedly at his fat, hairy hand on her forearm. He immediately released her. "Look, I'm sorry. I didn't mean it the way it came out. I... I'm sorry you're having such a hard time."

I bet. She stared at him, unblinking.

"Look, this can stop right here, right now. It's up to you."

"Actually George, since it's you who is suing me, it's up to *you*." She paused, wondering if it was even worth her breath to try to reason with him. "Gabe loved us both. Do you really think he'd want you to prevent me from having his baby?"

"Gabe didn't always know what was best for him. He..." Twin lines dug deep, vertical furrows into his forehead as he struggled to find the right words. "Just give up before things get ugly. I don't want anybody to get hurt."

Too late. "I'm hurt."

"You're hurting yourself. Look, I don't want to fight you. Just quit before it's too late."

Too late for what? "I want my husband's baby."

He frowned and pursed his lips. "Why are you being so stubborn about this? This is no game. Lawsuits are ugly. Lawyers play to win. They dig and pry into things that are nobody's business. Just let it be."

That part had been made crystal clear, but she'd been the one to show up to the fight unarmed; why was George warning her off? Had he found out something or was he just using scare tactics? "Are you threatening me?"

"Threatening you?" His eyes widened as if surprised. "Hell, no, I'm not threatening you. I'm trying to make you understand the can of worms you're about to open up. Look, we're reasonable adults. There has to be another way to settle this."

"Agreed. Drop the lawsuit."

"I can't do that." George sighed and looked away. His lips thinned as he reached into his coat pocket and pulled out a folded blue piece of paper. He smoothed his finger and thumb along the crease before thrusting it at Jenny.

Jenny unfolded the paper to see her name a line above a hundred thousand dollars. She stared at the check.

"I'm sure Gabe left you well-provided for, but... well, I don't know how else to change your mind."

Jenny crushed the check in her fist and threw it to the floor. Head held high, she descended the stairs without looking back, proud that she'd managed to ignore the urge to slap the old man's face—or cry. The heavy fire door shut and latched with a loud click that echoed with eerie finality in the vacant stairwell as if emphasizing her aloneness. She passed the first landing. What the world made George think he could buy her off?

For a while back there, she'd actually begun to second-guess herself. Maybe it *was* too complicated. Maybe it wouldn't be worth the humiliation and pain, but that was before that arrogant prick tried to buy her off.

How *dare* he? How dare George interfere in her marriage? She wanted to have her husband's baby and she didn't give a damn what that old man thought. She'd dig up the most ruthless attorney in Michigan. Just let him *try* and stop her.

Jenny struggled to hold onto the anger and push away the hurt. Did George really think so little of her? Was she really so unworthy of being a mother to George's precious descendants? Strangely enough, George had seemed genuine in his appeal. Yet if he was so confident he was right and would win, why try to buy her off?

It didn't make sense. Jenny burst through the ground floor door and out into the cold, dank parking garage. Her clicking high heels ricocheted noisily, sounding like a dozen people hurrying behind, chasing her. Nervous cramping in her belly intensified, and Jenny was out of breath by the time she reached the Jeep. With trembling hands, she unlocked the car and got in.

Calm down, Jen. You're fine. He's just a crazy old man—don't let him get to you.

She'd be okay. She could do this. She'd find an amazing attorney who would persuade that nice lady judge that she should have Gabe's baby and this time next year she'd be rocking their darling baby in her arms. Everything would be fine.

Then why did she feel so horrible?

Jenny propped her elbows on the steering wheel and dropped her aching head into cold trembling hands. Tears spilled from her eyes and dribbled down her cheek. How could her life have fallen apart so completely—again? What had she done wrong to deserve this?

A sudden knock at the window penetrated Jenny's misery. Mortified to be caught crying in her car, Jenny brushed the tears away. An older woman with blonde hair twisted into a loose topknot stood beside her car. Folded reading glasses hung from a silver-bead chain around her neck, standing out against the black turtleneck. She hunched into her gray herringbone wool blazer. Twin lines of concern creased her forehead. "Are you all right?"

"Fine. Thank you." Jenny reached for her keys and put them in the ignition.

"Mrs. Harrison, could I speak to you for a moment?"

Mrs. Harrison? She knew Jenny's name? She watched the lady closely while inching her hand closer to the door lock. "Have we met?"

"I'm Deirdre Hall from the *Lansing Daily.*"

Jenny punched the lock button.

"Can we go somewhere and talk?"

She stared at the woman.

"Is it true that you've had your dead husband's sperm frozen so you can have his baby?"

The reporter's words buzzed around Jenny's tired head.

"Is it true that a sperm bank in California was the only one that would accept your husband's sperm?"

She knew too much. Jenny fumbled with the keys, then started the car. The reporter backed away, still hurling questions at her as Jenny sped off. *Lansing Daily*? Why come all the way from Lansing to cover her story? How'd the press even gotten hold of her case?

Jenny quickly drove home and collapsed on the couch. Next to her, the answering machine blinked a red warning. She had eight messages. Somehow she doubted it was attorneys suddenly banging down her door to change their minds about taking her case.

Breathing in deeply, she pushed the play button. Most of them were from reporters promising her a sympathetic ear if she'd share her story with them. This had to be George's doing. Although she'd approached a lot of attorneys, she was certain that some ethical law forbade them from talking about her case, even after they'd refused her. It had to be George. She grabbed a pillow and hugged it tight against her cramping belly. Damn him.

ॐ ॐ ॐ

Jenny blinked, frowned, and then winced at the strip of bright light sneaking around the curtains, blinding her. Groaning, she pulled the covers over her head and flipped on her side away from the window. The doorbell rang, over and over again, making the chimes a demand rather than an announcement.

Throwing the covers back, she growled at the sound of something thwacking the wall. What'd she knocked over? She rolled out of bed and picked Gabe's watch up off the floor. She cradled it in her palm, carefully examining it for damage. No cracked glass face and the second hand still pivoted. Phew. She blew out a deep breath and gently returned it to her nightstand.

The doorbell rang again. Jenny jammed her feet into slippers and scuffled downstairs. "I'm coming."

It had to be a relative, Judith, her mother, or maybe even Alex—if she was really desperate or excited. Only a relative would dare be so annoying.

Ritz whined and pranced at the door, doing the doggie version of crossing her legs. Poor thing, it was early afternoon and Jenny hadn't let her out yet. She opened the door and as Ritz dashed outside to take care of business, her mother barged in.

Mary Campbell was a slight woman with short auburn hair and a profusion of freckles dotting her face. She had laser blue eyes that missed nothing. Jenny had inherited their mother's petite statue and light blue eyes, but she possessed her father's dark hair and compassionate nature.

"Mom. Hi." Jenny wrapped her arms around her stomach. Her hand snuck up to scratch her head as she, discretely as possible, checked her hair for knots.

"I thought I'd drop by for a little visit before picking Michael up for his dentist appointment at two-thirty." She walked in and dumped her purse on the stairs. With one eyebrow cocked, she stared at Jenny. "Didn't you go back to work this week?"

"Un huh. I'm working from home." She forced a bright smile. "How's semi-retirement going?"

"In your pajamas?" She propped her hands on her hips. "Are you just getting up?"

Jenny looked to the right of her mother at a clump of fur on the wood floor. "I haven't been sleeping well."

She turned away from her mother's steady, concerned stare. What could she say to get her to leave? She didn't need to be judged nor did she need the guilt that came from worrying her parents. "I'm fine, Mom."

She went to the door and whistled for the dog. So? She was just having a bad day. It was to be expected. She'd set her alarm so she wouldn't miss Michael's game. She'd have her sadness under control long before her evening tutoring appointment with Grammy J, but this morning she'd given in to exhaustion and depression.

Ritz trotted in and snuffled Jenny's hand to remind her she'd like to be fed.

Mom shut the door, took Jenny's arm and guided her toward the kitchen. "Well, of course you're not fine. Your husband died only a little over a month ago. Here, sit down and I'll make you some lunch. Scrambled eggs or peanut butter and fluff?"

Jenny went to the pantry and dumped a scoop of dog food into Ritz's bowl before sinking into the nearest chair. "I'm not hungry."

"I'm sure you're not, but you need to eat. You've lost weight."

"I'm fine. Eggs," Jenny said at her mother's frown.

Mom took out two eggs from the refrigerator. After cracking them in a small glass bowl, she lifted it and wrinkled her nose. "*Dear God.*"

She tossed them in the sink on top of the dirty soup pot and a week's worth of grimy glasses, plates, and silverware. Jenny hoped colorful mold wasn't fuzzing them but wouldn't be at all surprised if it was.

"Peanut butter it is," Mom announced.

"Third shelf on the right in the pantry," Jenny said, too tired to get it herself.

Her mom made the peanut butter sandwich and cut it in half. "I shouldn't have listened to your father. I wanted to come over weeks ago, but he convinced me you needed some time."

Bless Dad.

"But what do men know?" Mom slid the sandwich onto a plate and plunked it down in front of her. "Eat up and then we're going to have a little talk."

Jenny diligently chewed each mouthful carefully before swallowing, more to make a show of eating and putting off the talk than because she was savoring the subtle melding of crunchy peanut butter and sweet marshmallow fluff. She hadn't enjoyed the taste of food since Gabe died. Eating was just a means to keep her from getting queasy and for maintaining her strength.

Mom silently loaded her dishwasher and scrubbed her pots and pans. Knowing what a meticulous housekeeper her mother was—an unwelcome neuroses she'd passed on to her daughter, Jenny was surprised she wasn't mortified that her mother was cleaning her kitchen. Normally she would have been ashamed for her mother to see her sloppy housekeeping, but today she really didn't care.

Jenny ate the sandwich and drank the ice water her mother put before her.

When the dishwasher was running, pots and pans dried and put away, and the counters scrubbed until the black granite gleamed, her mother sat down at the table and pulled her chair close.

"So. I wanted to check on you and now that I have, I can see that I should've insisted you stay with us—at least for a little while. It's natural that you'd spend days in bed mourning, but you need somebody to take care of you."

"I'm fine, Mom. Is Dad in China or Ireland this week?"

"Ireland. You're not fine."

"You should go with him one of these trips. A second honeymoon. I'd be happy to stay with Michael."

"That's sweet—now stop trying to distract me. We were talking about you."

"I'm fine. I just need to figure things out."

"Like what?"

"Things. It's a little hard adjusting—okay, *really* hard," she confessed. "I'm so tired of it all. Tired of the tears, the emptiness, the *sadness*. I thought I'd be ready to go back to work by now, but I can't seem to concentrate on anything. I start out doing one thing, then get distracted by something else and before you know it, hours have gone by and I haven't accomplished anything."

"That's menopause," her mother muttered.

"What?"

"Nothing." She shook her head. "It's only natural. Everybody grieves in her own time."

"But it's been more than a month and I still can't work, even part-time? I need to work. I *need* to feel normal again. And it's weird going out now," she blurted, "even to the grocery store. I feel like people *know*. They know I used to be a part of a couple and now I'm not. I'm not a wife. I'm not an... anything.

"When I used my credit card the other day and signed Jenny Harrison, I felt like a fraud. Like now that Gabe's dead, I should give the name back. How weird is that?"

Her mother raised her eyebrows and inclined her head. "Well, *that's* a little strange, but kind of understandable. You'd only been married a couple of years. That's really not all that long."

"It's *weird*, Mom. I'm starting to freak myself out."

Mom pulled her close and rubbed Jenny's back. "I know. But you'll get beyond this. I know you miss Gabe terribly, but he's not coming back. You're no longer a part of a couple, so you need to learn to be strong and happy with yourself. You had a life before Gabe and you'll have a life after him. You're a smart, beautiful woman." She patted Jenny's hand. "You'll be happy again one day. You *will*," she said at Jenny's doubtful frown. "When you were single you were never one to need a man to make you happy. You had goals and ambitions. What were they?"

Life before Gabe? Hmm. She'd just started at the newspaper and hadn't even made enough money to pay her bills. She'd been in debt to Dad and carried balances on her credit cards. She'd been fighting with Mom over Michael's skateboard and accident. She'd been a royal screwup.

Gabe had been this good-looking, successful doctor who loved her. He would've given her the world if she'd asked. Marriage to Gabe gave her a fresh start and a chance to remake herself into a better person—and she'd taken it, as if changing her name would change the person she'd been inside.

"Jenny? What did you want out of life? You loved journalism," Mom prompted.

Jenny blinked. She *had* loved journalism—she'd sold a wonderful article on Steve to *People* magazine. That'd been nice, but all she'd really wanted was to be successful and feel good about herself. "To be a great wife and stepmother."

"And you were, but before Gabe. Who were you *before* him?"

Jenny frowned. She didn't want to remember those days—didn't like that person very much. "I don't know."

"Yes, you do." Mom patted her hand again. "What would you love to do? Right here. Right now."

"Have Gabe's baby."

"Something doable, honey. Something that involves just you. For you." Mom smiled encouragingly. "You're not a wife. Not a stepmother. Just Jenny. What would feed your soul?"

She'd been so intensely focused on being the best wife and stepmother, it'd been years since Jenny had really thought about herself. She couldn't even think of herself in that context. Besides, she was still a stepmom. "I... I don't know."

"What have you always wanted to do, but never made the time for? Travel? A hobby? Going back to school? Volunteering?"

Jenny blinked. Travel? Hobby? Too many choices. "I *don't* know."

"Sure you do. You have all the answers in here." She gently tapped Jenny's temple. "And here." She pointed at Jenny's heart.

"Not helpful." Jenny rolled her eyes up as if looking into her head. "Nothing's there." Her brain and her heart were empty.

Mom smiled. "It's there. You just have to find it."

"Don't you have to pick Michael up?"

Mom looked at her watch and jumped to her feet. "Yep."

Jenny walked her to the door and whistled for Ritz. She gave her mom a brief hug. "Thanks for lunch and the clean kitchen, Mom."

"You're welcome. See you at Michael's soccer game, tomorrow? It's home. Four o'clock."

"Today at four?"

"Nope, tomorrow. It'd mean a lot to him." She held Jenny's gaze. "He really misses you."

Determined not to let the big age difference deprive either of them of a close sibling relationship, Jenny had always made time for her little brother since the day he'd been born. She religiously attended Michael's home games, but with Gabe's death, well, she'd missed a few.

Way to pull the guilt card, Mom. Though she had every intention of making more of an effort to get to her brother's games, she didn't appreciate her mother using Michael to get her out of the house.

She wiggled her fingers in a wave. "Bye, Mom. You're going to be late."

She closed the door. That was one pushy Irishwoman, but she was well-intentioned and she'd made a good point. Volunteering? Hmm. As she leaned back against the door, a kernel of an idea tickled Jenny's brain.

Chapter 12

Sunday morning, Jenny woke to the rumbling of her garage door opening. She sat up and looked at the alarm clock. Eight-thirty. She cocked her head at the click, click, click of Ritz's nails as she trotted across kitchen floor. Then the back door quietly clunked shut. Jenny threw the covers back and tiptoed into the hallway. She peeked over the balcony railing. "Steve?"

She couldn't imagine Ritz allowing anybody else into the house without sounding an alarm. Rrr. Rrrr. A lawnmower purred to life, then the engine revved before it droned off across the front yard. Jenny hurried to her bedroom window and yanked the shade up just as Michael swung the mower around to cross the yard again.

Michael was cutting their grass? How come? Why wasn't he at church or soccer? Jenny jogged downstairs. In the kitchen, a small white pastry box from East Detroit Bakery sat on her island countertop. She flipped the box open. Glazed, Bavarian cream, chocolate, and sugar doughnuts—all her favorites. Jenny smiled at the strip of white receipt paper and the simple note scrawled across it: "Love you, Dad."

She picked up her phone and texted, *Thanks for the doughnuts, Dad.*

That was so like her dad, unobtrusive, yet there if she needed him. Snatching a chocolate doughnut from the box, she threw a jacket on over her PJs and slid her feet into flip-flops on her way out the back door. Michael's bike rested against the brick next to the open garage door.

Her phone chimed with the eerie Harry Potter music Michael had downloaded and chosen as her text alert. Jenny looked at the message. *Eat, little girl. Mother says you're wasting away.*

Mom *would* enlist Dad's help. He was probably on his way to China; he had to go there for work just about once a month. She texted a smiley face. *Safe travels.*

Seconds later, a smiley face popped up on her screen. No reprimands, no guilting her into being happy, just gentle acceptance—that was her dad.

Across the lawn, Michael, earbuds in place, trudged behind the lawnmower. Her eyes teared up at her sweet little brother cutting her grass. Not so little anymore—At nearly fourteen, Michael had just shot up six inches and was closing in on six feet. He was tall, lanky and skinny and had become endearingly shy as if uncertain in his new bigger body. With shocking blue eyes and dark brown hair, there was no doubt she and he were related. He pivoted the mower and set off across the yard again.

What was he doing here? He should be out enjoying his weekend, hanging with friends and flirting with girls at the football games, not cutting his sister's grass. Jenny frowned. Was this because she'd ignored his calls? She just hadn't been up to putting up a happy front, so she hadn't called Michael back. She didn't want to scare her baby brother with her tears.

Michael started high school a few months ago—maybe he'd wanted to talk. Maybe he had a crush on some pretty girl. Maybe he couldn't decide which classes to take. Maybe he was being picked on. Maybe he needed her and she'd selfishly ignored his calls. She hadn't been a very good sister lately.

Michel turned at the far end of the yard, cutting one last strip. Naw... he wasn't being picked on; her cute brother had always been well liked. Being a good-looking jock eased a kid's way in school.

Michael paused when saw her standing there. He pulled the earbuds from his ears, leaving them to dangle down the front of his shirt as he pushed the mower over and turned it off. His shy smile renewed her guilt for not making more of an effort with him lately.

Jenny forced a smile. "Hey. What're you doin'?"

He shrugged. "Your grass was gettin' long."

"Mom know you're here?" Mom was always complaining that Michael constantly had to be reminded to do his chores. She wouldn't be pleased that he was here working in Jenny's yard if he hadn't done his work at home.

"It was her idea."

Her idea? Wow, Mom *was* worried. "You don't have to. I..." she could get a service, but then again, it didn't take a genius to cut a little grass. "I was going to get to it."

Michael shrugged again, then looked away as if embarrassed. "I don't mind. We went to the bakery, then Dad dropped me off on his way to the airport."

She held out the doughnut she'd brought him.

He shook his head. "I ate mine."

"Since when do you turn down a chocolate doughnut?"

"You eat it."

She cut it in half and held out both hands. "I split, you choose."

Michael looked like he'd refuse, but she raised her eyebrows and tilted her head, letting him know she wouldn't tolerate any refusal. He reached for the one that was fractionally smaller than the other.

"Sorry I didn't make your game yesterday—I was catching up on work. How'd you do?" Jenny hated that it sounded like the hollow excuse it was.

Michael polished off the doughnut in two big bites. "One goal and two assists."

"That's great." She beamed, then suddenly felt sad to have missed it. "So what's it like being at the bottom of the food chain again?"

"All right." Michael shoved his hands deep in his pockets as if he didn't know what to do with them. "Look, Jen, I know Mom's bugging you about comin' to my games and everything, but it's okay if you don't. I get it."

Jenny cocked her head. "Get what?"

"That you're sad. Gabe was a good guy."

"Yeah, he really was."

"At first, you marrying my doctor was a little weird, but he was cool. He treated me like one of his kids. Helped me with my topspin and slice." He looked away at the road, then down at his shoes. "I figure if I miss him this much, you must really miss him.

Jenny nodded. "I do."

"Mom's always bugging Dad about calling and visiting you. She wants to bring you food and stuff, but Dad says you need time." He looked away. "When I screw up during a game or have a bad day, I'm so pissed off, I just want to be left alone." He looked at her. "It's not the same as someone dying, so you probably need more time."

Jenny swallowed a lump and blinked back tears.

"But I figured it'd be okay if I cut the grass or did some weeding. I could brush Ritz and walk her once in a while. She probably misses him too." He crouched down to pet the dog. "Don'tcha girl?" Glancing back at Jenny, he added. "I won't bother you. Okay?"

Jenny nodded.

"Oh," —he smiled and stood—"and don't let her make you feel guilty about not coming to my games. You're not missin' anything."

Liar. Michael made the varsity team as a freshman—that was huge. He'd scored a goal and she'd missed it. Starting high school was a big deal. She was the adult. She should be supporting him, yet here he was cutting her grass, brushing her dog and lying to spare her feelings. She didn't want to embarrass him with a sloppy display of emotions, so she ran a hand beneath her nose and took a deep breath. "So what's her name?"

"Who?"

"The girl you're showing off for at soccer games and don't want me to meet."

Michael grinned and turned away. "Come on, Ritz. Where's the ball? Find it."

There really *was* a girl? She'd just been teasing. "Is she pretty?" Jenny hurried after him. "Is she older?"

Michael blushed and walked faster. He scooped up a tennis ball from the asphalt and sent it sailing across the driveway deep into the backyard. He swiveled his Detroit baseball cap so the bill pointed backward and pushed the lawnmower behind the racing dog.

My God, he's such a good kid. Her parents were doing a great job raising him. Hopefully she'd be as good a parent to her and Gabe's baby. Jenny returned to the house and glanced at the clock on the oven. Just enough time to call Alex and see how she was doing before her afternoon match with Steve and Annie.

Jenny was impressed with how well Alex was handling her father's death—Ted too. They'd returned to school soon after the funeral, and Alex called weekly to check on Jenny. Ted was a little less communicative, but then he was a boy. Jenny would call him after Alex. Even though he was a young adult, Ted and his dad had been close and losing a father couldn't be easy for a son at any age.

That Ted and Alex were so protective of her was sweet. Jenny had really lucked out that they'd worked out any resentments about their father marrying a younger woman early on and became friends. A slow smile lifted Jenny's face. Cookies. She'd make them their favorite peanut butter surprise cookies while she talked to them. If she hurried, she could make a double batch and send some home with Michael.

Energized for the first time in days, she jogged up the stairs to get dressed. It'd been months since Jenny had sent the kids care packages. Every college kid loved mail and her kids deserved a little extra pampering.

ﾟ ﾟ ﾟ

Late that afternoon, Jenny headed through the hedges to Steve's. It'd been several weeks since operation "Trojan Annie," and Steve had apparently noticed Jenny's efforts at distancing herself from the couple. Her reasons for turning down his repeated invitations were starting to sound like excuses.

To avoid an awkward confrontation, Jenny accepted the invite to hangout with Steve and Annie. To be honest, she'd missed Steve. Missed his company, his conversation, and the way he teased her out of a bad mood. No matter how hard she worked or what projects she took on to keep herself busy, life without both Gabe and Steve was lonely. Really lonely.

Jenny gave a token knock as she twisted the doorknob and entered Steve's house. In the kitchen, bare feet and a jean-clad butt greeted her as Steve leaned into the refrigerator. An untucked, faded polo shirt completed his ensemble.

"Hey, Grant, ready to play?" Jenny looked around the room. "Where's Annie?"

"She bagged out. Word games aren't exactly her thing."

After our last tête-à-tête, I didn't think she'd leave me alone with you. "She knows I'm here, right?"

"Yeah, why? Coke Zero or a Genuine Draft?"

"Soda, please." She lifted her hips onto the counter. "Hey, can I ask you a personal question?"

"Sure." Steve set the beer and soda on the counter and shut the refrigerator door before facing her.

"What do you see in Annie?" She raised a hand as he shot her an annoyed frown. "I'm not being snarky, just curious. I mean, she's pretty and has a great body, but what do you two have in common?"

He leaned against the opposite cabinets and crossed his legs. "She's beautiful and smart and independent. She's a good mom." He lifted his gaze and smirked. "And she's crazy about me."

Women were crazy about Steve; he had his pick. "But she makes you happy, right?"

"Yeah. Of course." He paused a second too long before answering, then tilted the Heineken bottle and swigged his beer. Because she didn't make him happy or because Jenny's nosiness made him uncomfortable?

If there was a problem, it's not like he'd say anything to her anyway. He seemed the kind of guy to keep his private life private instead of soliciting relationship advice from his buddies.

"What about the kids?"

"What about them? You have stepchildren."

"Alex and Ted were sixteen and eighteen when I married Gabe. Annie's kids are still young. It's a bigger commitment. You'll have to help raise them, and you won't have much time alone with her."

"It's okay. Besides, I can't have kids of my own, so this'll be my chance."

"You can't have kids?" Her eyebrows lifted and the rude question popped out before the thought even consciously formed.

"Probably not. Had mumps in college."

"Oh." Well then, Annie's appeal became more obvious, but still, he was pretty nonchalant about being sterile. Somehow she'd expect a guy to be a little more macho about infertility. Jenny popped the top on her soda to avoid looking at him.

"What's with all the questions?"

She shrugged and slid off the counter. "Just curious. Where do you want to play?"

He stared, like he didn't quite believe her and thought she was up to something, but he didn't have enough to go on to accuse her. Steve pushed to his feet. "Set up on the coffee table, and I'll get chips."

It sounded like he was really going through with the marriage. In that case, she should make a bigger effort with Annie. "Do you think Annie would like it if I gave you guys a bridal shower?"

"She'd probably love it, but you don't need to do that."

"I want to. You're getting married and I'm happy for you." At least she was trying to be. Once Steve married, everything would change. Jenny forced a smile to her lips. "I'll call her after Thanksgiving and set it up."

"You don't even like Annie."

"I don't dislike her." Sometimes a little white lie was necessary. "*You* like her and she makes you happy. That's all that matters."

"Thank you." He gave her arm an appreciative squeeze, then turned her by the shoulders toward the family room. "But that's not gonna buy you any mercy."

"Just don't forget the chips."

In the family room, Steve handed Jenny a bowl of Fritos and sat down Indian style in front of the coffee table. With efficient flicks of his wrist, he helped her turn over the wooden Scrabble tiles and then mix them up like a scam artist running a street shell game.

They drew to see who'd go first. Steve spelled "howler," using the double letter with his *H*.

"So..." He arranged and stared at his new letters. "What've you been up to?"

"Went back to work this week. Wasn't great, but it wasn't as awkward as I thought it would be. I'm teaching a friend how to read, and then I've been thinking about getting a little more involved with the Donnatelli Clinic."

"The place where Gabe volunteered?"

"Yeah. The waiting room could use sprucing up, and they really need some way to entertain kids when the wait is long—which is most of the time. Hammer." Jenny laid down her tiles. "Seventeen times two is thirty-four." She picked six more tiles and arranged them on her holder. "Last time I was there, I read them a *Ranger Rick*. It was kind of fun."

"So you'd go there and read to kids?"

"I don't know, maybe. I haven't really thought it through."

"Don't they have a TV or toys or something?"

Jenny quirked an eyebrow. "It's a *free* clinic run mostly by volunteers. What do you think?" Her eyes lit up. "Hey, your firm wouldn't want to donate money for a children's center, would they?"

"I have no idea."

"So ask—or I'll ask—no, you ask. It'd be better coming from you."

"I'm just a junior associate, Jen. I'd rather write you a check myself."

"I'll take that too. Just think of all the positive publicity for the firm." She raised her hand as if spotlighting a header. "Local law firm helps inner city clinic." Jenny threw in a bone. "I'll even cover it for the paper."

"I'll ask." He tossed down his letters, spelling "warrior." "Eleven doubled is twenty-two."

"Great, thanks." Jenny used the *I* in "warrior" to make "infant."

"Hey, I forgot to ask." Steve's hand hovered over the board as he looked at her. "How'd your spa day go?"

"Spa day?" Jenny rearranged her tiles. Anyway she looked at it, she couldn't use more than three letters. Darn.

"With Annie. Last week?"

Her and Annie at a spa together? For a whole day? Was he kidding? She'd rather have a full body wax. "We didn't go to a spa."

He frowned. "She scheduled you guys a whole day at that place on the Hill."

Not with her, she hadn't. What was Annie up to? Didn't matter, she didn't want to get involved. "She suggested it weeks ago, but... You must have misunderstood."

"I guess. Maybe it's supposed to be a surprise. Don't say anything, would you?"

Not a problem. "Okay."

"When she tells you, act surprised, okay?" He laid down some tiles and picked four more.

"I can do that." Easily. But she highly doubted she'd need to. "Busy week coming up?"

"Yeah. The hazing case finally starts tomorrow." Steve popped a few chips into his mouth.

"Ready?"

"Yup."

"Ribbit. Ribbit." Jenny's cell phone croaked. "Excuse me." She pulled her phone from her pocket. "Hey, Michael." She waved a hand at Steve and mouthed "go ahead," as she continued to chat with her brother.

Steve laid out his word, wrote down his fifteen points, collected his letters and arranged them and still Jenny hadn't made a move. She fiddled with one of her pieces, flipping the blank tile over and over between her fingers while nodding at something Michael said.

"Are you going to play?"

She flashed him a quick frown and laid out her letters, spelling "burp." Pushing the phone aside, she said, "Eight," before collecting three more tiles and returning to her conversation.

Steve threw down his next word and recorded his sixteen points. "Your turn."

"Already?" Her expression lightened. "No, I was talking to Steve. We're playing Scrabble." She laid out three more tiles. "'Road.' Five."

"'Zephyr.'" He used her *R*, and laid the *Z* on a double-letter square. "Thirty-one."

She flashed a smile and nodded in appreciation before using his *P* to spell "pique" for sixteen points. Ha, if she hadn't been so careless, she'd have used that double word spot on the other side of "warrior." She would have seen it if she hadn't been talking on the phone.

He stared at "pique." "That doesn't look right. Is it spelled right?"

Jenny tilted her head sideways and took a second look before pushing her phone aside. "It's right." She went back to her brother. "So tell Mom it's too much. She won't care if you drop piano during soccer season."

Steve stared at the word, then reluctantly agreed. He added up her score and grinned; he'd shot ahead of her since she'd answered the phone. Apparently women weren't so good at multitasking when it came to playing games. They exchanged a few more turns over the next five minutes and now he had a safe thirty-point lead.

"Do you want to finish this later?" he asked.

"Michael, I've gotta go. I'll talk to you later. Love you. Bye." She slid the phone closed, surveyed the board and then her letters. "Is it my turn?"

"Still. And if you're not going to use that blank you've been flashing at me for the past ten minutes, why don't you trade it in?"

She frowned. "Stop looking."

"It's a bit hard when you put it right under my nose." Once you glimpsed someone's letters, you couldn't unsee them. Wondering where she was going to put that *X*, he glanced at the spot he'd picked out for his next turn, then quickly looked at a different spot on the board in case she was watching him.

"Fine." Jenny pulled the rack closer to her and quickly rearranged her letters. "Here you go. Wax." She slapped the eight-point *X* down on his triple letter space. "Three times eight is twenty-four, plus five, is twenty-nine. Eat that, hot shot."

Grinning, he put his *J* on the triple letter score and laid out the rest of his word. "Twenty-four plus," he added up the other letters, "eleven... is thirty-five."

"What's a 'jabiur'?"

"A bird. A stork, to be specific."

"Really? Hmm." Jenny studied the letters lined up on her rack and then looked at the board, then back to her rack, and then the board again. She worried her bottom lip between her front teeth as she rearranged her letters on the rack again.

Ribbit. Ribbit.

"Do *not* answer that." He glared.

She looked at the number of the incoming caller and ignored it. Frowning at the board, she laid down her tiles. "'Piscary.' Thirty points."

Sixteen points for "waxy" and then fourteen for "piscary." He wrote down thirty points and added it to her score, then added in her fifty-point bonus for using all her tiles. She was kicking his ass. What's a 'piscary'? 'Piscary' is not a word."

"Sure it is."

"What does it mean?"

"I forget. It has something to do with fishing or breeding fish or something."

"I've never heard of it."

"So? I couldn't *possibly* know a word you don't know?" She raised her eyebrows. "What's with you? I took your word about the bird."

"'Jabiur' is a real word. 'Piscary' isn't." He pushed her tiles back at her.

Jenny's eyes widened. "Come *on*. Do you really need to win that badly? Get a dictionary. Go ahead, look it up."

"It's not about winning. If you're going to play, you should follow the rules."

"You don't have to be so damn ruthless. It's only a game." She glared at him.

"You like that side of me well enough to want me to represent you in court or be your partner in tennis."

"This isn't tennis or court, it's a frigging board game." Her eyes narrowed and her cheeks flushed with anger as she stood, then stomped out of the room.

He winced at the loud crack of the slamming door. Steve stared at the kitchen doorway. She'd really left? This couldn't be about the game. Couldn't be about winning. What had he said? He'd just told her he didn't think her word was legit and she'd gone nuts.

Steve tapped an index finger on the table. She must be missing Gabe or something. He should have just let it slide, but he was sure she was wrong. Besides, who goes ballistic just because he challenged a call? She'd never make it in professional sports, that's for sure.

Steve picked up his phone and googled "piscary." Within seconds he slid the phone shut and fell back against the couch. His breath exhaled in a loud whoosh.

Piscary, a fishery. The right of fishing in waters belonging to another. Damn.

∾ ∾ ∾

Jenny stormed home and slammed the door behind her. What a jerk. She couldn't believe normally mild-mannered Steve became so competitive at a simple little board game. And he'd acted like an impatient child when she'd been on the phone. Sighing loudly, he'd fidgeted with the tiles and then stared at her, trying to bore holes through her with his eyes—as if she were totally obtuse and hadn't noticed his other antics. What's with that? Gabe never minded her talking on the phone during dinner or a movie; why was Steve getting so bent out of shape?

He'd acted like a spoiled brat, and she wasn't about to feed into that.

Chapter 13

Days before Thanksgiving, Jenny was taking a pie from the oven when she heard a "peck, peck, peck-peck." Woodpeckerish knocking. A Kleenex taped to a twig waved at her from the cracked back door.

"Don't shoot. I apologize."

She smothered a smile as Steve walked in the back door, a wrinkled dress shirt hanging over his faded jeans. He plunked down on a stool in front of the counter where she worked.

"I'm sorry I was such an ass." He looked up at her. "Forgive me?"

"I'll think about it. But I'm not playing Scrabble with you again."

"Yes, you will."

"Don't think so."

"We'll see." He lifted his nose to the air and sniffed a couple of times, like an animal scenting prey. "Pumpkin pie. Yum." He picked up a can of Reddi-wip. "Three?"

She plucked it out of his hand, scooped up the other two cans and put them in the fridge. "That's Michael's favorite part." She turned back around.

"Going to your mom's?"

"And to Judith's to see the kids afterwards." She narrowed her eyes, noting Steve's unshaven face and glum expression. "What's with the..." she swung her index finger in a circle aimed at his face, "stubble? Going for the bad boy, dangerous look?"

Steve cupped a hand around his jaw and rasped his whiskers. "Like it?"

Jenny wrinkled her nose. "As long as I don't have to kiss it. Kissing a guy and having his beard scrape your face and his moustache ram up your nose is a definite turnoff."

"Annie likes it."

"Well then, you *must* be made for each other," she joked. He was growing a moustache and beard for Annie? She wouldn't have pegged him for that kind of guy.

"I'm on vacation. Leavin' for the folks' tomorrow and didn't feel like shaving."

"Annie and the kids going with you?"

He shook his head. "They're spending the weekend with Ryan and his family in Florida."

"Annie too?"

"Yeah. She doesn't trust her ex with the kids."

Jenny frowned and leaned against the counter. "And he allows her to tag along?"

"Not for the usual visitation weekends, but there's no way Annie was going to let him take the kids out of the state without her."

"And you're okay with your fiancée spending the holiday with her ex and his family?"

"Why not? It's not as if they're alone. Ryan's a good guy and I trust Annie." He looked at her. "You're sharing the holiday with Gabe's ex-wife and his kids."

But she didn't used to be married to Judith and she was spending a few hours, not a long weekend, but whatever. O-kay. Then that didn't account for his glum look. She pushed the pies aside and leaned on the counter. "Sooo, I take it the jury's in and it didn't go well?"

"We lost."

"I'm sorry. Want a beer? Six beers? How about a martini? I make a killer lemon drop."

"No, but thanks." He sighed heavily and picked up her notepad. "I can't believe I lost. We had all the physical evidence." He riffled the pages with a thumb. "I thought my closing was brilliant, but apparently not brilliant enough. We should have won."

"What went wrong?"

He shrugged and stared at the counter as if watching a replay of the trial in the shiny, dark surface. "The medical testimony was solid. I thought I connected with all the jurors... I bet it was chair six." He raised his head to look at her. "He was a marine in the Korean War."

"How would an ex-marine hurt your case?"

"It was a hazing incident," he reminded her. "Hazing, brotherhood, toughness, hatred of homosexuals—it's all consistent with the marine mentality. He wasn't a career soldier and he served fifty years ago." He raked a hand through his hair, ruffling it until it stood straight on end. "Damn it, I should have struck him."

Jenny didn't remember enough about the specifics of the case to make the connection. "Remind me again."

"During rush, this Alpha Zeta Epsilon pledge was beaten. He spent a month in the hospital undergoing kidney dialysis and will probably need a transplant. He had to have surgery to repair his rectum, damaged when they sodomized the guy with a broom handle."

"Niiice. And, how did these guys get off?"

"The defendants lied under oath. I could *not* get them to come clean. The judge gave me no room on cross and I finally had to let it go—either that or piss off the judge and jury. And..."

"What?"

"It's no excuse really, but it pissed me off all the same." He shoved the pad across the counter. "The defense discovered that my client's gay. A little fact he might have thought to inform his counsel of beforehand."

"You didn't ask?"

"No." Steve washed a hand down his face. "It shouldn't have had any bearing on the case. The guy's back and butt were covered with bruises, he was admitted to the hospital in complete kidney failure, and his rectum was ripped for inches."

He arched an eyebrow and pointed an index finger at Jenny. "You don't get injuries like that from rough sex. It was a felony. Rape. Assault." He ticked off the charges on his fingers. "Those assholes should have been on the hook for the medical bills and jail time—instead they walked."

"Poor guy. He bravely revealed his sexual orientation for nothing."

"He revealed *nothin'*. The defense forced his disclosure."

"Why didn't you stop them?"

His eyes grew wide and his jaw dropped open in indignation. "I *tried*. I objected so loudly and so many times the judge threatened to hold me in contempt. When the whole gay thing came out, he kept overruling me. I was stunned. Never in a million years had it occurred to me that the guy was gay. He should have told me."

"So it's his fault?"

"Well, yeah. If he'd told me ahead of time I wouldn't have sat there yelling fabricated objections, like an idiot. Had I known he was gay, I would have anticipated the attack and prepared arguments to neutralize the impact it had on prejudiced jurors. I could have been prepared to protect my client, instead of sitting there like a dumbass, letting the defense make mincemeat out of him. I also would have taken it into consideration during the jury selection."

He shook his head and slumped over the counter. "But that's not really why we lost. I dropped the ball. One of the defendants had a history of a prior child molestation charge; I should have found a way to use it. I was afraid that going after the defendant would garner sympathy for him with the jury. It was a rookie mistake. A more experienced attorney would have found a way to get it in." He sighed. "Crap. My first real loss."

Jenny straightened. "Real sympathetic, Grant. It isn't all about the win or the loss."

He raised an eyebrow. "Uh-h-h-h. Yeah, it is."

"No it's not. It's about righting an injustice."

"Of course it is. An attorney's a hired gun—someone to do the fighting you can't do—or don't want to do. You *always* go into it for the win—and some people for the money."

"Nice. How shallow can you be?"

"Just bein' honest. Doesn't matter how honorable your intentions are if you can't win. If you can't succeed, the injustice doesn't even have a chance of being corrected, right?"

"What about hiring an attorney because he knows the law better than you, or to right a wrong, or for principles?"

"That's just motives. Motives don't really matter; it's results that count. It's the wins that earn a person the justice you want for them, or the mental peace they need to carry on after a tragedy, or the win earns them money to help pay medical bills—or to support their children. Or in some cases, the win grants a person's freedom."

"What a cynical viewpoint."

"Maybe, but it's reality."

"I don't like it."

"Sorry, that's the way it is."

"The poor guy's stuck with a ton of medical bills, your bill, humiliation beyond belief, and probably nightmares."

"Now we're gonna have to go after the fraternity and the school."

"After he lost? Why would you do that? They'll just lie again."

"But this time I'll be better prepared. I'll take my *voir dire* more seriously and be a lot more aggressive with my strikes. And we'll name the fraternity and the university as co-defendants and see if I can get them fighting each other."

"And your client wants to move forward with this? If he needs a kidney transplant, I wouldn't think he'd have the energy or emotional strength to go through that again."

"He has to. He needs the money, and we can't let them get away with it."

Jenny clasped her hands together and leaned forward on her elbows. "Maybe you should."

"Should what? Let them get off?"

She nodded. "Maybe he should put it all behind him and concentrate on healing and getting on with his life. He was beaten, raped, and had his sexual orientation exposed in a public, humiliating way. Maybe he's better off letting it go."

"That's crazy."

"That's *his* choice. You ought to respect your client enough to let him make that decision."

"I do and he did. He wants to go on. He hired me to stand for him and I won't let him down again." He narrowed his eyes. "What happened to your noble quest for justice—for righting a wrong?"

"I still believe that, but—" She paused, considering if she should continue. "Well... are you sure this is what your *client* really wants instead of soothing your ego?"

Steve's foot stilled from its shaking and his face froze in an accusing stare. "That's insulting."

"It's not meant to be, but I know how much winning means to you. I just can't believe this kid would agree to go through all that pain again unless you talked him into it."

Eyes narrowed and his forehead wrinkled in indecision. He blew out a loud sigh. "I'll talk to him again and make sure it's what he really wants. Satisfied?"

"Yes." She smiled sweetly.

"In turn, I'm gonna ask a favor of you."

Jenny stilled, cautious. "O-kay."

"I have to go to the firm's holiday party Friday night, and I don't want to go alone."

"What about Annie?"

"She's got Bunko."

"And she can't skip it?"

Steve shook his head. "Will you go? Nobody there knows you, so there won't be any awkward questions or condolences—no expectations."

"Does Annie know you're asking me?" Because if Annie knew that Steve had asked her to the fancy party, Jenny'd bet her eyeteeth she'd cancel Bunko in a heartbeat.

"Why would she care?"

"Because she's your fiancée. I'd be jealous if Gabe took another woman to a hospital party."

"Three points." He ticked each supporting argument off on his fingers. "You were married to Gabe—we're engaged, I asked her first and she turned me down, and you're not just 'another woman.'"

Jenny raised her eyebrows at his last item. "Thanks."

He waved aside her complaint. "You know what I mean. It's not as if this is a date. I just don't want to go alone. Don't want to go at *all*, but it's business. We don't even have to stay long. And you could use a night out. Come with me."

Jenny really didn't feel like going to a party. Her gaze drifted to a little sheet of paper clipped to the refrigerator door. *'Happiness is never something you get from other people. The happiness you feel is in direct proportion to the love you give.'*

Jenny had found the Oprah quote inspiring, so she'd typed it up and taped it to her refrigerator. Lonely as she occasionally was, Jenny didn't want to make meaningless chit chat with strangers, yet maybe that was exactly what she needed. She wanted to be happy again, and since Gabe's coming back to life wasn't an option, she had to make herself happy. She'd have his baby and give it all the love she'd given to Gabe. Meanwhile, she'd make Steve happy and keep him company at his party.

She smiled. "I'd be happy to. Thanks for asking."

 av av av

Steve left Jenny's kitchen, feeling more than a little disgruntled. He passed through the hedges between their houses wondering why women were so damn difficult. It was just a party. Where was all the Christmas spirit? Annie refused to go with him to the work party and he had to talk Jenny into going with him, when it'd be good therapy for her.

Steve rounded his house and headed to the patio. He lit the fire pit and sat back on the cold metal chair. When he'd first asked Annie to go to the party, the Bunko conflict came up right away, but when she found out it was strictly a work party with no famous clients attending, she'd been adamant that she couldn't cancel Bunko.

She couldn't even use the kids as an excuse, because Ryan had them, but Annie used them still, refusing to attend a function thirty minutes from home, claiming it was too far from Ryan's—in case the children needed her. Which she was *always* certain, they would.

As if Ryan wasn't capable of caring for his own kids for a weekend. From what Steve could see, he was a decent dad. Annie was so obsessive about her ex-husband's inability to handle the kids alone that Steve couldn't decide if she was a control freak or if she was still in love with her ex.

Either way, she wouldn't go with him, and he didn't want to go to the holiday party alone, so he'd asked Jenny. Propping his feet next to the fire, Steve pulled his jacket tighter to shield him from the brisk November breeze.

He hadn't planned on asking Jenny; it'd been a spontaneous idea, but one that felt right as soon as he'd suggested it. Damn it, it shouldn't feel right. His fiancée should be going with him, not his friend. But Jenny wouldn't be bored with the conversation like Annie would. In fact, Jenny never backed down from a good debate.

He winced, thinking about her earlier accusation about his need to win. Was he being unreasonable? He bit his lower lip, thinking. Naw, she's off base. Being competitive was a trait that stood him well in professional baseball and was also an essential characteristic in a successful attorney. He wasn't wrong this time.

He stared into the dancing flames. An engaged man shouldn't be taking another woman to a party—even if she was just a friend. Even though it wasn't a date, it probably wouldn't look right to others. But Jenny'd agreed. He hadn't really thought she would, but she had—and she'd smiled. A soft, hesitant smile, as if she'd almost look forward to the party. He wasn't about to recant that invitation.

∾ ∾ ∾

Thanksgiving with Jenny's family passed uneventfully. The holiday had been more somber than usual, but given Gabe's death that was to be expected. She still hadn't found the right time or words to tell her parents about her pending court case, sure they wouldn't understand. She vowed to tell them soon.

Most of her month of reprieve was up, and although she still hadn't located a lawyer willing to take her case, the press was heating up. They'd initially allowed her rebuffs but had become noticeably more persistent since the holiday. She'd have to tell her parents before they read about it in the newspaper.

Jenny ignored the banging at the front door, but it continued relentlessly. Clicking the save button on her computer, she pushed away from the desk, cursing the person causing all the racket. Grabbing her cell phone, she went to the door.

"Ritz, quiet. No bark," she whispered at the dog growling at the door.

If it was another reporter, she was calling the police. She'd had more than enough of their harassment. As a journalist she'd interviewed distraught people in sticky situations, but she'd never invaded their privacy to get the story. What was their problem? Jenny pressed her face close to the peephole before shooing Ritz back and opening the door.

"Judith. Hi."

Wearing a black woolen double-breasted dress coat topped by a lovely peach scarf, Judith stood on the front porch, clutching a paper bag to her chest. "Took you long enough to answer the door. What're you doing?"

"Working."

"Don't you answer your phone anymore? I've called a dozen times in the past week and left as many messages." She breezed by, wafting the unmistakable smell of Chinese food.

"Come on in." Jenny shut the door and faced Judith. "What's wrong? Are the kids okay?"

"They're fine." Judith stared at her. Her keen brown gaze traveled up and down Jenny's body.

Jenny fought the urge to squirm. Inwardly cringing, she pushed back the sleeves of Gabe's sweatshirt and folded her arms across her narrow waist. She smoothed an errant lock of hair away from her face. With no makeup and wearing old sweats that hung on her, she knew she looked rough.

"You look like shit," Judith said. She unwound the scarf and unbuttoned her coat. "You've lost fifteen pounds and you're pale. Your hair's even lost its luster. Haven't you been eating?"

Jenny raised her chin. "I've been busy and I haven't been hungry."

Judith draped her coat across the staircase newel. "For God's sake, Jenny, how're you going to convince a doctor to inseminate you when you can't even take care of yourself?"

Jenny fought the urge to hunch over to try and disappear into Gabe's huge sweatshirt, ashamed that she'd let herself deteriorate to such an obvious degree. It had never occurred to her that the judge might think her unfit if she didn't look healthy. She vowed to move that to the top of her list, right next to finding an attorney.

"Have you contacted a fertility specialist yet?"

Jenny drew her cold hands further into the sweatshirt sleeves until they were completely covered. No need for Judith to see her chewed-off nails too.

"No. Reporters have started following me. I didn't want them to scare the doctor off with all their questions. I'll take care of it later."

Jenny trailed after Judith as she moved into the kitchen. She might have been offended by the way the older woman nosed about her cupboards, pulling out plates and silverware, but was amused instead. "I take it you're staying for dinner? What about Dave and the kids?"

"Dave took them out for pizza and a movie." Judith opened up the paper bag and began pulling out the folded white boxes. Again and again, until six Chinese boxes lined the countertop. She'd brought enough food to feed ten people.

Judith shrugged. "I wasn't sure what you liked, so I got a variety."

"You didn't want to go to the movie?"

She wrinkled her nose. "Those stupid slapstick comedies aren't my thing. Now come eat."

Why didn't that surprise her? If Judith had a sense of humor, she hid it well. Jenny instantly felt ashamed of the uncharitable thought. Judith had brought her dinner and was checking on her. That was nice. Jenny pushed off the counter, poured Judith a glass of iced tea and popped the top on a soda for herself.

Settling at the table, she spooned a small portion of sweet and sour chicken over pan-fried noodles. "Their loss is my gain."

"What're you working on?" Judith took a bite of her egg roll.

"I'm researching a new homeopathic cure for jet lag."

Judith nodded, chewing. "How's the case coming?"

She thought about reassuring Gabe's ex-wife that everything was wonderful and she had everything under control—but it was a fleeting thought. Judith wasn't stupid. "Horribly. For the life of me I can't understand why George is putting me through this. It's none of his business."

Judith waved her fork. "That's George. He's probably OCD to some degree. Can't stand for things to deviate from his routine or the expected. It's not surprising that your unconventional choice of procreation sent him into a tailspin."

"You seem to get along with him well enough."

"Since I'm no longer married to Gabe." She chewed and swallowed. "And he gives you that impression to needle you. He didn't like me anymore than you. In fact, as soon as he found out I was pregnant with Ted, he tried to talk me into getting an abortion. When that didn't work, he went on this obsessive campaign to get Gabe to have a vasectomy."

"You're kidding." George had wanted Gabe to have a vasectomy? A man trying to convince another that he should have surgery on his testicles? That was *so* odd.

"Nope. Couldn't stand the fact that Ted was an accident. He hated me so much he wanted to make sure I didn't tie Gabe to me any tighter with more children."

"That's ridiculous."

"That's George. I think he was happier than I when we divorced."

"How'd Gabe react?"

Judith shot her a quick look. "He didn't do it—ever. In case you're wondering if that's why you didn't get pregnant. Well, at least not that I know of," she added.

Given that she'd lost their baby, Jenny was certain he hadn't had a vasectomy, but she didn't feel the need to share that with his ex-wife. Why would Judith think she wouldn't have known something that personal about Gabe? Did she suspect that they hadn't had complete honesty and disclosure in their marriage or was that just her overactive guilty conscience?

"It never occurred to me. I just remember how furious Gabe got when George tried to get me to sign a prenup. A vasectomy's so much more personal." Jenny smiled, imagining Gabe's fury at George. "He must have been livid."

"At first he laughed it off, but when George persisted year after year, even Gabe's patience wore thin." She shook her head. "Actually I kind of pity the guy. Must be an exhausting way to live." Judith took a sip of her iced tea. "So. Find an attorney yet?"

"Nope." Her chicken suddenly became a monumental effort to chew. She pushed the plate aside.

"Aren't you running out of time?"

"Yup." She loathed admitting it. "Nobody wants to touch my case."

Judith moved the plate back in front of her. "Eat. Who've you tried?"

"More like who haven't I tried." Jenny picked up her fork and speared some noodles. Slowly, she spun them around her fork.

"It can't be that bad."

She reached over to the desk behind her for a yellow legal pad with two pages of names crossed out on it. Wordlessly she tossed it onto the table in front of Judith.

Judith's gaze sharpened and she did a satisfying double take at the sheer volume of attorneys Jenny had approached.

"There's nobody left in the area to contact," Jenny said. "They act like they'd catch gonorrhea from taking my case."

"Wow. Every lawyer I've ever heard of is on here. Even that jerk who sued me for malpractice a couple of years ago." She put down her fork and pushed the plate away, frowning. "There's got to be someone."

"Monday I'm going to call and set up appointments at the law school clinics."

Judith shook her head. "You need someone with experience."

She arched her brows and sat back in her chair. "I don't have a lot of choice here. I can't represent myself."

"What about your lawyer friend next door," Judith tilted her head toward Steve's house. "Won't he help you? Alex said you guys used to be like the three musketeers."

The three musketeers? Yeah, she guessed they had been. She, Gabe and Steve had spent a lot of time together. Steve and Gabe had raced each other through the Pointes early each morning. They'd boated together, played tennis, barbequed, celebrated the kids' graduations and professional achievements, and they'd been in and out of each other's houses as if related.

And Jenny couldn't press him. Much as she hated to admit it, the afternoon of Annie's tirade, she had been right about one thing.

She relied on Steve too much. He helped with the condolence notes, he fixed the glitch with her computer, he kept her active, getting her out of the house to play tennis or check out a movie each week, he brought in her newspapers when she let them pile up at the end of the drive, and he called several times a week to be sure she was okay.

Jenny probably saw more of Steve than Annie did, and much as she appreciated it and as comfortable as it was, it really wasn't right. It wasn't fair to Steve—or Annie. Jenny returned her attention to her meal. "Steve turned me down."

"Why?"

"Inexperience." She chewed and swallowed. "And he wasn't sure I was doing the right thing."

"Bull. Why don't you try him again? He's had some time to get used to the idea. And what he lacks in experience and knowledge, he'd make up for with the passion his friendship would bring to your case. Try him again."

"Maybe." When associated with Steve, the words passion and friendship made her uncomfortable.

"Go ahead," Judith pushed.

"I will."

"Now."

"Why now?"

"Why not?" Judith wiped her mouth on her napkin. "I'll go with you."

Chapter 14

Maybe it wouldn't be such an imposition, Jenny thought. She'd pay him—it wasn't as if she'd ask Steve to do it pro bono. It had been several weeks since they last talked about it; maybe Steve had changed his mind. Or maybe Judith could change his mind. She could be very persuasive. "I don't know."

"What've you got to lose?"

"A friendship? Maybe this isn't such a good idea. Sort of like you shouldn't go into business with a friend."

"Don't be ridiculous. There are millions of successful businesses run by friends."

"All right. But I'm warning you, it'll be a waste." She insisted on calling Steve and asking if they could come over, thinking it only fair to warn him before springing Judith on him. Although they'd met a couple of times before the funeral, Judith's take-charge personality took some getting used to.

They crossed the yard, and Steve met them at the back door. He offered them a drink that both declined, then they sat around his coffee table in front of a small fire.

"So what's up?"

Jenny handed him her list of lawyers. "I've been turned down by just about every family attorney in town. Can you think of anyone I've missed? Or maybe you know somebody out of state that might represent me?"

"It's not likely an out-of-state attorney would take your case, Jenny. He'd need to be familiar with Michigan law." Scanning her list, he shook his head and sat back in his chair. "Geez, I'm sorry,

Jen. I can't think of anybody. I have to admit I'm a little surprised. I didn't think it'd be this tough to find someone." He rubbed a thumb against his lip. "I don't know what to tell you."

"Why don't you take it?" Judith suggested.

"It's out of my league. I'd do more harm than good."

"I disagree. Jenny's got nothing to lose by going with you. Besides, you're a good friend of the family who knew Gabe well. Who better to fight for her?"

"I explained to Jenny that I wouldn't be the best advocate for her, because I'm still not convinced what she's doing is right."

"Why not?"

Steve hesitated, clearly not wanting to explain himself to Judith, but her set expression must've told him she wouldn't leave without an answer. "She took his sperm without consent."

Judith made a face. "Oh, come on. They'd been trying to have a baby when he died."

Steve's gaze snapped Jenny's way. He knew she'd been pregnant when they went away for the weekend, but she'd never told him they'd been *trying* to have a baby—she'd never told him the baby was an accident either. He was probably wondering why she hadn't told Judith about the miscarriage.

Ignoring the fact that the pregnancy had been an accident, Jenny perpetuated the lie with a curt nod. "Actually, I *was* pregnant. I lost the baby right after the accident."

Judith looked at her sharply. "You were? Why didn't you say anything?"

Jenny shrugged. "There was a lot going on. I..." *And I couldn't bear another loss. I didn't want to think about it.*

Steve had been the only other person to know about the baby, so why tell anybody about the miscarriage? Nobody else needed to know her shame—that they'd argued over a hypothetical pregnancy and her running off had gotten Gabe killed.

"Do you have proof?" Steve asked

Jenny blinked at Steve. "Proof?"

"That you were pregnant. Of the miscarriage."

"I guess. I went to the ER hoping they could stop the bleeding. They ran tests confirming the miscarriage."

Judith turned to Steve, triumphant. "There's your proof."

"That helps," he admitted, "but it's not conclusive proof that Gabe would want her to have a baby under these circumstances. Anything else? A visit to an obstetrician? Fill a prescription for prenatal vitamins? He didn't tell me, but might Gabe have told anybody else that you were trying to get pregnant?"

She frowned and shook her head. No vitamins. No OB visit.

"Why?" Judith asked.

"If there was some kind of written proof that Gabe had purposefully gotten her pregnant, it seems she'd have a better chance of winning. Without clear, indisputable proof of his intent, I don't see how this decision could be made except by witnesses testifying to what they *thought* Gabe would have wanted had he conceived of this scenario before his death."

"So it'll all come down to George's word against mine?"

"It could," Steve said. "Are you sure you want to do this? Think about the child. This trial's going to attract nationwide attention, if not worldwide. You won't be able to escape it. How do you think your child's going to feel when kids make fun of her saying she was mixed up in a test tube from a dead man? They'll label her a freak."

Freak was a bit harsh, but kids could be mean. She frowned. There had to be a way to protect her child. "I'll prepare her. I'll tell her she's a special gift from her daddy in heaven. She'll be strong enough to ignore them."

"Really? Bullying is a rising problem and by doing this, you're making your kid an easy target. Aren't you afraid she'll resent you for making her a curiosity?"

"She'll be *fine*," Judith said. "Jenny can get counseling from child experts beforehand so she'll be prepared."

"What makes you think they'll know how to handle it? This situation's pretty rare."

"This isn't so different from test-tube babies. I'm sure they have a support group Jenny can join." Judith dismissed his argument.

Jenny's head whipped back and forth like a spectator at a tennis match. For every valid concern Steve lobbed, Judith smashed it down with a ready answer.

Steve turned to Judith. "What's your stake in this? Why're you helping her? You two weren't bosom buddies before Gabe died."

"No nefarious reason. Jenny needs the support. It'd make Gabe happy to know I'm looking out for her... and," she smiled ruefully, "maybe I'm making up for past behavior."

"Or maybe you're keeping her close to keep an eye on your kids' inheritance," Steve suggested. "Nothing wrong with that. I'd expect it of a shrewd woman. What about Alex and Ted? How do you think this will affect them?"

What? She'd *never* even thought that. What was Steve doing?

A flush blotted Judith's face, unbecomingly. "They've been expecting Jenny and Gabe to announce a pregnancy ever since they married."

"But that was a natural conception with a baby being born into a family. A different thing altogether," he pointed out. "You don't think that they'll be embarrassed, if not angry, that their half sibling was conceived in such a perverted, public way? I think you're fooling yourselves."

"You want to know what I think?" Judith paused, staring intently at Steve. Tension charged the room. "I think you're afraid of losing. Losing such a high-profile case would make you look bad." She arched her eyebrows, looking superior. "You pretend to be Jenny's friend, but underneath, you're just a jock afraid of losing." She stood up. "Come on, Jenny, he's not going to help."

Jenny gasped. How could a simple debate have deteriorated into this angry insult-flinging argument? She just wanted to have her husband's baby, not start a war. "Judith, that's not fair."

"He hasn't denied it."

Jenny looked at Steve. He sat, jaw locked, glaring at the fire. Her heart ached for him, knowing how much the accusation must have hurt.

"He shouldn't have to defend himself—especially when we're asking for a favor. Let's go." Jenny was reluctant to leave, but after Judith's vituperative comment, she was anxious to get her away from him. Judith meant well, but she'd been unnecessarily cruel. She glanced at Judith's retreating back and then touched Steve's shoulder in passing. "I'm sorry."

As soon as they closed the door at Jenny's house, Judith sat in a chair looking thoughtful.

Jenny took the chair opposite her. "What was that? He didn't deserve that. He was just playing the devil's advocate."

"You think so?"

"Of course. That's what lawyers do. Steve's a friend; he'd help if he could."

"I don't know about that." Judith stared at her as if puzzling out a curious problem. "He was a bit too dogmatic," she mused, "too emphatic in his objections." She put a finger to her lips, tapping. "He wasn't objective enough... as if it was personal. Personal?" Her expression lightened. "It *is* personal. He's jealous. He doesn't want you to have Gabe's baby. He must have feelings for you himself. Of course. Now it makes sense."

"That's ridiculous. We're just friends. Besides, he's engaged."

"Nooo." She warmed to the idea. "I saw the way he watched you. And when I told him you'd been trying to get pregnant, he got a sick, funny look on his face."

"That was confusion. He knew I'd lost the baby and was just surprised you didn't."

Judith shook her head. "No—it was more. He paled and tensed. And he went out of his way not to touch you, which means, of course, that he wants to. Nope, he's attracted to you—it's the only thing that makes sense."

"Steve's not attracted to me; he's engaged. If anything, he treats me like a little sister."

"Nope." She leaned forward, suddenly serious. "I was wrong to insist he help you—not wrong, I didn't know how he felt about you. You can't trust him. Forget him, we'll find someone else. After Christmas I'll get on it. You're still coming over for dinner aren't you?"

Steve jealous? He was her friend. That's all he could ever be.

Judith snapped her fingers in front of Jenny's face. "Christmas eve? Dinner?"

Jenny hesitated. Christmas eve dinner with Gabe's family would emphasize his not being there. If she just spent the holiday alone with her family, perhaps old memory cells would kick in to past, familiar Christmases before Gabe and it wouldn't hurt so much.

Judith leaned forward. "Look, I know we got off on the wrong foot. Gabe's remarrying after all these years took me by surprise, and I know I didn't react very gracefully—"

"You accused me of teaching Alex the different sex positions," Jenny said flatly.

A bright red rash climbed Judith's neck. "I was upset."

Jenny raised her eyebrows.

"*Very* upset." Judith waved a hand. "Okay, I'm sorry. I was out of line. But we've both come a long way. We're family. Come over."

Jenny frowned and bit her lip, considering. "I think I'd better pass, but thank y—."

"We're all going to be sad. Gabe's only been gone a few months; it's okay to mourn. But you're stronger than you know."

"Me?" Jenny pointed at her chest and raised her eyebrows. "I'm a coward."

"You used to be, but you've changed. You single-handedly organized Gabe's funeral. You wrote an amazing tribute for his obituary and a beautiful eulogy. I couldn't have done that." Judith raised her eyebrows for emphasis. "No way could I have spoken in front of all those people, sharing private memories of my husband."

She shook her head. "That took real courage. If you can do that, you can eat dinner with us on Christmas."

She *could* do it, but did she want to? Holidays were time for celebrating with loved ones. Gabe would want her to appreciate the love he'd brought into her life through his family. Besides, she couldn't wait for Alex and Ted to open their presents. "Can I bring an appetizer? And maybe some champagne?"

"Absolutely. Gabe always appreciated a toast with some bubbly." Judith stood and gathered her coat. "Five o'clock. And don't worry, Dave and I will find you a lawyer. Stay away from the jock."

∾ ∾ ∾

Steve watched Judith's Ford Focus pull out of the drive. He washed a hand down his face and sighed. When had his life gotten so damn complicated? When Jenny and Gabe moved next door. He'd been messing up ever since.

First he fell in love with his friend's wife, then he found Annie and got his life back on track, only to have it messed up again when Gabe up and died on him. Suddenly he was falling asleep with Jenny in his arms, and now she wanted him to be her lawyer, and he couldn't. A good friend would help her. But right now, he wasn't even sure he was capable of being a good friend to Jenny. He was trying, but damn it was hard.

When Jenny came home from Saugatuck alone and they'd spent that night together on the couch, he'd been consumed with guilt—as if he'd betrayed his friend and his fiancée. But thankfully, Jenny couldn't possibly know that a good bit of his grief was fueled by remorse. She'd bravely forged ahead, with the little support he managed to give her. And God forgive him, he'd admired her that much more.

He hadn't wanted to love Jenny. Lord knows he tried hard to unlove her. Loving Jenny was fruitless and painful—so incredibly painful. Until Jenny Harrison moved in next door, the precipitous ending of his baseball career had been the most difficult adjustment in his life—but having to hide his feelings and still be her friend and confidant was hell on earth.

The greatest blow had struck months before Gabe's death when she'd come over asking for help. They often traded favors, bring in the mail, take out the garbage cans, watching the dog; but this was different, brutally different...

"I want a baby," Jenny blurted out.

Steve leaned back against his cold granite countertop and crossed his legs at his ankles. He carefully schooled his expression to something neutral and bit his lip to keep from grinning. "Ahhh... isn't that something your husband should help you with?"

"Funny, Grant." She scowled at him before her expression turned pleading. "How do I tell Gabe? Before we married I told him I didn't want children. Besides, I don't think he wants any more."

Steve suspected she was right. His buddy was pretty happy with life the way it was. But Gabe adored Jenny and if a baby was that important to her, he'd probably be willing to start all over again. "Talk to him. Tell him how important it is to you."

"I can't."

"Why not?"

"Because—" She bit her lip and looked away. "He thinks I'm a good person, and—oh, forget it. You wouldn't understand." Jenny turned away and rushed toward the door.

Steve didn't want to get involved in their personal lives, but she was upset. Jenny didn't know that her problem with her husband was scoring his heart like dozens of painful paper cuts. Steve forced air into his lungs to push aside his pain and caught Jenny at the door. He wrapped a brotherly arm around her shoulders and redirected her toward the couch in the family room.

"What wouldn't I understand?"

She studied him carefully, frowning as she sized him up. "When I was fourteen, I got pregnant. Michael's my adopted brother—and my son."

"Oh." Brilliant response, he derided silently, but he seemed incapable of anything more coherent. "And Gabe doesn't know?"

"Of course not. And you can't tell him." Her eyes widened in alarm. She looked at him, pleading. "I was just a kid. It was a mistake. I mean, it wasn't a mistake, because Michael's a great kid, but the pregnancy was a mistake. Gabe wouldn't understand."

"I'm sure he didn't think you were a virgin when you married."

Fear streaked across her face. "Did he say that?"

"Of course not." He sighed and sank down on the couch next to her.

"Good." She blew out a deep breath. "Turning Michael over to my mother in the hospital was the hardest thing I've ever done. But it was best for both of us. I tried to keep perspective and not love him, ya know? But I couldn't. He was a part of me—and so stinkin' sweet. It wasn't his fault I was an idiot and got pregnant."

He did know. He knew exactly how hard it was to love someone he shouldn't.

"The only way I could deal with it was to convince myself that Michael really was my adopted brother. I never ever let myself think of him any other way. But I can't help remembering what it was like to be pregnant." She stared off at some distant point. A smile softened her lips and a hopeful glow lit her eyes. "It'd be so much better with Gabe. I can care for a baby now. I have a husband. We could be a family. I could be a real mom this time." Turning to him, her joy melted into a frown. "But how can I convince Gabe without telling him about Michael?"

He was proud of Jenny's amazing, selfless love for her child. Why couldn't she share this with Gabe? He should know something this intimate and profound about his wife. Steve looked sideways at her and held her gaze. "You can't. Tell him the truth. He'll understand."

"That I've been promiscuous and lived a lie for the past thirteen years?" She pursed her lips and shook her head. "I maybe could have told him before we got married, but now it's too late. He has no patience for immoral teenagers. He came home from the clinic one night really angry about this sixteen-year-old patient who aborted her baby because she was sick with gonorrhea. It was her third pregnancy by three different guys.

Gabe was so angry at her—on the dead baby's behalf. He reported her to social services and wished it was legal to sterilize girls like her." She paused. "He would not understand."

"Your situation's a little different, Jen. Tell him. He'll understand. He loves you."

Indecision, frustration, and fear flashed across her face. She dropped her head as if shamed. "He won't understand. He'll think I tricked him. He'll be angry and feel betrayed."

"Betrayed? Isn't that a little strong?"

"He'd hate me for not telling him sooner."

"Gabe could never hate you. Tell him."

"I can't. He'll be disappointed beyond belief. I can't take that chance. Besides, it doesn't just involve me, it involves my whole family." She looked at him, pleading for understanding.

"You told me."

"Only so you'd understand why this is so important. I thought you'd be able to help me find a way to convince Gabe to have a baby."

Steve froze. His sympathy evaporated in that wounding instant. Jenny told him so he'd help her, not because she'd been compelled to share something that personal. His gut burned with jealous angst. He wanted to tell her that if Gabe didn't want to have a baby with her, she should leave him, and Steve would do his damndest to get her pregnant—and love every minute of it.

You can't give her a child, his conscience reminded.

For her I'd find a way; he rebutted the annoying, persistent voice.

But she didn't want his child, she wanted her husband's. She loved Gabe, not him. Maybe marriage to Annie and her children was what it would take to loosen Jenny's grip on his heart. Maybe then he could stop hating himself and be happy again.

Or not. A dog barked loudly in the stillness of the night. Steve shifted in his chair. Now his best friend was dead and he hated himself even more. With Gabe gone everything was different between him and Jenny. Steve didn't know how to act around her anymore, so he sat back and continued the older brother/best friend role and redoubled his effort to transfer his affections to Annie. Between him and Jenny nothing had changed, yet everything had changed.

And his relationship with Annie wasn't going as planned either. He wasn't being a good friend to Jenny nor did it seem he was succeeding at being a good fiancé. Both women deserved better. He'd always prided himself on being an honest, upfront guy, yet the uncomfortable aching in his stomach told him he wasn't being honest with either woman—or himself. Shit.

Chapter 15

Jenny read the *Oprah* magazine from cover to cover, hoping for inspiration. She tossed the magazine to the side of the bathmat and rose from the bubble bath. Facing the mirror, she examined her small breasts and flat tummy, then arched her back, thrust her hips forward and pushed her stomach out. She smiled and caressed her belly. Pretty soon she'd have real boobs and their baby would swell her stomach in a perfectly round ball.

She sighed and snagged a fluffy towel from the hook. First things first. She had to win her court case and before that, she needed to retain an attorney and survive Christmas. One day at a time—like a step program for addicts. Baby steps. She smiled. How apropos.

Her first big step on the way to recovery was going to Steve's Christmas party tonight. She'd push all thoughts of babies to the background, be supportive of her friend, and prove she could be okay in public again.

She'd smile and be confident and charming and send all kinds of good vibes out into the cosmos. Maybe it'd come back to her or maybe it'd just make her feel good to focus on something other than her loss. Either way she won, and that was progress.

Jenny dried herself and threw on Gabe's maroon robe as she padded to her closet. She searched the racks, pulling out a midnight blue velvet strapless dress—too sexy. She wasn't dressing up for her husband. Her hand lit on an elegant gray suit she'd worn to her first interview—too staid. She reached for her favorite black leather pants. Too casual? Then Jenny found a simple scarlet dress. Red stood for power or romance and the classic lines hinted at curves and hugged her breasts before plunging sensually in the front—in this case, it shouted romantic feminine power. Hmm.

Exasperated, Jenny grabbed the clothes and marched out of her closet. She threw them across her bed, fanning them out in a colorful array. Crossing her arm over her chest, she picked up the phone. Steve would know what would be most appropriate.

"Come *on*, Jenny." Her thumb stabbed the 'off' button. "You're not some pitiful woman who needs someone to pick out her clothes." She sank onto the bed and stared at her choices. "It's Christmas and you're going to a party. What do *you* feel like wearing?"

∾ ∾ ∾

Steve pulled into Jenny's driveway at six forty-five. As he pushed the gear into park, Jenny rushed out the front door. She trotted through the cold night and met him as he rounded the car. He stretched around her to open the car door just as Jenny reached out. Their hands bumped and she pulled hers back.

Flashing him a quick smile and a murmured "Thanks," she slipped past him, gracefully swinging into the mustang. The light, sweet scent of her perfume tickled his nose and toyed with his mind. Sexy. Fresh. Steve shook his head to clear his senses. Hustling around the car, he got in his side and turned up the heat.

"On time. I'm impressed."

"You should be. Don't ever expect it to happen again," she joked, though they both knew Jenny loathed being late.

"What's that?" He nodded to the hexagonal box sporting an elaborate pink satin bow resting in her lap.

"A gift for you to give your hosts." She shrugged. "I didn't know if you'd think of it. If you already have something, we can leave it in the car, or maybe you'd rather not—"

"What'd we get them?"

"A pound of Elan's Candies by Maralyn. You can't go wrong with candy."

"Thanks," he said. "I knew you'd come in handy."

Her lips twitched and she looked at him from the corner of her eyes. "Anything to help."

They made chitchat for a little while, then drove the last ten minutes to his boss's summer house in silence, with Steve trying not to look at Jenny. He wondered what she was wearing under that thick winter coat. With her hair curled and piled on top of her head and diamond earrings in her ears, Jenny'd clearly gone to some effort with her appearance.

Until that moment, he hadn't known what to expect. He hadn't seen her out of sweats and grubby clothes since Gabe died—he would hardly have been surprised if she hadn't gotten dressed up. Steve flattered himself that she'd gone to the effort to please him, though his conscience denied it. They drove up a long driveway, and Steve relinquished his car to the valet. With a hand at Jenny's back, he guided her up several steps and through the front door.

A black-and-white uniformed maid smiled politely. "May I take your coat, ma'am?"

Steve took the box of chocolates Jenny handed him, helped her out of her coat, and then handed it to the waiting maid before pocketing the claim ticket. Turning back to Jenny, he froze. She wore a black and gold, gauzy, shimmery top that crisscrossed her breasts, leaving a tantalizing V opening. A delicate heart-shaped diamond cluster nestled just above her breasts.

Black clingy pants hugged her slim figure and dropped to strappy high-heeled sandals. Recent weight loss and skillfully applied makeup accentuated her cheekbones and made her skin appear flawless. Her light blue eyes seemed huge in her small face. A very slight dusting of glitter in her hair gave her a fairytale, enchanted aura. The whole package whispered classy elegance. She took his breath away.

He took her chin in his hand and lifted her face toward the chandelier light. "You're wearing makeup."

A flush colored her cheeks better than any blush could. Jenny slapped his hand away and laughed. "Shut up."

"Wow."

"Close your mouth, Grant. I can look presentable when I need to."

He raised an appreciative eyebrow. "That's more than presentable, Jenny. You look fantastic."

She fidgeted with her beaded purse, then glanced at him from beneath long black lashes. "You're looking pretty dapper yourself tonight. A tux?"

The tux was a remnant from his celebrity days. Steve backed up, unbuttoned his jacket and pulled it aside so she could admire his scarlet cummerbund. He posed first from his right and then from his left. Crossing his legs, he executed a Michael Jackson style spin, and arched an eyebrow over a cocky, playful grin. "Glad you approve."

Jenny laughed at his clowning. Her husky chuckle warmed his heart. It was great to hear her laugh again. This was going to be a fun night.

"And you must be Annie." A lady in her mid-fifties stood behind Jenny, holding out her jeweled hand. Her husband stood at her back. "It's so good to finally meet you. I'm Patricia Corbridge—Daniel's wife."

Steve swore under his breath. It'd never occurred to him that people might think Jenny was his fiancée, but before he could correct his boss's wife, Jenny smiled graciously and shook her hand. "Hi. Jenny Harrison—sorry to disappoint you, but I'm just standing in for Annie tonight."

Steve hastily buttoned his jacket and introduced Jenny to his boss, Daniel Corbridge. "Jenny's a friend. Annie's son got sick and she had to stay home with him."

Jenny glanced at him out of the corner of her eye at the white lie but luckily didn't contradict him. Steve couldn't take a chance that Mrs. Corbridge might feel slighted that his fiancée decided to forego her party for Bunko night. Some of the partners' wives were easily offended, and Patricia Corbridge took her husband's social engagements very seriously.

"Nothing serious, I hope," Daniel said.

"Just a fever. I'm sure he'll be fine in a few days."

Mrs. Corbridge stared at him, her polite smile never reaching her shrewd eyes—she wasn't buying it. Steve resisted the urge to loosen his necktie and squirm.

"Jenny Harrison..." Patricia turned to her husband. "Why do I know that name?"

"Ms. Harrison is coordinating the firm's gift to that inner city clinic."

"The Donnatelli Clinic," Jenny supplied.

"Oh yes, it sounds like a fun project. What exactly are you going to do?"

"Well, we'd hoped to buy some books and a few toys to keep the children occupied in the waiting room. Since it's a free clinic, it's packed—as you can imagine—so the wait is often quite lengthy."

Patricia turned to her husband. "And how much is the firm donating?"

"We hadn't set an amount yet. What would you suggest?"

"Well, toys are nice, but easily broken and taken home. A television might work well—perhaps the clinic could run some informational/educational tapes occasionally, and a fish tank built into an open space, like at the dentist's office, is always entertaining to children. And of course a fresh paint job with a nice cheery color, and maybe some subscriptions to *Ranger Ricks* and *Highlights*?" She put a hand on Jenny's arm and leaned in. "Those were always favorites with our children." She pursed her lips, considering. "I'd say ten thousand should do."

Ten thousand dollars? Jenny briefly lowered her gaze to hide her popping eyes before turning to Patricia's husband in polite inquiry.

He smiled and inclined his head. "I think we can manage that. We'll get you a check made out to the clinic on Monday."

"Thank you. That's very generous."

Daniel rocked back on his heels. "We do what we can for the community."

"And it's a tax deduction and creates goodwill," Patricia added dryly.

"There *is* that," he acknowledged with a chuckle.

"Well, it's not ten thousand dollars, but..." Steve handed Patricia the box of candy. "Jenny thought you might enjoy this."

She turned and smiled at Jenny. "Candies by Maralyn. I love the toffee. Thank you."

Jenny waved her hand dismissively. "It's just a little something. It's kind of you to open up your home this way. It must have been a lot of work." Jenny said with a bright smile as she made a show of looking around. "Your house is absolutely beautiful, Mrs. Corbridge."

The older woman beamed. "Why thank you, dear. It's no trouble, really. I love to entertain. And please, call me Patricia."

"You certainly do it well. Look at the fresh greenery and all the candles, and the stunning tree." She sighed in wonder. "It must have taken you weeks to put all that up."

Steve very much doubted that Patricia had contributed more than a directing finger and a hefty check toward the elaborate decorations Jenny gushed over, but her appreciation seemed to please his boss's wife.

Patricia blushed. "Oh, I didn't do all this myself. I had help. I'm so glad you like it."

Daniel turned to him. "Tough break on the hazing case—that was yours, wasn't it?"

"Yes, sir."

Daniel clasped him on the shoulder. "Well, you know the old saying: you're not a real litigator until you've lost a million."

Steve nodded, though he hated the sentiment. "I'll try to keep that in mind."

"When're you filing on the university and the fraternity?"

He cleared his throat, acutely aware of Jenny's rapt gaze. "The client's health is unpredictable at the moment. I thought I'd wait until after the holidays."

"Don't wait too long." He leaned in and lowered his voice. "And I trust you're going to bill the client this time."

Steve resisted the urge to glance at Jenny. "The firm didn't lose out."

"I know, son. But the firm does a certain amount of pro bono cases and the rest..." He shrugged. "Have to find other representation."

"He couldn't afford it."

"Can he afford it any better now?"

He thought about lying to his boss. What should he care where the money came from as long as the firm got paid. He shook his head. "No, sir."

The older man gave him a steady look through rheumy eyes. "Then this'll be your pro bono case for the year. You cannot pay for all the losses. You do your best for the client and then move on." His raised eyebrows generated a wealth of wrinkles on his forehead. "Understand?"

Again he nodded. Steve hoped Patricia's chatter had kept Jenny busy so she hadn't overheard his boss's little lesson.

Daniel raised his voice and slapped him lightly on the back. "What a shame to ruin a perfect record. You were batting a thousand."

Steve nodded. Were these guys always going to talk to him like he was still a jock?

"Do you play pool?"

"A bit."

"We'll have to play a little eight ball later on my Christmas present." He squeezed his wife's shoulder. "While visiting her sister in North Carolina, Patricia got me a Vitalie Limited Edition—only one hundred made." He puffed out his chest. "The Patriot. She's a real beaut."

"Looking forward to it."

"Daniel, why don't you be a darling and get me and Jennifer drinks," Patricia said.

Jenny's lips locked in a stiff smile as she stared at Steve, trying to silently convey a meaningful message that, for the life of him, he couldn't decipher.

Daniel nudged Steve. "That's our cue—the ladies want to talk. White wine?" At his wife's nod, he turned to Jenny. "Jennifer, what can we get you?"

Jenny tore her annoyed gaze from Steve's and smiled at Daniel. "It's just Jenny. Nothing as elegant as Jennifer, I'm afraid—unless my mother's annoyed with me. Beer, please."

"Be right back," Steve said. He hated to abandon Jenny, but didn't see any way around it.

When the men left, Patricia linked her arm through Jenny's and walked her toward the living room where people gathered around the fireplace. A woman broke away from a group and moved toward them.

"I saw Steve going to the bar with Daniel." She gave Jenny a sideways look. "So is this the fiancée?" she asked in a stage whisper.

"This is Jenny Harrison—a friend of Steve's. Jenny, meet Vivian Foster—an attorney at the firm."

Jenny chuckled at Vivian's crestfallen face. "Sorry—not the fiancée."

"But there really *is* a fiancée?" she asked, clearly not wanting there to be.

"There really is." Jenny silently commiserated with the other woman.

"Well that's sad."

"It is."

Vivian's eyes narrowed suspiciously on Jenny. "Just friends? Steve hasn't taken his eyes off you since you arrived."

She'd been watching them? That was a little disconcerting. "He worries about me. My husband died recently."

"I'm so sorry," Vivian said.

"Condolences," Patricia said.

"Thank you." She could tell they were dying for details about Gabe's death, but Jenny didn't feel like satisfying their curiosity. "Gabe and Steve have been friends for years. Since Gabe died, Steve doesn't seem to notice that I can take care of myself, but truth be told," she lowered her voice, confiding, "his bossiness is getting a little old."

Vivian leaned forward, closing their little circle. "I know a few women that wouldn't mind him bossing her around."

"Who can blame them? He's gorgeous and rich," Patricia said.

Not to mention funny, smart, and sweet, Jenny added silently. She sought Steve out at the bar where he stood with his boss. Though facing Daniel, he was looking over the other man's shoulder at her. She smiled and nodded to reassure him.

Jenny had to admit Steve was the most handsome guy in the crowded room. Not only was he good looking, but the way he stood with his shoulders back exuded confidence, and he moved with the natural grace of an athlete. Steve could be very charming; she didn't doubt he had every woman's heart aflutter. He reached forward to accept drinks from the bartender and Jenny turned her attention back to the ladies.

"And coming this way." Vivian and Patricia shared a private look, then stared quizzically at Jenny.

Steve handed Patricia her drink before giving Jenny her Corona. "Viv, can I get you a drink?"

"No, thanks, I'm good."

He reached out a hand to Jenny. "We're going to check out that fabulous buffet in the dining room." He tugged on her arm playfully. "She gets mean when she's hungry."

Jenny turned back to the ladies. "Would you like to join us?"

"No, thanks. You two run along. And if you like meat, the prime rib is superb," her hostess added.

"I'll remember that, thanks." Jenny turned away and leaned into Steve, whispering, "What's that all about?"

"From the looks of that huddle, I assumed you needed rescuing."

"Where were you when she called me Jennifer?" Gabe would have corrected the mistake immediately.

"What?"

"Never mind." She drew him aside. "You paid the college kid's legal fees?"

Steve tugged on her hand, pulling her toward the buffet. "Let's eat."

Jenny was tempted to draw the moment out and make Steve admit that beneath that competitive spirit and analytical lawyer brain lurked the soul of a really decent man, but instead she gave in to his obvious embarrassment and patted him on the back. "I'm proud of you, Grant."

They crossed the large, open living room where a saxophonist, drummer, cellist, and harpist squeezed in around a grand piano in the right hand corner. The furniture had been cleared to create a dance floor. An elaborately decorated twelve-foot Nordic spruce stretched to the ceiling on the other side of a long wall of windows that looked out over Lake Huron.

Jenny wandered down the elegant buffet to the dessert table that offered crystal cups of chocolate mousse, white bowls of crème brûlée, three different cheese cakes, tiered platters of cream puffs and assorted pastries, and silver platters piled high with colorful fruits and a variety of cheeses.

At the other end of the table, Steve held his plate out as the chef carved a thin slice of beef off the huge roast sitting under the glowing orange warming lamp, and draped it carefully on his plate as if bestowing a precious gift. With a grin, Steve thanked him and moved toward the seafood area offering caviar, oysters, and bowls of huge shrimp.

Next to that stood steaming chafing dishes of roasted vegetables and rice pilaf. Wait staff circulated with bacon-wrapped chestnuts, little crudités with brochette, flaky triangular pastries, and crab-stuffed mushrooms.

Steve filled his plate to overflowing, but she was a bit more judicious with her choices. They went to the bar to refill their drinks before joining a group sitting near the fireplace. Steve made the introductions and after a few initial polite inquiries about what Jenny did for a living, the conversation turned to trials and office gossip.

Jenny took a bite of the mushroom and sighed. "This is amazing. Have you tried the mushrooms?"

Steve swallowed. "I don't like crab."

"You can hardly taste it. Here, try." She speared the other half of her mushroom and held it out to him.

Steve opened his mouth and she fed him the appetizer. He chewed quickly.

"Good, eh?"

His head bobbed. "Not bad. I like the prime rib better. Here." He cut off a little slice and offered it to her.

She winced. "Too fatty. It upsets my stomach. But the roasted veggies are wonderful. Do you think Mrs. Corbridge knows how they were prepared?"

He raised an eyebrow and shook his head.

"Too bad." Jenny set aside the empty plate and dug a small teaspoon into her cup of mousse. She closed her eyes, savoring the creamy rich chocolaty amazingness. "Oh, now *this* is pure heaven," she purred.

Steve stared, his expression amused and something else...

"What?" She frowned. "Do I have something in my teeth?"

He shook his head and smiled. "It's just good to see you enjoying food again."

That's all? You'd have to be a zombie not to appreciate this spread. "Are you kidding? This is amazing." She popped another spoonful into her mouth.

He raised a spoon to her glass and she swiveled to the side, stretching her arm to keep the cup out of his reach. "Get your own."

"You're not gonna eat all that."

Probably not. She narrowed her eyes, took a heaping spoonful of the mousse, and then handed him the glass. "I have to get the name of her caterer." A caterer would make Annie's shower so much easier.

With a whisper to Steve, Jenny slipped away to the restroom. On her way back, she stepped into the empty library. She felt instantly comfortable in this cozy room with floor-to-ceiling shelves lined with books—everything from bestseller paperback fiction and leather-bound classics to nonfiction. A whole wall was dedicated to law and management books. Crossing to the window. Jenny touched the frosty pane and admired the white lights illuminating the glittering trees in the backyard.

This time last year, she and Gabe had been freezing their butts off stringing lights around the pines and crab trees in their backyard. They'd strung the pines with multicolored lights and the deciduous trees with twinkling white lights. Jenny had had to use a little creative persuasion in the form of kisses and backrubs to convince Gabe to help her, but once they were done, snuggling together on the porch with warm mugs of hot chocolate, Gabe had agreed that he loved the festive lights reflecting across the sugary snow, creating their own private wonderland.

This year the porch remained closed off and the yard dark. Maybe she'd decorate it next Christmas for the baby. Or maybe she'd wait a year. Next Christmas the baby would be too young to appreciate it. Jenny sighed.

This isn't doing you any good, moping around. Go find Steve. Taking a deep breath, she forced a smile to her lips, raised her chin, and left her sanctuary.

The group from the fireplace had disassembled, leaving a scattering of china, silver and cloth napkins. Jenny looked at the bar; he wasn't there. She followed a few men toward a staircase to the lower level. Rounding the stairs, Jenny found Steve, standing beside an ornate pool table.

He'd discarded his jacket and stood relaxed, holding the cue stick at his side. Steve smiled, catching her eye as soon as she rounded the stairs as if he'd been watching for her. When she reached his side, he leaned down, murmuring, "Okay?"

She nodded. Daniel Corbridge was right; that certainly was a unique table. Now she understood the moniker, the patriot. The table's slate top was covered by navy blue felt. A circle of stars sat beneath the side pocket and was flanked by red and white painted wood carved to remind one of a rippling flag. Perfect for a politician.

"Good shot," he said to Daniel.

"Stripes or solids?" she asked. There were far more stripes on the table than solids. As the words left her mouth, Daniel nudged in the solid purple four ball.

"Stripes," she answered her own question.

Daniel missed the next shot and Steve moved forward. Ignoring the fifteen ball sitting in front of the end pocket, he tried a bank shot that just missed the ten ball.

"Too bad," Daniel said. "Why didn't you go for the fifteen? It was all set up for you."

"I like it blocking the pocket. I can go back and get it anytime," Steve said.

Daniel leaned over the table and eased in the yellow two ball. "Take 'em while you can get 'em, son."

Daniel sank another solid and then missed his next shot. Steve sank the twelve and then again tried for a more skillful shot. Banking the cue ball, he smacked the eleven, but it rolled just past the side pocket. After he missed, his boss tisked, tisked and sank his last ball.

"Eight ball in the side," he called out. He missed. With the table pretty much cleared, Steve sank his last two.

"Eight in the corner." With a quick punch, the black ball shot into the corner and the white ball promptly rolled in behind it. He lost.

"Easy, man. This isn't like pitching. You need a little finesse." Daniel patted him on the back. "Billiards is like a woman. Ya get a lot further with a little sweet talkin' than yellin'. Know what I mean?"

Steve nodded. "Yes, sir, I do."

What a condescending ass. Jenny burned on Steve's behalf. As if pitching required no skill. She was surprised and proud he didn't show any annoyance. Was he inured to such insults or did he really not mind?

Daniel put his stick away. "I'd better check on the missus. You keep practicing and pretty soon you'll be a shark."

"Thanks," Steve said.

"Hey, Steve, ready for another lesson?" a short balding man called out. With an arm firmly wrapped around a pretty brunette's waist, he smirked.

"No, thanks, Doug." He walked toward the rack. "I've ignored my guest too long."

"Not afraid to lose are you?" Doug turned to his date. "Steve here used to play professional ball, but apparently he isn't as gifted with his fine motor skills."

Steve's lips tightened as he continued putting the cue in the rack.

Jenny walked over, whispering, "I don't mind waiting, but you don't have to prove anything."

"What'd ya say, pal?"

Pal? Jenny hadn't thought that word could sound so insulting. If this was a sample of what Steve put up with at work on a regular basis, she wondered why he stayed.

Steve reached for the cue. "One game." He chalked his stick. "You can break."

"No, we'll lag. Don't want it said I took advantage." He shrugged out of his suit coat and handed it to his girlfriend.

Doug won the lag and Steve backed away from the table to lean against the back of a chair. Doug took an easy shot and then grinned at his date sitting nearby, cheering. He lined up his next shot and punched it in. Swinging the stick behind his back, he leaned backward over the table and punched another stripe ball in the pocket. He beamed and slapped Steve on the shoulder. "That's how it's done, old man."

Steve nodded. "Nice shot."

Doug sauntered around the table to line up his next shot.

"It's not looking good for you," Jenny whispered.

He took a sip of his beer. "He's about through."

Four striped balls lay scattered about. Doug didn't look done. The guy missed a shot and Steve moved forward, silently scanning the layout. He crouched over the table and, with a loud crack, shot the three ball into the corner pocket. In two smooth steps, he moved around the table to sink the nine and seven balls in rapid succession. Jenny silently cheered as Steve wordlessly, skillfully cleared the table.

"Eight in the end," Steve said as he lined up the shot.

"You're never gonna make it; the fifteen's in the way."

With one smooth stroke, Steve rolled the cue into the black ball, which glided between the fifteen and the bumper before plunking into the corner pocket.

Doug clamped his jaw shut, then slapped a fifty-dollar bill on the table. "Another? How about we make it interesting?"

Steve unrolled his sleeves and reached for his jacket. "Some other time."

"What? Afraid of losing?"

Steve felt Jenny freeze at his side, knowing she worried he'd rise to the bait. He shoved his arms into the jacket and took his time adjusting it. Not with this prick. He wasn't worth it. "Why would I waste time playing pool with you when I could be dancing with a beautiful woman?" He turned Jenny toward the stairs.

As soon as they'd climbed a few steps and were out of sight, she said, "You're really good at pool."

"Yep."

"You let Daniel win, didn't you?"

"Yep."

She stopped, blocking the stairs. He looked up at her and she brushed a hand across his cheek. Pride shone in her beautiful eyes. "That was very sweet. You're a pretty nice guy, Grant."

"Save the halo, Jen. He's my boss. I'm not stupid." To forestall more talking, he turned her and nudged her up the stairs. They threaded their way through half a dozen dancing pairs. Needing to burn off some energy, Steve swung her around to the jazzy tune of Glenn Miller's "In The Mood." He pulled her in close.

"I don't remember how to jitterbug."

"Fake it." He pushed her away, then pulled her close for an underarm turn before twirling her out again.

"Where'd you learn to dance?"

"My sisters made me dance with them, but I drew the line when they came at me with makeup."

Jenny grinned. She liked to dance. He hadn't known for sure but thought she might. He loved the way she gave herself over to the music with complete abandonment, closing her eyes and moving in perfect time to the song.

A singer joined the band, and in appreciation of the dancing couples, the group played a quick succession of popular fast songs by Van Morrison and Bob Seger. As they wound down, Steve inclined his head toward the bar and held out his hand. Jenny put her hand in his and they wound their way through the couples.

At the first few bars of the next song, Jenny pulled him back. "I love this song."

She tugged him back onto the dance floor to dance to Starship's "Nothing's Gonna Stop us Now." Jenny closed her eyes and swayed to the music. Lip syncing about determined lovers willing to pit themselves against the world to live their dream together, her hips rocked sensually from side to side.

He stifled the urge to rest his hands on those sexy curves and pull her close so they could get lost in the music together. He pulled her in, then whirled her out to break the romantic spell. Seeing the sparkle shine in her eyes and the glow in her cheeks made everything worthwhile—even if it was only temporary. Anything to make her smile again.

Then the music slowed to a ballad from the Phantom of the Opera—"All I Ask of You." Jenny's eyes became luminous, and she reached a hand out to him. Steve folded her into his arms and tucked her close to his chest. He resisted the impulse to close his eyes and drop his head to rest on hers, savoring the bliss. The rich tones of the trumpet, violin, and cello wrapped around them, cocooning them in sweetness. They waltzed around the floor until Steve whirled Jenny around and around to the swirling of the harp.

God, he was happy. He was really having fun. Too much fun. He should be dancing and enjoying tonight with his fiancée, instead of being glad she'd chosen Bunko over his work party.

Over the top of Jenny's curls, he scanned the dancing couples, thinking he should put a little space between them. He didn't want spiteful office gossip to hurt Annie. Then again, nobody was paying attention to them, and he hadn't the heart to push Jenny away.

Jenny nestled against Steve's chest, then looked up with huge sad eyes that squeezed his heart painfully.

Chapter 16

God what an idiot. How could Steve have forgotten this was Gabe and Jenny's song? For two months straight, he'd awakened to the sound of Gabe playing "All I Ask of You" on his piano. While Jenny slept, Gabe got up extra early and let himself into Steve's house to practice the song before they went on their morning bike ride. He'd learned it for their first anniversary. No wonder she was teary-eyed.

As the refrain came to an end, regardless of possible watching eyes, Steve dropped a kiss on Jenny's forehead. "Let's get out of here."

"It's okay." Jenny smiled, but it didn't reach her eyes. "I'm okay."

She might be okay but the festive mood was gone, intruded on by bittersweet memories for them both. He tugged her hand. "I've had enough. Let's go."

She flashed him a look of relief. They found their hosts near the buffet and said their goodbyes before retrieving Jenny's coat and the car. Once seated in the mustang, Steve turned up the heat.

Jenny settled back and closed her eyes. After a few minutes, she rolled her head sideways to peer at him through the dark. "Do you believe in destiny?"

Steve looked both ways before heading out into the street. "Destiny as in our lives are all scripted out for us and we're just puppets fulfilling some master plan?"

"Yeah. Perhaps I'm just destined to be alone. Maybe that's the way it's supposed to be and I should stop fighting it. I mean first, I had to give up Michael, then Gabe died on me and now this fight over the baby... maybe I'm not supposed to have a really close love."

Steve thought of the precipitous end of his baseball career despite the extraordinary precautions he'd taken to avoid tearing his rotator cuff, and then falling for his best friend's wife. Neither was anything he'd chosen to put himself through. Maybe he did believe in fate.

As they pulled up to a stoplight, he looked at her. "You're hardly alone. You've got friends and family who love you." He glanced back at the light. Still red.

"But no special love. Maybe I'm being greedy, after all I had Gabe for almost three great years. Maybe that's it."

A car honked, Steve glanced up at the green light and pressed his foot to the accelerator. "You're not being greedy." He paused, gathering his thoughts. "I believe we each have our own path to travel. Sometimes we make false starts and detours, but we have this internal compass that knows our true path. We just have to listen to it." He hesitated. "If your internal compass keeps pointing at this baby, then you need to do it. But you're not supposed to be alone."

"Ya think?"

As much as his gut protested against her having Gabe's baby now, he also saw that Jenny radiated love. It was like a positive comforting energy that wrapped around her. With Gabe gone, it seemed her energy needed to be expressed in their child. He got that. Even before Gabe died, she'd wanted a baby. He sighed. It all kept coming back to her need for their child.

As much as he hated to encourage her, he nodded. "Listen to your heart; you'll know what to do."

She pursed her lips. "Okay then."

They raced up the off ramp, and Steve pointed the car toward the lake. Suddenly Jenny smacked his arm. "You could have let me know you're really good at pool." She pouted. "I actually worried that jerk might beat you."

Steve grinned. He'd enjoyed Jenny's defensiveness on his behalf. And he had to admit he'd shown off to impress her. "What fun would there have been in that?"

"Jerk."

"Thanks for going with me tonight, Jen."

She yawned. "Thank *you*. It was fun. I'd forgotten how much I love to dance."

He'd like to take her dancing again, but he wouldn't. In April he'd be a married man. "Sorry about the misunderstanding—them thinking you were Annie."

She waved aside his concern. "Not your fault."

"You handled it well."

"What'd you think I'd do? Dissolve in a fit of embarrassment."

"I don't know." He glanced sideways at Jenny before patting her hand. "I'm proud of you. Ya done good, kid."

"I'm proud of me too. I actually had a good time."

He pulled into Jenny's drive and put a hand on her arm. "Wait."

He hurried around the car and opened the door before extending a hand to help her out.

She yawned broadly again. "You don't have to walk me to the door."

He followed her up the walk and then reached around her to open the screen door. "My mom raised a gentleman."

She snickered. "I'll remind you the next time you burp in my face." Jenny took keys from her purse, opened the door and turned back to him. "Thanks. Sleep well." She popped into the house and closed the door.

Steve stood there a few seconds, watching for the lights to turn on as she walked through the house, then allowed the screen door to swing shut and walked back to his car. He shoved the passenger door closed and got in his side before reversing and then turning into his own driveway.

Steve shut the garage door and went into the house. In the family room, he flipped a switch to turn on the fireplace, and then shrugged out of his jacket before tossing it on the couch. He twisted his bow tie off and threw it on top of the jacket. With a quick flick of his wrist, he undid the top two shirt buttons and dropped into the leather chair.

What a perfect night. He hadn't enjoyed a night out this much in years. Hell, he'd never enjoyed a work function as much. He probably wouldn't have had half as much fun with Annie. She thought lawyers were boring and rarely went out of her way to hide her feelings, whereas Jenny seemed to mix well with his colleagues.

Jenny. He rubbed an index finger across his upper lip. Damn, she'd looked beautiful tonight. He'd dated beautiful women before—Annie was gorgeous—but none of them could compare to Jenny tonight. He found himself looking for any little excuse to touch her; help her on and off with her coat, dancing—now that had been a mistake. Watching Jenny lose herself in sensual abandon to the music brought out unwelcome desire he'd thought was long buried.

Desire you have no business feeling, prick, his little voice whispered.

I know.

And even though bittersweet memories of Gabe's song wrecked the romantic mood, Jenny hadn't broken down weeping for her deceased husband. She'd smiled, and laughed, and enjoyed herself—with him. He'd put that smile on her face.

Tonight he was king. Tomorrow he'd try harder with Annie.

∾ ∾ ∾

Annie came downstairs as Josh let Steve in. Steve's face lit in a smile and he held out a lovely bouquet of flowers as he unzipped and shrugged out of his coat.

"Does this mean I'm forgiven for missing last night's party?" She drank in the scents of roses and pine prigs. Evergreens and scarlet roses lay nestled between sprays of snowy chrysanthemums in the

Christmas bouquet. "Maybe I should beg off on more events if it gets me flowers."

She held out her hand for his coat and hooked the jacket on the coat rack.

"It was fine. Jen stood in for you so I didn't have to go alone."

"You took Jenny?" Annie paused on her way to the kitchen. A part of her was a little perturbed that he'd taken Jenny instead of going alone, then the other part was a little gleeful that Jenny'd had to suffer through the boring night. Then again, as a doctor's wife, she was probably used to those dull duty events.

"Yeah. It was good for her to get out and be with people who didn't know Gabe. The food was good. You would've loved the chocolate mousse."

"Did they have Christmas cookies?" Josh asked. They moved into the kitchen and he climbed onto a counter stool.

"Not as good as your mom's." Steve sniffed appreciatively and picked up one of the un-iced sugar cookies.

Annie swatted his hand. "Those are for decorating."

"Mom and me made the icing and got the dec-rations all ready."

"You did?" Steve rolled up the sleeves on his shirt. "Well, let's get to it." He looked around. "Where's Soph?"

"Shopping with Ryan. He's going to drop her off after lunch." To her surprise, Ryan had insisted on taking Josh and Sophie Christmas shopping and to lunch separately, so he could have a little one-on-one time with each of them. Despite herself, Annie was impressed.

"She didn't want to decorate Christmas cookies?"

"She can't do it—she's just a baby," Josh said disdainfully, stirring the green frosting.

"You were a baby too and I let you help," Annie reminded. "We'll save some for her to decorate after her nap."

Steve settled on a stool and reached for a cookie. He ducked his head as Annie slipped an apron over him, then tied it in the back. "There. All set."

"My mom called and asked about our Christmas plans." He swirled white frosting in three globs on the snowman. "I told her we were having Christmas Eve with your folks. Seeing how this was our first Christmas together, I told her we'd probably be busy in the morning with opening presents and then we'd want to have brunch alone, but dinner was a possibility." He looked at her with raised eyebrows. "Is that okay?"

"Uhhh..." Annie picked up a pastry bag full of red icing, and leaned over her cookie to buy some time. She'd intended to talk with Steve about their holiday plans a little later—in private.

"Don't forget Daddy," Josh piped up.

Out of the corner of her eye, Annie saw Steve's head come up and immediately gave her cookie her full attention.

"I thought Ryan was going to be in Florida with his folks."

She bit her lower lip and studiously gave her snowman his carrot nose, then switched bags to the black icing for eyes and buttons as she tried to find the right words to explain the arrangement she and Ryan had negotiated.

"Nope. We're gonna have a great big sleepover." Josh swung his arms wide. "With you and Daddy, and me and Sophie and Mommy."

"We are?"

The silky cautious tone of Steve's question went right over her son's head as he nodded enthusiastically and reached for another plain cookie, but Annie felt Steve's hard stare and knew she had to tread lightly.

"Daddy's gonna sleepover just like you." Josh raised shining eyes to Steve. "Isn't that great?"

Steve looked at Annie as he stood. "My snowman needs a peppermint nose. Help me find it in the pantry."

Josh wrinkled his nose. "Peppermint? Snowmen have carrot noses."

Annie was tempted to tell Steve she didn't have any peppermint, but followed him to the walk-in pantry.

"Not this snowman." Steve took her wrist, pulled her into the pantry and closed the door behind them. "Ryan's spending the night?"

She shrugged. "It's Christmas. I couldn't tell him no."

"Why the hell not?"

"He's their father."

"He can come by later. He doesn't have to spend the night."

She bit back the instinct to point out that *he* was spending the night, but as her future husband, it was natural Steve would sleep over. Josh and Sophie were used to sleepovers with Steve.

"That's what the kids wanted and Ry wanted to be there first thing in the morning."

"Is that what you want?"

She shrugged. "It just worked out that way. It's simpler."

"It's not what I want. It's intrusive and weird."

"I thought you liked Ryan."

"My liking Ryan's not the issue. I'm marrying you and the kids, not him."

"Ryan's a part of the package, the same way Jenny comes with you. Jenny's your friend. Ryan's the father of my children. Neither of us was willing to give up Christmas morning with the kids, so we have to share."

"How about..." Steve pursed his lips and frowned.

She watched warily, waiting for his idea.

"After they wake up with us and open their presents, we take them over to Ryan's?" he suggested.

Annie shook her head, tamping down on rising impatience. She and Ryan already hashed this out and this was the best solution. "Santa only comes to one house, and we both want to be there when the kids open their stockings and Santa presents."

Jaw tightening, Steve's frown deepened. "I'm not spending the next ten Christmas mornings with Ryan."

Annie didn't like the hard edge in his voice or the unspoken ultimatum. She crossed her arms. "Well, you're going to have to."

"Hey, are you guys gonna help me?" Josh called out.

Annie raised her voice to be heard through the pantry door. "Be there in a minute, Joshie."

"Tell Ryan it's just us this year, he can have the kids next Christmas."

"I don't want to miss Christmas morning with my kids. The solution we came up with works just fine."

"Not for me. I get that Sophie and Josh come with you, but I draw the line at including your ex-husband."

"That's unreasonable."

"And I don't want to honeymoon in Bora Bora."

Her head whipped around. "What?" How'd they jumped from Christmas to Bora Bora? "What's wrong with Bora Bora? We discussed it and you agreed."

He shook his head. "There was no discussion. You told me what you wanted and booked it—just like the rest."

"But you liked it all. I told you—"

"You *told* me—you didn't ask what I wanted." He tilted his head to the side. "Why'd you even agree to marry me?"

She frowned. "What?"

"What's my favorite color? Favorite drink? What music do I like?"

"Beer. Uh..." She made a stab, "Blue? Favorite music... I have no idea." Anger built in her at the grilling and she lashed back, "You don't know me any better."

His head bobbed up and down. "That's the point. We don't really know each other very well."

"We have our whole lives to get to know each other." Isn't that what marriage was about? Growing old together?

"Why'd you accept my proposal, Annie?"

His proposal? "How could I not? You proposed on national TV in front of millions of people. The band playing that song... You went to so much trouble to set up an amazing proposal and then you got me my dream ring... what was I supposed to say?"

He cocked his head. "So you said yes to save me embarrassment?"

"Yes—no!" She shook her head, confused. "What girl wouldn't want to marry you? You're gorgeous, generous, financially stable, reliable," Unlike Ryan—well, the old Ryan. Now that his dad retired and handed him control of the family boat shop, Ryan seemed to have matured quite a bit. He was even a pretty good dad. Steve had always been good dad material. "And you like Josh and Sophie."

"Okay." He nodded as if putting together puzzle pieces.

"Okay what?" What was *wrong* with him? Steve had always been so sweet and amenable. He'd always liked her plans. Why was he picking a fight now? She frowned and blinked back the tears burning her eyes. "I don't understand. You never complained about anything before. Is this because I missed one business dinner?"

"No—it's not about the dinner." He leaned back against the shelf. "Look, if this is going to work, we have to be a team. We've got to want the same things. I get that your children are the most important people in your life, but I have to be next in line—not Ryan."

"This isn't about Ryan." Ryan was her *ex*-husband. He was off sailing most of the time. She had no idea what this was about, but it wasn't Ry.

"I agree. It's about teamwork and loyalty. It's about us and our commitment to each other."

Was he saying she wasn't committed to him? She was marrying the guy; what more did he want? She looked up at him. "I don't understand."

"We need to be a better team. Equals—not you making decisions and letting me know about it. I want to be included in any discussion that affects us. I deserve as much say as Ryan."

She quieted, finally getting it. "You think you should have a say in decisions we make for Josh and Sophie?"

Steve nodded. "Okay, maybe not an equal say, but I should at least be consulted when the decisions affect us—me and you."

Eyes widening, she looked away. It was hard enough working with Ryan and now Steve thought he should be able to tell her what to do with her kids? Or what? She didn't care if the wedding was all planned, Steve was *not* going to call the shots when it came to Ryan and her kids. And she was standing by her decision.

Ryan would be with them Christmas morning. It was only fair. He'd changed. Their time together at Thanksgiving had shown her that. He earned the right to spend Christmas morning with his kids and Steve was just going to have to accept it.

She raised her chin. "I'm not telling Ryan he can't spend the night. He's the father of my children, and he'll always be a part of my life. And if you can't accept it, then..." She took a deep breath and twisted the ring from her finger. "I can't marry you."

Steve looked at her hard, thinking, then reached for the pantry door handle.

Annie grabbed his arm. "Wait!"

"You made your decision." He left the pantry, whipped the apron over his head and threw it aside as he moved toward the door.

"Where're you goin'?" Josh asked.

Steve snagged his coat and yanked the front door open.

Annie jammed the ring back on her finger and hurried after him. "That's it? You're going to give up so easily?"

He thrust one arm in his jacket, then the other. Without looking at her, he calmly walked out the front door. Annie followed him into the cold and slammed the door shut behind her. Joshie didn't need to see or hear this. She couldn't believe Steve hadn't given in. She'd thought for sure he'd back down. Tears choked her throat. He was really going to allow Ryan to come between them?

She trailed after him, swallowing around the lump in her throat. They'd lose their deposit on the Yacht club—she already had her dress. He was really going to let her go?

"Do you want to see a therapist? Maybe talking to somebody could help us figure things out. A therapist can teach us how be a family."

Steve stopped by his car, turned and studied the ground. Finally he raised his head and shook it, sadly. "A therapist can't help us fall in love. It was stupid to ever think we would."

"Love? Of course we're in lo—Oh." Annie felt sucker punched as what he was really saying sank in. He wasn't *in love* with her. Well. *That* was... sobering. And a little hurtful. But so what? So Steve didn't love her? She knew he cared about her. Love was overrated. She and Ryan had been in love and look where it'd gotten them. Divorced.

She shrugged and rubbed her hands together. "That's okay. I don't need that 'in love' stuff. It's romantic nonsense—what we have is more... better."

"I need it," he blurted out, then looked away as if embarrassed.

"Oh." Annie crossed her arms over her chest, suddenly freezing. Well, maybe it *was* a deal breaker. She frowned and bit her lip. They had a great sex life; that was usually enough for most guys. Steve needed to be in love? Really? She'd been in love and wasn't about to go there again, not for anybody.

She traced backward through their whole fight. This had all started because of Ryan. Ryan. The kids. Nope; love wasn't their problem, this was a power struggle. Steve was just pissed because he wasn't getting his way. She breathed in deeply and allowed righteous anger to push away the confusion and tears. She was not about to let another man run her life.

Annie looked up as Ryan's car pulled in the drive. Sophie jumped out of the car. "Hi Steve." She flew past him and launched herself at Annie. "Mommy."

Annie caught her daughter and whirled her around. Squeezing her tightly, she relished the weight of her sweet baby in her arms. This little girl, her kids, were the most important thing in her life. "Hi, sweet pea. Did you have fun with Daddy?"

Sophie nodded. "We got you a present and we had hotdogs for lunch."

"You did? What a lucky girl." She set Sophie on her feet. "Go inside with Daddy and I'll be in in a minute and you can tell me all about it."

"'Kay." Sophie spun away, grabbed her father's hand and led him into the house. "Let's go, Daddy."

Steve silently watched father and daughter. Annie hardened her heart against the pain on his face. He'd made his choice. Josh and Sophie would be confused by their breakup, but they were young and Ryan would help smooth things over.

"Do you want to tell Josh and Sophie now?" he asked.

"No." She couldn't resist one hurtful jab. "Ryan and I will tell them tonight."

Steve scowled and looked like he wanted to argue.

Don't even go there, buster. They're my kids.

"What're you going to tell them? I don't want them to think this is their fault."

"I don't know." She shoved a hand through her hair. She was still taking it in; she had no idea what she'd tell the kids. "Don't worry, I won't make you out to be the bad guy. I'll tell them..." How could she simplify something so complex?

Steve looked at her, waiting. She sighed, winging it. "We'll say something like... it had nothing to do with them—there were a lot of adult reasons... You still love them... but you just can't be around anymore.

"Maybe we'll go to Florida for Christmas—it'll be a great distraction and help them forget..." "You" seemed unnecessarily cruel. At least she still had her kids; Steve had nobody.

His face had become a handsome blank mask she couldn't read. "Would it be okay if I took them to the park or sledding, and eased out of their lives?"

"I don't think that's a good idea." It'd be painful seeing Steve— she'd prefer a clean break, but what would be best for Josh and Sophie? She'd see what Ryan thought. "I'll think about it."

He nodded and turned to leave.

"Wait!" She looked down at the beautiful, sparkling diamond winking up at her and twisted it off. She held the amazing engagement ring out to him. "Here."

He shook his head. "Keep it."

She paused, tempted, then grabbed his hand, pressed the ring into his palm and folded his fingers around it. Keeping his ring would make her look mercenary. "I don't want it anymore."

Annie swiped at hot tears and turned to run back to the warm house.

∾ ∾ ∾

Steve drove around awhile. Not ready to go home yet, he parked at the Yacht club. Looking toward the barren dock reminded him of Ryan, so he left the property and walked along the lake. Maybe if he burned off some energy and cleared his head, this would all make sense.

He probably should be relieved, but he wasn't. Anger burned in his gut and sadness weighted down his shoulders. He'd sensed for a while that he and Annie weren't right, but he'd ignored the signs. He'd wanted marriage to Annie to work, damn it. Even knowing he didn't love her and she didn't love him, he'd ignored the fleeting thought that he could be her rebound relationship and had forged forward with his plan.

Annie was right; he'd made sure she wouldn't turn him down. His lips tightened in self-loathing. He'd carefully calculated his proposal, making it impossible for her to say no. The large diamond in his pocket poked his thigh with each step. From the impressive ring to the band and the public proposal on TV... she'd never had a chance.

Emotional bullying is what it was, you asshole. You've got no one to blame but yourself.

And to make matters worse, he'd dragged Josh and Sophie into it. He'd really fallen for those munchkins. They were good kids; they didn't deserve this. He should have been more careful. The last thing in the world he'd ever want to do was hurt them. Shit.

They'll get over you. Don't flatter yourself; you're not all that great. Besides, they have Ryan.

Probably. Kids were resilient. Josh and Sophie were young. And Ryan was stepping up. It wouldn't be long before he was just a faint memory of a fun guy that passed through their lives. How depressing. He let out another deep breath and closed his eyes one long moment. He'd remember them always.

Steve stopped his march along the shoreline, turned into the wind and faced the lake. He'd set himself up for failure. Failing again left the bitter taste in his mouth. He blew out a deep breath. Bending, he picked up a stone and threw it as far into the choppy gray waters as he could. He threw another and another until his arm ached. He embraced the pain in his shoulder; serve him right if he tore his rotator again. His doctor would be pissed. He could join the crowd.

Fucking shit! First Jenny and now Annie. Gabe and then Ryan. He was so damn tired of coming in second—of being second best. Yet he kept making the same damn mistake. He rolled his head and thrust his hands deep into his pant pockets. Was he a masochist or what? Why'd he keep choosing emotionally unavailable women? Why keep setting himself up for failure?

Would he never learn? God *damn* it.

Enough. Enough pity. Enough women. He was going to forget about relationships and concentrate on something rational, something he could be successful at, something simple... like the law.

Steve spun on his heels, stalked back to his car, and headed into work.

Chapter 17

Christmas Eve day found Jenny in the basement surrounded by bags of gifts, wrapping paper and bows. She turned on Christmas music and made hot cocoa, determined to embrace the spirit of Christmas—or consumerism, as it were. As if pretty packages and rich food could distract her from missing Gabe.

Not helpful, Jen. Be grateful for the blessings you have.

She bit her lower lip and redoubled her efforts in tying the intricate bow on Alex's present. Alex would appreciate the prettily wrapped gift. Jenny peeled away the label and stuck it on. Snatching up the pen, her hand hovered over the sticker a minute before dropping to the tabletop. After a lengthy mental debate, she scrawled "Jenny," swiped away an errant tear and set the wrapped gifts aside without adding Gabe's name.

Next she packaged up Gabe's stethoscope and tennis racquet for Ted and signed the tag, "Love, Dad." For Alex, Jenny had framed a favorite picture of Gabe and Alex taken last spring break in Cancun. For her other "Dad" present, Jenny had the perfect gift in mind. She drew Gabe's watch from her pocket.

Jenny caressed the smooth, gold metal back, remembering how Gabe had worn it every day. Lovely and reliable and Gabe's. She put it in a soft cloth bag, then into a square box. Alex had teased Gabe constantly about using the old relic, but Jenny knew she treasured it. She smiled and patted the package. *Alex will love you well.*

Jenny nodded in satisfaction, happy to have found a positive way to include Gabe.

Christmas Eve Jenny shared dinner with Judith's family, Alex and Ted. She found a few minutes to pull Gabe's kids aside to give them their gifts. Ted nodded gratefully as he fingered the strings on Gabe's racquet, then immediately draped Gabe's stethoscope around his neck as soon as he freed it from the box, but it was Alex's reaction that had been everything Jenny could have hoped for.

When Alex opened her father's watch, she'd pursed her lips and batted back tears before grabbing Jenny in a fierce hug, whispering, "Thank you." The kids' appreciative reactions shamed her, making her feel like she'd been hording Gabe's things. Well, no more. She invited the kids over to dinner and to go through Gabe's things to see if they wanted any more mementos of their dad.

A little after nine, Jenny gathered Ritz and scooted over to her parent's house. For the first time in years, Jenny awoke Christmas morning in her old childhood room.

She was pretty sure Michael had set his alarm for six a.m.—no teenager naturally woke that early—even if Santa still came for him. Michael's enthusiasm was a tad overplayed, but it was contagious and before long Jenny couldn't help responding in kind. Surprisingly, she didn't have to fake it. Jenny had always loved Christmas and making her family happy never failed to lift her spirits.

Though she appreciated the busy, familiar Christmas day routine of presents, church and brunch, followed by afternoon football and early dinner, Jenny was happy to be home. She wrapped herself in old flannel pajamas and Gabe's terry robe before meandering downstairs out onto the enclosed porch. Strategically placed lighting illuminated the softly falling snow. Six inches of new snow blanketed the ground like fluffy white feathers.

It had never snowed on Christmas day while she and Gabe lived here. Their first snowfall together in this house, Gabe brought home two huge plastic disks. He'd covered her eyes, led her outside and sat her on one, then given her a big push. She'd gone sailing down the hill and nearly into the lake.

She took a deep breath. The pain in her stomach had eased with time and regular meals. Since Judith's visit, Jenny had gone out of her way to take care of herself. She'd regained much of the weight she'd lost, so she had breasts again. She still had trouble sleeping, but she'd bought a treadmill. She walked every night, sometimes five miles, before following up with a hot lavender bubble bath that usually helped her sleep.

She'd made an appointment with the fertility specialist Judith recommended, for after the holidays. Although that might be a moot point if Jenny couldn't get an attorney to represent her, or worse yet, if she lost her case. She wandered into the living room and turned on the Christmas tree lights. Alex had brought her a noble fir, insisting that Gabe would have wanted Jenny to celebrate her favorite holiday.

Sitting Indian style in front of the colorful twinkling lights, Jenny allowed emotions she'd held at bay all day to swamp her. Tears blurred the colorful reds, blues, greens, oranges, and whites, till they blended like a kaleidoscope and the crisp pine scent transported her back to the intimate talks she and Gabe had shared, sitting in the dark near the tree, softly discussing life... love... their future.

She pulled her knees up, hugging them close, missing Gabe's strong arms. Christmas was romantic—a time for sharing and celebrating life with special people. But her special person was gone. Cold loneliness consumed her, carving her out like a hollow shell, empty and alone. Tears dribbled down her cheeks. Ritz whined and lay her head on Jenny's foot.

When a knock sounded at the back door, Jenny got up and grabbed a tissue. On her way through the kitchen, she wiped her tears and blew her nose. Knowing it was pointless to try and pretend she hadn't been crying, she clutched a hand full of tissues and let Steve in. Not even attempting a smile, she backed away from the door.

Dressed in dark blue slacks, a sweater, and loafers, he'd probably just gotten home from dinner with his family—or maybe Annie's.

"Driveway looks good." He brushed some snow off his shoulders and shut the door behind him. "You shovel it?"

She shook her head. "Michael."

Steve took in her disheveled appearance and shifted a gold box sporting an elaborate bow in his hand. "I can leave if you want me to."

Jenny blew her nose again and shook her head. Sitting around feeling sorry for herself hadn't made her feel any better. Besides, Jenny was anxious to see how Steve liked his presents. She forced a wobbly smile. "Come on in."

She led Steve through the living room onto the patio, turning on the room lamps as she passed. The Christmas tree magic was her and Gabe's special thing; she wasn't ready to share it. On the couch, she tucked slipper-clad feet under her. "Why does everyone say that crying's good for you? It always makes me feel like shit. My eyes get all gritty and my stomach kills. Wha's so good about it?"

Steve shrugged. "Got me. Makes me feel like I've got the flu and a hangover at the same time. Maybe because crying's a physical release and it exhausts you?"

She blew out a deep breath through her mouth since her nose was stuffed. "'S not worth it."

"I agree."

She threw the used tissues on the coffee table. "I am sooo tired of crying."

"It's getting easier."

"Slowly."

He sat down next to her and jostled the wrapped box in his hand awkwardly. "This might cheer you up."

She retrieved Steve's presents from under the tree and handed them to him. "Merry Christmas."

Jenny lifted his gift and gently shook it. "What is it?"

"Open it."

She pulled the ribbon and bow aside then ripped the wrapping off to reveal a beautiful wooden music box with a picture of Gabe,

Jenny, and Steve encased in the lid. Out on the boat, a grinning Gabe sat between Jenny and Steve with an arm thrown around each. When she raised the lid, it played James Taylor's "You've got a friend." Jenny gasped and put a trembling hand to her mouth. *How sweet.*

"Gabe was the best friend I ever had." Steve cleared his throat. "We had some great times together. I don't want to forget our friendship—either of us."

"It's beautiful," she whispered and stroked the polished wood.

"You missed something." He opened the lid and pointed to the cream business card nestled on top of the maroon velvet lining.

Jenny fingered the crisp card with embossed black script. "Helen Johnson, Attorney at Law?"

"Your attorney. If you want her." He paused. "Helen's been retired a few years, but when I explained your case, she was intrigued and agreed to meet you."

"How'd you find her?"

"She's the mother of a baseball buddy. I helped her son out of a little trouble years ago."

"You called in a favor, for me?" Tears swamped Jenny's eyes, stinging her aching sockets.

"Don't make too much of it. Being a bit out of practice, she's not the most ideal attorney for you, but she has a solid track record and she's sharp."

"And she's willing. That's the amazing part."

"Call her. See if you can work with her."

"You got me an attorney for Christmas?" She frowned and pursed her trembling lips. "Even after the terrible things Judith said to you."

Steve looked away. A flush crept up his neck. "She was right. A part of me is afraid of losing. Maybe I'm a coward, but losing for you would be a lot worse than if it were just me." He shook his head. "I won't risk it."

"You got me an attorney." Jenny covered her mouth with one hand and sniffled. She grasped the lapels of her robe and closed them tightly around her neck, needing the comfort.

"Helen might not be what you want," he warned.

"I can't exactly afford to be picky. And you'd never recommend someone incompetent. I'm sure she'll be perfect." She smiled brightly, touched by his gifts. "Thank you so much. They're both wonderful."

Jenny hugged him close as she'd done a hundred times before, but this time she detected a wariness—almost stiffness—in this embrace that had never been there before. Prior to Gabe's death, Steve's big body had been nothing more than a comforting brother-shoulder to cry on; now, something was different.

Backing away, Jenny pushed aside the observation and smiled regretfully at her own gift. "Your present isn't nearly so special."

Successful people fascinated Steve, so she'd thought he'd enjoy reading Bill Gates, Michael Eisner's, and Steve Jobs's biographies.

Ripping into them like an eager boy, he carefully examined each hardback, reading the jackets and first pages. "How'd you get Bill Gates's signature?"

She flashed a wry smile. "I waited a very long time, in a very long line, on a very hot day outside Barnes and Noble when he was in town last summer."

Steve nodded, eyes still glued to the books, then looked up and slowly smiled. A lopsided smile so beautiful it pulled at her heartstrings. "Thank you. It's great."

"Too bad you'll breeze through them in a week or two."

"I'll read them again."

"After I do. The one about Gates sounds interesting."

He chuckled. "If you've had it that long, I'm surprised you didn't already read it."

"Before you? That'd be rude." Jenny handed him a long, slim, flat box. "This is from me and Gabe."

"You and Gabe, eh?" He tapped the light box in his hand and raised an eyebrow. "You got me a tie?"

"Just open it."

Steve flipped the lid off and stared at the box. "Red Wing tickets?" He stared in awe at the pack of season tickets.

"He'd want you to have them. I would have given them to you earlier, but I only found them last week."

He carefully folded the tissue paper over the red tickets, put the lid on and handed it to her. "This is too much. I can't accept it."

"Yes, you can. You love hockey. For god's sake, you've practically got a shrine to Wayne Gretzky in your rec room."

His arm dropped to his lap. "That was your and Gabe's thing."

"Not really. I never really liked hockey."

"Yes, you did." He tilted his head and narrowed his eye, clearly skeptical. "You never missed a game."

She shook her head. "Nope. I just went for him."

"Gabe thought you were a diehard fan."

She shuddered. "Too violent. Now if they got rid of checking..."

"Nobody would go." Steve stared at the oblong box several seconds, then lifted his head. A deep frown contrasted with the hope and excitement gleaming in his eyes.

"Enjoy. Freeze your butt off. Revel in the violence."

"Sooo I take it you're not going to go with me."

"Not a chance. Take Annie." Jenny couldn't help the smile that curved her lips, hoping it didn't look as evil as she felt.

"Hockey's hardly Annie's thing."

She widened her eyes in innocence. "No?"

He reopened the box, his gaze settling on the tickets, and he absentmindedly shook his head. "Row six, section one twenty-four? That's right on the blue line. Thanks, Jen."

"You're welcome." She smiled, glad he was pleased with the gift.

Jenny ran a finger around the edge of the gold-trimmed business card while studying the picture of the three of them. She looked up and caught Steve watching, a wistful but contented look in his blue eyes. Lord, he was a handsome man. A good man. He deserved to be happy.

"How're the wedding plans coming along?"

"They're not. We called it off."

"What?" She must have heard wrong.

"Called it off." Steve methodically smoothed the red tissue paper back across the tickets and fitted the gold lid back on the box. He lifted his head and met her gaze. "She wasn't ready to give up her ex-husband, and I wasn't willing to be that accommodating—even if he is the father of her children."

Jenny suddenly felt lightheaded with relief, but one look at his sober face reminded her that her friend was hurting. No wonder he'd been so subdued. Selfishly wrapped up in her own pain, she'd that assumed Steve was grieving for Gabe, when the truth was he'd suffered a more personal blow.

She scrambled for something appropriate to say when she really wanted to know all the nitty-gritty details. *Who broke up with whom? When? How?* She hoped Steve had done the breaking up, though either way hurt. "I'm sorry. I know how attached you were to her kids."

"Yeah. They're great little guys. It's not really fair to them." He blew out a deep breath and looked at her. "I thought you'd be thrilled—you never liked Annie."

"I—" she wanted to deny it, but he would know better—"I want you to be happy. I want you to experience what Gabe and I had."

"Yeah, well, we might not have been a perfect fit, but I really thought we could make it work." Steve looked at her. "Great relationships don't have to be like yours and Gabe's. Love looks different on different people."

Thinking about her parents and other happily married couples she knew, Jenny pursed her lips and nodded. She had to give him that one. "You okay?"

"I've had better Christmases." He lifted a corner of his lip in a little smile.

"Amen to that." Jenny searched for a happier topic of conversation. "Gianna told me they collected twenty-five thousand dollars in Gabe's fund. Joe and Gianna suggested investing it in prenatal education or updating the clinic's trauma equipment. What do you think?"

"Either sounds worthy. Gabe would have appreciated it."

"You know," her voice lowered, confiding. "Some days I forget. I know it's silly, but I feel terrible for forgetting him for even a day."

"It's natural. Maybe that's why I got that," he nodded at the music box and photo. "I don't want to forget."

She brightened. "Exactly. But then something sets me off. Last week I got the most touching letter from the man who received Gabe's heart. The Organ Donor society forwarded it to me. Sometimes I wish they wouldn't, because these people are so damn grateful and their stories are so touching that it makes me feel guilty I didn't want to donate his organs.

"This man was only thirty-five-years old and his own heart had been destroyed by some virus. He'd been on the waiting list for three years and was losing hope, spending more time in the hospital than outside." She ran across the room, pulled the letter from the bombay chest drawer, and handed it to Steve. "He's got two little girls— aren't they precious?"

Steve scanned the letter and looked at the family picture. "You're a special lady."

"No, I'm the lucky one." She tucked the letter away carefully. "This is the fifth letter I've received. These people live through hell. Every time I feel sorry for myself, I read one of these letters and I feel so fortunate."

Unable to argue that, they fell into a companionable silence, watching the snow fall.

Chapter 18

The only thing Jenny dreaded more than being late was arriving late and sweaty. Just gonna have to take that chance, Jenny thought as she power-walked through the cold January day.

She rushed past a huge bronze statue of a muscular near-naked guy in an impossible yoga-pose, holding a shiny golden sun in one hand and mini people in the other, into the Coleman Young Municipal Center. She probably should know the story behind that statue—undoubtedly it had a real name. She'd check it out on her way home, but right now she wasn't entirely sure of where she was going and she was late.

After asking directions from a guard, she took the elevator to the tenth floor and the appropriate courtroom. An iron-haired older lady carrying a generic brown leather briefcase immediately approached her. Smiling, she held out her hand. "Jenny, I'm Helen Johnson. It's nice to finally put a face to your name and voice."

Jenny shook her hand. Slightly rounded, with a no-nonsense walk and handshake, Helen wore an expensive navy tailored suit with a colorful cloisonné frog pin—impeccable taste. Jenny got a warm and fuzzy feeling from her, grandmotherly like, and worried if she could be tough enough. She instantly felt comfortable with Helen, so hopefully that was a good sign.

"There's no need to be nervous. This is just a pretrial hearing. He is going to fix the date for the trial," Helen explained.

"He? My judge is a woman. Christina somebody-or-other."

"She was appointed to the appellate court. Apparently Judge Limber retired and recommended her. Andrew Delaney is the new judge presiding over our case."

Judge Limber? Could that be George's friend he was always bragging about? "Isn't that rather sudden? I mean, I would have thought something like that would have been executed more slowly."

Helen shrugged and settled in her seat. "I guess he had some health problems that worsened."

"I'll bet." Jenny's eyes narrowed suspiciously at George, lounging comfortably with his attorney, looking for all the world like he was a Wednesday regular here. She looked around the courtroom, intimidated by the formal surroundings. "Why are we in here? Last time we met in the judge's chambers."

Helen patted her hand. "It's all right; some judges prefer the formality of the courtroom. They're paranoid about being accused of shady dealings going on in chambers, so they have everything out in public. Or if a judge has a heavy schedule, he'll often fit these hearings in here rather than run back and forth between his chambers and court."

"All rise, Honorable Judge Andrew Delaney presiding," the bailiff called out in a bored voice. Jenny stood. Mouth dropping open, she nearly flopped back in her seat when the judge entered the room.

"That can't be the judge," she whispered. "He's my age."

Andrew Delaney had a long, smooth face—too smooth. Was he even old enough to shave? Not a hair out of place, he was impeccably groomed from what she could see beyond his black robe. He couldn't have been long out of law school. And he wasn't wearing a wedding band. Great. Just great. How could some hotshot, bachelor judge sympathize with her?

Before Helen could reply, the judge sat and fixed steady brown eyes on them. "Is there a problem, counselor?"

"No, Your Honor." Helen tugged Jenny down into her seat.

With raised eyebrows, he stared a minute longer before turning back to his open case folder. "Very well then. Bailiff read the docket, please."

"Harrison versus Turner. Are all parties present?"

"We are," the attorneys said.

The judge looked at each party. "Taking into account the unusual nature of this suit, I'd think ninety days should be long enough to get your expert witnesses and prepare."

George's attorney stood. Or one of them stood. For the first time, Jenny noticed that a chic-looking young brunette had joined George and his attorney. All of a sudden he needed two attorneys? Were they trying to intimidate her with this show of power?

The woman addressed the judge. "Excuse me, Your Honor. Due to the lack of precedents, we're going to have to rely heavily on witnesses to discover the decease's exact intent, and this will take time."

The judge consulted his calendar. "Sixteen weeks from today is April twenty-third. The final pretrial conference will be May eighth. That should give you plenty of time for depositions. If anything comes up in the interim, file a motion." He picked up the gavel and pounded it, signaling their departure.

Jenny rose, confused. "That's it? That's all there is to it?"

"That's it. Now the work comes. Since I don't have an office, do you want to go back to your house or work at mine?"

"Mine."

Jenny led the way home, immersed in uneasy feelings. A male judge? A handsome, single guy. What bad luck. She'd bet her last dollar luck had nothing to do with it. George was already playing dirty. Did Jenny's sweet-looking grandma lawyer even know how to play dirty?

At home, she put on a pot of coffee as Steve came in the back door. "Hi, Jen. Helen, how'd it go?"

Jenny looked up in surprise. "What're you doing here? It's only three."

"What's to do?" Helen shrugged. "Trial's set for May tenth." She smiled warmly and pulled Steve to her for a hearty hug. "It's good to see you, kiddo. You get handsomer and handsomer. Lawyering must agree with you."

Jenny could swear Steve blushed. "You need to put on your glasses, lady."

These two certainly were chummy. "What're you doing here?"

He smiled and sat in the chair next to Helen. "Just checking on you."

"Change your mind?" Helen asked, hopeful.

"Nope."

"You'd be a big help."

Steve reached for a chocolate chip cookie. "Sorry."

"How about doing some research on the side?"

"Nope. Sorry." He didn't sound in the least bit sorry. In fact, he sounded rather carefree, as he sat in her kitchen, munching the cookies she'd baked that morning to wear off nervous energy before the hearing.

Helen turned to Jenny. "I wanted Steve to take the case and I would second chair. Having a young, single male arguing your case would be better for you from a psychological standpoint. But he flat-out turned me down. So we'll have to make do with things the way they are."

"And I told her that I'm not experienced enough. I've only tried eight cases—and I lost one." Steve pushed back in the chair to balance on the two rear legs. "So how'd it go?"

"They switched judges on me," Jenny complained. "At the pretrial, I'd been assigned this nice lady judge, then today we found she'd gotten a promotion because an appellate judge *suddenly* decided to retire—and he recommended her as his successor. And our new judge, this Delaney guy, is some single stud barely out of law school. Annnd," she drew out, "the judge that retired is a fishing buddy of George's. Coincidence? I think not."

"So you think that George's fishing buddy rearranged his career and retirement just to help a friend and to spite you?" Steve asked.

When put that way, Jenny felt a little silly.

"Though I'll admit that you'd probably have had a better chance with a female judge." He turned to Helen. "You could file a motion for judicial recusal."

"That would just antagonize Judge Delaney. It would draw more press and word would get out that we're difficult." Helen looked pensive. "We'll do okay with Delaney."

"Probably. You'll need to offer indisputable proof of Gabe's intent. And you've got the ace right here." Steve lowered the chair and reached for another cookie. "They'd been trying to have a baby—Jenny, in fact, *had been* pregnant, at the time of Gabe's accident." He looked at her. "Right?"

Jenny nodded.

ભ ભ ભ

Great, she was their trump. Weeks later, Steve's words still haunted Jenny. Her lie was their ace. Just great. She might not have to lie. They might assume she and Gabe had planned the baby she miscarried. But if they didn't, could she lie? Convincingly?

Jenny sat on their bed, struggling to remember how that conversation by the lake had gone. Maybe if she could remember *exactly* what Gabe had said and how he'd said it, she'd convince herself that had he known about the baby, he would have wanted it and, in fact, been happy about her pregnancy, and *that* would justify the lie. Nobody knew the truth but her. The only glitch was her conscience.

Jenny leaned against the brass headboard and drew her legs up to her chest. That morning by the lake, Gabe had been so quiet and introspective she knew he'd given the decision a lot of thought. And she'd honestly thought he'd tell her no—which he initially had.

Then he'd come up with that stupid compromise that had infuriated her—which shouldn't have angered her since she was already pregnant. It was the motive beneath the compromise that upset her so. If she'd held her temper and not allowed hurt feelings to swell out of proportion, Gabe would be alive today.

He hadn't been dead set against the idea of a baby, but he'd hardly been enthusiastic. He'd specified no artificial help in getting pregnant, proving he really hadn't wanted a child. O-r... maybe he was a purist, wanting to leave it completely up to fate. In which case he would have embraced her pregnancy, knowing she'd gotten pregnant despite using protection, she thought with growing elation.

Unless he thought she'd gotten pregnant on purpose. Perhaps he specified no assisted conception because he'd been worried about multiple births. Twins or more would have been a lot to handle, she admitted. That must be why he came up with the all-natural stipulation.

She smiled and rested her chin on her knees. They'd loved each other; he would've been happy about the baby. If only she'd told him. If she'd told him, they wouldn't have argued and she wouldn't have run off and Gabe wouldn't have been killed. They'd have celebrated with a romantic dinner, instead of living a nightmare. After the shock wore off, Gabe would've been happy about the baby. She knew he would. The phone beside her rang.

"Hello?"

"Hey. What've you been up to?" Steve asked.

"Not much. Working. Went to Ann Arbor and took Alex and Ted to dinner last weekend; that was fun. Mom's coming over next week on her day off to help me go through Gabe's stuff, but other than that, not much. What about you?"

"Work. Estate and tax planning." He sounded as if it were deadly boring work. "I need a vacation."

"Poor baby. Aren't you the guy who used to complain you never had any work?"

"*Interesting* work, Jen. Interesting," he emphasized. "What'dya say we take the afternoon off tomorrow and play hooky? We could go to lunch, go bowling, a movie, window-shopping, whatever. I could use a break."

"Sounds great, but I can't tomorrow. I've got a one o'clock deadline and a doctor's appointment in the afternoon."

"Are you sick?"

"No. I'm seeing a fertility specialist to check out in vitro fertilization."

"Creating embryos?"

She heard the pause before his carefully worded question. She was expecting his pessimism, yet he cared enough to find her a lawyer and he was her friend, so she was willing to share this information with him. She pushed the covers aside and scooted down in the bed. "It may be the best way to get pregnant."

"Before you do anything, you'd better talk to Helen. Creating embryos is probably a whole different ballgame in court. The storing of sperm is different than embryos. It's a human rights argument that might really complicate your case—even jeopardize it. You don't want to do anything before you actually win in court."

"Check with Helen before even exploring pregnancy options? Are you kidding me?" When had her attorney become her guardian?

"Not if you want to win."

"Chill out, Grant. I'm just gathering information while I'm waiting."

"Okay," he said, sounding relieved. "So, how about tomorrow night? Want to catch a movie?"

"What? Tired of your own company already?" she teased. "It's only been a month."

"A little." He sounded sheepish. "It's quiet without the kids."

That she could believe. A movie at night sounded a bit like a date, but Steve was always good company and needed a distraction. Being single was lonely. It took some getting used to.

"Come on. It'll be your good deed for the week."

"Sure, why not."

"Great. Check the paper and let me know what, when, and where, and I'll pick you up."

"What do you want to see?"

"Action or comedy. Something to get my mind off things."

"'Kay. Text you tomorrow."

"'Night."

Steve dropped the phone into the cradle and pushed back in his lounge chair, exhaling loudly. "What're you doing, Grant?"

When Jenny first passed up his offer to the afternoon off, he'd pressed until she'd agreed to go out with him. Pressed too hard? Things had been good between them lately. It'd taken them four months to get beyond the awkwardness of the night they'd spent together, to form a new bond. A new silken link, thin, pure, and strong.

He was perversely tempted to get involved in Jenny's case. He was good in court but couldn't help worrying that if he helped with her case and they lost, she'd blame him. Being brutally honest with himself, he wasn't ready for a case of this magnitude and exposure. And he was too emotionally involved to do a good job. Plus he still wasn't convinced she was right. If it'd been him married to Jenny and he died, the more he thought about it, the more he was inclined to believe he wouldn't want her to have his baby.

If he died, he'd be in a better place, waiting, watching over her. He'd want Jenny to get on with her life. He'd want her to find another good man who would love and cherish her—someone she could share herself with. He'd want her to start fresh.

Jenny had a tremendous capacity to love, and he wouldn't want to see this hampered by an obsession to hang onto him by fixating on having their baby. Besides, raising a child alone was difficult. His sister did it because she had to—Ralph left her. But to choose to do it alone to memorialize your dead husband wasn't a good enough reason to put either Jenny or a baby through those long years of additional stress. It might work out just fine, but he wouldn't choose it for her. However it wasn't his decision; it was Jenny's. As much as it went against his every instinct, he had to respect her feelings.

∾ ∾ ∾

"Jenny, are you sure Ted wouldn't want any of his father's things?" Holding up a couple of silk ties, her mom left Gabe's closet. "A few ties? A sweater? The sweaters are still in very good shape."

"He said not, but let's save a few things and I'll ask him again."

Watching her mother disappear back into Gabe's closet, Jenny folded a worn flannel shirt. How could she tell her about the trial? She had to tell her soon, before Mom read about it in the paper, but she just didn't know how to bring it up. And she didn't want to ruin the truce they'd established.

Mom had been so supportive since Gabe's death. She helped when Jenny asked, but gave her lots of space. She didn't want to wreck this new friendship and was very afraid that's exactly what would happen when she told her mother she was going to have Gabe's baby.

She sat on her bed with Gabe's folded shirt in her hands while her mother made several more trips in and out of the closet. Coming out again, Mom stuffed Gabe's bathrobe in the charity box. Jenny jumped up and snatched the terry robe. "This stays."

"All right," her mother said, pacifying, but looking puzzled.

"I've kept a few of his shirts and sweatshirts too. I wear them when I'm bloated." She loved the way her favorite Gabe shirts and sweatshirts felt so soft and still smelled of him. She refused to wash them for fear they'd lose his scent. Wearing them made her feel happier and more secure.

"Anything else?"

"No." Then she smiled, sheepish. "His jacket. I love that leather jacket. Actually, it always looked better on me than him." She chuckled, embarrassed, as she hung the robe in her closet. "Listen to me. Someone would think I paid that guy to run Gabe over just so I could get his clothes."

"Jennifer Lyn, that's morbid!"

"Joking, Mom." She left the closet and sat on the end of the bed. "But there *is* something I need to tell you."

"That sounds grim."

"I should've told you a while ago. But we'd been getting along so well, I didn't want to upset you."

Mom sat next to her and patted Jenny's leg. "I've really enjoyed the peace between us too." She looked away and bit her lip. "While we're being honest, I should admit that I was wrong about your marriage." Mom took a deep breath and wiped a tear from her eye, muttering, "Boy, this is hard." She cleared her throat. "It's just that, well, I was certain that once you were happily married, you'd want to take Michael."

"Take Michael? Tell him the truth and raise him myself?" Searching her mom's face, Jenny saw the naked fear in her eyes and the truth in her expression. She'd really worried they'd take Michael from her and Dad. "That's crazy. Mom, you know that would never happen. We agreed he should never know—at least not until he's an adult."

"I know. But you were so young, and I could see how hard it was for you to give him up and still live in the same house. I just thought..." Mom sniffled and waved her hand in a never-mind gesture. "That's neither here nor there. Anyway, I'm sorry."

"O-h, Mom." Jenny gathered her close in a tight hug, made all the tighter in anticipation of her mother's negative reaction. Slowly she released her. "Hold that thought, 'cause I'm involved in some litigation that's going to get nasty and very public in a couple of months when we go to trial. I just want you and Dad to be prepared."

Her mother stiffened. "It's the estate, isn't it? Judith's contesting Gabe's will."

Jenny smiled at her fierce tone and shook her head. "No, Judith's been surprisingly good. In fact, she supports me in this. It's about our baby. I was five weeks pregnant when we went to Saugatuck... and then I miscarried."

Her mom put an arm around her shoulder. "Oh, baby, I'm so sorry."

"That weekend, I lost not only Gabe but our baby too. I felt utterly alone and cheated. But as it turns out, the doctors were able to save and freeze Gabe's sperm for me, so I can be artificially inseminated. I may have lost Gabe, but at least I can still have our baby."

"After he's dead? That's a bit unusual, isn't it? I mean, I've heard of test tube babies and cloning, but this is... different."

Relief swept through her that her mother hadn't told her she was crazy. "Yeah. It's unusual, which is why the press will be all over the trial. There've only been a handful of women in similar situations."

"It's not illegal is it?"

"No, but George is trying to say it is. He's furious that I donated Gabe's organs and he couldn't stop it. So he's taking me to court to keep me from using Gabe's sperm. He's just being spiteful."

Jenny watched Mom carefully, trying to gauge her reaction. For much of her life, or so it seemed, they'd been at odds. She should be used to disappointing her mother and doing without her encouragement, but apparently she was more of an optimist than she'd ever known, because she really wanted her mom's approval this time.

"It's really none of his business," Mom finally announced.

"What?"

"It's none of his business." Mom raised her chin defiantly. "You should go for it."

Eyes wide, Jenny stared. "Really?"

"Of course. Gabe was a wonderful man and you'll make a wonderful mother. A baby from the two of you couldn't help but be a little angel. Go for it."

"Sooo... you don't think it's weird to have Gabe's baby after he's dead?"

"Of course it's weird. But you've the means to support this child. If you're sure that's what you want, then you should do it."

"I was sure you'd think I'm crazy."

"Your father might. Men are squeamish when it comes to their testicles and such. Don't be disappointed if it takes him a while to come around."

Dad might be a problem? What a twist that'd be. Maybe she had a point with it being a squeamish thing. Judith, her mom, Amy the organ donor lady, they all got it. But George had been appalled and Steve pensive... almost confused.

"You know, you might be right. It must be a male thing. Steve's been against this from the beginning."

"Is he representing you?"

"No—he flat-out refused, but he found me an attorney." A female attorney. Hmm, interesting. "He's been sweet actually. Although he's trying, he just doesn't get it. I think you're right, Mom. It must be a testosterone thing."

"Well of course it is." She patted her hand. "Now let's finish up here and you can go home and tell your father."

"Do we have to?" she joked.

"Yes."

"Can't you tell him for me?"

"Not a chance. He was traumatized enough when I suggested he get a vasectomy." She chuckled. "Nope, this is your baby—literally."

∾ ∾ ∾

The winter months passed quickly as Jenny kept herself busy fitting her depositions and strategy meetings with Helen around work. She and Steve avoided playing any games—or when they played Euchre with Alex and a friend, they made sure to be on the same team.

Steve slowly returned to his cheerful self but declined her offer to set him up. Maybe she'd get him a subscription to Match.com for his birthday if he still wasn't dating by then. She'd heard good things about that company.

They joined a weekly tennis clinic at Steve's club, Wimbledon, to keep in shape and burn off some nervous energy. Occasionally they played tennis at the Hunt Club, but mostly they played at his club. She was thinking about dropping the Hunt Club membership—without Gabe she hardly ever used it. Jenny approached May with growing trepidation.

The week before the trial, she spent hours being coached by Helen until both felt confident she knew what to expect and could handle any questions thrown her way, no matter how slyly worded.

Friday afternoon Jenny emailed in her last assignment, turned off her laptop and blew out a deep breath. Now, onto cleaning the house and putting boxes of Gabe's old clothes onto the porch for tomorrow's Vietnam Vet pick up.

She carefully made her way downstairs with her third box when it was lifted from her arms. Jenny gasped and stumbled back, plunking down hard on the carpeted steps. "Sheez! You scared me."

"Sorry. I thought you heard me come in." Steve held out a hand and hauled her to her feet. "You want this on the front porch with the others?"

"Yeah, thanks." They retrieved another box of Gabe's clothes from the bedroom and then two boxes of medical books from his study.

"This it?"

Jenny put her hands on her hips and looked around Gabe's library. "For now. The clothes were easier to go through than his desk. It all looked important and felt so personal that I ended up not getting rid of very much."

"There's no rush."

"I guess. So what brings you here?" Jenny pivoted and headed out of the room. "I'm dying of thirst. Want a soda?"

"Sure." As they walked past the hall, Steve snatched a manila folder. "Helen wanted me to take a look at the P.I.'s report on George."

"She had George investigated?"

Steve pulled sheets from the envelope and turned them upright, as he walked. "Hmm. I'm sure George's attorney had you investigated too."

Jenny's head jerked up. "Would they find out about Michael?"

"Doubtful. They'll be looking at your finances, credit history, work history, stuff like that." Steve straddled a stool as Jenny poured their drinks.

"So why'd Helen give you the report? Shouldn't that be confidential?"

"She wanted a second opinion." Steve pinched his bottom lip between his thumb and forefinger. "This is interesting."

Chapter 19

"What's interesting?" Jenny set Steve's drink down and craned her neck sideways to read the report.

"George's charitable deductions."

"George has charitable deductions? That *is* surprising."

"Not that. Last year he donated five hundred dollars to the University of Detroit—his alma mater, a thousand to Grosse Pointe Memorial Church... there're a few other piddly donations... then two thousand to the American Heart Association—"

"His wife, Adele, died of a heart attack."

"So that makes sense," he drew out. "But what doesn't make sense is this last one Helen highlighted." He raised his head and looked at her. "He gave fifteen thousand to the Huntington's Disease Association."

"Thousand?" Jenny reached for the paper. "That must be a mistake."

Steve handed her the sheet. "No mistake. According to Helen's note, he's been donating for more than ten years and has been increasing the donation about a thousand dollars a year."

Jenny handed him the paper. "What's Huntington's Disease? Think he has it?"

"Don't know. Where's your laptop?"

Jenny retrieved her Dell and they settled shoulder-to-shoulder to read the Huntington's Disease Association website.

"It's fatal. Peak age of onset, thirty-five to fifty with death generally within ten to twenty years of the first symptom. Autosomal dominance inheritance." Jenny read. "Look at these symptoms." She pointed at the screen. "Clumsiness, forgetfulness, ticks, jerking, fidgety movements of limbs and body and slight personality changes, then later on lurching, uncontrolled movements. Eating can be tiring, frustrating and messy due to mouth and diaphragm muscles not working properly, so they choke easily."

"They're prone to infection, illness, and muscle-wasting." He pointed at the screen. "Then we get to the behavior issues. Who wouldn't be irritable, depressed and angry trying to cope with all that?"

"Sounds horrible. Like Parkinson's and Alzheimer's rolled into one." Jenny raised an eyebrow to Steve. "George doesn't have any of these symptoms."

"Then who?"

"I don't know, but Judith might." Jenny pulled out her cell phone, scrolled down her list, and pushed call. "Maybe I can catch her on her way home."

"Dr. Sterling."

"Judith, this is Jenny. Who in George's family might have had Huntington's Disease?"

"Huntington's Disease? Nobody I know of, why?"

"George gives huge amounts of money to the Huntington's Disease Association every year. He has to have a personal connection. Adele died from a heart attack, but could she have had Huntington's as well?"

"If she did, I never heard of it."

"What about George's parents?"

"Huntington's? Not that I know of." Judith paused as if thinking. "They both died before I met Gabe; I don't really know much about the family history. I'm home now; I've got to go in for dinner. Sorry I'm no help."

"No worries. Thanks." Jenny slid the phone shut. "She didn't know anything."

"So we're back to George's wife." Steve mused. "They never had children. Because she couldn't or because they didn't want to pass Huntington's on to their kids?"

"Adele died of a heart attack."

Steve raised an eyebrow. "Doesn't mean she didn't have Huntington's disease."

∽ ∽ ∽

The day of the trial dawned beautifully. Cloaked in Gabe's warm bathrobe, Jenny sipped her coffee out on the porch and watched the sun come up. Clear and soft, the orange ball crested Canada, stretching its golden rays across Lake St. Clair to touch and warm her. The beauty and purity reached right to her soul, calming her. It would be a good day.

After showering, Jenny dressed in the navy suit and white linen blouse she and Helen had picked out. She completed the outfit with sensible heels, determined to present herself as a competent, levelheaded young woman. She wove her hair into a neat French braid and lightly applied her makeup. She couldn't remember taking such care with her appearance since that first date with Gabe.

Jenny rinsed out her coffee mug and went to the bathroom to check her makeup one last time. Gathering her coat and purse, she stood in the middle of the kitchen, wondering what she was forgetting, when Steve knocked and came through the back door. Dressed in a pinstriped suit and a blue silk tie that brought out the color of his eyes, he was the picture of a handsome, successful attorney. "Ready?"

"What're you doing here?"

"Driving you to court."

"What about work?"

"I'm on vacation for the next week."

"A-n-d..." She waited for him to complete her sentence. "You're in need of entertainment?"

He reached out a hand to her, which Jenny gratefully grasped between sweaty palms, trying not to clutch it like a nervous child even though she felt like one. With a quick flick of his wrist, he checked his watch and ushered Jenny out the door to his waiting convertible.

"Not entertainment; support. My friend is going to court today and I wanted to be there to support her."

"Ahhhh," Jenny drew out. "This must be a very good friend if you're getting dressed up and wasting a whole vacation day on her."

He held open the car door and his eyes locked on hers. "She's a very special lady who's gotten a raw deal."

Jenny's chest tightened and her breath quickened. "Lucky lady."

"Lucky me."

Mindful of her carefully styled hair, he put the Mustang's top up. Going home they could enjoy the freedom of the breeze, but he didn't want her arriving at court all disheveled.

Steve held the courthouse door open for Jenny and ushered her inside. Dozens of people stood around the room, talking in small groups, creating a low buzz. Some intently leafed through documents as if cramming before a final exam while others sat around waiting. Jenny located Alex and Ted up front, sitting behind Helen, separated from her by a half-wall. Helen was seated at a thick wooden table. Her worn leather briefcase rested on the floor next to her chair. She leaned on the wall, talking to Alex, probably reassuring the girl.

Dressed in her favorite black pants and cherry-red cashmere sweater, Alex swiveled her head around, scanning the room. Relief eased her taut face as Jenny approached. She moved over to make room for them, and her sterling bangles knocked loudly on the wood railing. Alex smiled brightly.

Alex scooted close, whispering, "Jenny, Mom's supposed to be here this morning. They subpoenaed her too, but she had an emergency."

Helen smiled and patted Alex's hand. "Don't worry. They'll work around her." She turned to Jenny. "You'll need to sit up here when we start."

Alex leaned close until their heads almost touched. "Are you nervous?"

"Scared to death," Jenny whispered back.

"This is so freakin' weird," Ted muttered. He sat with hands clasped between bouncing knees, looking around the room through wide eyes under arched eyebrows.

"Oh look, there's Grams and Pops," Alex said.

Gabe's children had taken to Jenny's parents, immediately dubbing them Grams and Pops. With Gabe's parents and his Aunt Adele deceased, Alex and Ted had never really known grandparents besides Judith's parents. So when they'd married, even though the kids were teenagers, they latched onto Jenny's mom and dad, and her parents had been delighted with their new step-grandchildren. Her mom might not have been thrilled about their marriage, but she'd been thrilled to be a grandparent. It'd been love at first sight.

Jenny stood to greet her parents while Steve took her place chatting with Ted and Alex. It was strange seeing her parents in court in their Sunday church clothes. Her mother kept fingering her purse strap.

"Mom, don't worry. It'll be okay."

"I hate this," she muttered through tense lips.

She looked so miserable that Jenny felt compelled to put aside her own anxiety and reassure her agitated mother. "It's okay. Just answer the questions as best you can."

"But it'll sound so..." she struggled to find a tactful way to verbalize the truth. "I feel so helpless."

"I know. But I *did* make mistakes. I was immature and made some poor decisions; there's no getting around it. Don't worry, it'll be okay."

Her mother nodded abruptly, but didn't look very reassured as she took the seat next to Alex. Her dad smiled and squeezed Jenny's shoulder before sitting beside them. At a gesture from Helen, Jenny excused herself and walked uncertainly toward the long table where Helen sat.

After lowering herself onto the cold, hard chair, she looked up in surprise when Steve took the seat on her other side. She returned his smile, feeling more secure flanked by friends. Did he get to sit with them because he was an attorney?

The bailiff called, "All rise, the honorable Judge Delaney presiding."

Judge Andrew Delaney swept into the room, moving to the bench in lithe, unhurried strides. He still looked as young as Jenny remembered. She glanced at the empty seats where the jury would sit—except there was no jury in this case. Her fate completely rested on the wisdom and sympathy of this young stud.

What'd he know about life and the law? What'd he know about being fair? She searched his unlined face, sure he'd never felt tragedy. How would he know what it was like to lose your whole life? He didn't even have a hair out of place.

Totally composed, he sat and scanned the room like a king surveying his subjects. "You may be seated. Bailiff?"

"Turner vs. Harrison, case number CJ99-1214."

"Are the parties present?"

Helen and George's attorney rose, and Jenny was shocked to hear Steve's deep baritone chime in, "We are, Your Honor."

She stared at Steve in astonishment, but he'd already reseated himself and was concentrating on the judge. What was Steve doing? He wasn't a part of this. He didn't approve of her having Gabe's baby and didn't want to his name linked to her controversial case, yet he'd just publicly declared his allegiance to her. What was going on?

She turned to ask Helen, but the older woman was busy sketching on her legal pad, drawing a... Jenny leaned closer. A long, skinny flower of some sort. With sure quick strokes, she quickly penciled in something else over it. Another flower?

As George's lady attorney stood, preparing for her opening argument, Jenny sat totally perplexed. What was going on here? Suddenly she had two attorneys, and one was so unconcerned about the whole proceedings she was doodling all over her legal pad, drawing flowers and... Jenny tilted her head to better see. A bird? A humming bird hovered over the flower. What kind of a lawyer drew nature pictures in court, instead of listening sharply, planning cutting witty arguments to make the plaintiff look silly?

And her other attorney wasn't even supposed to be there. What was going on? Confused, Jenny wanted to call a timeout, but nobody else seemed to have a problem with the way things were proceeding. When and how had she stepped through the looking glass into this topsy-turvy world?

Jenny fished her own pen out of her purse. Hesitating a second, she worried about ruining Helen's drawing before deciding that she was paying Helen to lawyer, not draw. She reached over to write on Helen's pad in quick tense print. *Since when is Steve on our team?*

Helen barely paused in her shading to answer in flowing loopy script: *since we filed an appearance of additional counsel.*

Why?

Wanted to, she wrote back before sketching a long flowing stem.

He wanted to? *Well that was insightful,* Jenny thought. She wanted to pursue it further, but needed to pay attention to the opposing counsel's opening statement—someone had to. She cast a worried frown at Helen, who was busy adding another hummingbird to her picture.

Ms. Blair, a statuesque lady wearing the standard navy suit and pumps, had coiled her burnished light brown hair into a long, tight twist held together with a gold clip. She wore a two-toned watch and gold hoops in her ears. Her facial features were unremarkable, neither too long nor short, nor too heavy or scant, just ordinary. But as she began to speak, Jenny was mesmerized by the soothing deep timbre of her voice. Her voice was anything but ordinary.

"Your Honor, the deceased, Gabe Harrison, was orphaned when only twelve years old. At that time, he went to live with his mother's brother, George Turner, as stipulated in her will. Gabe's uncle and aunt had not been blessed with children of their own and welcomed their nephew into their family, showering him with love.

George's wife died unexpectedly when Gabe was only a teenager. Despite the inherent difficulties of single parenthood, Gabe and his uncle grew even closer. The reason I've explained all this history is to prove that George Turner, the man who raised Gabe Harrison during his formative years, is the *one* person who knew and understood the deceased best.

"It is our belief, and we will prove, that Jenny Harrison is an immature woman incapable of raising a child on her own. We will prove that Gabe Harrison would not have wanted more children and furthermore, he'd certainly never want his child to be raised by a single parent. We contend that in coercing a urologist to recover her husband's sperm, Jennifer Harrison violated her husband's rights of procreational choice and committed an unconstitutional invasion of his privacy.

"Furthermore, we will prove that Mrs. Harrison's desire to have her dead husband's baby is motivated by greed. In addition, we will demonstrate that creating a child and raising it under these less than ideal circumstances is not in the best interest of the potential child. Nobody but Jennifer Harrison would benefit by this course of action, and if allowed, it's possible that a great many people could be damaged by it—not just this family, but all those in the future who would be affected by such an ill-advised precedent."

She gathered her notes and, without a glance their way, sat down and folded her hands in front of her.

Ms. Blair was so fervent in her statements that when she ended, Jenny had the impulse to yell "Amen" and clap. Instead, she wrapped her arms across her knotted stomach. Surprisingly, on cue, Helen dropped her pen and replaced Stephanie Blair at the podium—without any written notes, which worried Jenny.

For the first time since the judge walked into the room, her attorney looked aware of her surroundings and proceedings. Worried about what Helen might say, Jenny didn't know whether to be heartened or dismayed.

Helen pushed back her jacket to bury her hands deep in her skirt pockets. She took a deep breath, looked at the plaintiff through wide eyes and raised eyebrows one long minute before turning to the judge.

"Wow," she said. "How dramatic. Ms. Blair would have us believe that the fate of thousands of unborn children lay on the outcome of this trial. I think the plaintiff is reading far too much into the circumstances. The situation here is really very simple, Your Honor.

"The facts will show that Jenny and Gabe Harrison had a wonderful, loving marriage. By all accounts, they adored each other. This is an indisputable fact," she said, letting it sink in. She strode out from behind the podium. "They went away one weekend last October to celebrate their second wedding anniversary and Jenny's pregnancy, when Gabe was suddenly tragically killed in a bicycling accident." She raised her eyebrows, her glance sweeping over both the plaintiff and the judge. "An accident that might have killed Jenny too if not for her husband's quick response in pushing her out of the way of the oncoming vehicle. And then Jenny suffered a miscarriage.

"As I said before, this situation is quite simple. It's not fraught with Shakespearean subterfuge or deep dark secrets. When Gabe Harrison was suddenly killed, his wife was denied not only her husband, but also the child they'd created. A terrible double loss. All we're asking is that she be allowed to recoup a little of what she lost that heartbreaking weekend.

"We will prove, beyond a shadow of a doubt, that Jennifer Harrison will make a model parent, given the chance. And although they knew each other only three years, the unique and intimate bond that Gabe and Jenny shared transcends time. As Dr. Harrison's devoted wife, Jenny is the perfect person to know her husband's will. She's the *only* person to judge his intent in this situation.

"Mrs. Harrison's desire to have her husband's child is perfectly normal and natural. And yet, we're here today because of the machinations of a jealous, bitter man who is bent on keeping others from gaining solace during this difficult time of grief."

Pausing, Helen's face tightened with the long, hard look she gave George. "We will prove that George Turner is a man so steeped in his own rage and grief that he'll do anything to prevent Jenny Harrison from conceiving his nephew's child. Mr. Turner was furious that Mrs. Harrison honored her husband's wishes and donated his organs despite Mr. Turner's objections, so he's trying to punish her.

"It's sad." She sighed. "But it's as simple as that. There are no devious plots here, Your Honor. Jenny Harrison doesn't want a thing from anybody, except the opportunity to create and love her and her husband's child." Helen finished and returned to her seat.

Not bad, Jenny thought. Helen's logical, passionate appeal appeased her, renewing her confidence in her attorney.

"The plaintiff may call his first witness," the judge said.

Ms. Blair stood. "The plaintiff calls Mary Campbell to the stand."

The bailiff swore her mother in. Mom sat in the witness box; nervously fingering the pearls Dad gave her for their thirtieth anniversary. She looked quite matronly in her black dress and lacy white blouse. She squared her shoulders as if suddenly aware she was the center of attention or as if preparing for an unpleasant combative task.

Ms. Blair smiled sweetly. "Good morning, Mrs. Campbell."

Jenny's mom watched her warily, as if looking for a double meaning in the greeting. "Good morning."

Ms. Blair quickly led her mother through several basic background questions. Then, "Mrs. Campbell, how would you describe your relationship with your daughter?"

"We're close."

"Have you always been close?"

She shifted in her seat. "Not always. No, but then most parents have difficulties with their children at one time or another."

Ms. Blair raised an eyebrow. "And when were these difficult years?"

"Mostly during her teenage years."

"Mostly? Isn't it true that you opposed your daughter's marriage?"

"Yes."

"Why was that?"

"Because I was bothered by the age difference between her and Gabe."

"And?"

"And what? I was wrong. Jen—"

Ms Blaire took a few steps toward the witness box. "Isn't it true that you thought your daughter was too immature for marriage to anybody?"

"I—"

"Didn't you make a comment similar to that?"

"I don't remember. I may have," her mother mumbled.

"Yes or no?"

"Yes."

"Yes." Ms. Blair backed away, satisfied. "So you weren't happy about the proposed marriage between Dr. Harrison and your daughter?"

"Not at the time."

"If the thought of your daughter marrying a much older man with grown children of his own bothered you, it stands to reason that you might have been concerned about their having children. Were you concerned about any possible children that would come of the union?"

A worried look flickered across her mother's face as she shifted in her seat. "Maybe. I guess so."

"And what did your daughter say in response to these concerns?"

They'd gone back and forth about this question, but there was no way around it. Her mother's gaze sought hers, silently apologizing. "Jenny and I were angry with each other and not getting along at that point."

"What did your daughter say?" Ms. Blair pressed.

Her mother sighed. "She said that she didn't intend to have children."

"She didn't intend to have *any* children?" Ms. Blair sounded shocked.

"Yes. But Gabe—"

"She didn't want to have Dr. Harrison's child?"

"Not then, but she changed her mind, obviously since she—"

"After he died. Yes, we know. That's why we're here today."

"No, before," her mother protested. "Don't forget the miscarriage. She'd been pregnant."

"Ahh—the miscarriage. At five weeks," she said, as if five weeks wasn't actually pregnant. But she'd seen the ER report during discovery. She knew Jenny hadn't made it up. "Did your daughter confide in you that she and Dr. Harrison were trying to start a family?"

Her mom shook her head. "No."

"No? As close as you two are?" Ms. Blair feigned surprise, then tilted her head to the side, as if curious. "When *did* your daughter give you the happy news that she was expecting?"

"When?"

"Yes, when did Jenny tell you she was pregnant?"

"Gosh, I don't know exactly," Mom stalled.

"An approximation will do."

Her mother frowned. "I guess it was when I helped Jenny sort Gabe's things."

"And when was that?"

What did it matter? Jenny wondered.

"After the holidays."

"January? February? March?" She raised her eyebrows, as if shocked. "Four months after Dr. Harrison died?"

"I guess."

"Four months after your son-in-law's death is the first you learned of your daughter's pregnancy. Then it stands to reason that you didn't know about the miscarriage until then either, correct?"

Jenny saw where Ms. Blair was leading them. Good God, did she have to drag it out?

Mom paused, as if realizing she'd been trapped. Her finger and thumb rubbed the pearls harder. "Yes."

"Your daughter suffered the traumatizing loss of her baby, yet didn't tell her own mother about it until months later? Don't you find it a bit strange that she wouldn't have mentioned it sooner?"

"No. Not strange at all." Her mom raised her chin, trying to protect Jenny. "Jenny was grieving for both her husband and baby. Grief's a very private thing. We all express it differently."

Ms. Blair moved on. "Mrs. Campbell, your son was rather seriously hurt in a skateboarding accident spring of 2011. Isn't it true that you held your daughter responsible for the accident?"

She nodded. "Yes."

"Why?"

"Because I'd forbidden Michael to get a skateboard."

"Why'd you forbid your son from having a skateboard?"

"They're dangerous."

"So, why'd you blame Jenny for your son's accident?"

"She bought Michael the board—along with a helmet and pads," her mother added quickly before the attorney could interrupt her again.

"So, knowing that you had forbidden your son to own, or ride, a skateboard, *because it was dangerous*," she stressed, "Jenny ignored your wishes? She ignored the potential danger to her minor brother and gave him a skateboard?"

"Yes."

"What exactly were your son's injuries as a direct result of his skateboard accident."

Her mother licked her lips. "He had a concussion, a broken wrist, and a ruptured spleen,"

"Along with an assorted variety of bumps and contusions," Ms. Blair looked at her. "Correct?"

"Yes."

"And your son required surgery and a protracted stay in the hospital due to his injuries. Isn't that true?"

"Yes." She nodded.

"Isn't it true that you were so enraged by your daughter's immaturity and defiance, her reckless endangerment of your son, that you banned her from his bedside?"

Jenny was comforted by the regret covering her mother's face. "No. Jenny stayed with her brother at night so I could get some rest."

"Did you worry about your son's safety while she was with him?"

"In the hospital?" Her mother looked confused. "No."

Helen stood, "I object. This whole incident is collateral and of marginal relevance. Your Honor, at this point counsel is attempting to elicit opinion testimony."

"I agree." The judge turned to Ms. Blair, giving her a censorious look. "Move on, counselor. You've made your point."

"No more questions."

Helen rose and walked toward Jenny's mother. "Mrs. Campbell, when Ms. Blair asked you why you opposed Jenny's marriage, you were going to add something when she interrupted you. What did you want to add?"

"I was wrong. Because Jenny was fifteen years younger than Gabe and because he was a sophisticated doctor with teenagers from a previous marriage, I thought Jenny couldn't handle marriage to him and being a stepmother." Her eyes met Jenny's, with an expression both warm and full of pride. "But I was wrong. Jenny's become great friends with Gabe's children, and she and Gabe had a wonderful marriage," she paused to glare at the plaintiff, "despite the trouble George Turner tried to cause. I was the wrong one, not Jenny."

"And when she asked you about Jenny's intentions to have children, you were going to add..."

"At that time, Jenny was upset and angry with me. She said things she didn't mean."

"Objection," Ms. Blair inserted. "The witness can't possibly judge if her daughter meant what she said or not."

"Objection sustained." The judge bent to her mother. "Mrs. Campbell, you may testify only to the facts of what was said."

Helen looked at Jenny's mother. "What was Gabe's reaction to Jenny's rash proclamation that she didn't want children?"

"He said that Jenny might not want children right then, *but*," she paused to make sure she had everybody's attention, "if they should change their minds, they'd be fine. Then he reassured us of how much he loved Jenny and that he'd take care of her and do his best to make her happy," she finished, sniffling and blinking back tears.

"And did he make her happy?"

"Objection, calls for opinion."

"I'll rephrase. Mrs. Campbell, did you ever witness a fight or disagreement between your daughter and son-in-law?"

"No."

"Did Jenny or Gabe ever tell you that they'd had a disagreement?"

She lifted her chin, as if proud of their solid marriage. "*Never.* Gabe was crazy about Jenny. In fact, he was quite protective of her. While we were having our difficulties, he *always* supported her in everything."

"No more questions."

Jenny's mom left the witness box and sat between her father and Alex. Alex put an arm around Mom's shoulders and squeezed in support. Jenny smiled encouragingly at her. Having her mess with

Michael rehashed in public was a little embarrassing, but Jenny'd come to terms with her mistake long ago. Having to say anything that might hurt her chances in the trial visibly upset her mother, and Jenny's heart went out to her.

Chapter 20

Alex looked relaxed and defiant as she raised her chin at Ms. Blair's first question. Jenny hoped that Alex's natural chattiness wouldn't land her in trouble, like the time at the hospital when she'd tried to console George and let slip that Gabe would have wanted her to have his baby. Helen had spent hours preparing Alex for this testimony, but under stress and in her desire to help, Alex could easily say the wrong thing.

"Ms. Harrison, were you sixteen when your father married the then twenty-six-year-old defendant?"

"Almost seventeen," Alex corrected.

"Is Jenny a good stepmother?"

"That depends upon what you mean by good. She's more of a friend than a stepmom."

"What do you mean?"

"At first I thought it was kind of weird—their getting married. I mean, my friends used to joke about my dad being hot, but he's so old and Jenny's so pretty and so much younger. I just didn't get it."

"You weren't embarrassed or humiliated by her?"

She held her breath, hoping Alex wouldn't bring up her jealousy at her graduation party when the guy Alex had a crush on asked Jenny to dance.

"No." Alex frowned, puzzled. "Why would I be?"

Ms. Blair gave Alex a sharp look, but ignored the impertinent question. Briefly referring to her notes, she approached Alex and began speaking tentatively as if choosing her words carefully. "It sounds like your relationship was a combination friend/stepmom...

did you ever see, or hear, Jenny do, or say, anything that caused you to wonder about her capabilities as a stepmother?"

"Objection, opinion," Helen spouted.

"It does call for opinion testimony," Judge Delaney agreed. "But in this case, because I'm called upon to assess the defendant's capabilities as a mother, I'll allow some latitude." He turned to Alex. "Please answer the question."

Alex's head swiveled between the attorney and the judge as she followed the exchange. "No. Jenny never acted strangely or inappropriately."

"Did she ever discipline you?"

"She never grounded me, if that's what you're getting at."

"What about signing permission slips for school or giving you permission for things requiring a parent's signature?"

"No. My mom, stepdad, or dad always did that stuff."

"Take you to the doctor's, dentist or orthodontist?"

Alex raised an eyebrow and gave the attorney a superior, you're-stupid look. She'd had her driver's license the whole of their marriage—which she apparently thought that Ms. Blair should have known, if she'd done her homework. "I drove myself."

She walked closer. "Did you share confidences? Did she ever offer you advice?"

Alex's smile waned, seemingly along with her confidence, to be replaced by an almost palpable wariness. "Yeah."

The attorney, sensing she was onto something at last, calmed. She stopped pacing and watched Alex closely. A predatory gleam narrowed her eyes. "What advice did she give you?"

"To put my mom, dad, stepdad, and Jenny's cell numbers at the top of my speed dial list—for emergencies."

Ms. Blair's jaw clenched. "Anything else?" she snapped. "If you and Jenny were friends, surely you must have talked about boys? Dating?"

Alex's mouth tightened. She looked to Helen in a silent plea, not wanting to answer the question. Helen gave her an encouraging nod.

"Just once. When I wanted to go on this camping trip my junior year."

"What did you talk about?"

"My mom didn't want me to go because she hated my boyfriend, so I went to Dad for permission."

"Was the fact that your mom didn't like your boyfriend the only reason she didn't want you to go?"

"Objection." Helen stood. "Your Honor, I don't see the relevancy here."

"Mrs. Harrison's relationship with her stepdaughter bears on how well she'd raise her own child," Ms. Blair claimed.

"Be brief, counselor. I'm tiring of this line of questioning. Objection overruled," he declared.

"Ms. Harrison. What were your mother's other objections to your proposed camping trip?"

Alex shifted in her seat and avoided the attorney's gaze. "She was worried we'd spend the weekend having sex."

Ms. Blair's expression lightened, looking interested. "And did you tell your stepmother this?"

"Yes."

"And what was her response?"

Alex glanced at her. Jenny smiled encouragingly.

"She asked me if I was sexually active."

"And?"

And what? Was she asking Alex if she was indeed sexually active? Jenny looked at Helen, amazed she wasn't protesting. In fact, she could have sworn she even saw Helen wink at Alex. What was she thinking? This was no game; this was her life.

Alex smiled at Jenny, a familiar impudent grin. "I asked her if she'd had sex with my dad before they married."

Ms. Blair raised her eyebrows, following Alex's gaze to Jenny. "What was her response?"

Uncomfortable with the turn the questioning had taken, Jenny wanted to squirm, but with everybody watching her, she refused to give them the satisfaction. Her and Gabe's sex life was none of their business.

Alex smirked at the attorney. "Basically she told me it was none of my business. She said if I was smart, I'd get on the pill and use a condom so I wouldn't end up pregnant."

"So she told you it was okay for you, a high school junior, to have sex?"

"No. She told me *if I chose* to do it, to use birth control because a baby would wreck my life."

"Having a baby would wreck a woman's life?"

"No," Alex glowered at the attorney who seemed bent on misinterpreting her words. "*My* having an *unplanned* baby at *my* age and place in life would wreck *my* life."

Seeing that she couldn't trick Alex into saying anything else incriminating, Ms. Blair changed her line of questioning. "Ms. Harrison, did you ever hear your father or stepmother mention that they were trying to conceive a baby? Before your father's accident," she amended.

Alex shook her head. "No."

"Did you know Jenny was pregnant before she miscarried?"

"No."

"Did they ever talk about starting their own family?"

"No."

"Did you ever hear your stepmother say she *didn't* want to have children?"

"Never."

"Did you ever hear her say that she *did* want to have children?"

"No," Alex conceded.

"Have you ever seen your stepmother with young children?"

"Yes." Alex smile in triumph, pleased with the opportunity to say something good about Jenny. "She babysat my friend's baby."

"And how did she behave with the child?"

Alex frowned. "Fine."

"Did she seem to know what to do?"

Alex gave her another impatient look. "Well, she didn't drop him."

"Was she awkward with the baby?"

"Not at all. Jenny was a natural with him."

"No more questions."

Jenny shifted in her chair, wishing Alex hadn't stretched the truth so much. She hadn't been totally comfortable with baby Adam. She hadn't been inept, just a little nervous.

Helen looked up from her drawing and rolled the pen between her hands. "Alex, did you ever hear you father and stepmother seriously argue?" she asked, matter-of-factly.

"No. They were great together."

"No more questions."

The judge dismissed Alex.

Ted's testimony was understandably brief since he'd started college the year Jenny and Gabe had married. Jenny hadn't had nearly the contact with him that she'd had with Alex. In fact, Jenny wondered why the plaintiff even had him testify at all. The judge looked bored and eagerly dismissed Ted when Helen finished her cross.

"We'll break for lunch now. Court will resume at one o'clock." The judge pounded the gavel and they all rose as he left the room in a swirl of black robes.

Jenny grabbed Steve's sleeve, excused them and pulled him to the side at the front of the room. "What're you doing? How come you're listed as my attorney?"

He had to bend his head close to hear her clipped whispers. Steve straightened, looking over her head thoughtfully. "It's good strategy."

"But you still don't agree that I should have the baby?"

He slowly shook his head. "No."

She folded her arms across her chest. "Why didn't you tell me?"

"You'd find out soon enough."

"I had a right to know."

"Now you know."

"But why? I don't understand."

He looked away, reluctant to explain. "It's just better this way."

"What if we lose? You said this is a tough case. We could lose. You hate to lose."

He shrugged. "I'll live."

"Your boss won't like your name linked to this case."

"The firm's not listed, just me."

"But this could cost you your job," Jenny insisted. "The reputation you've worked so hard for."

"Don't worry about it." He took her arm and tried to turn her. "Let's get some lunch."

It just didn't make sense. Jenny stood firm, pursing her lips stubbornly. "Why'd you do it?"

Steve sighed, looking annoyed. He abruptly sat against the table so that they were at the same eyelevel. Pulling her close until their faces were mere inches away, Steve raised his eyebrows and spoke slowly. "If I'm listed as your counsel, the plaintiff cannot subpoena me to testify against you."

He watched her carefully as if waiting for her to get some secret meaning.

She frowned. "Why would *you* testify?"

He stood and turned so that his body blocked the curious press milling around them. "Jenny, we've been friends for years. I live next door and would have heard any arguments you two may have had. It's natural that they would question me about your relationship. And once I was under oath, they'd be able to ask me all kinds of questions I don't want to answer." He raised his eyebrows and stared at her hard. "Understand?"

Jenny's hand covered her mouth as comprehension set in. Under oath they could ask Steve about his relationship with her and he'd be forced to tell the truth.

"Oh my God. If they found out about that night I spent with you—even though we really didn't—" she whispered, feeling faint.

"Not to mention the times you confided in me that you *didn't* want to have children. *And why.*" Steve murmured and gave her another meaningful look.

Oh, boy. Under oath, he might have been forced to reveal her family's secret. She'd lose her case for sure if they knew about Michael. And she didn't even want to contemplate the damage to her brother—especially should he learn the truth under those circumstances. She felt Steve's attention as the full horrifying force of his implications hit her.

"But that *can't* happen," Steve said, gently. "I'm your counsel and they can't ask me to testify against you."

Tears filled her eyes at the magnitude of his sacrifice. Steve was risking his job and his reputation on a case he didn't even believe in, just to protect her. "I don't know what to say. Thank you is so inadequate."

"There's nothing to say. Everything's fine." Steve leaned over and took the tissue Helen held out to him and handed it to her. "Alex and your mom did great. Now paste a happy smile on your face and let's go to lunch."

"I don't think I can eat," she mumbled.

"You can and you will." With a hand firmly at her back, Steve moved her to the waiting family.

After lunch, Jenny's parents stayed for support. Alex and Ted, having just finished final exams and the move back home, had to unpack and get to their summer jobs, so they left and Judith replaced them. Sliding into the seat next to her parents, Judith quizzed them about the morning's testimony.

The judge returned and called the court to order. The plaintiff called the paramedic to detail Gabe's injuries and testify that he'd never regained consciousness. Then she asked the young emergency room resident similar questions before calling Dr. Collins, the neurologist, to the stand.

Ms. Blair asked the neurologist the same questions as the previous two witnesses before asking about Gabe's treatment. "So

Dr. Collins, could you please explain to the court exactly what constitutes brain death in the state of Michigan."

Resting her elbows on the arms of her chair, she lightly laced her fingers and crossed her legs, as if totally at ease in the courtroom. "According to the State of Michigan Determination of Death Law, a person is considered dead if two physicians declare that, based on ordinary standards of medical practice, there is an irreversible cessation of the spontaneous respiratory and circulatory functions."

"What ordinary standards of medical practice are used to determine this?"

"The patient must be in a deep coma without any response to internal or external stimuli. Respiratory movements and spontaneous limb movements must be absent. We then confirm the clinical assessment with two EEGs to verify the loss of cerebral cortical function," she recounted the procedure in a professional, unemotional voice.

"When did Dr. Harrison meet these criteria?"

"We performed the first EEG in the ER and then we did a second one approximately eight hours later. At Mrs. Harrison's request, we did a third one twelve hours later, with exactly the same results. On Dr. Harrison, we also did a formal four-vessel cerebral angiography to confirm complete cessation of circulation to his brain."

"And then?"

"Then Mrs. Harrison asked Dr. Stanley, St. Francis's head of neurology, to consult. His exam substantiated our findings that Dr. Harrison's condition was irreversible. At that time, Dr. Harrison was declared legally dead. He was left on the ventilator until Mrs. Harrison could be approached about donating his organs."

"You stated that Dr. Harrison never regained consciousness, therefore he was unable to consent or object, to the recovery of his sperm, correct?"

"Obviously that's right."

"And Dr. Collins, this might sound obvious, but when Dr. Harrison is brain dead, he is completely at another's mercy, correct?"

"Of course."

"He was incapable of making any decision, incapable of protecting himself. He was completely helpless. Correct?"

"As helpless as a dead person can be," she agreed equitably, obviously considering the attorney's repeated questions silly. "His body, his organs, were only kept functioning because we were notified that he was a potential organ donor."

"But in his condition, he was utterly helpless. Correct?"

Helen's head came up and her hand stilled over the drawing. She turned her attention to the proceedings. "Judge, asked and answered."

"Point made, counselor. Move on," the judge instructed.

"In your fifteen years in practice, approximately how many people have you declared brain dead?"

Dr. Collins looked almost bored, as if she thought this whole procedure a waste of her time. "I can't be sure. Maybe twenty-five to fifty."

"And of those twenty-five to fifty, how many spouses have requested the deceased's sperm or ova be recovered?"

"One."

"For Dr. Harrison?"

"Yes."

"So would you say that this was a highly unusual request?"

"Yes, but—"

"The constitution guarantees everyone the right of procreational choice and the right to privacy. Don't you consider taking Dr. Harrison's sperm, in his condition, an invasion of his privacy?"

"Objection. You can't invade the privacy of a dead person," Helen observed.

"But if that person is still breathing and his bodily organs are functioning, he's not dead in the true meaning of the word," the attorney pointed out.

"Your witness just testified that he was dead. Dead is dead," Helen argued.

"*Brain* dead. She testified that he was brain dead, not dead."

Helen slapped down her pen, reached in her briefcase and withdrew a beat-up old red and blue paperback dictionary. "Webster defines 'dead' as no longer living, without life, lacking feeling, emotion, or sensitivity, being unresponsive, not having the capacity to live, devoid of human activity and no longer productive." She slammed the dictionary closed. "I'd say Dr. Harrison met most of the criteria for being dead. So nobody could have invaded his rights because dead people have no rights."

"Enough." Judge Delaney glared at both attorneys before centering his attention on Helen. "Ms. Johnson, you are not the witness; stop testifying. I will not tolerate any bickering in my court. You are both to address *me* only. Now, this argument goes to the ultimate issue in the case and I'd like to hear what the witness has to say. Objection overruled."

Ms. Blair turned back to the doctor. "Wouldn't you say recovering his sperm was an invasion of his privacy?"

"No more so than recovering his other organs." Spoken like a true scientist.

"No more questions," Ms. Blair said.

Helen passed up her opportunity to cross-examine the witness, having nothing to refute. Gabe had been at their mercy, and if a dead person still has rights, then it could be argued that his had been violated.

They took a break, and when they came back, Ms. Blair put Dr. Steinmetz, the urologist, on the stand. She questioned him about his professional qualifications: what medical school he attended, where he did his residency and fellowship, about his professional achievements, and current practice.

"Dr. Steinmetz, please tell the court how you became involved in Dr. Harrison's case."

"Amy Bromley, the coordinator from Save a Life, the organ donation organization, approached me and asked me to review Dr. Harrison's case and see if I'd be willing to help Mrs. Harrison."

"And what did you find?"

"Dr. Harrison had suffered extensive brain damage. After I reviewed his chart and x-rays, read Dr. Stanley's note, and talked with Dr. Collins, it was clear that he was brain dead."

"And then what did you do?"

"I spoke with Mrs. Harrison regarding her request that her husband's sperm be recovered. I listened to her reasons and told her what I could do for her."

"Which was what?"

"With several different procedures, I could probably recover enough sperm for, maybe, three attempts at insemination."

"And then?"

"After she signed the addendum to the organ recovery, I took the sperm, froze it, and sent it to the sperm lab."

"You operated on a patient without his explicit knowledge or consent?"

He blinked, then stared at Ms. Blair through sparkling round wire-rimmed glasses. "Dr. Harrison was declared brain dead. As next of kin, his wife signed the consent."

"But that was not your patient's consent. Not the donor's consent. You operated on Dr. Harrison without his direct consent?"

Dr. Steinmetz shrugged. "If you want to look at it that way, I guess so. But then, the all the doctors on the transplant team took his organs too—without the legally-declared-dead patient's explicit knowledge and consent."

Ms. Blair ignored his sarcastic answer. "The Human Fertilisation and Embryology Act 1990 strictly prohibits the preservation of sperm without the decedent's prior written consent. Did it ever occur to you that removing Dr. Harrison's sperm without his consent was a gross breach of ethics and an invasion of his privacy?"

"Objection," Helen stood. "First, Dr. Steinmetz is not on trial here. Second, in the United States, there is no law forbidding postmortem sperm retrieval. The Human Fertilisation and Embryology Act is a law in the United Kingdom and has absolutely no bearing upon these events."

"Objection sustained."

"Excuse me, I'd like to answer the question," Dr. Steinmetz said.

The judge turned to the witness. "The objection has been sustained, you may not answer." He glared at Ms. Blair. "Counselor, approach the bench."

Jenny couldn't hear what the judge whispered to Ms. Blair, but judging by the stern look on his face and the color flooding hers, she was getting quite the dressing-down. Helen and Steve exchanged knowing looks.

What'd she do wrong? Jenny scribbled on Helen's legal pad.

Attempted to mislead the court. Very unethical. She smiled broadly. *Apparently Delany doesn't appreciate her trying to make him look like a fool.*

Ms. Blair returned to the stand and studied her notes for a minute, taking time to recover her composure before continuing her questioning. "Dr. Steinmetz could you explain to the court exactly how you extracted Dr. Harrison's sperm?"

"Objection," Helen said. "It's irrelevant. The sperm already exists and is frozen. The issue now is my client's right to it."

"Goes to prove the procedures were a clear invasion of the deceased's privacy."

"Overruled. The witness is instructed to answer the question."

Dr. Steinmetz shifted in his seat. "Given that the deceased's physiological processes were still intact, I used electroejaculation to extract the sperm, which was then cryopreserved in a one to one dilution of TES and Tris-yolk buffer with six percent glycerol."

"What exactly does electroejaculation entail?"

"To obtain sperm, a probe is inserted into the rectum and delivers electricity through the rectal wall, inducing seminal emission."

"So you stuck a probe up Dr. Harrison's anus and repeatedly shocked him until he ejaculated?" Ms. Blair asked, sounding outraged.

"Essentially, yes," he admitted matter-of-factly.

"Electroejaculation sounds like a barbaric invasive procedure."

"Not at all. It's a means to simulate a natural ejaculation. Besides, Dr. Harrison didn't feel anything; he was dead. It's certainly no more barbaric than organ removal."

Ms. Blair crossed her arms and stared at the witness quizzically. "Dr. Steinmetz, did you have any moral qualms about this case?"

He met her gaze, with an open, honest look. "No."

"Did you know that five Michigan sperm banks refused to take Dr. Harrison's sperm because it was recovered without his consent?"

Dr. Steinmetz went utterly still before softly admitting, "No, I did not."

Jenny's heart dropped. Damn, Judith and her sage advice. *She should have been honest with him*, Jenny thought. But if he'd refused to help, they would have been even worse off than they were right now. It'd been a gamble.

"You were *not* informed of this difficulty before performing the procedure?" Ms. Blair clarified.

Dr. Steinmetz gave her a steady, unreadable look. "No."

"Don't you consider it unethical of Mrs. Harrison and Amy Bromley not to have informed you of the difficulty they were encountering finding a sperm bank willing to take Dr. Harrison's sperm?"

He bridged his fingers and raised an eyebrow. "Unethical? Perhaps."

"Yes or no?"

"Yes."

"Had you known that the California sperm bank was the *only* one they contacted willing to store his sperm, because of the lack of donor consent, would you have had any qualms about this case?"

He thought for several seconds. "Possibly."

"Yes or no?"

"I can't say. I'd have to think about it."

"Yes or no, doctor?"

Dr. Steinmetz glared at her. "Yes. I would have had doubts about performing the surgery."

"If you'd been fully informed of the difficulties Mrs. Harrison had in finding an institution willing to breach ethical standards, would you still choose to become involved in this case?"

"To be honest, it didn't occur to me that there would be this much made of it. But had I known about the resistance to storing Dr. Harrison's sperm, I probably still would have performed the recovery."

At this unexpected turn in her witness's disposition, Ms. Blair quickly wrapped up. "So at Mrs. Harrison's request, you stuck a probe up Dr. Harrison's rectum and repeatedly shocked him until he ejaculated. Without his expressed consent?"

"Yes," he agreed, looking bored.

"And you didn't think there would be any legal repercussions from that unusual procedure?"

"No. It seemed a private issue to me."

"No further questions."

Helen rose. "Dr. Steinmeitz, why did you choose electroejaculation over other available techniques?"

"Because it's the simplest, least invasive method. The other techniques involve surgery."

"The *least* invasive?"

He nodded. "Yes, ma'am."

"Doctor, why'd you recover Dr. Harrison's sperm?"

"I believed it to be the right thing to do." His brows arched high over the gold wire-rimmed glasses. He turned to the judge. "Mrs. Harrison had just suffered a miscarriage as well as having just lost her husband. She had the economic means to provide for a child. Mrs. Harrison's love for her husband and compassionate nature led me to believe that a child nurtured by that woman would be well-loved and wanted—something that isn't necessarily true in all duel-parent families. So I performed the procedure for her."

Jenny felt uncomfortable under his warm and understanding look. She'd tricked him—or certainly been less than honest with him, yet he still understood and supported her in court.

Dr. Steinmetz continued. "I'd like to remind the court that she has a finite amount of sperm and the various means of assisted conception are not guarantees that she can conceive with the amount of sperm she has."

"You performed the procedure about seven months ago. There's been a lot of publicity since then, and I'm sure some people have given you a hard time for what you did. Do you regret your decision now?"

He shook his head. "No."

"Thank you. No more questions."

The urologist's kind remarks astonished Jenny. He'd understood right from the beginning. She was touched that, even after discovering they'd withheld pertinent information from him, he'd still have performed the surgery. Why couldn't everybody see it like he did? She wanted to hug him.

Next, the plaintiff put the director of a sperm bank that refused to store Gabe's sperm on the stand. She testified that she'd refused to accept the sperm because of the lack of the man's consent. Ms. Blair had her run through their policies, emphasizing in a superior tone, that a man's written consent was required before they would accept his sperm.

Like a woman could steal sperm and secretly save it, Jenny thought. She pictured women having sex, using a condom to save the sperm in, and then running it to the freezer for deposit in the sperm bank the next day. How ridiculous.

After this lengthy and boring testimony, they quit for the day.

Chapter 21

"Please state your full name for the record," Ms. Blair requested.

George lounged in the witness box with his legs stretched before him, crossed at the ankles, and his folded, plump hands resting on his stomach. Jenny could still smell the lingering scent of his Old Spice cologne from when he'd sauntered by.

"George Aloysius Turner."

"How are you related to the deceased?"

"Gabe Harrison was my sister's son. I'm his uncle and became his legal guardian after his parents died when he was twelve years old."

"Your wife died when your nephew was a teenager, leaving just the two of you, correct?"

"That's right."

"Was it difficult raising a teenager on your own?"

"Well, sure. For both of us."

"How was it difficult for your nephew?"

"Objection. Irrelevant," Helen said.

"Your Honor, of course it's relevant, it goes to the deceased's intent. If the deceased had a difficult time being raised by a single parent, it stands to reason he wouldn't want his own child to be raised that way. If he had no trouble with it," Ms. Blair shrugged, "then I'm wrong."

If you were wrong, then you wouldn't be pursuing this line of questioning with your witness, Jenny thought.

"Objection overruled." The judge turned to George. "Answer the question, please."

"It was hard on Gabe," George admitted. "I missed a lot of his football games and award ceremonies 'cause I had to work. A lot of times I couldn't get home early enough to make dinner, so either Gabe made it or we made it together and ate late. A lot of jobs fell to Gabe once my wife died.

"It wasn't easy and, though Gabe didn't rebel or anything, I could tell it was tough on him." He narrowed cold small eyes on Jenny. "He'd never want his children raised that way." He turned to the judge and smiled triumphantly. "As a matter of a fact, he mentioned lots of times how happy he was that Judith married such a good man to help her raise Alex and Ted when he wasn't around. Between the three of them, he felt they had the bases covered."

"Mr. Turner, did you ever hear or see anything to indicate that your nephew and his second wife did not have a happy marriage?" Ms. Blair asked.

George hitched himself up in the chair and tucked his legs under his seat. "Naw, Gabe was infatuated with her. She had him totally fooled. She married him for his money and, hell, he gave her everything money could buy, so why wouldn't she be happy?"

"Objection. Opinion," Helen said.

"Sustained." The judge turned to George. "Mr. Turner, you may testify only to the facts."

"Yes, sir," George said, managing to look contrite.

"Mr. Turner, did you hear or observe anything to indicate that Mrs. Harrison married your nephew for his money?"

George snorted and pointed at Jenny. "You can see that rock on her finger. That diamond must of set him back twenty grand. And as soon as they got married, she went out and bought a brand new Jeep and that house on the lake. He took her to Maui for their honeymoon. She was constantly spendin' his money.

"Gabe was a miser. Before meeting her, he lived simply. He drove a 2001 station wagon and rented a tiny two-bedroom house on Mt Vernon. Just ask Judith; he didn't buy *her* a whopping diamond and they never vacationed in Hawaii. My nephew was *not* in the habit of spending money, but he sure spent it on her." He jerked a thumb in Jenny's direction.

Heat flushed Jenny's cheeks and she stifled the urge to cover her engagement ring. She hadn't asked for the stunning two-carat diamond—Gabe picked out her ring.

"Did you ever hear your nephew mention that he intended to have children with Jenny?"

"No. Never." George shook his head emphatically. "In fact, I was having dinner with them one night when Jenny was doing this story on the foster care system." He shifted in his seat, crossed one leg over the other, and leaned forward as if enjoying himself. "Well, anyways, she felt sorry for these kids she'd interviewed. She told Gabe that she wanted them to become foster parents."

Jenny glanced sharply at George. That's not exactly the way it happened. When she'd told them about the kids, she'd thought that *George* would be a good candidate for foster parenting. She hadn't really thought about herself and Gabe being foster parents until George suggested it.

"And what was your nephew's reaction?"

"He told her no way," George stated, proudly. "He'd raised his kids and didn't want to take on any more—especially high-maintenance kids. He told her they were too busy to do it and that they couldn't get personally involved with every needy cause she wrote an article about."

Jenny leaned over to write on Helen's pad, but the picture of a sailboat nose-diving in rough seas momentarily distracted her. She flipped the page and scribbled on Helen's legal pad, trying furiously to remember Gabe's exact words that night last summer when they'd discussed foster parenting.

Gabe automatically rejected the idea of their being foster parents, claiming they had no time or energy. His close-mindedness annoyed her such that she'd told him she worried about his reaction should she accidentally get pregnant—not that *she* had wanted any children at that time, but she'd been shocked and really upset by his instantaneous autocratic rejection of the idea—as if she had no say in the matter. His total disregard for her feelings or opinion had been so uncharacteristic of Gabe that it'd really thrown her.

Her pen paused over the pad. But then they'd talked it out and come to a mutual agreement. She'd been appeased by their discussion and the way the conversation had ended. Maybe Jenny could make this work in her favor. She scribbled more notes for Helen.

"Did they argue about it?" Ms. Blair asked.

"Nope. Jenny was always overemotional—a real bleeding heart, but she knew when Gabe made up his mind. She let it go."

"No more questions."

Helen read what Jenny wrote. Looking thoughtful, she stood and walked over to George. "Mr. Turner, you testified that your nephew spent quite a lot of money buying his wife gifts. Did you ever hear her *ask* for the gifts or coerce him into giving them to her?"

"No, but I wasn't privy to what went on in their bedroom, if you know what I mean." He snickered.

Helen ignored his tasteless remark. "You told the court that Gabe didn't want to be a foster parent, but at any time during that conversation did Gabe mention how he'd feel about a child of his and Jenny's?"

"Nope."

"Think harder. Are you sure?"

"I can't recall."

"Isn't it true that Jenny felt it unfair that Gabe refused to help these children because they had emotional issues?"

"Y-eah." He frowned, seeming confused by the question.

She looked down at Jenny's notes. "And didn't she then ask Gabe what he'd do if it was *their child* who had emotional issues?"

"I guess."

"And what was his response?"

"Something along the lines of, if it was their kid, then he'd deal with it."

"Could he have said that if it were their child, it would be, quote, 'totally different'?"

"He might have." George made a face. "So what?"

"So he *did* think about the possibility of having a child with Jenny, and that their child would be a totally different situation than being parents to a foster child."

"Yeah, but he still told her no way."

"No more questions."

The judge dismissed George, who strolled back to his table. Jenny was furious at his remarks and insinuations—especially that crack about her using sex to manipulate Gabe. She would have loved to trip him and laugh as he landed in an ungainly heap in front of everybody. The humiliation would do him good—her too. Especially her.

Next, Ms. Blair called Judith to the stand. The bailiff swore her in. Ms. Blair approached her smiling. "Dr. Sterling, how long were you married to Dr. Harrison?"

"Ten years."

"And you had two children together, correct?"

"Yes."

"Was Dr. Harrison an involved father?"

"Very. Because we both had demanding careers, Gabe helped out a lot with the children."

"How?"

"He read them books, bathed them, helped with their homework, and went to their school events as his schedule allowed."

"Parenting is exhausting," Ms. Blair said, sounding sympathetic.

Jenny doubted she would know. She'd be surprised if the callous attorney even had a pet.

"Do you remember Dr. Harrison ever making any comment expressing his relief at the milestones your children achieved?"

"Yes."

Jenny smiled at the way Judith answered the question but wasn't about to volunteer anything.

"And what were those comments?"

"Well… after Alex's graduation party, Gabe did remark that he was glad she was the last, but everybody makes comments like that after an emotional event. They don't really mean it," Judith said.

"He said that he was glad that she was the last?"

"Yes."

"In the ten years that you were married, did you ever hear Dr. Harrison express a negative opinion about single parents?"

Judith hesitated. "Yes."

"Tell us about it."

"Gabe's aunt died when he was a teenager and he felt the stress of only having one parent to love and provide for him."

"So Dr. Harrison did not approve of single parenthood?"

"Objection. Irrelevant, and calls for conjecture and opinion," Helen said.

"Sustained," the judge said.

"Okay, let's move on. Dr. Sterling, did you ever witness Mrs. Harrison saying or doing anything inappropriate regarding your children?"

"No."

"Not even your daughter?"

"No."

"Did she advise your daughter to use birth control?"

"I have no first-hand knowledge of any conversation like that."

"Did your daughter ever tell you that Mrs. Harrison had advised her to use birth control?"

Judith inclined her head. "Yes."

"Did she give her any other sexual advice?"

"Not that I know of."

"Did you ever hear or witness anything that would lead you to believe that Dr. Harrison and Jenny Harrison had a less than ideal marriage?"

"Objection. Calls for opinion," Helen claimed.

"Sustained," the judge agreed.

"Dr. Sterling, aren't you at all concerned that should Jenny win this case and get pregnant, she will invade your children's inheritance?"

"Objection." Helen rose. "Her opinion is neither proper testimony nor relevant here. Moreover, counsel seeks to mislead the court because, according to the Uniform Probate Code, the child must be in gestation at the time of death of the father and survive one hundred-twenty hours after birth to inherit by intestate succession. So it's a moot point. Any child Jenny conceived from artificial insemination would be ineligible to make a claim upon her husband's estate."

Ms. Blair glanced nervously at the judge. "I'll withdraw the question. Dr. Sterling, did you ever hear Dr. Harrison express any intention of having more children?"

"No."

Ms. Blair consulted her notes. "What kind of an engagement ring did Dr. Harrison buy you?"

"None. We didn't have the money."

"Dr. Harrison inherited quite a bit of money when his parents died. In fact, some might say that he was independently wealthy. He didn't have money to buy you an engagement ring?"

"He may have had money, I don't know. We lived off what we made."

"Later then. Surely in the ten years you were married, he could afford to buy you jewelry?"

"We could afford it, but I don't care much for jewelry."

That was the truth. She'd rarely seen Judith wearing more than her plain gold wedding band. It was probably a pain, since she couldn't operate with jewelry on.

"Very well. What kind of car did you drive while you were married to Dr. Harrison?"

"A Volkswagen bug."

"Did Dr. Harrison buy it for you new?"

"I bought it. It was three years old, but only had ten thousand miles on it."

"A used car." She nodded. "And where did you honeymoon?"

"Niagara Falls."

"He took *you* to Niagara Falls for your honeymoon. Not exactly Hawaii, is it?" Ms. Blair asked sadly, as if feeling sorry for Judith.

Judith looked at the judge, to see if she need answer the question.

He nodded.

"No, it's not Hawaii."

"So you had no engagement ring, drove a used car, and honeymooned at Niagara Falls. Dr. Sterling, Mr. Turner testified that he thought Dr. Harrison was a miser, would you agree?"

"Objection," Helen called out.

"Withdrawn. No more questions."

When Helen declined cross-examination, Judith was excused and the judge decided to dismiss them early.

Steve bent backwards and murmured something to Judith as Helen leaned close to Jenny. "Is it okay if we go back to your house? We have some things we need to discuss."

"Sure. What's up?"

"We just got the P.I.'s report back. I know why George gives money to the Huntington Foundation."

ᘒ ᘒ ᘒ

"Gabe had Huntington's Disease? Are you *sure*? Are you *absolutely positive*?" Judith asked. Standing in Jenny's family room, her arms circled her stomach as if she could ward off the blow.

"Since his body was cremated, we can't test him for it, but we're reasonably certain." Helen said. "Once we find out who Gabe's pediatrician was we can subpoena his records. If George had him tested, we'll know. What we know for sure is that Jan Harrison had it."

"*Sh-it.*" Judith looked away. "If Gabe had it, Alex and Ted are at risk. Even if he didn't have it, they're still at risk. Damn it," she whispered. She looked at Helen. "You're absolutely certain his mom had Huntington's?"

"I'm afraid so."

"That's why we wanted to talk to you. We wanted to give you a chance to speak with the kids or keep them out of court during George's testimony," Steve said.

The thought that Alex and Ted could have that horrible disease sent chills through Jenny as if she'd been electrically zapped. She frowned, trying to remember the exact odds of inheriting—something like fifty percent? Whatever it was, it was way too high. She couldn't imagine giving a kid barely out of her teens this kind of news. They had their whole lives before them, and it shouldn't include a nightmare like Huntington's. And it absolutely shouldn't be public knowledge—they deserved privacy.

"We don't need to bring it up," Jenny said. Alex and Ted didn't have to find out—at least not that way. It was bad enough that one of them could have inherited the disease without the people in that courtroom being privy to something so personal. They just wouldn't use the information to discredit George.

"Of course you're going to use it," Steve said.

"But why?" Jenny asked. "What's to be gained? If we keep quiet, Judith can tell the kids in her own time and her own way. George has already had to live with knowing Gabe had this death sentence hanging over him all these years. He's suffered enough."

Judith stepped stiffly forward. "No wonder the bastard tried to get me to have an abortion. He knew. He knew all along that we'd be passing it on and he didn't say anything!" She glared at Jenny. "You have to use it. George has to be stopped. Who the hell does he think he is?" She paced away, then spun and faced them. "What about the organ recipients? Are they at risk? I doubt they'd test for Huntington's." She muttered almost as if to herself. "I'd *think* they should be okay—it's not a communicable disease, but I don't know."

She glared at Jenny again. "His little secret could cost dozens of people their lives—including my children. You'll have to contact Amy what's-her-name right away and see if it's a problem. God, what a mess."

"Oh, no." Jenny's eyes widened and she put a hand to her mouth. "I hadn't even considered that."

As many as fifty people could be helped by his gift, Amy's words echoed in her mind. Jenny looked at the desk where she kept the recipients' letters. All those grateful, sweet people who'd sent her letters might be at risk? Ted and Alex? Jenny blinked back tears.

"How am I going to tell Ted and Alex?" Judith sank into a chair. "What've I done?"

"Nothing." Jenny sat and put a gentle hand to Judith's back. "*You* haven't done anything. You didn't know."

"That doesn't change anything." She looked through hard eyes. "I should've known. *Gabe* should've known. George had *no* right to keep that from us. We're doctors."

"Then it's over. He wins." Jenny softened her expression in apology as she looked at Judith. She didn't want to add to her pain, but she couldn't *knowingly* gamble with her child's life that way. "I'll have to give it up; it's not worth the risk."

"Don't be silly. You just have to do IVF and have the embryos tested." Judith scowled. "You're fine."

"But Jenny, we still have to use it," Helen softly spoke. "This offers indisputable proof of George's domineering character. He made important, life-altering decisions for your husband—and Judith and their children. And he's trying to do the same here with you. This could nail it for us."

But at what cost? Was having Gabe's baby worth bringing more pain to her family? Judith, Ted and Alex didn't deserve to have their private business drawn into this. She could not allow them to become collateral damage. Jesus, she'd just wanted Gabe's baby, how could so many people be hurt?

Jenny stared at them. But even in the face of Judith's devastation and Ted and Alex's uncertain future, she couldn't help the tug of sympathy for George. She'd made her share of huge mistakes that ended up with someone getting badly hurt. She'd kept family secrets.

Chapter 22

Jenny took a deep breath, raised her right hand and repeated the oath after the bailiff. She leaned back and watched Ms. Blair expectantly. Although Steve and Helen had worked with her, she was wary of the woman.

"Mrs. Harrison, when you met your husband, you were a freelance journalist, correct?" Ms. Blair began.

"Yes."

"Your annual income was approximately twenty-one-thousand dollars, correct?"

"No. I made about twenty-four thousand."

"Okay. Twenty-four thousand. Not a lot to live on. Yet you chose to reject the opportunity to save rent and live with your parents?"

Jenny smiled. "Yes. Like most young adults, I wanted to be on my own. And I shared an apartment with a roommate."

"But after paying bills at the end of the month you didn't have a lot of money left over."

"I had enough."

"Yet you spent one hundred-fifty dollars on a skateboard for your brother?"

"Yes." Was being generous a fault?

"You knew that your mother had forbidden your brother to have a skateboard, didn't you?"

Jenny nodded. Everybody knew that, thanks to earlier testimony. "Yes."

"You knew that your mother forbade him to have it because she thought it was dangerous and that he'd get hurt?"

"Yes." She'd truly thought the risk minimal.

"And still you defied your mother and spent your hard-earned money to buy a skateboard for him?"

"Yes."

"And were you with your brother when he was critically injured in a skateboarding accident?"

"I was."

"Is it true that your mother was angry with you for your part in his accident and didn't want you to visit him in the hospital?"

"Objection. Irrelevant and calls for speculation—how can this witness testify to her mother's thoughts?" Helen asked.

Jenny ignored Helen's objection, wanting to answer the question. She had no hesitation about taking responsibility for her mistake and refused to allow anybody to make her mother out to be the bad guy. "My mother was justifiably angry with me. She needed a little space so—"

"And did you stay away from your brother?"

"No. Michael wanted me near. He—"

"Mrs. Harrison, there's a fourteen-year age gap between you and your brother." Ms. Blair paused dramatically. "Is Michael your son?"

Jenny went utterly still, even forgetting to breathe for several long seconds. Her mind blanked, white and empty. She forced herself not to look at her mother. How would Ms. Blair even think to ask that? "Pardon me?"

"Is Michael your son?" she repeated, slowly and clearly.

Jenny flashed a trembling smile. "No, of course not."

"Then you lied to the hospital security guard when you claimed that Michael was your son?"

Relief made Jenny lightheaded. She shifted in her seat. "Yes."

"Did you deliberately withhold information from Dr. Steinmetz, not informing him that you were having difficulty finding a sperm bank willing to store your husband's sperm, due to the fact that you could not obtain his consent?"

"Yes."

"So you lied to the guard and lied, by omission, to Dr. Steinmetz?"

"Yes."

"You bought your brother a toy against your mother's wishes, knowing she considered it a danger, and then when he was critically injured using the skateboard, you impersonated your mother so that you could sneak into the hospital? This sounds like irresponsible behavior, wouldn't you agree?"

Impersonated her mother? Not exactly. "Partially. I snuck into the hospital—"

"Yes or no, please. Wasn't your behavior irresponsible?"

"Some of it, yes."

"Yes." At Ms. Blair's slow nod of satisfaction, Jenny clenched her teeth.

She'd made a few mistakes, but her intentions were good. Jenny hadn't maliciously hurt anybody; she'd just wanted to make Michael happy. And she'd learned from her mistakes. Didn't that count for anything?

Ms. Blair referred to her notes. She then asked Jenny a series of questions about her engagement ring, her car, and the house, all of which answers corroborated George's claim that Gabe had spent a lot of money buying her expensive things. But what husband didn't if he could afford it?

Jenny had bought Gabe several expensive presents too, but if she mentioned that, they'd probably point out that her gifts were bought with Gabe's money.

"Mrs. Harrison, did you marry Dr. Harrison for his money?"

Jenny stared at her stunned. Even if she had, did the attorney really think she'd be stupid enough to admit it?

"No, of course not." *But even if I had, that doesn't mean he wouldn't have wanted me to have his child.*

"Mrs. Harrison, was marrying an older man and being a stepmother of two teenagers difficult?"

"At times."

"Is it true that you advised your, then sixteen-year-old stepdaughter to use birth control?"

She clasped her hands together in her lap. "Yes."

"Is it true that people often mistook you for your husband's daughter?"

"Often?" Depends upon one's definition of often, she rationalized. "No."

"Did more than two people ever mistake you for your husband's daughter?"

She nodded slowly. "Yes."

"Did you act like his daughter?"

She bit back a sarcastic comment. "Of course not."

"Did you suggest to your husband that you become foster parents?"

"Sort of. I told George that he—"

"Yes or no?"

"Yes," Jenny snapped, tired of being interrupted.

"Was he opposed to the idea?"

"Yes."

"Why?"

None of your business. Jenny hated having to justify private things to this woman. "Because we didn't have the time or energy to help such troubled children."

"Dr. Harrison thought that the two of you didn't have enough time and energy to devote to a foster child?"

"Yes."

"But now, with your husband dead, you think that alone, you would have the time and energy to devote to raising a child?"

She shifted in her seat, tucking one leg comfortably under her. "Yes, I do. And I have all the free time I used to spend with Gabe. I have plenty of time to raise a child."

"You agreed with your husband that you didn't have the time and energy for a foster child, yet you claim to have plenty of time for a child now. Would *your husband* think so?"

Jenny wanted to shout that the situations were different. That troubled foster children; possibly terribly abused children, were a different prospect than raising an innocent baby of their own. She raised her chin and sent Ms. Blair a challenging look. "He would."

"Both Dr. Sterling and Mr. Turner claim that your husband found it difficult being raised by a single parent. Did he ever say anything to you indicating this?"

"Gabe mentioned that his childhood had been difficult, but—"

"Are you implying that Mr. Turner did a poor job raising your husband?"

Jenny shook her head. *I never said that.* "Not at all. I'm saying that—"

"Mrs. Harrison, did your husband ever express an opinion to you about single parenthood?"

Jenny thought back to the night Gabe had come home discouraged about the preemie that'd died at the clinic. He'd wanted to sterilize the teenage mother. He'd been angry and upset on behalf of the dead baby and her neglected children, but that wasn't the same as a single mother with a good job raising a child in a warm and loving environment.

With a twinge of guilt, she looked at Ms. Blair. "No."

"Mrs. Harrison, is it true that when you married, you told your husband that you *never* wanted to have children?"

"Yes."

"And now, after he's dead, you do?"

"No. I changed my mind about six months before Gabe died. But—"

"So you changed your mind about wanting children six months before your husband's accident. How long had you been trying to get pregnant before you successfully conceived?"

"Uh... not long." *At all.*

"Was the baby an accident?" She asked in a soft, solicitous voice.

The buzzing in Jenny's ears grew. Why had she even thought to ask that question? Her hesitation must have given her away. Jenny moistened dry lips. "Pardon me?"

"Was your pregnancy the result of you and your husband deliberately trying to conceive a child?"

"Objection, Your Honor, relevancy," Helen called out. "Whether a previous child was intentionally conceived or not has no bearing on determining whether Dr. Harrison would want his wife to have a child *now* after he's gone."

"Goes to character," she argued. "Did she trap him with the child that miscarried? Was he happily anticipating that child or was he upset about it? It all goes to determine his state of mind, Your Honor."

"I'd like to hear what the defendant has to say. Objection overruled."

"Ms. Harrision, was your pregnancy the result of you and your husband deliberately trying to conceive a child?" she repeated.

Jenny raised her chin. "Our baby was very much wanted."

Ms. Blair narrowed her eyes and quietly stalked closer, like a lion circling her prey. "I didn't ask you if the baby was *wanted*. Was it *planned*? Did your husband willingly have unprotected sex with the explicit intention of getting you pregnant?"

Oh, geez. That was specific enough. "I... uh... I—"

"Yes or no?"

"Objection, Your Honor." Steve jumped to his feet. "Ms. Blair is badgering the witness."

"I'll allow the line. I think the question is pretty straightforward."

This was it; all she had to do was say, yes. Yes, they'd had unprotected sex resulting in the pregnancy. Nobody could prove differently. Jenny wanted to drop her head in her hands in despair. She'd tried so hard to keep away from this question. "No."

"No?" The attorney's eyebrows shot up and victory lit her ice-cold blue eyes. "The child was not deliberately conceived. Then the baby you miscarried was an accident?"

"Asked and answered," Steve spat out.

Jenny's head whipped up at the sound of Steve's angry voice. He leaned on the table with his hands clasped tightly together—no doubt wishing they were around Jenny's neck. Head turned sideways, he glared at Ms. Blair.

She should have told them. She knew he and Helen were counting on that pregnancy to be proof of Gabe's intent, but they'd needed strong evidence so badly that Jenny'd hoped George's attorney wouldn't think to ask. And if she did, Jenny'd thought she could lie.

"Yes," she softly admitted.

"An accident." She paused to let the truth sink in. "So when you first married, you didn't want any children, then about six months before your husband died, you decided that you *did* want children, then you accidentally got pregnant—which resulted in a miscarriage, correct?"

"Yes."

"So in the two years you were married, you *never* had unprotected sex with your husband in an attempt to get pregnant?"

"Your Honor!" Steve shouted. "This has already been covered by the witness, now Ms. Blair is testifying."

"Objection sustained." The judge turned to Jenny. "You don't need to answer that." The judge gave Ms. Blair a steady, warning look. "Move on counselor."

Jenny looked away, humiliated by the constant battering and enumeration of all her mistakes. She rubbed her cold clammy hands together and concentrated on the next question.

"You lied to the guard about being your brother's mother and you lied by omission to Dr. Steinmetz. You seem to think nothing of lying to get your way... did you lie to your husband about the pregnancy being an accident when in fact you got pregnant on purpose?"

"No. It was a surprise to me too. We'd been using birth control."

"What was Dr. Harrison's reaction to your pregnancy?"

"He didn't know. I didn't have the chance to tell him before the accident. I'd just found out the morning we left and was waiting for the perfect time to tell Gabe."

She let her eyes stare unfocused at the parquet courtroom floor. She couldn't look at Steve, too afraid to see the disappointment and anger in his face. They'd always been honest with each other and now he knew that she'd lied to him, letting him think the baby had been planned. A lie of omission, but still a lie.

Ms. Blair consulted her notes. "Are you currently working as a freelance journalist?"

Jenny raised her head. Thank God, she was moving on. "Yes."

"And that requires you to do some traveling?"

"Rarely."

"If you were to get pregnant with Dr. Harrison's child, do you still intend to work?"

"Yes. I have a very flexible job. I'd like to work part time."

"And who would watch the baby while you were working?"

"There's a chance my mother could watch the baby or I'd hire a nanny. Either way, I'd be with the baby most of her waking moments."

"And you can afford this?"

"Yes."

Ms. Blair watched her thoughtfully, before reluctantly releasing her. "No more questions."

Helen rose. "Jenny, did you marry your husband for his money?"

Warmth and reassurance eased through her in remembering Gabe and the very simple reasons that she'd married him. Jenny smiled. "No. I married Gabe because he was a good man. He was incredibly supportive of me and he loved me with all his heart. He made me happy." She paused, trying to clear the huskiness from her voice. "He was kind. And wonderful. And I loved him very much," she finished in a whisper.

"Jenny, tell the court why you defied your mother's wishes and bought Michael the skateboard."

She took a deep breath, amazed at how one bad decision could keep returning to haunt her. "Michael had written this persuasive essay on why he should be able to have a skateboard. It was well written—he got an A on it. I was proud that Michael had done so well at something I'd chosen as a career and I wanted to encourage his writing, so I thought it appropriate to reward him with the skateboard."

"In the same situation today, let's say he wrote a persuasive essay about why he should be allowed to own a dirt bike, would you do the same?"

"No. I've learned from my mistake."

"Jenny can you tell the court why you felt compelled to break the hospital rules and visit Michael in the hospital?"

"He needed me. Michael and I are close. In the hospital, he was scared—especially at night. Michael was calmer and slept better when I was with him. I felt responsible for his accident and since Mom was with him all day, she could use the rest at night."

"You defied hospital rules for your little brother and mother's benefit?"

"Yes." Jenny raised her chin in defiance, not caring if she hurt her case. "And *that*, I would do again."

Helen stuck her hands deep in her skirt pocket. "And when you approached Gabe about foster parenting, what was his response?"

"As I said earlier, it was really George's idea. Gabe did shoot it down for the reasons George listed, but when I played the devil's advocate and asked Gabe what he'd do if we had a child with some psychological problems, Gabe said that would be totally different. It would be *our* child and he'd love it and take care of it. So Gabe was always open to the idea of our having a family. It was me who didn't want it in the beginning."

"And why did you change your mind?"

"Because I realized what a great dad Gabe was and that I'd missed out on such an important life experience. I realized I could be a good mom and I very much wanted our baby."

"Jenny, why didn't you tell Dr. Steinmetz about the difficulty you'd encountered in finding a willing sperm bank?"

"I hated deceiving Dr. Steinmetz, and for that I *do* sincerely apologize." She searched the crowded courtroom for the doctor but couldn't find him. Of course he'd have gone back to work after testifying.

"I didn't have a lot of time to convince him that I was doing the right thing. Though I suspected he probably wouldn't have changed his mind, I couldn't take that chance. The stakes were just too high. I needed his cooperation to get my baby."

"No more questions." Helen walked back to their table.

Turning to the judge, Ms. Blair said, "Your Honor, the plaintiff rests."

"We'll break for lunch and when we come back, the defense can present their first witness," the judge said.

Jenny slowly came off the stand and crossed to where Helen and Steve were shoving legal pads into their respective briefcases. Steve clicked his pen closed and slid it into his breast pocket. He didn't look up at her approach, but Helen gave her an understanding look.

"I'm sorry. I should have told you," Jenny choked out.

Helen wrapped a plump arm around her shoulder. "You did fine; it's not a big deal."

Jenny sank into her embrace and took a few seconds to compose herself before daring to look at Steve. Steve stood silent, studying the crowded courtroom, waiting for them.

Helen laid her briefcase strap across her shoulder. "Let's get some lunch."

Jenny glanced at Steve. "In a minute."

When Helen started walking away, Jenny moved close to Steve until the smoothness of his suit coat jacket brushed against her bare arm. Steve stepped back, bumping his chair into the railing.

"I'm sorry," Jenny whispered.

He refused to meet her gaze. Sliding his briefcase from the table, he took her arm in a tight, impersonal hold and turned her to follow Helen.

Jenny pulled back. "Wait. We need—"

"Not now," he bit out before nudging her forward.

Chapter 23

During lunch, Jenny could hardly eat. Steve ignored her and participated in the conversation only when Helen asked him a direct question. He ate his Ruben while deep in thought. He must really hate her. Although she had excellent reasons for the times she'd lied, Ms. Blair had done a good job of discrediting her. Jenny knew it. And now the judge knew it. Steve and Helen didn't say anything, but her small deception had made their job harder.

Steve sacrificed a lot to be with her throughout the trial—maybe even the job at which he'd spent so much time and energy proving himself. If they lost, that'd be an additional burden she hadn't counted on and really didn't want to bear.

Jenny thought hard. That was about all the lies Ms. Blair could possibly uncover. Luckily, there was no way they could know about that night spent on the couch with Steve. Thank God Steve couldn't testify. She didn't think she could damage her case any more.

After lunch, they took their seats and Jenny prepared to be impressed by Helen. It was their turn to prove that Gabe would have wanted her to have his baby. Helen brought out Alex, Ted, Judith, Jenny's mother and father and brother, all of whom quickly and succinctly testified that Gabe loved Jenny passionately and that they'd had a wonderful, solid marriage.

Then Helen called Anthony Pope, the director of Save a Life Foundation, to testify. After her introductory questions, she paused and looked at him. "Mr. Pope, in the twenty years you've been involved with organ donations, how many times have your people been requested to coordinate the recovery of sperm from a brain-dead donor?"

Mr. Pope was a very proper sort of gentleman. Jenny kept expecting him to speak with an English accent. He wore his dark hair slicked back and parted in the middle. Spotlessly shiny rimless glasses perched on an impossibly sharp nose. He sat stiffly in the chair in his three-piece herringbone suit and maroon bow tie. He was clean-shaven, as if he was one of those men who shaved several times a day, needed or not. And his angular features seemed to be arranged in a permanently haughty look, which probably rarely softened in a smile and certainly never in anything as playful as a grin.

"One other time," he said.

"When Ms. Bromley called you with Mrs. Harrison's request, why did you give your approval?"

"I couldn't see any reason not to." He inclined his head slowly, regally. "The request was certainly unusual, but I didn't see any harm in it—especially in light of Mrs. Harrison's recent miscarriage."

"So you weren't bothered by the lack of consent involved?"

"No. Due to his incapacitated state, his wife, as next of kin, had the right to approve or deny both donations."

"And if she denied consent to recover his organs?"

"Then we absolutely would *not* have touched him. Mrs. Harrison had complete authority in this instance. Under the Anatomical Gift Act, the next of kin of the deceased may make a gift of all or part of the body, *unless* the decedent either at the time of death or prior to, had made an unrevoked refusal to make that gift. In other words, unless he put it in writing that he did not want his organs donated, the decision was up to his wife."

"Since Mrs. Harrison had full authority to donate Dr. Harrison's organs under the Anatomical Gift Act, it didn't seem unreasonable that she be able to make a gift of his sperm to herself?"

"Exactly."

"Objection." Ms. Blair called out. "In Davis versus Davis, the judge ruled that sperm is entitled to special respect because it is unlike other human tissue in its genetic material, and because of its potential for human life. Therefore the witness's assumption is wrong."

Helen turned to the other attorney. "Maybe wrong, but not illegal." She addressed the judge. "And in Davis versus Davis, the dispute was over cryopreserved *embryos*, not sperm—a totally different ballgame."

"Objection overruled." The judge sent Ms. Blair a sharp look to let her know she was pushing him, but he did not call her forward for a formal reprimand.

Helen continued. "Mr. Pope, if family members are not in agreement about making a gift of the decedent's organs, who has the ultimate authority?"

"The next of kin; usually the husband or the wife."

"Dr. Harrison's uncle strenuously objected to the donation, yet it went through. Could you explain why?"

"Dr. Harrison's wife wanted to make the gift. Under those circumstances the uncle has no authority to dictate events."

"Thank you. No more questions."

Ms. Blair wisely declined cross-examination, so the next witness was called.

"The Defense calls George Turner to the stand." Helen waited patiently for George to be sworn in.

Jenny scanned the room behind her, happy to see that Judith had sent Ted and Alex home. She'd cancelled her afternoon surgeries to listen to George's testimony. Back rigid, expression closed, Judith sat in the front row next to Jenny's parents, where George could easily see her. Jenny turned around, sad for her. Sad for them all.

"Mr. Turner, why did you and your wife never have children of your own?"

George pursed his lips, then shrugged, as if the answer was obvious. "Arlene never got pregnant."

"Did you want children?"

"Of course." He scowled as if insulted.

"Was there a medical reason you could not have any children?"

"No. She just never got pregnant."

"Earlier, you testified that you and your wife became Dr. Harrison's legal guardians in nineteen eighty-two, when he was orphaned at age twelve, but that's not quite true, is it? You became his legal guardian in nineteen seventy-nine, three years *before* Gabe was orphaned. He was nine at the time."

"So? I was off a couple of years. Jan was on the old side when she had Gabe." He frowned and looked into space. "She and her husband weren't about to let a kid keep them from traipsing all over the world with the Peace Corps, but I finally convinced them that that was no life for a child. He needed stability and normalcy. So they left Gabe with me and Adele and came back to visit the boy for holidays."

Helen paced to the right. "Again, not quite true. Mr. Turner, your sister and her husband's affiliation with the Peace Corps ended in nineteen seventy-eight, at which time she and her husband moved to New York so your sister could participate in an experimental treatment program for Huntington's Disease."

"Objection, relevancy," Ms. Blair called out.

"Approach the bench." The judge beckoned them forward.

Jenny couldn't hear their whispered discussion, but it was quickly resolved and Helen continued.

"Mr. Turner, isn't it true that the real reason you were given custody of your nephew is that your sister was dying of Huntington's Disease and your brother-in-law took her to various clinics throughout the world for experimental treatments before ultimately putting her in a New York facility that specialized in caring for those with Huntington's Disease?"

George raised his chin and narrowed his eyes. "They *did* work for the Peace Corps."

"Yes, but not up to her death, as you told everyone."

"So? What does it matter?"

"Isn't it true that your sister, Dr. Harrison's mother, died from complications associated with Huntington's disease, not amoebic dysentery as you told everyone?"

"Sam did. He got dysentery in Somolia."

"We're not disputing Dr. Harrison's *father's* cause of death. Isn't it true that Jan Harrison died from complications from Huntington's disease?"

George deflated. "Yes."

"So you lied to Dr. Harrison, his wife, and to everyone about the true cause of her death. You lied," she turned and looked at Jenny, "like Jenny did, when she claimed to be her brother's mother, to protect a loved one. Didn't you?"

"Yes."

"When did you tell Dr. Harrison about his mother's illness?"

"Objection. Your Honor, Mr. Turner is not on trial here," Ms. Blair said.

"Goes to character," Helen shot back.

"Objection overruled." The judge turned to George. "Please answer the question."

George scowled and looked down. "Never."

"You *never* told Dr. Harrison that his mother died of a deadly *hereditary* disease? Why not?"

George clasped his hands together until the knuckles turned white. He fixed his fierce gaze on the railing surrounding the witness box. "He didn't need to know," he bit out.

"He didn't need to know," she repeated. "Mr. Turner, did you ever have Dr. Harrison tested to find out if he had inherited Huntington's disease from his mother?"

George shifted in his seat then glared at Helen for forcing the truth. "I did."

"And what were the results?"

George frowned and tightened his lips. His head jerked a little from side to side.

"Mr. Turner? Did Dr. Harrison test positive for Huntington's Disease?"

George scanned the courtroom until his gaze landed on Judith. Looking away from her censorious expression, his Adam's apple bobbed under his jowls. He slumped and blinked several times, then stared at his folded hands.

Helen looked at the judge.

Jenny's heart sank in sadness. Sadness for George, but she was infinitely more distressed by the truth. Ted and Alex were at risk—as her baby would have been if they hadn't uncovered the truth. Thank God Helen hired the private eye.

Judge Delaney leaned down to George. "Mr. Turner, you must answer the question."

George's frown deepened. He looked up and scowled at Helen. "He had it, okay? Are you satisfied?"

Satisfied? Hardly. They all would have given a great deal for a "no."

"When did you have the testing done?" Helen asked.

"The year after his mother died."

"And you never told him the results?"

George's eyes bulged. "Are you kidding? He was fourteen. Why would I tell a kid somethin' like that?"

"That's understandable, but what about when he became an adult? Had you told him by the time he graduated medical school?"

"No."

"Before he married Dr. Sterling?"

George shook his head. "No."

"Before they had children?"

Jenny could understand George's silence up to that point, but once Gabe married Judith, he had a moral obligation to tell Gabe the truth. That should have been the time. At that point George's continued silence morphed from protective parent to coward.

"No."

"No?" Helen raised surprised eyebrows. "When *did* you tell Dr. Harrison that he had Huntington's disease?"

George raised his chin. "I didn't. I kept up with all the research. They hadn't found a cure in forty years, so what was the point?"

"The point was that Dr. Harrison was a grown adult; he had the right to know. As a doctor he was in a better position than most— than you—to understand the complexities of his disease. The *point was* that as an adult who knew he had a terminal illness, he might have chosen to have a vasectomy and not risk passing the disease along to his children—or to have embryos genetically tested for Huntington's and avoid the risk of perpetuating the disease. The *point was* that knowing that his life span would be greatly limited he might have chosen to live his adult life differently.

"*The point was*, as a surgeon, Dr. Harrison's livelihood and people's lives, depended upon the steadiness of his hands. You could have jeopardized his patients and made him vulnerable to lawsuits, simply because he didn't know that the tremor in his hands was more than an excess of caffeine."

George's chin thrust out, belligerent. "I was watching for signs. Gabe was just starting to get the shakies. He's a smart man, he would have found out for himself soon enough."

"But perhaps there was medication he could have taken or treatments to delay the onset of the symptoms. Now we'll never know, because *you* took that choice away from him. Gabe Harrison was an adult and a doctor, and he died at age forty-three never knowing that he had a deadly hereditary disease and possibly passed it on to his children."

"See? He lived his life happy never knowing. Do you know how many people with Huntington's Disease commit suicide?" George asked. "Plenty. About half the people with the disease die never having been tested. They don't *want* to know. Gabe lived a full, happy life 'cause he *didn't* know. I still say it was the right thing to do."

"I've never doubted that you had your nephew's best interest at heart, Mr. Turner. But when Dr. Harrison became an adult, he had a *right* to know he had Huntington's disease."

"Objection, Your Honor," Ms. Blair called out. "Mr. Turner is not on trial here. Besides, this testimony has no relevancy—"

"It is *completely* relevant," Helen shot back. "By withholding that information, he took away Dr. Harrison's right to decide for himself if he wanted to know if he had inherited the disease." She swung around to face George. "*You* took that choice from him in a violation far greater than his wife taking his sperm."

"Objection sustained. Move on, counselor," the judge said.

"Are you kidding me? Look, you can judge me all you want, but I was protecting Gabe—and even her." George jerked his head toward Jenny. "It'd break her heart to find out she had a baby with Huntington's Disease. Now that you brought it out, Alex and Ted are going to find out and have to deal with it too. I was *protecting* them. All of them." He glanced at her, then back at Helen. "Sometimes ignorance *is* bliss."

"You could have done a better job protecting your family had you told Dr. Harrison about the Huntington's."

"Who are you to judge me?" George pulled himself up tall in his seat. "And when should I have told him? One minute Gabe was a teenager, the next, Judith was pregnant. Should I have told them then so she could abort the baby?"

Yes—if that's what they would have chosen. The decision should have been Gabe and Judith's—not George's. But Jenny could sympathize. Time seemed fly, like a freight train gathering momentum. Not long ago Michael had been a crying infant and now he was a teenager. It seemed like just yesterday she married Gabe: now he was gone. Their time together had been far too brief.

"Perhaps they would have chosen to abort the baby. It wasn't *your* decision to make, it was theirs—or should have been theirs." Helen stated. "As for Jenny, once she gets her husband's sperm, she can have the embryos genetically tested and implant only those free of Huntington's. If you'd only been honest with them all from the start, there'd been no need for any of this." She waved her arm at the courtroom.

"Yes, there is. What she's trying to do is *still* wrong and none of this has anything to do with her having his baby."

"Of course it does. It's all about choice and rights—your nephew and Jenny's husband's rights. And her rights as Gabe's wife and next of kin. Moving on." Helen consulted her notes.

Jenny was already worn out. Gabe had had Huntington's. His trembling hands hadn't been the result of excess caffeine but the beginnings of a terrible debilitating disease. She tucked that reality away to examine later, as she focused on Helen's continued questioning.

"Your wife died when Gabe was fifteen, leaving him your only living relative?"

"Yes."

"Life must have been difficult for you after your wife died." She watched him, expectant.

"Me and Gabe were fine," he said in a gruff voice, as if not wanting anybody to pity him. "We had each other."

"You had each other. You and Gabe must have grown quite close?"

George's generous lips lifted in a smile as he nodded with pride. "Very close. I was best man at his first wedding."

"Best man? Wonderful." Helen appeared to be impressed, then crossed her arms and paced in front of the witness box. "Please bear with me a moment as I digress," Helen said in a thoughtful voice. "Mr. Turner, was Adele Williams your wife?"

"Yes."

"She was the daughter of renowned chef Joseph Williams, yet had acquired some eminence in her own right as a chef?"

"Yes. Desserts were her specialty." He smiled fondly. "Nobody made chocolate mousse like my Adele."

"Mr. Turner, how did your wife die?"

His smile evaporated. "She died from a broken heart. That scumbag reporter killed her."

Helen's eyebrows rose in a look of surprise. "A reporter killed her?"

He nodded. "Adele was a good woman. She never hurt anybody. And that restaurant meant the world to her. Her and her pa used to argue about how to run it. When he retired, 'cause he had a heart attack and couldn't stay on his feet that long anymore, Adele took over.

"She wanted to prove she was as good as the old man, when she was really better. Hands down," he said with pride. "But she worked so hard. I tried to get her to slow down so she wouldn't end up like her pa, but she wouldn't listen.

"Anyhow, there was an outbreak of Salmonella, and this reporter put it in the newspaper that these sick people had been poisoned at Adele's restaurant. It wasn't true, but people believe what they read. Nobody would eat there anymore, and my poor Adele was heartbroken. She fretted herself right into that stroke. Thinking people blamed her for all those sick people, she lost her will to live." He paused, his eyes turning cold. "All because of that lyin' reporter."

"Did the salmonella come from her restaurant?"

He scoffed. "Of course not. But by the time they figured that out, the damage had been done. Nobody would eat there and Adele was dead."

"And you blame the reporter for her death?" Helen asked.

"Of course." His eyes narrowed and his lips curled in contempt. "If he hadn't printed those lies about her, she'd be alive today."

"You must not have a very high opinion of the press?"

He snorted. "No, I do *not*."

"Then you must not have liked the fact that your nephew married a journalist, did you?"

"Not particularly."

"Is it true that, without your nephew's knowledge, you coerced Jenny into having an attorney draw up a prenuptial agreement?"

"I didn't force her to do anything."

"But you did try to persuade her to obtain the document?"

"It was my idea," he conceded. "But it was for her own good."

"Her own good?" Helen raised her eyebrows. "Jenny didn't have any assets to protect. The prenuptial agreement would have benefited only your nephew."

"Okay," he shrugged. "So I was mostly looking out after Gabe. However, it *would* have proved to those mean-spirited people that she wasn't marrying him for his money. Nobody could have called her a gold-digger—if she'd have signed."

And she would have signed it if Gabe had wanted it. Jenny hadn't cared about his money. It was Gabe who had been outraged by the prenup—not her.

"The prenup was never drawn up. Why?"

He stared hard at Jenny, suspicion deep in his eyes. "'Cause she went running to Gabe, acting all confused, tellin' him it was my idea, usin' it to try and turn him against me."

Liar. It had been all Gabe objecting—rather ripping up the sample document. She'd never tried to interfere in Gabe's relationship with his uncle. Even though George had never been one of her favorite people, he was her husband's family and she'd always respected that. He'd been welcome in their home.

"And did Jenny turn Gabe against you?"

"Naw." Bushy gray eyebrows drew together as George pursed his lips. "Gabe was sore with me at first, but he got over it. It'd take more than a woman to come between us."

"Mr. Turner, were you in favor of donating Gabe's organs?"

George visibly stiffened in his seat. "Definitely not. Which was why she did it behind my back."

"Did Jenny know your feelings about organ donation before the accident?"

"I don't know, but she sure as hell knew that day."

"What happened when you learned that it was Jenny's decision and that you had no say in it?"

"I told her not to."

"You *ordered* her not to," Helen clarified.

He scowled. "Told, ordered. Whatever. I told her to stop it."

"And what did you do when she refused?"

"I got on the horn to my attorney."

"Isn't it true that Jenny's donating your nephew's organs enraged you?"

"Of course," he snapped. "They carved him up. It's inhuman."

"Isn't it true that you could care less about your nephew's wishes regarding his organ donation and this baby? That you filed this lawsuit to try to keep Jenny from having his baby out of revenge?"

"No. Gabe had two kids already, he was against single parenthood, and he would *never* want a kid of his brought into the world that way. He just wouldn't." He frowned. "In fact, he only married Judith 'cause she was pregnant. He didn't want his son being raised by a single parent."

Jenny gasped and resisted the urge to turn around and look at Judith. That was more than anybody needed to know. She was glad Ted wasn't here to be hurt by his great uncle's insensitivity.

Helen looked thoughtful. "Mr. Turner, you sued the reporter that ruined your wife's professional reputation for defamation of character and wrongful death, correct?"

Crossing his ankles and tucking his legs under the chair, George scooted back and sat up straight. "I did."

"Did you prevail in the suit?"

"No. The mor—" he glanced at Judge Delaney, apparently choosing his words carefully, not wanting to alienate him—"the judge didn't see things my way."

"In fact, the lawsuit was dismissed before ever getting to trial?"

George clenched and unclenched his jaw before forcing the answer through taught lips. "Yes."

"No more questions." Helen turned to Ms. Blair. "Your witness."

Ms. Blair rose. "Mr. Turner, when your nephew was orphaned, you didn't *have* to take him in; he could have gone to foster care. Why did you bring him into your home and raise him like a son?"

George pulled back, frowning, clearly affronted at her question. "Well, that's a *stupid* question. He's family. He was my responsibility."

Ms. Blair's cheeks reddened at George's insult. Her tone became a bit harder. "And did you have feelings for your young nephew even before he lived with you?"

"Of course."

Ms. Blair did a good job of hiding her impatience with her client. He had to be frustrating her; he certainly wasn't making her job any easier by making her drag every little bit of information out of him. George's rudeness, even to his attorney—his only ally—was incomprehensible to Jenny, but Ms. Blair remained calm and moved on.

"And what exactly were those feelings you had for your orphaned nephew?"

"I loved him, of course. Adele did too."

"You loved him." She nodded. "Mr. Turner, was it out of love that you lied about how your sister died?"

"Of course."

"Mr. Turner, why did you conceal Gabe's mother's disease?"

George swallowed hard before answering. "Our Dad had Huntington's, and we didn't have money to put him in a nursing home, so me and Jan had a front row seat in seeing how bad it gets." He shook his head and blew out a deep breath. "It was brutal."

"Brutal? How so?"

"He was bossy and controlling and his paranoia got so bad Mother couldn't go to the grocery store 'cause he was sure someone was gonna kill him when she left." Frowning, he bit his lower lip and stared at his hands before raising his head and continuing. "He got depressed. Couldn't hold a job. He'd shout and hit us when we'd try to help him.

"In the end he couldn't walk, couldn't feed himself, messed his bed. He wouldn't—or couldn't—talk. He just lay in bed like a lump, waiting to die." He looked up at Ms. Blair with tears in his eyes. "It was hell to live through. Jan, she didn't want to scare Gabe like that, so... so..." His throat muscles worked as he tried to continue.

"So her husband took her away and you concocted the story about them serving in the Peace Corps?"

George nodded. "Yeah."

"Before they left, did your nephew ever notice his mother's illness?"

George shook his head. "He didn't say anything. In the early days you get good at making up excuses for the clumsiness and shakies. It's only later that it's impossible to hide. But it's the in between..." He raised his head and looked at directly at Jenny. "The in between is bad."

Jenny wondered what George was thinking at that moment. Was he thinking that she was lucky to have been spared watching Gabe go through that hell? Perhaps dying young had spared Gabe the indignities and suffering Huntington's promised, but that didn't mean she shouldn't have his child. They could test the embryos. The devastating legacy could stop with their child.

"Mr. Turner, did you sue that reporter out of petty spite?"

"No."

"Did you sue him in hopes of retaining a hefty monetary settlement?"

"No."

"Did you sue him to get revenge?"

Another swift denial was what Jenny—and apparently Ms. Blair had been expecting, because she closed her eyes, to maybe count to ten, while George considered her question.

George looked away. A hardness in his eyes belied the weariness wrinkling his face.

"Partly," he admitted. "I sued him because he destroyed the woman I loved more than anything on this earth. I didn't want his money. I wanted to teach him a lesson. He didn't take his job seriously enough.

"You can't just prance around writin' things about people that aren't true. He had a responsibility to print the truth, and maybe *not* print the truth if it'd really hurt somebody. He had a responsibility to do his job keeping in mind human decency. This was people's lives he's screwing with. Some things the public does *not* have a right to know—does not need to know."

Wow, Jenny could almost respect George just then. She glimpsed the decent side of him that he kept well hidden behind a thick wall of abrasive rudeness. And she had to agree with him; reporters should be sensitive and respectful of the people they write about. It was a thin line they walked sometimes.

She felt sorry that one reporter's poor judgment had such a disastrous effect, but there were crummy people in all professions. It wasn't sensible or healthy to hate all types of people just because one had hurt you.

Ms. Blair looked resigned. "No more questions."

"Redirect?" The judge asked Helen.

"Yes." Helen stood. "Mr. Turner, you just claimed that a reporter has a responsibility to do his job keeping in mind human decency. That some things the public does *not* have a right to know. Correct?"

"Yes."

"Well, don't you think that the same human decency and right to privacy applies to this case too?" She raised a hand, keeping him from replying. "No. Just think a minute, before you answer."

George watched Helen through steady, angry eyes.

"Jenny Harrison's life has been torn apart by the loss of her beloved husband; just like yours was when your beloved Adele died," Helen began.

"Jenny's been so devastated by the loss of the man she loved more than anything on earth," Helen said, pausing, allowing the deliberate use of his words to sink in, "that she wants to have his baby. And because you can't respect their love and her loss, you've dragged her into court, and forced private discussions, mistakes, and tragedies to be laid wide open in the most public way." Helen paused a moment for effect. "How is what you're doing to Jenny any worse than what was done to you?"

George didn't answer right away. His mouth pinched in a tight, angry line. Jenny imagined that single long hair protruding from his bushy eyebrows even quivered with his emotions.

"This trial does invade her privacy, bringing out things that are none of the public's business." George looked straight at her with raised eyebrows, layering his forehead in wrinkles. "And I *am* sorry for that. And I hope to hell you all know what you've done in telling poor Alex and Ted about their dad. I tried to protect them, but... well what's done is done. But my privacy and my life are being invaded by this trial as much as hers. My family's business and mistakes have been exposed too. But it's the price I have to pay to see justice done.

"I sympathize with her loss, but what she's trying to do is still wrong. To be honest, I didn't know embryos could be tested so she doesn't have to worry about passing the Huntington's on, but what she's trying to do is irresponsible and defies human decency. I'm sorry we had to go to court this way, but she *needs* to be stopped. Before anybody else gets hurt."

Helen backed away. "No more questions."

"Okay, let's break early today. Tomorrow we'll have closing arguments." The judge smacked his gavel. "Court adjourned."

Chapter 24

Jenny climbed into Steve's Mustang and turned her face from the cameramen pressing close, trying to take her picture. She huddled in her seat, feeling truly awkward with Steve for the first time ever. He'd been coldly polite to her in front of others, putting up a professional lawyer front, but now that they were alone Jenny didn't know what to expect from him.

After fifteen minutes of silently reassessing her miserable situation, Jenny was unable to endure the quiet any longer. She turned in her seat to face him. "Say something."

Steve looked straight ahead.

"Please."

Several long uncomfortable seconds passed. "What do you want me to say?"

"I don't know," she nearly wailed in frustration. "Yell at me. Say you hate me. Tell me I'm a selfish bitch. Say *something*. Please."

Stopping for the light at the Yacht club, Steve looked straight ahead. "I don't hate you, Jenny."

He accelerated through the intersection. But she was a selfish bitch; he hadn't denied that. Jenny shrank back, wounded. He *should* be pissed. She wanted his anger—she deserved it. His disappointment hurt so much more.

Steve flipped on his blinker before turning into his driveway. They rolled up the long drive and parked in front of the garage. Without a word to her, he got out of the car and walked toward his house.

Jenny jumped out and rounded the car. Grabbing his arm she swung him around to face her. "You *should* be angry. I withheld important information that nullified our advantage. And I made you look foolish in court."

He stopped and looked at her. "So why'd you do it?"

Jenny's hand dropped to her side. Ah. The million-dollar question. "I just wanted the baby so badly. You and Judith said it was our ace. I never thought they'd ask if the baby was an accident— you didn't." She shrugged. "I didn't really think about what it would mean to you—to our friendship."

"You want the baby that badly?" He stared at her with steady penetrating eyes that seemed to bore into her, yet gave nothing away as to what he was thinking.

"It was an accident, really. Judith assumed that Gabe and I'd been trying to have a baby, and I didn't see a reason to correct her. I wanted it to be true." She shrugged; it was simple, really. "After a while, I almost convinced myself."

"Do you do that often?"

"Do what?"

Steve watched her carefully, studying her as if she were a curiosity. "Convince yourself that a lie is true."

"No. Well... maybe. I convinced myself Michael really was my little brother and not my baby. But not often, no."

"So, when something's really important to you, when you really want to win, you go to such lengths that you delude yourself into believing a reality that doesn't exist?"

He made it sound as if she was unbalanced. There was nothing psychotic in what she'd done. Just an assumption gone awry. "No, I—"

"You get on me for being competitive, but this is no different." Catching his bottom lip between his teeth, he nodded. "But I get it."

Get what? He didn't get it at all. Her nerves hummed at his calm understanding. She didn't know what he *thought* he understood, but she had a feeling it wasn't what she'd meant. She was *not* a bad person. She hadn't started out to deliberately mislead anybody.

"That's *totally* different," she said. It was different, but there was enough similarity to prick Jenny's conscience. Perpetuating a false assumption to get people to give her what she wanted wasn't so different from winning a game or a lawsuit—regardless of the cost. Both involved manipulating people. Jenny hung her head in shame.

"You're right, it *is* different." Steve folded his arms across his chest. "This was personal. One question. Why'd you tell the truth?"

"What?"

"Why'd you tell the truth about the baby being an accident?" When he looked at her, a lock of hair fell across his forehead, giving him a boyish look. "You didn't tell us."

"Why didn't you ask?"

"Yeah, that's on me. We should've asked, but to be honest," he bit his lower lip, "I didn't really want to know. Also if she asked, I figured you'd lie—nobody would've been able to prove otherwise."

"I thought about it. I tried," she confessed. "But I just couldn't do it."

"Why not?"

"I would've known. Gabe would've known. It just seemed wrong."

Hurt shimmered in his steady eyes. "But you had no problem lying to me."

Jenny's heart clench at his obvious pain. Nausea roiled in her stomach and she hated herself for hurting this sweet man. She opened and closed her mouth wordlessly before shrugging. "I didn't really lie to you and Helen—it was more an oversight. An assumption. It just kind of snowballed."

"Oh, come on." Steve's look of disbelief turned to ugly disgust. "We've shared a lot of personal stuff, Jen. We might have disagreed about things, but we've always been honest and trusted each other. At least we had that."

Steve spun on his heel and walked into the garage without a backward glance. How could she tell him that even though he was her lawyer, he was about the last person she could tell the truth to— *because* they were so close. The pregnancy, her and Gabe's fight, and then her running off that caused his death... she was so ashamed at how badly she'd handled it. It was too raw and it'd *all* been her fault; she couldn't bear admitting that to Steve.

"Wait. I'm sorry." She hurried after him, trotting by his side.

Steve waved a hand and didn't look back. "Not now."

"But—"

He went in the house and shut the door. The click echoed loudly in the garage. Jenny stared at the gleaming brass deadbolt. He'd locked her out.

Tears stabbed the back of her eyes as she stared at the scraped garage door. They'd had spats, but he'd always been willing to talk. She reached out to knock on the metal door, then drew back. He'd never turned his back on her before. He was really angry.

And he wondered why she hadn't told Gabe about Michael? *That* was exactly why. Gabe would've felt betrayed and disappointed in her. He probably would have shut her out just like Steve had. The truth would have wrecked her marriage just as this little lie wrecked her and Steve's friendship. And it would have hurt at least this much.

Jenny walked back to her house, his words echoing in her head. *We've always been honest with each other. At least we had that.* She'd really screwed up this time.

∾ ∾ ∾

Stephanie Blair walked through her apartment, kicking off her high heels on the way to the kitchen and her favorite beer. She quickly cut a wedge of lime and squeezed it into her Corona. Untucking her white silk blouse as she walked, she sipped the beer, savoring the tangy bitterness from the lime. She dropped onto the overstuffed denim couch and sighed loudly. Unclasping the plastic clip holding her twisted long hair, she ruffled it, massaging the roots that had been pulled all day long. She bounced one leg restlessly, rehashing her disastrous day in court.

George Turner was a royal pain in the ass. No wonder the partners pawned him off on her. They'd told her they were giving her the case because it'd be better having a woman represent him, but now she knew the truth; he was a pain in the ass they didn't want to deal with. It's a good thing this wasn't a jury trial, 'cause good old George was so offensive that even if they had an ironclad case, which they didn't, the jurors would've found an excuse to hang him.

And the Huntington's? Shit. How could she possibly have guessed that? And there'd been simply no way to defuse that bomb. Thanks again, George.

She propped her aching head against her fist and wiggled her toes. She needed a foot massage. She'd spent half the day on her feet questioning her client, racking her brain for any question that might remotely make him look good. And he'd called her stupid.

Something sharp snagged her foot.

"Youch!" She launched herself off the couch in time to see her cat dash away.

"Damn it, Clover." She inspected her foot. Sure enough, a long run was laddering up her calf. She groaned. "Another pair of hose ruined. Thanks a bunch."

The midsize calico came over, butting her head against Stephanie's calf, winding around her in apology. She picked Clover up and returned to the sofa.

"*Now* you want love? You're psychotic, cat. I don't need this abuse; I've got George Turner, thank you very much."

She sipped her beer, depressed. She'd gone into it knowing the case would be tough, but now it didn't look as if they had a leg to stand on. The Harrisons had had a perfect marriage by all accounts. Gabe Harrison had adored his wife and was probably up in heaven wondering what the hell we stupid mortals were doing.

Sometimes, when things were going particularly badly, she could almost imagine him yelling down, "Give her the damn sperm, you fools!"

And then there had been the embarrassment of having that prick Delaney chew her ass up and down over a simple misunderstanding. Embryos? Sperm? They were close. She hadn't deliberately tried to slip anything by him. How mortifying.

The only chance she might have is to play up Jenny Harrison's proclivity for lying. As a witness, she came across as the perfect grieving widow. And her attorneys had prepared her well. Why couldn't *she* be her client, instead of good old George?

The only time she'd seem Jenny's composure falter was when Stephanie had taken a shot in the dark and asked if she was Michael's mother. Jenny'd denied it of course, like she knew she would, but she'd paled and gotten this funny look on her face. At least she'd succeeded in throwing her off balance. Jenny had been totally unprepared for her next question and had to admit that she'd lied to the guard. But she sure had looked funny... almost sickly. Almost as if it were true.

Her thumb moved back and forth, wiping the condensation from the beer bottle, then suddenly stopped. My God, it couldn't be true, could it? Could she have perjured herself? If Michael was her son, she would have been a pregnant teenager. If she perjured herself and already had a child, her case would be blown out of the water. No judge in his right mind would give her the sperm.

Sick, Stephanie, really sick. You're grasping at straws now. Really desperate. But... what if it's true?

Crazier things happened. She'd check it out first thing in the morning. She picked up the meowing cat and poured a little beer in the empty candy dish on the coffee table to shut her up. Maybe she'd get lucky. Just maybe she could salvage this mess yet.

She smiled and raised her beer to the cat. "Cheers."

∾ ∾ ∾

Jenny dragged herself out of bed the next morning, wondering if she'd be driving herself to court today. She'd called Steve four times last night, trying to apologize again, but he refused to pick up. She'd marched across the driveway three times, but each time she chickened out before she got to his door. He was really mad. She had no idea what he'd do if she forced her presence on him.

As the garage door rolled up and Jenny opened the Jeep's door, Steve's car pulled up the driveway. He politely got out and opened the passenger door for her. Jenny shut her car and the garage doors and climbed into his car. Without the slightest glance in her direction, Steve backed out of the driveway and headed downtown.

Though Steve hadn't abandoned her, he wasn't ready to breech the chasm between them either; ten minutes of her nervous chatter was met with monosyllabic answers. Jenny couldn't stand the way he shut her out. "Steve, please. We have to discuss this."

"Not now."

"Then when?"

"Look," through hard eyes, he looked at her for the first time that morning, "you stepped over the line. What you did was not only stupid but manipulative—and that's what I'm having trouble with.

"As your attorney, that was key information we should've had. It was our mistake in overlooking it—that's what comes from being emotionally invested in the client—but you deliberately withheld it. You made us look stupid. I know this baby means a lot to you, but I won't be made a fool and I won't be manipulated." He raised an eyebrow. "Not even by you."

"I'm sorry. I didn't mean to hurt—"

"Back off, Jen." He looked at his hands wrapped around the steering wheel, squeezing until his knuckles turned white. "You still want that baby, don't you?"

"Of course, but—"

"Then concentrate on that."

"But—"

"*Shut* up." A muscle at his jaw pulsed. "Please."

Jenny felt empty, totally bereft. Gone was her best friend and in his place was this cold stranger-lawyer person. And she'd done it. She had no one to blame but herself. The interminable ride downtown finally ended, and for once, Jenny was glad of the distraction the swarming reporters provided. Now that the trial was winding down, the press seemed more energized than before, as if expecting a spectacular finale.

Depressed, Jenny took her seat next to the ever-present Helen and was surprised to see that George's attorney wasn't there yet. Ms. Blair hurried in just as the judge called the room to order. She tossed her raincoat over the back of her chair and slid into her seat.

He inclined his head toward Ms. Blair. "Nice of you to join us, counselor. Are we ready for closing arguments?"

"No, Your Honor." Ms. Blair smoothed a hair back into her twist as she withdrew a document from her briefcase. "We request leave to reopen the case due to new evidence that goes directly to the credibility of the defendant."

"What new evidence? Your Honor, I object," Helen said, standing.

"Counselors approach the bench."

Jenny looked uncertainly at Helen, who ignored her. Steve rounded the table from his side and joined them in front of the judge. A nervous chill quivered through Jenny's stomach. Helen looked concerned. Uh-oh. Her gaze went to Helen's blank legal pad. Empty. No new picture; Helen had been paying close attention instead of doodling. The judge and attorneys discussed the new evidence with hushed whispers Jenny couldn't hear.

Finally, the attorneys returned to their tables. The judge called the bailiff forward and whispered something to him, who in turn went to the court reporter.

"Counselors, Mrs. Harrison, join me in my chambers, please. Ms. Johnson, you have five minutes with your client."

"What's going on? What's the matter?" Jenny whispered.

Helen moved her and Steve toward the front of the courtroom, away from the crowd. Turning her back to the room, Helen grabbed her arm in a firm grip. "They've got Michael's birth certificate. They know you're his birth mother."

A buzzing sound filled Jenny's ears and she felt the blood drain from her face, leaving her lightheaded. She glanced at George's attorney. How had they found out?

Over her reading glasses, Helen's serious blue eyes stared at Jenny. "We're moving into chambers for your testimony. The judge will issue a gag order to protect Michael, but you're going to have to come up with some pretty solid answers—fast."

Judge Delaney's chambers were similar to Judge Moore's without the plants and homey touches. Definitely a much more stark, no-nonsense kind of room. The judge seated himself in a cushy high-backed leather chair behind his desk and motioned for Jenny to sit on his left. The other attorneys took seats nearby.

The bailiff swore her in and Ms. Blair began. "Mrs. Harrison, are you Michael Campbell's mother?"

"No." Her answer was swift and sure.

Ms. Blair reworded the question. "Did you give birth to Michael Campbell?"

"Yes."

She handed Jenny the birth certificate. "Do you remember filling this out?"

"Yes."

"So you lied yesterday when you said that Michael was not your son?"

"No. He isn't my son. I signed adoption papers when he was three days old. My parents are his legal parents. Michael was raised as my brother. I never mothered him and I have no parental rights. All I did was give birth to him." *And love him.*

"How did you come to be pregnant?"

"The usual way." Jenny couldn't resist the Alex-like answer.

"Objection, relevancy," Helen said.

"Goes to character."

"Sustained. Move on, counselor."

"Mrs. Harrison, have you given birth to any other children?"

"Not live birth."

"Have you ever been pregnant besides that one time and the one resulting in the miscarriage?"

"No."

"How many men have you had sexual intercourse with?"

"Objection," Helen called out, indignant.

Jenny closed her eyes in despair; this was getting *really* personal. Three, Michael's father, Jake, a guy she'd dated for three years in college, and Gabe.

"Goes to character." Ms. Blair raised Michael's birth certificate and waved it in the air. "The witness has already proven herself to be a consummate liar. If she's also promiscuous, she's certainly not suitable to raise children."

Helen turned to the judge. "Your Honor, we're not here to determine if Jenny Harrison is suitable to raise children, the issue is if Gabe Harrison would have wanted her to have his child. Pursuing this line of questioning is pointless.

"Sure, in her youth Jenny made some stupid mistakes and got pregnant, but she did *not* have an abortion. She did the responsible thing and gave her baby up for adoption—to people she knew to be loving, caring parents. She should be lauded for her courage. It took selfless love and bravery to put the well-being of her baby above that of herself. Yesterday Jenny answered Ms. Blair's question about Michael's parentage truthfully. She is *not* the child's mother.

"Michael Campbell is fourteen years old—still a minor," Helen continued. "He's had a wonderful childhood being loved by his adopted parents and his adopted sister. He's happy and well adjusted. He doesn't know that Jenny is his birth mother, and I ask that you honor his parents' right to tell him about his true lineage when they feel the time is appropriate."

"Objection sustained." He turned to Ms. Blair. "Counselor, unless you have new testimony to elicit, I suggest you rest."

"But, Your Honor, she lied under oath!"

"She did not. Jenny Harrison has *no* legal rights as the child's mother," Helen said.

"She's an unreliable witness," Ms. Blair sputtered. "She lied to—"

"I'll take your comments under consideration, counselor. Anything else?"

Ms. Blair clamped her jaw together before forcing out a "No, we rest."

"Okay. To protect the rights of the minor, Michael Joseph Campbell, everything disclosed in this testimony is to remain confidential." Judge Delaney looked around the room. His glance rested on Ms. Blair. "I assume I need not remind you that I will be listening closely to closing arguments to be sure you're following the strictest letter of my gag order." His stern gaze held Ms. Blair's, warning, "*Do not stray*, counselor."

The judge addressed Helen. "If you feel, at any time, anyone is in danger of violating my gag order simply say, 'objection goes to the court's previous ruling,' do *not* use the words, 'gag order'." He gave each attorney in turn a prolonged, serious stare. "Am I clear on this?"

"Yes, Your Honor."

Wow, Jenny was impressed by his emphatic determination to protect Michael and her family. Maybe he was a compassionate man after all. If this information leaked to the press, there would be an ugly frenzy. Judge Delaney's career could be immeasurably enhanced with a notorious precedent-setting case—especially if it had been sensationalized. But he had done the honorable thing and at least tried to protect them. Her previous animosity toward him evaporated, leaving only respect and hope.

"Very well." He checked his watch. "We'll break for lunch and begin closing arguments at one p.m."

Jenny left the room feeling confused yet relieved that Michael had been protected. Judge Delaney might be a young, uptight yuppie, but he'd put the fear of God into her. She'd hate to be the person that violated his gag order. Maybe things would be okay after all. She peeked at Steve and Helen. They looked pretty grim.

Jenny pulled Steve aside. "Helen didn't seem surprised to find out about Michael."

"She wasn't."

"How'd she know?"

"I told her."

Her eyes widened and her jaw dropped open. "But I told you that in confidence."

"And I told Helen in confidence. It was privileged client information she needed to know."

"She's *my* attorney. It wasn't up to you to tell her."

"Exactly." He gave her a hard look. "*You* should have."

"You had no right."

"Actually, I did." He pinned her with a steady look. "What're you so indignant about? It worked in your favor."

"But you betrayed my trust."

He cocked an eyebrow. "Hurts, doesn't it?"

Chapter 25

"Your Honor, we have provided indisputable proof of Jenny Harrison's immaturity, impulsive nature, and propensity to circumvent the truth," Ms. Blair began. "Jenny Harrison and her mother and father all testified that Mrs. Harrison defied her mother's wishes in buying her brother a skateboard, then broke hospital rules by sneaking into the hospital after hours, and then by impersonating her mother. All acts indicating her immaturity and poor judgment. Jenny Harrison is an overemotional young woman flighty in her endeavors, as indicated by her desire to become a foster parent simply because the need existed and she was writing an article about it at the time.

"Changing her mind about wanting children after two years of marriage is further evidence of her capricious nature. That she accidentally got pregnant and then never shared that joyful news with her husband before he was killed and she miscarried is evidence of her immaturity and manipulative nature. Being impulsive and overemotional is not in and of itself hurtful, although in the instance of her brother it very nearly proved fatal, but Mrs. Harrison carried it to a detrimental level.

"When Jenny Harrison was denied the opportunity to have the baby she'd *recently* decided she was desperate for, she selfishly had her defenseless husband's body repeatedly shocked until it gave up the sperm she needed for assisted conception. The paramedics, neurologist, and urologist all testified to Dr. Harrison's helpless state and to the fact that he never regained consciousness to give consent for his wife to have his sperm. Both Dr. Harrison's uncle and his first wife testified that Gabriel Harrison did not enjoy being raised by a single parent and would not have wanted it for his own child.

"Two times that we know of, Jenny Harrison either lied outright or lied by omission, to get her way. She lied to the hospital guard, claiming to be her brother's mother, so she'd be allowed to visit him, and she lied by omission to Dr. Steinmetz, not informing him of the great difficulty she was encountering in finding a sperm bank willing to store Dr. Harrison's sperm.

"How can the court trust the testimony of this witness? Especially when all we have is her word that Dr. Harrison would want her to have his child. You can't. The court can't give much weight to the testimony of a witness who has lied at least twice.

Ms. Blair sighed, as if feeling sorry for Jenny. "It's not that Mrs. Harrison is a bad person, but her record of poor decisions as testified to over the past few days by her family and Mrs. Harrison herself indicates that she's not a responsible person and that it is not in a child's best interest to be raised by her alone. Even if she had the money and time to devote to the child, she lacks the maturity to safely raise one.

"And finally, as Mr. Turner and Dr. Sterling testified, Dr. Harrison most likely did *not* want more children. He raised two children and was glad to be done. There's no evidence, other than Mrs. Harrison's unreliable claim, that he's ever changed his mind about this."

Ms. Blair gathered her papers and sat next to George.

Helen rose and approached the bench. "Your Honor, this isn't about Jenny Harrison's maturity. She admits to having made mistakes in her youth; who of us hasn't? But she *has* taken full responsibility for the mistakes and has demonstrated that she's learned from them. Case in point is her handling of her stepdaughter's dilemma concerning sexual relations. She educated her and urged her to use birth control. That sounds responsible to me.

"This case is about life, love, and revenge. In attempting to coerce Jenny into drawing up a prenuptial agreement, which her husband knew nothing about, George Turner proved himself a manipulative, jealous, interfering old man. In withholding information that Dr. Harrison had a deadly hereditary disease, again Mr. Turner proved himself to be manipulative and arrogant. He took away Dr. Harrison's choice to make critical life decisions for himself that affected not only Dr. Harrison, but his first wife and their two children.

"The death of his wife left Mr. Turner bitter and prejudiced against journalists in general. He clung to Gabe, his sole living relative, and was jealous of the love Gabe showered on Jenny. George Turner never liked Jenny. He didn't want her to help other people by gifting Gabe's organs and was furious because he had no control over it, so he's punishing her now by trying to deny her her husband's child.

"It's as simple as that. Under the Anatomical Gift Act, the law recognizes Jenny's right as the deceased's closest relative to donate his organs so that others might live. Why should this situation be any different? Is it right that Jenny can donate her husband's organs, helping as many as fifty people, yet she can't save his sperm to conceive just one child for herself? I think not.

"Jenny Harrison is a compassionate woman. Her husband recognized the goodness in her and loved her very deeply, so deeply that he gave his life for her. He took her place and pushed her out of the path of a truck. His *very last* thoughts were of Jenny. He loved her that much.

"Every single witness testified that Gabe and Jenny had a wonderful, loving relationship. Why would anyone ever assume that Gabe Harrison, who apparently doted on his wife, would deny her their child? He wouldn't. He'd want her to have the chance to conceive their child, knowing that the loving generosity she brought to their marriage would flow into her relationship with their child.

That's what Gabe Harrison would have wanted." Helen returned to her seat.

The judge took a moment to look over the courtroom. "Thank you very much, I will give everything careful consideration and issue my ruling in due course. Court dismissed." He smacked the gavel and left the room.

Jenny looked at Helen. "That's it? What's 'due course'?"

"It's as long as he takes. Could be a day, could be a month."

"A month? Great." She stood. "Will we have to come back to court to hear his decision?"

"Probably not. We'll probably get his decision in the mail."

"In the mail?" After the drama of the past week, how could things end so anticlimactically?

"Sorry."

"So... what do you think our chances are?" Jenny asked.

"It depends upon how compassionate he is and how much he disliked Ms. Blair. He had to about hate George; I can't see how anyone wouldn't. Since there are no precedents to go by, Judge Delaney pretty much gets to make his own decision. I think we made a sound case." Helen patted her arm. "There's nothing more we can do. You go home and relax."

As if she could. When they exited the courtroom, Helen waved them off and rushed away to a luncheon meeting. Jenny and Steve weaved their way through the lunchtime crowd, heading for the garage.

Suddenly a young woman thrust a microphone toward Jenny. "Mrs. Harrison, how'd it go?"

At the question, several other reporters ran over, swarming them. "Were there surprises in closing arguments?"

"If you win, how soon do you plan on trying to get pregnant?"

Jenny's head whipped from side to side, trying to identify who had asked which question, but the questions came fast and furiously.

"No comment." Steve put a guiding arm around Jenny's shoulder and pushed his way past.

The reporters followed, shouting more questions but eventually trailed off. Steve hustled them through the garage to his car. He quickly unlocked the car door and all but stuffed Jenny inside. She looked around the garage, then sighed in relief. No sign of reporters.

Jenny was grateful Steve had been by her side and she hadn't had to face those reporters by herself. She was used to being on the other side of the questions, being the hunter rather than the hunted—as it was. As an ex-baseball player, Steve undoubtedly had more experienced in evading the press than she had.

Jenny peeked at his set jaw and solemn expression. He was still mad. Throughout the trial, Steve maintained his silence. Now that the trial was over, even though he was still angry, he shielded her from the reporters. Was he being kind or did he pity her, thinking she didn't have a chance in hell of winning?

Suddenly it occurred to her that this messy trial could cost her not only her chance to have Gabe's baby, but her best friend. Head bowed, Jenny turned to the window and blinked back tears. When he pulled into her driveway and threw the gear into park, she put a hand over Steve's to keep him from getting out of the car.

"I know you need some time, but I need you to know that I'm sorry. Truly sorry." She reached out and put a hand to his cheek and turned his face so he looked at her. At his blank expression, she took a deep breath and forged on. "I perpetuated Judith's assumption that we'd conceived the baby on purpose 'cause I didn't see any harm in it, but then when it became the cornerstone of our defense, I didn't have the nerve to tell you it was a lie. I was too ashamed to tell you the truth and I'm very, very sorry.

"I know you need time to forgive me, but I need to know what I can do to make it up to you. There's this big gap between us and I can't stand it. I stayed up all last night, wracking my brain trying to find a way to make things right between us, and I'm at a total loss. I want things to be the way they were before."

Steve stared ahead one long minute before answering. "Things will never be the same between us."

Jenny's heart dropped, leaving a sick feeling in the pit of her stomach.

"We can't pretend this never happened—just like we couldn't pretend that night on the couch never happened. I didn't forget. You didn't either." He raked a hand through his hair, then looked at her. "I don't know what to tell you."

"Tell me you forgive me and we can move past this."

"I forgive you." Steve got out of the car and walked around to open her door.

"And we can get past this," she repeated, refusing to get out of the car until he agreed.

"I've got to get to work."

"We *will* get past this." Jenny wouldn't accept any less. She *would* find a way to rebuild the trust she'd shattered.

"I hope so," he said softly.

She had to be satisfied with that. Unbuckling her seatbelt, Jenny climbed out of the car but stood in the opening so he couldn't shut the door. "Dinner tomorrow night? I'll grill steaks."

"I'll be home late. Work piled up while I was gone."

"How about a movie Saturday?"

"Hockey game."

She held onto the car door. "Wednesday's the unveiling of the new children's corner at the clinic; I don't suppose you'll be there?"

"I doubt it."

"Your firm donated the money," she persisted.

He waited, silently watching her, waiting for her to get out of his way.

"Okay." Jenny backed out of the opening, allowing Steve to slam the door closed. She stood still, watching him back out of the driveway, praying he wasn't backing out of her life as well.

∾ ∾ ∾

To help pass time while she waited for the verdict to come in, Jenny threw herself into work, tutoring Grammy J, and volunteering at the clinic. Two mornings a week she read to children waiting to see the doctor and then worked on last-minute tweaks of the children's corner remodel. The other days, she researched her article on teenager sleep deprivation as associated with electronics in their lives.

Jenny took Judith to lunch to thank her for her help during the trial and to see if she'd made a decision about telling the kids about the Huntington's Disease. Judith, though still angry, was calmer. She and Dave elected to tell Ted and Alex that they may have inherited Huntington's after Alex graduated college or before either of them married or got pregnant—at least that was the plan, barring any unforeseen pregnancies.

Once the kids were told, they'd have to decide for themselves if they wanted to be tested. Either way, Judith and Dave felt it imperative that Ted and Alex have a college degree, and telling them while they were in school would be a formidable and unfair distraction. Jenny thought it was probably the best plan given the circumstances and offered Judith an understanding ear and shoulder to lean on anytime she needed it.

Sadly, Jenny's fight with George suddenly felt petty in light of what Ted and Alex would soon face. She'd gladly give up the chance to have Gabe's baby if it meant Ted and Alex never had to worry about Huntington's; unfortunately she couldn't make that deal, their destiny was already sealed.

Wednesday morning, Jenny wore a loose cotton dress and sandals. She pulled her hair back in a ponytail and applied a little lip-gloss. In the kitchen, she snatched her cell from the countertop. Pausing, she hefted it in her hand. Her thumb hovered over the screen. Should she call him? Would he answer?

She tossed the phone in her purse. Jenny opened the garage door to let Ritz out and looked at Steve's silent house. He was probably already at work. Sighing, she loaded up the Jeep with Danishes, muffins, and fresh fruit from Costco and headed downtown.

For their ten thousand dollars, Patricia Corbridge suggested that it might be nice to have a little unveiling ceremony. Gianna joked that for a fifty thousand dollar donation, she'd name her next child after Patricia; an appreciation ceremony was little enough to ask. So before opening for business that morning, they'd planned a little pomp and circumstance.

Jenny slowly rolled down her driveway and paused one last time to look in her rearview mirror at Steve's garage door and empty driveway. Steve had been conspicuously absent these past few weeks and she missed him terribly. Gosh, how much time did he need? She blew out a deep, sad breath before pulling out onto Lakeshore Drive and heading south.

Twenty-five minutes later, Jenny swung into the handicapped parking space in front of the clinic, and Max, the security guard, came out to help unload the Jeep before she moved her car to the parking lot. Inside, Gianna and the receptionist were spreading a tablecloth over a long table as Patricia Corbridge directed them by gesturing with the colorful flower centerpiece in her hands. A few strangers already milled about the room.

A van bearing the logo of the local TV station pulled to the curb. She smiled and walked through the clinic doors. Patricia Corbridge must have been a marketing magnate before marrying Daniel, 'cause she sure knew how to work an event.

Jenny scanned the freshly painted, pale yellow room, looking for any last minute details that might need attention. A huge tarp tacked to the ceiling hid the cozy rug and rocking chair in the new reading corner.

An assortment of children's books and magazines lay neatly stacked in the new magazine rack on one wall, while a large square sheet of steel had been bolted to the other wall so children could play with the alphabet and assorted magnates there.

The tarp stretched around the corner, hiding the colorful fish exploring their new home in Patricia's built-in fish tank. A local artist had donated her talents to paint vivid, adorable murals of children reading and playing. It started in the waiting room and continued along the hallway into a few exam rooms.

A TV combo DVD player now hung from the ceiling near the receptionist/sign-in counter, and Gianna had gotten several educational tapes about childcare and hygiene to run in it when they weren't playing children's DVDs. Twenty new, cushioned chairs lined the walls and divided the center of the large room, and a few live green plants composed the finishing touches.

People trickled in off the street, but Jenny's quick scan of the room failed to locate Steve. He wasn't coming. She pasted a smile on her face and looked for something to do.

Gianna showed up at her back and put an arm around her waist. "Looking for someone?"

Jenny shook her head. "Not really."

"Too bad." Gianna leaned in and raised an eyebrow. "Look who just walked in."

Jenny's head jerked toward the door and her heart lifted. Expecting to see Steve, her gaze skimmed right over Grammy J and Clarisse as she searched the few men. She looked back at the Johnsons. Oh, that's whom Gianna was referring to. Gianna didn't even know Steve.

Jenny smiled and moved forward, greeting them with big hugs. "Hi. How're you guys?"

"We wanted to stop by and celebrate your big unveiling."

"What about work?" She turned to Clarisse. "And school for you, young lady."

"I told Ms. Kingsly I'd be an hour late today and she said it'd be all right," Grammy J said.

Jenny put an arm around the elderly woman's shoulder. "I'm glad to see you."

Gianna moved close, murmuring, "Just about time to start. Patricia's got the camera crew where she wants them."

More people entered the room until it almost achieved its thirty-person capacity. Gianna stood in front of the tarp and raised her voice. "Good morning, everybody. My name is Gianna Donnatelli Scarfili, and I'd like to welcome you to the Donnatelli Clinic. Ten years ago, my father opened this clinic in memory of my mother, who suffered from multiple sclerosis.

"I won't bore you with all the family history, but my father's gone now, so my family and I run the clinic to preserve his vision of quality medical care for all. But we couldn't do it without private donations and the generosity of our volunteer doctors and nurses. We're here today to unveil the efforts of several other people who have selflessly and thoughtfully supported us."

Gianna looked at Patricia and then Jenny, who blushed and studied her feet. "Dr. Gabe Harrison was one of our staff doctors who volunteered several times a week. As you might know, we lost Dr. Harrison this past year, but his wife, Jenny, picked up where Gabe left off.

"Jenny brought some friends in for treatment on a particularly chaotic day and took it upon herself to entertain the waiting children—and she's been doing this nearly every week since." Gianna made it sound as if the clinic was hard-up for patients and that Jenny had done them a huge favor.

"But not content to stop there, Jenny solicited the help of Patricia Corbridge and her husband's law firm to fund this wonderful transformation we're about to reveal. So our sincerest thanks go out to Jenny Harrison and Knight, Corbridge and Howe."

Grinning broadly, Gianna raised her hands and clapped. Jenny looked at Patricia and joined in. It was Patricia who'd really wrung that huge donation from her husband; Jenny just started the ball rolling.

Beyond Patricia, just inside the front door, Jenny spied a tall light-haired guy. Steve. He stood at the back, behind two young mothers with children on their hips, clapping. His gaze locked on hers and he nodded in approval.

Jenny's heart swelled; he'd come. Her attention was snagged by the gust of air generated by the fluttering, dropped sheet.

"At the firm's suggestion, we had this plaque made up in honor of Dr. Harrison and thusly christen this children's corner, 'Harrison's Hideaway.'" Smiling at Jenny, Gianna gestured to a carved and painted wooden sign hanging on the wall.

Jenny eyes widened in surprise and she couldn't stop staring at the beautifully crafted sign. Gabe would've been embarrassed at the honor, but she appreciated it. Gabe would not be forgotten.

"This concludes our ceremony. Please, enjoy the refreshments while Mrs. Johnson, one of our newest volunteers, breaks in our new corner and reads to the children."

A slow, proud smile broke across Jenny's lips as Grammy J took Clarisse's hand and moved to corner.

"Come along. Gather 'round," she called to the children. Selecting a book from the rack, she eased into the rocking chair and settled in. Looking around the children gathered at her feet, she said, "We're going to read a story about a bunch of silly dogs."

Jenny moved forward as Grammy J began the simple Dr. Seuss book. Her delivery wasn't quite smooth and she tended to supplement the text with questions for the children, but she was reading. Jenny caught her eye and gave her a thumbs up. It took guts to learn to read at her age. What a wonderful example she set for her grandkids—for all of them. Brave lady.

Jenny headed toward the door, anxious to brag about her friend to Steve, but he wasn't there. She looked right, then left, and over her shoulder, but he wasn't at the refreshments table either. He'd left. But at least he'd come. That had to count for something.

Jenny pushed aside her disappointment and, with one more glance at Grammy J, she went to get a glass of juice.

"That's something, eh?" Gianna said. "They love her."

"I'll say. A few months ago, she couldn't read a word."

"I know. She told me." Gianna nodded. "She came to us about a week ago and said she couldn't read too well yet, but she wanted to do something to repay us for taking care of her and her grandchildren. She said the children like your reading so much that she thought maybe she could read to them once a week." Gianna raised her shoulders. "How could I say no?"

"*Why* would you say no?"

"Exactly."

"That's my friend." Jenny beamed and stood a little taller. "Isn't she amazing?"

Chapter 26

Jenny left the pharmacy and sat in her car. She slumped in her seat and stared at the ovulation kit. Surgery. Shots. In vitro. The words bounced around her brain like boomeranging lottery ping pong balls. She pressed her head back and sighed heavily. It all sounded so painful. And complicated.

Should she trust that the judge would rule in her favor and move ahead with the egg extraction or wait for his ruling? Would fresh collected eggs work better than those collected months ago? She hadn't even thought to ask the doctor that.

Where was Gabe when she needed him? He could've helped her navigate these medical decisions, and she'd be confident that they'd have made the best choice. If Gabe had known about the Huntington's, he would have insisted on IVF.

More likely he would have been adamantly opposed to having more children, her little voice whispered. *With good reason.*

Living with Huntington's would have been increasingly difficult for them. Jenny spent days on the Internet researching the disease: symptoms, progression, current treatments, and prognosis. The Internet was an endless supply of information, and bless those brave people who bared their souls and unselfishly shared their experiences on Huntington forums and message boards. They gave her the unvarnished truth about what Gabe would've faced, and a brutal glimpse into Alex and/or Ted's potential future challenges.

Gabe would have needed to devote all his energy to exploring new treatment options, not caring for a baby. Given Gabe's condition, she probably would have put off having children so she could take care of Gabe and enjoy the time they had left together.

Even with the worst-case scenario, Gabe would have had another ten to fifteen years and that would have made Jenny thirty-eight to forty-three. Old to start having kids. Jenny blew bangs out of her eyes. Obsessing over what might have been was a waste of time.

Gabe was gone and she was here, and she could have his *healthy* baby. She picked up the purple box and turned it over in her hands. She tapped it lightly against the steering wheel. Now, dare she risk proceeding before getting the judge's ruling?

Who could she go to for advice? Not Steve. He'd been avoiding her since the trial ended. Jenny hated the distance between them but clung to the hope that he'd forgive her in time. Sooner than later would be better. She missed him terribly. She missed the way he made her laugh, missed his teasing, his company at meals or watching a movie. Steve was right: when he finally forgave her, things between them would be different. They were different. She was different. This time she'd cherish and respect his friendship and trust.

Deep down, Jenny sensed Steve cared for her more than just as a friend, but she wasn't ready for that complication—he wasn't either. He seemed recovered from the breakup, but he'd moped around for months. Steve lost not just Annie but her kids too. He'd had a double whammy just like when both Gabe and the baby died. She knew what that felt like.

Jenny hadn't realized Annie's divorce had been so recent or she'd have recognized Steve was her rebound guy. They never had a chance. She should be sad for the pain her friend went through but was selfishly glad they'd called the engagement off. She'd had Steve's undivided attention for these difficult seven months.

Jenny turned on the hot car and rolled down the windows to catch the breeze. Hmm. She'd had Steve's support, but what'd she given him? Cookies? Companionship? A sounding board and willing ear when he needed to discuss work? Not much. She'd used him.

First to jump start her career with the article for *People*, then for comfort when she'd spent the night with him to avoid facing her and Gabe's empty house, and most recently she'd used his lawyer skills to get the baby she so desperately wanted. Jenny winced. *I am one selfish bitch.*

She tossed the ovulation kit into the passenger's seat in disgust. Steve was a good man. He deserved better than her. But he refused to look for anyone better. Because of her? Jenny didn't know how long he'd cared—didn't want to know—but she had to do better with Steve.

Her gaze dropped to the ovulation kit. Her old confidant couldn't help her on this one. Maybe her mother could. Mom had had trouble getting pregnant with Jenny and then had had multiple miscarriages after her birth. Maybe she could help her decide what to do.

Reaching for her seatbelt, Jenny buckled in and headed for her parents' house. Since Mom semi retired last year, she spent the majority of her days in the yard, tilling, planting, weeding, pruning, raking, fertilizing, mowing—doing it all. While they could afford a lawn service, her parents refused to even consider it, maintaining that they did a far better job than any service. Jenny couldn't argue that; they had the most beautiful yard on the block. It was something they enjoyed doing together and that was important.

She found her mom weeding in the back yard. Crouching down next to her, Jenny pulled out a tall weed hiding beneath a tomato plant. "Missed one."

Her mother jumped. A gloved hand flew to cover her heart. "Good Lord, Jennifer Lyn, you scared me. What're you doing here?"

She sat Indian-style on the grass next to the garden and pulled a scraggly weed. "I need advice."

"About what?" Mom sat with her legs folded to the side and pulled off her gardening gloves, giving Jenny her full attention.

"Pregnancy. Conception, really."

"Not exactly my strong suit, if you recall."

Jenny brushed the dirt from her hands. "I have to use in vitro fertilization to get pregnant. I'll have to give myself hormone shots every day and have all kinds of blood tests. Then when the time is right, have general anesthetic to laproscopically remove some of my eggs to mix with Gabe's sperm in a petri dish. Once we see how many eggs are fertilized, they test them for Huntington's, and then we decide how many of the healthy embryos to implant."

"It sounds involved."

"Yeah." She ran a blade of grass through her fingers. "You know that now they can even take a single sperm and help it penetrate an egg to almost ensure fertilization? It's amazing."

"But?" her mother asked gently.

"It's so clinical."

"You knew getting pregnant with Gabe gone wouldn't exactly be natural."

"At first it seemed so simple. Save Gabe's sperm, take it home, squirt it up, and after nine months I get a sweet baby to love. I get a forever reminder of Gabe and our love and my own little family—me and the baby." Jenny licked her lips and frowned. "But it keeps getting more and more complicated. What should have been simple and private has become complicated and public. And painful."

She scanned Jenny's face. "Are you having doubts about wanting the baby?"

"No. I *want* the baby." She paused, swamped in confusion. "But how do I know what I want is what I should have? Like a kid *wants* all kinds of candy and goodies, but it's not good for him to eat all that." She looked at Mom, hoping for an epiphany. "How do I know having this baby's the right thing to do?"

"That's a toughie. Life doesn't come with a road map or guarantees. You just have to look at the situation from all sides and make the best decision you can."

"It's sooo complicated. And it keeps getting worse. It was bad enough fighting George, but now finding out about Gabe's Huntington, artificial insemination's out and I *have* to do in vitro."

"Then do in vitro."

"But then I'm creating embryos—little prebabies. And they'll discard the ones that test positive for Huntington's and only implant the healthy ones."

"Ah..." Mom's frown, smoothed and her expression lightened. "So that's the real problem. You're upset at discarding unhealthy embryos."

"I guess." She sighed. "It doesn't seem fair. They're embryos I created. It's not their fault they're not healthy. It's my fault, yet they'll have to pay the consequences for my decision to create them."

"You know embryos don't have any cognitive processes—no feelings. Some would debate that they're not really even alive since they're not viable outside a womb."

"I know, but we don't know for sure they don't have feelings. They undoubtedly have souls. And I know that giving birth to a flawed, painful life is choosing to make them suffer and it's probably better for them to never be born," She made a face. "But it seems so heartless and wrong." She sighed. "Then you freeze the healthy ones you don't use right away—that seems a bit barbaric. And thirty to thirty-five percent of those don't survive the thawing to implant, so it's almost like killing them. And I might get twins or triplets." She turned to her mother, pleading. "Tell me what to do."

Mom's glance sharpened and she pulled back. "Ho ho. Not a chance. You're not putting this on me. This is one of those damned if you do and damned if you don't moral decisions that I don't think has a clear right or wrong answer." She paused. "You're making a decision for you and your future child. Ultimately you're the only one who can puzzle this out 'cause you've got to live the rest of your life with the choice you make. And Dad and I will support whatever you decide."

"Hey, Jen." Bowl in hand, Michael came out the sliding glass doors. He shoveled a heaping spoonful of cereal into his mouth, mumbling, "Wha's fo din'r, Mom?"

Mom shaded her eyes against the lowering sun and looked up at him. "Leftover spaghetti."

"After that huge bowl of cereal?" Jenny asked.

He hefted his bowl at her. "Snack." He shook his head and plunked down on a boulder near them. "I ate the spaghetti for breakfast. Dad home?" He tilted the bowl, scraping the last of the cereal.

"Not till tomorrow night. I guess we're having pizza." She turned to Jenny. "Want to stay for dinner?"

"Sure."

Mom looked at Michael. "Call Nona's and order what you want."

"Buddies pizza?"

"Fine."

Michael stood. "Can I drive?"

Mom picked a clump of grass and shook the dirt off it. "Sure, Jenny'll go with you while I clean up."

Michael pumped a fist in the air and turned toward the house.

"Bowl," Mom yelled after him.

"You want me to drive with him?" She hadn't driven with Michael since he'd finished Driver's Ed last month. He was well-coordinated and had good spatial recognition, so she bet he had a good feel for driving, but...

"Take my car. Just be careful on Mack Ave. He has a tendency to gun it through yellow lights instead of stopping." Her mother smiled slyly. "Here's a little taste of parenting."

"Great." A parenting lesson seemed a bit premature when she couldn't even decide *how* to get pregnant. "I still don't know what to do about the baby."

"Let me ask you this." Mom tossed a weed in her bucket, then looked at Jenny. "Do you want *a* baby or Gabe's baby? If the judge decides against you, would you get a sperm donor who had Gabe's characteristics and have a baby?"

"No." She frowned. "I mean, I don't think so. It never occurred to me." Just *a* baby? It would certainly cure her loneliness, give her something to love and keep her busy... "No. I only want Gabe's baby."

"So this isn't about experiencing pregnancy and being a mom."

"No." She shook her head. "But I'm not so sure I should have it if it involves IVF with genetic selection. I mean logically I know it's the only way to ensure a healthy child, but..."

"You're overthinking it. Deep down, you know what's right for you."

Jenny sat, trying to silence the conflicting thoughts so she could feel the right answer. The deep green grass blurred before her eyes, and she suddenly realized the other part of her dilemma. She wiped her eyes, but couldn't look at her mother, somehow feeling ashamed.

"I don't *really* know what Gabe would want either. I told the judge I did—I thought I did, but now I'm not so sure. I know *I* want it, but..." She knew Gabe hadn't wanted *them* to have a child. He hadn't wanted to do the work of raising another child, hadn't wanted to share her or saddle them with the responsibility, but would he have been in favor of Jenny having his child and sharing her life with him or her in his stead? She didn't really know anymore. She raised worried eyes to her mother. "I *think* he would."

"Honey, Gabe's gone. I don't mean to be cruel, but he really isn't going to have any impact on this child's life. He'll just be a story to the child. This is going to be *your* baby."

She was right. Whether Gabe would've approved or not really didn't affect her having their baby. If the judge gave her the right to his sperm, it didn't matter what Gabe wanted, only what she wanted. After all, she'd be the one raising it. Jenny lifted her head and stared at her mom. "Am I making this harder than it needs to be?"

"Not this time, sweetie. It's a hard decision; one you can't undo."

They sat silently looking over the neat rows of swiss chard, lettuce, and beans. Jenny dragged her index finger through the warm dirt, drawing a heart. Why couldn't life be simple? Why was her life full of shady spots, poor soil, and weeds?

"If I actually win, I've gone through so much to gain this opportunity." So much time, expense, heartache... It even affected her relationship with friends and family. Steve. The trial spilled over into all aspects of her life. "How can I not do it? Otherwise it was all for... what?"

Mom threw a weed in the basket and turned to Jenny. "I don't know; that's for you to figure out."

Jenny looked sideways at her mom. "I liked it better when you had all the answers."

"I never had all the answers." She smiled. "You just thought I did."

ᖇ ᖇ ᖇ

Jenny thought about the conversation with her mom many times over the following weeks and decided to leave it up to Fate—or Judge Delaney. If she won, it would be a sign that she was meant to have Gabe's baby; if he didn't decide in her favor, then it wasn't meant to be. She could live with that.

Jenny decided to adopt a proactive, positive stance and to take the shots and at least go as far as harvesting her eggs. If she didn't win, she'd simply discard them. Nothing wrong with being prepared.

Several weeks later, Jenny let herself into the house after having taken a long walk with Ritz. She was washing down a couple of extra-strength Tylenol since fresh air hadn't eliminated her splitting headache, when she heard a voice leaving a message on the answering machine. She rushed to the receiver and picked it up. "Helen?"

"Jenny, you're home?"

"I just got in. What's up?"

"His ruling's in," Helen said without preamble.

"And?" She held her breath. *Please, God. Please, God. Let it go my way.*

"And... we won."

"We won? I got it?"

"You got it." Jenny heard the smile in Helen's voice. "He ruled in your favor."

"So... I can do it?"

"Any time you're ready. I'll send you a copy of his ruling. He says, 'in light of the evidence presented and my review of relevant law, it is my determination that Mrs. Jennifer Harrison has every right to exercise ownership over the property of the deceased, her husband, including his sperm.' You've won. Let's celebrate."

She'd won! Wow. She could have Gabe's baby! Jenny took back every mean word and thought she ever had about the young judge. Apparently he was a very sensitive, sensible, compassionate man— with excellent judgment. A great judge.

A mom. Wow. She could have Gabe's baby.

"Does Steve know yet?" Jenny asked. They'd not quite recovered their earlier comfortable relationship, though Steve had stopped avoiding her and the awkwardness was slowly melting with each interaction.

"He should. I've had reporters calling already. I sent them a copy of the ruling."

Why didn't he call me himself? Jenny wanted to ask, a little hurt that Steve hadn't wanted to break the good news to her. Was he upset or happy? Or was he just relieved to have it over with? He should have been thrilled; he'd won.

"So where do you want to meet?" Helen asked.

"How about Antonio's?"

"Great, I love Italian food. What time?"

Jenny looked at the wall clock. "Six thirty?"

That would give her time to call the doctor and give him the good news, take a hot bubble bath scented with lavender and chamomile to clear the remnants of her headache before dinner.

"Okay. Should I call Steve or do you want to?" Helen asked.

"I'll call."

"Great. See you later."

"Thanks, Helen."

They'd won. Jenny lifted Ritz's front paws and danced her around the kitchen on her hind legs, chanting, "We won, we won. We're gonna have a baby, Ritz."

Jenny pulled her close and hugged her until the dog squirmed and tugged away. Dropping her paws, she picked up the phone and dialed Steve's work number. "Hi, this is Jenny Harrison, is Steve in?"

I'm sorry, Mr. Grant is no longer with Knight, Corbridge, and Howe. Could I connect you with someone else?" The operator recited in a bored monotone.

"Pardon me? Since when?"

"I'm not allowed to give out that information."

"Did he go to another firm?"

"I'm not allowed to—"

"Forget it," Jenny cut in. She poked the off button, then dialed Steve's cell. When he didn't pick up, she left a message about dinner.

He'd left Knight, Corbridge, and Howe? How come? Why hadn't he said anything? Had he been fired because of her? But they'd won. A high-profile case—that should please the partners.

When she'd seen Steve two days ago, he hadn't said anything about a job change. Why hadn't he said something? They always shared that kind of news. Unless... he'd been fired because of her. Then he wouldn't tell her. Deep in thought, Jenny sat on a kitchen stool. Did Helen know that Steve was no longer with his firm?

Jenny checked the time, and saw that she barely had enough time to change before meeting Helen. She pushed the gloomy thoughts away. Maybe Steve had gotten a better job offer and hadn't told her because he was waiting for the ruling to come in. Maybe they'd be celebrating his new job and her win. Cheered by that thought, Jenny headed upstairs.

After quick calls to her parents and Judith, Jenny exchanged her T-shirt for a peach tank top to wear with her favorite capris. She slipped her feet into flip-flops. A baby. Jenny hugged herself, and with a flying leap, she squealed and dove onto their bed. She was going to have Gabe's baby.

Jenny arrived at the restaurant just as Helen got out of her car. Grinning broadly, she ran over and gave the older woman a big hug. "Thank you *so* much."

"You're welcome. Actually it was a lot of fun," Helen confided. "Almost makes me want to come out of retirement."

Jenny followed her into the restaurant. "You should. You're a terrific attorney."

"You're only saying that because we won. You might've thought differently had we lost."

Jenny thought about Helen's drawings and seeming inattentiveness during the trial and her own doubts about Helen's competency. Given Helen's laid-back court demeanor, Jenny had to admit that she was probably right. She instantly banished the confession. They'd won. It was time to celebrate.

While waiting for Steve, they had a glass of Chianti and Jenny's favorite appetizer. They savored the scarmorza, lingering over the rich, lemon, butter, cheesy bread creation, topped with black olives and capers, until it was gone. Having waited twenty minutes, they went ahead and ordered dinner.

She watched Helen carefully. "Did you know Steve's no longer with Knight, Corbridge, and Howe?"

Iron eyebrows arched high. "No. How'd that come about?

Judging her surprise genuine, Jenny relaxed. "I don't know. I was hoping you could tell me."

"I had no idea."

"Think he got fired, because of me?" Jenny asked softly.

"O-h, I doubt it. But why wouldn't he have said something?"

Jenny's heart clenched. "He didn't want to make me feel bad."

She pursed her lips and nodded. "That could be."

Then Steve materialized at their table. "Sorry I'm late." He took a chair between them. "There was an accident on ninety-four." The waiter appeared at Steve's side, gave him a menu and took his drink order.

"We figured it was something like that, so we went ahead and ordered," Helen said.

"Why aren't you at Knight, Corbridge, and Howe anymore?" Jenny blurted.

Steve turned his tawny head toward her and took a sip of his water. "Hi to you too. Congratulations." He enveloped her in a quick, tight hug.

"Did they fire you because of me?"

"You won. Aren't you thrilled?" Steve patted her hand twice.

Jenny snatched her hand away, unwilling to be cheered or distracted. She wanted the truth. "Why aren't you with the firm anymore?"

"You knew I wasn't happy there. They just hired me for my name."

"Did you get fired?"

"I got tired of being used, so I'm opening my own firm. I found this great office downtown in the Ren Cen." He ripped off a chunk of bread and swirled it in olive oil, then looked at Helen. "You wouldn't be interested in being one of the founding partners, would you?"

"Seriously?" Her eyes widened.

He nodded. Chewing quickly, he swallowed and licked the oil from his thumb. "I know you're retired, but you could work a couple of years and get us up and running, then faze out as you want to. After this win I don't think we'll have trouble getting clients."

"You'd want an old lady like me for a partner?"

"It'd be a chore..." Steve teased, then reached for another piece of bread. "I'd love to have a cunning, experienced woman like you for a partner."

"Excuse me," Jenny broke in. "Did you quit or get fired?"

"Be still my heart." Helen's eyes twinkled and she blushed like a schoolgirl. "I just may take you up on that offer."

"I'm counting on it." His head bobbed as he poured more olive oil on his bread plate.

"Let me think about it and I'll get back to you." Helen glanced at her watch. "I've got to get to my daughter's in time for cake—it's my granddaughter's birthday today."

"Why didn't you say so? We could've done this another time." Jenny hated that Helen was missing her granddaughter's birthday party for her. She shouldn't miss a family event on her account.

The waiter brought Steve his wine.

"Nope, had to be tonight. It's tradition." Helen raised her glass to Jenny. "To your good health, happiness, and motherhood." She then turned to Steve, "And best of luck with your new venture."

"*Our* new venture, partner," he corrected as he clinked his glass with hers.

Jenny raised her glass to Helen and then to Steve. Steve smiled warmly, mesmerizing her with twinkling blue eyes. If he'd been fired, he didn't seem too broken up about it.

"Well, children, I've got to run." Helen stood and motioned Steve back into his seat when he stood politely. She turned to Jenny. "Take care. And I expect to be invited to the baby shower."

"Of course." She got up and hugged the older woman close, suddenly shamed by her doubts. "Thanks again."

Helen patted her back. "You're welcome, honey. Have some Tiramisu; I hear it's wonderful."

Jenny sat down feeling somewhat bereft. Alone with Steve, she felt unexpectedly awkward and shy—then annoyed when she remembered how he'd avoided answering her questions. His good mood confused her. After being mad at her for weeks, it appeared that he'd finally forgiven her—which was good—but she didn't know where they stood.

The waiter came and took Steve's dinner order. Jenny watched Steve closely. Was he really happy, or just putting up a front? He hadn't wanted her to win.

Steve smoothed the cloth napkin back across his lap and smiled. "Well. You did it."

"I didn't do anything. You and Helen did it—despite me." Jenny looked at him, hoping he'd see the sincerity in her expression. "Thank you."

"*I* did very little. You saw it through and fought for something you believed in. That takes guts."

"I didn't make it easy for you." Jenny briefly rested her hand on his arm. "I'm sorry."

"Forget it. So, where do you go from here?"

The waiter delivered Steve's veal and Jenny declined dessert. "Well, amazingly enough, this couldn't have come at a better time. I'm going in for egg extractions in a couple of days." She raised her eyebrows, "So we're good to go."

Thank God. Hopefully she wouldn't have to go through another month of taking drugs. Even though the expected mood swings had been minimal, nasty headaches associated with the hormone treatment had been anything but minimal. She wasn't going to miss that.

Steve's chewing slowed. "So soon? Are you ready?"

More than ready. Feeling a little strange talking about such an intimate thing as if it were just another doctor's appointment, Jenny tucked her hands under her thighs and leaned forward, lowering her voice. "Yup. The doctor says we'll have just enough time to get the sperm."

"Well... that's great then." His smile seemed a little uncertain, forced.

"What's the matter?"

Steve stabbed another mouthful of pasta, but instead of eating it, he twirled the fork around and around in his hand. "Nothing."

"But?"

"But nothing. I'm happy for you," he insisted, but Jenny sensed his withdrawal.

"What about you? Where do you go from here?"

"I signed the lease on my new office. So I'll be busy interviewing staff and setting up shop."

"It seems a bit risky. Can you afford to do this?" She squirmed, hoping he wouldn't think she was prying into his finances.

"I'll be okay—at least for a few months."

"This is all my fault. I'm sorry. I—"

"Jen. I was just teasing." He paused. "I made enough money playing ball that, if I were *really* frugal," he fixed her with a serious look, "I could probably get by for... the rest of my life and the next one, without working." He grinned broadly.

Jenny swatted his arm. "Jerk."

"It's sweet of you to worry."

"Just worried about my property value. I don't want them selling your house as a foreclosure," she said airily.

He laughed. Finishing his meal, Steve paid the bill, stood and stretched out a hand to her. He clasped her hand in his and then pulled her out of her seat toward the door. As they left the restaurant, he didn't let go.

Jenny relished the feeling of his big warm hand wrapped around hers. It was comforting, yet at the same time strangely intimate. They walked down the street toward her car. She looked at their clasp hands and her diamond winking at her. Did people assume that they were married?

As an only child, she'd grown up feeling a bit isolated. After Michael was born, those feelings magnified fivefold, until she'd married. Jenny loved being a part of a couple. She'd loved being married to a wonderful man, feeling that she belonged to someone. She missed that companionship and special rapport. She peeked sideways at Steve. What would it be like to be married to him?

She and Steve shared a lot. They'd always had a definite affinity. Besides Gabe, he'd been her best friend. He still was.

At her car, Steve opened her door. "So, when's the big day?"

"Probably a couple of days."

"Is your mom taking you?"

"No." Jenny wrinkled up her nose. "I want to do it alone. It's kind of personal."

He nodded, but she didn't think he really understood. "If you need anything, call."

"Thanks." Shoving her hands deep into her pants pockets, Jenny looked up at him. "For everything."

Jenny knew Steve wouldn't acknowledge the grief she'd caused him professionally. Now that he'd forgiven her, he'd let it go. Jenny wracked her brain to think of something she could give him or something she could do to show Steve how thankful she was. She needed him to know how much his friendship meant to her, but so far she'd come up empty.

Steve brushed bangs from her eyes. She froze, holding her breath as his fingers skimmed her cheek, trailing lightly down her jaw in a lingering caress. She closed her eyes as he bent forward and pressed a light kiss to her lips.

"You're welcome. Drive carefully."

Jenny's eyelids flew open as she felt him move away. He'd kissed her. A sweet gentle kiss, intimate and deliberate, blowing all thoughts from her mind.

He'd kissed her on the lips, then walked away? What the heck?

Chapter 27

Steve couldn't sleep. Again. For the third dang night in a row. He rose up on his elbow. The neon green three thirty-seven on his alarm clock mocked him. Damn it. He punched his pillow and flopped onto his back. The past month, keeping busy setting up his new practice had allowed him a decent measure of sleep, then one little dinner with Jenny, she mentions insemination and it's blown to smithereens. He dreamed about Jenny and a newborn. Gabe's newborn. He wanted it to be his. Why shouldn't it be his?

Gabe was gone, damn it. Steve's jaw clamped shut. Why shouldn't he love Jenny? He couldn't come up with one solid reason, except that she wasn't ready for a committed relationship with anybody. But she hadn't said so... This baby, being a single mom, certainly was a new life direction. Maybe she *was* ready.

Are you ready to raise Gabe's baby? His annoying conscience asked. *Didn't work out so well with Annie and her kids, now did it?*

That was different. But alike enough to give him pause. How did Jenny even feel about him? Did she ever think of him as more than a friend? They had fun playing tennis and games together. They liked the same movies—for the most part. They enjoyed talking together, sharing work. They had a lot in common. She cared; he'd bet his house on it.

They'd had an amazing time at the Christmas party—that'd been romantic. And over the past few months he'd caught her looking at him oddly, as if noticing what had been under his nose all along. That was encouraging.

Unless you're making it up 'cause you're desperate to believe you might have a chance with her.

No, he pursed his lips and shook his head. There was something there; otherwise she'd have slapped him for kissing her. Hard. The impulsive kiss he'd given her after dinner had surprised her, yet Jenny hadn't pulled back or pushed him away. That was a good sign. There was definitely something there.

She's going to have his baby, his little voice reminded.

Yeah, but maybe she wouldn't, if she knew how much he loved her.

But she doesn't know, now does she, numbnut? 'Cause you've never told her.

Wha—He stopped breathing with the realization, then blew out a deep breath of frustration. He'd never actually said the words. Would it make a difference? *Should* it make a difference? Shit, he didn't know, but she should know how he felt. He had to tell her before her doctor's appointment—if it wasn't too late already.

Steve threw himself out of bed, slipped his bare feet into sneakers, pulled on the first shirt his hand landed on, put his watch on and was halfway across the drive before he realized it was still dark outside. He held up his watch to catch the streetlight's glow. Four in the morning. Jenny would be sleeping. Clenching his teeth, he returned to his house to wait until a decent hour.

At seven o' clock, Steve couldn't stand the inactivity another second. Fueled by three cups of coffee, he showered, shaved, and dressed. Nervous thoughts combined with the caffeine jumped around his brain, having him nearly vibrating out of his skin.

He fixed eggs and bacon to push around the plate, hoping food would take the edge off his jitters. It didn't. Finally, after watching the sun slowly crest the lake, he strode out the door and retrieved her morning paper.

Breathing deeply to prevent hyperventilating, Steve wiped his sweaty palms on his pants and marched toward Jenny's house, feeling as nervous and ill as he had when he'd pitched his first professional game in front of fifty thousand people.

He rapped twice on the screen before trying the door. Locked. He knocked again. Dressed in a white robe, Jenny opened the door and smiled in surprise.

"Newspaper boy. New profession?" she asked as she looped a lock of hair behind her ear.

Steve took in her mussed hair and sleepy face. She looked so cuddly wrapped in a new white terry robe. At least she wasn't still wearing Gabe's; he tried not to attach any great significance to the observation but failed.

He returned her smile. "I was out getting mine and thought I'd save you the trip." Never mind he only had her newspaper in hand.

Jenny took the paper he handed her. "Want some coffee?"

More coffee to fuel his nerves? That was exactly what he didn't need, but this was one of those times when his brain had absolutely no control over his mouth. "Sure," he followed her in and closed the door behind him.

"You're pretty perky for this early in the morning."

Perky? Zinging, jazzed, humming, buzzing, hyper.

"I've been up a while." Steve rolled back off the balls of his feet where he'd been nearly bouncing and forced himself to stroll into the kitchen. He stretched his neck from side to side, then took a seat at the table.

Jenny handed him his coffee with cream and sat across from him, tucking her legs under her until just her painted pink toenails showed. Lips puckering, she blew on her coffee before taking a tentative sip. "How come?"

His eyes concentrated on her luscious lips. "Huh?"

"How come you've been up for hours?"

The perfect lead-in. He'd rehearsed a half-dozen ways to bring up the subject and he needn't have—she'd done it for him. Steve looked at her, relaxed, slouching in her chair, waiting for his answer, and his courage almost failed him.

She was comfortable with him. What if he ruined that? What if she hated him? He looked at the corner of the table, unwilling to see the confusion settle in her eyes.

"I couldn't sleep. There's something I need to tell you—something you need to know."

Jenny put her coffee down. "I already know. I've always known."

His head snapped up. She knew? Why didn't she say something? Because she didn't care for him or because she wasn't ready for another relationship? He snapped his slack mouth shut. "You do?"

She nodded. "How come you're admitting it now?" She took another sip of coffee.

"I, uh, I thought you should know—have you gone to the doctor's to..." He swallowed hard. "For... it?"

Jenny shook her head. "This afternoon."

"I just thought you should know before then."

"Why." She cocked her head to the side. "What difference does it make?"

Wha—? His heart dropped. "I thought it might make a difference to—to your decision to, um."

Jenny put the coffee cup down, frowning. "What does your getting fired have to do with my in vitro?"

"Fired?" He didn't know whether to be relieved, exasperated, or scared. "Jen. That's not what I was going to say."

"You *didn't* get fired because of my case?"

He frowned; exasperation won out. "Yes, but that's not it."

"Then what?"

"I love you."

"I love you too." she said, too quickly to have really thought about it.

"No, Jenny." He paused, gaining her full attention. "I'm *in* love with you."

"Oh." Her eyes grew wide. "*Oh.*"

Steve stared at his hands, wrapped around the coffee mug as if it were a lifeline.

"*Oh.*" Her cheeks turned dusky rose with the realization.

Oh. Not exactly the response he'd been hoping for, but not revulsion either. He hurried on. "You might not be ready yet, but I think there's something more than friendship here. I know the timing stinks." He breathed out, trying to calm down so that he could rationally present his case. "But you should know how I feel before you go through with it."

Eyes solemn, Jenny studied him. "So... you're telling me *now* because you don't want me to have the baby?"

"Yes." He washed a hand over his face. "I know it's totally selfish of me. I want you to be happy and I know how badly you want a child. I just wish that the baby could be mine. Gabe was a great guy, and I respect the love you guys had, but I'm sorry." He looked to where Ritz lay on the floor across the kitchen before forcing himself to face her. "I don't want you to have it. I want a chance.

"I've loved you and hated myself for years. Had Gabe lived, I would've found a way to get over you. I would *never* have tried to come between you and Gabe—you gotta believe that." Steve stared at her, needing her to read the truth in his eyes. "But he's gone and I'm still here. And I love you. And all I'm asking for is a chance."

Jenny's eyes clouded. "A chance?"

"To be with you. To see if we have a future together." He hurried on. "The other night when I kissed you, you felt something—well, at least you weren't repulsed. And we're good friends. A lot of marriages have started out with less."

"Marriage?" Now her eyes popped open wide.

"Not right away," he hurried to assure her. "First we'd date a while and then let things develop naturally. I just wanted you to know that I'm—I'm—" he floundered, "not afraid of commitment or anything."

"Steve..." Jenny's mouth opened and closed several times. She shrugged. "I don't know what to say. I mean, obviously I care for you—a lot. You're my best friend. But the *in* love, and... marriage is—Wow. I don't know."

Remind her, his conscience whispered. *She has a right to know.*

"In the interest of full disclosure... I should remind you that there's a good chance I could be sterile." He looked her in the eye. "I probably can't father any children."

Being sterile had never really bothered him before, but in the face of Jenny's desire for Gabe's baby, he felt like a huge failure. He couldn't give her what she wanted most, yet here he was, still asking her to give them a chance.

"There's medicine I can take," he blurted out, "but even if it worked, it'd involve surgery and probably in vitro fertilization still. I'd be willing to do it, but it still might not work."

A deep frown puckered Jenny's brow while she rimmed her coffee mug with one index finger, thinking. "Hmmm. If we did have difficulty conceiving, we could use Gabe's sperm," she raised eyes lit with hope and purpose. "It's perfect. Like it's our destiny. This makes sense of Gabe's death."

"What?"

"You probably can't have children, and I have Gabe's sperm. That solves the problem."

"No. I don't want you to have his baby. Ever."

Jenny frowned. "Why not? That's unreasonable."

"Maybe, but that's the way I feel."

"That's ridiculous."

"Ridiculous?" He fisted his hands on the table. "I'll tell you what's ridiculous. I was a decent guy before you came along. *You* move in next door and suddenly I'm a fucking asshole who loves a married woman—not just any married woman, but my good friend who trusted me and whom I liked and admired. Very much." He paused, letting the truth sink in. "Do you have *any* idea how hard it was to watch you with Gabe, wishing it was me who'd met you first? Wishing it was me you loved?

"For the first time in my life, my self-control deserted me. I hated myself until I got engaged to Annie, and well, you know what a mistake that was. Then Gabe died and I had to wonder if maybe I hadn't subconsciously wished him gone so I'd have a chance with you. How fucking despicable does that make me?

"I tried to make amends. I tried to be a good friend. I helped you win your lawsuit. But God help me, the thought of his baby growing in you—especially when we both know he probably didn't even want it, makes me sick to my stomach."

He scowled until his eyes ached. "I know it's unreasonable. I could raise Gabe's kid. But after what I went through with Annie... You'd always see this baby as yours—yours and his. You might not think it now, but I wouldn't be a real dad to his child—especially if it looked like him.

"What if it was a boy? What if you accused me of being unfair to him because I was jealous he was Gabe's, not mine? What if I resented the baby? What if I wasn't strong enough? It could easily come between us and that wouldn't be fair you, me, or the baby."

He sighed and raised scared eyes to her. "The truth is... a part of me wants you any way I can have you. But a larger part of me says you have to choose. I'd take the medicine and have surgery. I'd even be willing to consider insemination with a stranger's sperm—just not Gabe's. We need to let him go. I *need* you to choose me."

Finishing, his heart pounding like he'd run the sixty-yard dash in six point three seconds, he wiped sweaty hands on his jeans.

Jenny sat silent, looking stunned. "I... don't know what to say."

Steve ran a hand through his hair. "I know I'm a selfish prick. But I have to know you love me as much as him." *I need proof that I'm at least as important to you as he was.*

Jenny looked at him, confusion and hurt imprinted all over her expressive face. "That's not fair."

"I know." Steve nodded and pursed his lips, never hating himself more.

"You can't make me choose."

He had to.

Jenny bit her lip and then looked at him, suddenly hopeful. "You might change your mind."

"No." He'd learned that from Annie. He wasn't going to settle. He'd rather be alone than with the wrong woman.

They were quiet for a few moments. Neither looked at the other for fear of what they'd see. Finally she broke the miserable silence. "If I choose to go through with the in vitro?"

He bit his lower lip. Nausea boiled in his gut. "I'd have to leave." Steve steeled himself against the tears brightening her eyes.

"So I have to choose between loving you or having children?"

He shook his head. "You don't get to choose who you love. You have to decide between a future with me—possibly without children, and life without me but with Gabe's child—maybe."

"But assisted conceptions are okay?"

Steve fisted his hands tightly at his side to keep from grabbing her and pulling her close. If he touched her, he wouldn't stop and their physical attraction would only further muddle things. He stared at her as if he could burn the truth of his feelings into her with the strength of his gaze and will.

"Jenny, I love you more than I can say. If we were together, I'd consult every medical expert, try *whatever* it took to have a child with you. But if everything failed, I have to know you'd still love me."

Jenny digested this new information. "What about adoption?"

"*Adoption*," he drew out the word thoughtfully, "is an alternative."

"Just not Gabe's baby."

Steve pursed his lips, feeling every bit the bastard he was. "I know it's unreasonable, but that's the way I feel."

She ringed her coffee cup before looking up at him. "Your timing really sucks, Grant."

"I know." He stood, looked at the crown of her silky brown head.

Disappointment commingled with resignation. Well, what'd he expect? That he'd throw her life into turmoil again and she'd fall all over him with declarations of love and devotion?

It hadn't even been a year since Gabe's death—only eight months. He wasn't looking forward to that anniversary. Jenny probably wasn't ready for another relationship, but it was only right that she knew how he felt. He'd presented his case as best he could; now it was up to her.

Steve couldn't stop himself from moving forward and cupping the back of her head. Closing his eyes, he pressed a soft kiss to her forehead. "See you later."

At the sweet smell of her hair, fresh from the shower, he leaned close again to nuzzle her temple. He moved to her soft lips, which parted in welcome as her arms clutched his shoulders pulling him closer. Her tongue darted across his lips until he ground his mouth into hers in a primitive urge to take his mate.

One hand gripped the back of her chair while the other bunched her robe at her throat, crushing it together to keep him from yanking it off. Her soft moans of pleasure and fingers furrowing in his hair shot hot currents of desire through his hardening body. Panting with need and restraint, Steve turned his mouth aside and rested his forehead on hers.

Don't do it, man. Play fair.

No matter how badly Steve wanted to brand her with his scent, touch and kiss her until her lips were swollen and all desire for Gabe left her forever, he wouldn't. He watched his hand at her throat rapidly rise and fall with her respiration. Her pupils were dilated, eyes soft with desire. She was as turned on as he. He could pick her up and carry her to bed right now and make love until they were both exhausted and sore. But he wouldn't. Not this morning.

Forcing his fist open, Steve stretched his fingers wide, releasing her robe. With trembling, damp hands, he meticulously smoothed the wrinkled fabric and slowly straightened. He looked into her luminous eyes, soft with passion. "I love you."

Chapter 28

Jenny drove down the road toward Saugatuck. Windows down, the wind threaded through her hair like comforting fingers, tingling her scalp. She glanced at the passenger's seat, half expecting to see Gabe slouched there as she had the last time she'd gone on a road trip. The long, solitary drive comforted her. She hadn't been away since Gabe's death.

Saugatuck was definitely a summer community. People were everywhere, walking along the roads, playing on the beaches or in the water, boating, or riding bikes. You name it; they were everywhere. She preferred the sleepiness of the fall.

Steve's declaration of love and his ultimatum had taken Jenny through the full gamut of emotions during the past week. Needing time to think, she'd cancelled her appointment for the egg extraction. The staff had been surprised and, unable to come up with a satisfactory explanation for the doctor, Jenny had pretended to be ill with a virus.

Incapable of thinking with Steve right next door or in the house filled with memories of both men, Jenny packed up Ritz and left. Without a word to Steve or anybody else, she'd run.

Jenny turned from the coast and drove leisurely inland. A couple of miles from the inn, she slowed, pulled onto the shoulder, and glided to a stop. Eyes never leaving the pavement, she studied the wide black skid lines still marking the road nearly a year later.

Ignoring Ritz's high-pitched bark, Jenny turned the ignition off and left the car. She walked to the end of the skid marks and squatted, touching the ground where Gabe had lain. As if a ghost, the large black car seemed to materialize, idling in front of her. She smelled the burning rubber and exhaust, and heard the young man's horrified voice.

A car approached, dissolving the phantom images. Jenny stood and moved out of the road. The driver slowed and rolled down the window. "Do you need help?"

She smiled at the young woman. "No, thanks. Just stretching my legs."

"Okay."

Jenny moved to the embankment and peered down the slope. It looked different without the blanket of leaves. She expected to maybe see a path where she rolled down, but the forest looked undisturbed. With a long sigh, Jenny turned back to the car, when something caught her eye.

She slipped down the incline, bracing her hands on tree trunks, until she came to a tree about fifteen feet down the slope. Bending over, she crouched beside the dirty, black plastic helmet. She picked it up and stood, fingering the frayed ribbed strap. Closing her eyes, Jenny pulled the old helmet to her chest and rocked back against the tree. She stayed that way for a minute before picking her way up the hill and returning to the car. She placed the helmet on the seat next to her and Ritz nosed it, snuffling loudly.

"Still smell like him, girl?"

Ritz whined and pawed her arm. Jenny patted her head before starting the car.

"It's okay. We're almost there."

∽ ∽ ∽

Jenny spent the next several days walking through the forest, with only Ritz and her jumbled thoughts for company. Sometimes she carried the old helmet with her, as if it were a good luck charm or a magic lamp that might spew forth answers instead of a genie. After a few morning walks on the beach, before sunbathers and young kids took over, produced no inspiration, Jenny left the helmet in her room and returned to the forest.

She found her way to their log by the pond, where she spent hours trying to become Steve. Lying back, balancing on the hard, rounded log, she closed her eyes and let the warm sun, buzzing bees and twittering birds transport her to a place where she could visualize the past couple of years from Steve's perspective. She didn't much like life from his shoes.

Whereas her years before Gabe's death had been wonderful, filled with contentment and personal growth, she imagined Steve's to have been fraught with jealousy and self-loathing.

Those confidential talks she'd shared with Steve about her insecurities as Gabe's wife, her desire to have Gabe's baby, baring her soul about her past, must have been really painful for him, yet Steve had managed to be the perfect friend, putting her happiness above his own.

To be honest, she'd always been aware of Steve on a sexual level—most women are when around handsome men. Steve could have tried to capitalize on that attraction. He could've tried to come between her and Gabe. They'd trusted him and he'd had plenty of opportunity to abuse that trust, but he'd been a steadfast friend to both of them, asking little in return.

Yet he was asking a lot now.

Steve or Gabe's baby—she couldn't have them both. The selfish part of her wanted to rail against Steve, but the fair part of her sympathized with his pain. Forcing her to choose wasn't something he'd enjoyed. She could tell by his rigid body and scowling face that challenging her had filled him with self-loathing.

He was asking her to make him her world. He demanded that she be totally committed to him and him alone. Was that unreasonable? Sighing, she sat up and looked at the dog lying at her feet. "What do I do, Ritz?"

At the sound of her name, Ritz came to her feet and rested her golden head on Jenny's thigh. "Steve's my best friend. He's always been there to listen and help. From the beginning, there was a connection. I could tell him anything and he never judged me." She rested a hand atop the dog's head.

"I told him things I was afraid to tell Gabe. I told him about Michael, but I couldn't tell Gabe." She released the dog and straddled the log. "Why not? Why couldn't I tell Gabe? I loved him so much and I *know* he loved me. Why was I so afraid that knowing the truth about Michael would ruin what we had? Would it have?"

Jenny slid off the log and sat with her back against it. She looked around, hoping Gabe would walk out of the woods, if only for a few minutes to give her some advice.

"If I'd told you about Michael, would it have destroyed us, Gabe?" Ears straining, she searched the trees for the answer in the softly rustling leaves. "You were so good to me. When we first married, I was so insecure and pitiful, but you believed in me and that meant *everything*.

"Your love freed me. You gave me confidence and security. You were always so proud of me; I had to become a better person. But I was so afraid to tell you I was pregnant. Things were great between us and I was scared to death it'd ruin it—and I was right. Our argument got you killed. I got you killed." Jenny's eyes filled with tears.

"I wanted us to be able to share everything, but I couldn't risk it. Why couldn't I risk it? God, I miss you." She rested her head on bent knees, her jeans greedily soaked up the hot tears slowly trickling down her cheeks. "Our baby would keep you alive. Just to look in his face and see your eyes or your smile. It'd mean everything to me.

"I can't smell you in your bathrobe or sweaters anymore. I can't remember your laugh. I listen to your messages on the answering machine every now and then, just to remember the sound of your voice." With her sleeve, she wiped the gentle tears pooling at the corners of her mouth. "I still love you and miss you like crazy, but it doesn't hurt as much—just makes me sad." Jenny drew in a deep breath and stroked Ritz's soft head. "What should I do about Steve?"

"He's a good man and a great friend, but... Even though you've been gone almost a year, it seems... disloyal." She sighed. "As happy as you made me and as much as I loved being married to you, I was always afraid I'd do something to blow it. Steve and I are easier. I can be me. And that's such a relief. I could love him, but I still love you too." She banged her head against the log, hoping to pound in some sense.

"Gabe, tell me what to do, 'cause I'm seriously at a loss here. I didn't show you the trust you'd always given me and I should have." She froze and her eyes opened wide. "Well, I'm trusting you now. You're still with me—I feel you in my heart. Show me what to do."

Jenny felt a big wet drop on her head. She jerked her face to the sky and felt her head. Had a bird pooped on her? Another drop landed on her cheek, and then her leg. It was raining. Jenny scanned the clear, blue sky. Rain? Raining in sunlight meant a rainbow somewhere. A happy ending.

"Rain tears for a fresh start or tears of sadness saying don't let me go?" Jenny looked skyward. "A little more help, please."

∾ ∾ ∾

Steve coasted through the amber light and turned onto Lakeshore Drive. Rubbing tired eyes, he was thankful for the absence of late night traffic, knowing he was incapable of concentrating. His own stupidity and Jenny's disappearance whirled around his brain, worrying him so he'd been unable to think of anything else for days.

He wanted to find Jenny to apologize for being such an ass and to retract that dumb ultimatum. Driven by fear of a life without Jenny's laughter and friendship, he'd gone to her house to apologize, but she and Ritz were gone. And she wasn't answering her cell phone. Three days later, they still hadn't returned.

Jenny had probably gone into hiding to lick her wounds. Or maybe she was resting somewhere peaceful after her egg extraction, praying that they'd made lots of Huntington's-free embryos. His empty stomach clenched.

He'd called Jenny's editor, but only found out that she had no pending assignments. He'd put off calling her parents; if they didn't know her whereabouts, he didn't want to concern them, but he was beginning to worry. Where was she? Did she hate him? Did she need him?

Where the hell are you, Jen?

He turned into his drive and drew up short. For a brief second, his headlights illuminated something strange on the Harrison's lawn. He peered through the dark and with only the distant streetlight to see by, he made out the distinctive shape of a For Sale sign.

Almost absentmindedly, he noted that Jenny's house was lit when it'd been dark and empty the previous nights. Thrusting the gear into park, Steve glared at the sign.

Jenny was selling her and Gabe's home? She loved that house; why would she sell?

To escape you, his inner demon whispered. *Well, there's your answer, dumbass. You made her choose. All because you're afraid you couldn't measure up to a dead man—a dead man, for Chrissake.*

As if in a trance, Steve turned off his ignition. Leaving the door wide open, he left the car in the middle of his drive and stalked over to the wooden stake holding the tasteful green and white sign advertising a local realtor.

Gritting his teeth, he rammed his arm into the pole. It took three more furious thrusts to shove the sign to the ground and that didn't begin to satisfy him. Steve marched to Jenny's door and pounded loudly against the solid wood. The pain in his clenched fist barely registered. He flinched as the bright porch light temporarily blinded him; fueling his anger.

Jenny's welcoming smile quickly evaporated, replaced by a wary look. Not happy to see him, eh? Was she expecting someone else? His roiling feelings must have showed on his face, because she stepped back in surprise. The caution flickering in her eyes deflated